# Stars & Stripes

## Cut & Run Series Book 6

### By Abigail Roux

RIPTIDE PUBLISHING

Riptide Publishing
PO Box 6652
Hillsborough, NJ 08844
http://www.riptidepublishing.com

This is a work of fiction. Names, characters, places, and incidents are either the product of the author's imagination or are used fictitiously. Any resemblance to actual persons living or dead, business establishments, events, or locales is entirely coincidental.

Stars & Stripes (Cut & Run, #6)
Copyright © 2012 by Abigail Roux

Cover Art by L.C. Chase, lcchase.com/design.htm
Editor: Rachel Haimowitz
Layout: L.C. Chase, lcchase.com/design.htm

All rights reserved. No part of this book may be reproduced or transmitted in any form or by any means, electronic or mechanical, including photocopying, recording, or by any information storage and retrieval system without the written permission of the publisher, and where permitted by law. Reviewers may quote brief passages in a review. To request permission and all other inquiries, contact Riptide Publishing at the mailing address above, at Riptidepublishing.com, or at marketing@riptidepublishing.com.

ISBN: 978-1-937551-58-2

First edition
August, 2012

Also available in ebook:
ISBN: 978-1-937551-42-1

# Stars & Stripes

## Cut & Run Series Book 6

### By Abigail Roux

RIPTIDE PUBLISHING

*For my Little Roux. Because family is worth fighting for.*

# Table of Contents

Chapter 1 .................................................... 1
Chapter 2 .................................................. 13
Chapter 3 .................................................. 39
Chapter 4 .................................................. 69
Chapter 5 .................................................. 99
Chapter 6 ................................................ 117
Chapter 7 ................................................ 141
Chapter 8 ................................................ 181
Chapter 9 ................................................ 209
Chapter 10 .............................................. 247
Chapter 11 .............................................. 271

# Chapter 1

The waitress came up to their table in the middle of an argument. "Would you like some more iced tea?"

Zane Garrett looked from his ranting partner to the waitress and smiled. "Thanks." He slid his glass across the small bar table so she could fill it from the pitcher she had in her hand.

"No problem, Zane. More wings?"

"Yeah, but just the medium ones this time. I'm not too hot on the honey barbecue kind."

"Bad pun penalty," Ty Grady muttered from across the table.

"Shut up."

The waitress laughed. She set a pint down in front of Ty and he pointed at her with his celery stick.

"Designated Hitter or real baseball?"

"I'm cutting you off," she answered before turning away.

"No!" Ty called out, and Zane laughed, the sound almost lost in the midst of the mid-week revelry. Ty turned a glare on him, dipped his celery into a plastic cup of ranch dressing, and then pointed at Zane with it, sending drops of dressing flying. "You know what we should do next weekend?" he asked without seeming to notice he'd sprayed Zane with ranch.

Zane grabbed a napkin and wiped up the splatter on his shirt. These weekly outings were the only time Ty drank around him, and he seemed to make up for lost beers at them. Zane didn't mind. After a few months of regular Wednesday night baseball viewings at the local bar, he was used to Ty's semi-drunken antics. He had to admit, he enjoyed Ty when he was drunk. And as long as Ty stuck to beer or wine, and Zane continued his AA meetings, he didn't even fight cravings.

"Was that a rhetorical question?"

"No. We should go get me another tattoo."

Zane loved to see Ty's mind at work. At first blush, it seemed there was no rhyme or reason to it, but once he'd started paying attention, he could see the tracks Ty's thoughts followed. Sometimes Ty jumped a track and surprised him, though. Like now. Ty had never mentioned getting another tattoo, had never been caught admiring anyone's body art. The only reason Ty had gotten the bulldog on his arm was because it meant something dear to him.

Zane watched him for a long moment, entranced by his lover just as he always was. What did people see when they looked at the two of them sitting here in the bar? Two friends, watching the game, hanging out? Maybe they sat a little closer together than some guys would, maybe their shoulders brushed more than casual friends' should. Maybe people saw two men in love. Zane hated living in fear of what other people might see, but until he or Ty retired, that was their life.

Zane looked at the bulldog on Ty's arm and raised an eyebrow. "What would you get?"

Ty threw back what was left of his beer, then set the glass down hard, rattling the unstable bar table. He met Zane's eyes. "Ballgame's over. I've been cut off by Designated Daisy. Let's go home and look for trouble."

Zane swallowed hard as Ty's purr hit a chord deep inside him that only Ty had ever been able to reach. He pulled out his wallet, picked through some cash, and tossed a few bills onto the table. "Ready when you are, Bulldog."

Ty slid out of his seat, and when Zane came around the table, Ty's arm snaked around his waist. Most likely it was to keep himself from weaving as they left the bar. Over the months, Ty had grown more comfortable being demonstrative in front of strangers, and it warmed Zane to his toes every time, but it still sent a shiver of nerves through him. Ty had always been the more careful of the two of them, and even he was growing more careless as time went on. What if they were seen by someone who knew them? What if they were found out? Everyone at work knew they were living together, though no one thought anything of it yet except that they were sharing the cost of the mortgage. But they were destined to be outed eventually. The real questions, the ones that haunted him, were, would it matter, and would he even care?

The summer heat hit them when they exited the bar, even though the sun had long ago set and a salty breeze was blowing in off the nearby harbor. Ty's arm tightened on Zane's waist, and Zane slid his hand around Ty's shoulders as they headed for their row house on Ann

Street. He was struck yet again by just how happy they were, despite the obstacles and worries hanging over their heads.

There were moments when it was all surreal. He'd never expected to live with another person again, never expected to fall head over heels for someone again. For over two months now, he'd been waking to Ty's arms wrapped around him every morning, and sometimes he wondered if he deserved it.

Other times he pondered how many tranquilizers it would take to bring Ty down, and whether he could do it before Ty killed him, but those moments passed quickly.

Now Ty's body was hard and warm against him, but his movements were loose and relaxed. He was humming under his breath, and Zane knew it would soon turn into a song. He couldn't help but smile as he pulled his lover closer. It might just be the rose-tinted color of love's glasses, but there wasn't a thing about Ty he didn't find fascinating, amusing, or smoking hot. He loved it when Ty sang because Ty had a beautiful voice, drunk or not.

"It's funny, you know?" Ty said. "How much things have changed."

"What do you mean?"

"A couple years ago, at this point in the night, I'd be back in that bar with someone in the supply closet."

Zane snorted and shook his head. "And now you just have to go home with me."

"No," Ty said, serious as he stopped and turned to look at Zane. "I don't *have* to go home with you."

Zane raised an eyebrow and cocked his head.

"I *can't wait* to get home with you. Even if it's just to crawl in bed and watch that stupid-ass show you like so much, I don't care. Whatever I do, I'm glad I'm with you."

Zane knew he was grinning like a fool, but sometimes Ty still managed to surprise him with his romantic, sentimental gestures.

Ty took his arm and continued to walk. Zane watched him out of the corner of his eye, amused and warmed all over.

"I love you," Ty said out of the blue, his voice almost sing-song.

Zane laughed. "You're drunk."

"I loved you before I was drunk."

Zane stopped walking and pulled Ty around to face him. The evening was full of the noises of summer night revelry, but the sidewalk was empty. He smiled and leaned in to kiss Ty. "I can't remember a time that I was happier than I am right now."

Ty smiled against his lips, his eyes closed as he wrapped his arms around Zane's neck. "I bet we can top it when we get home."

Zane growled and squeezed Ty's ass before releasing him. "Let's go find out."

Ty lay tangled in the sheets of the bed he shared with Zane, his head under his pillow. His entire body ached from the gymnastics of the night before. He had carpet burns on his knees. He could feel every place that Zane's fingers had dug in to hold him down. He was fairly certain there were teeth marks on his shoulder. His insides were a mash of aching, lingering pleasure, and his head was full of cotton. They had to work today, but not for a few hours. He didn't intend to move until something worthwhile compelled him.

A rough hand settled on the small of his back. Ty hummed and started to smile. That was compelling.

He raised his head, letting his pillow slide away as he turned to peer at his bedmate. Zane was still asleep, his handsome face relaxed in the shadows of the early morning. Ty took the opportunity to stare. He'd never expected to have the privilege of waking up every day to someone he loved so dearly. Now that he did, he tried to appreciate it when he could.

Zane's hair had grown longer, almost unruly. He'd taken to slicking it back when he worked, and the ends would curl around his ears. Ty loved it. He loved even more that Zane had lost the lines of stress he'd carried for so long, and there were threads of silver hair growing in near his ears that Ty found incredibly sexy.

He reached out to slide his fingers over Zane's lips. Zane scrunched up his nose and jerked his head away, grunting in his sleep. Ty bit his lip to keep from laughing and reached to do it again. Zane swatted at him this time, barely missing his hand, and then shifted and twitched his lips.

Ty waited a moment, then touched Zane's lips again, letting the tip of his finger brush against them with the utmost care.

Zane snorted and swatted at him again, smacking himself in the nose and waking with a start and a grunt. Ty pressed his face into his pillow and tried not to let his laughter shake his shoulders.

He felt Zane move, and peeked over his pillow at him. Zane was watching him, his dark eyes like sleepy obsidian in the morning light.

"You're an ass," Zane muttered, closing his eyes and turning his head.

Ty laughed and scooted closer, resting his chin on Zane's chest and wrapping around him. He dragged his foot along Zane's calf and slid it against his toes, enjoying the intimate contact and soaking in Zane's warmth and calm.

For all that they enjoyed their rough-and-tumble sex, they were both surprisingly good at cuddling.

The bed jostled at their feet.

"Oh God," Zane whispered.

Ty shushed him, holding his breath to keep still. They'd been caught off guard, with no covers over their naked bodies. They were defenseless. Ty bent his leg until his knee was covering Zane's groin, but that was all the movement he was willing to risk as the bed jostled again.

Smith and Wesson had awoken.

The two fluffy orange cats were Ty's "temporary" wards, but much to Zane's chagrin, they'd been here for months now. They were exceptionally large and ill-tempered, and though they seemed to have developed a certain loyalty and affection for Ty, Zane insisted they were trying to kill him. Ty had never witnessed them doing anything spectacularly evil, but he would admit they pounced and hissed at Zane with unusual frequency. And if it was time for their breakfast, they weren't averse to biting the tip of Ty's nose and sinking their sharp little teeth into other sensitive areas.

Ty had a special interest in keeping Zane's tender spots unscathed, hence his knee over Zane's fun parts.

"I thought you closed the door last night," Zane whispered.

"I did."

"Oh Jesus. Can they open doors now?"

Ty wouldn't have put it past these cats.

Zane's phone began to ring from the bedside table, but neither man dared to move.

Ty grunted as one of the cats began walking up his body, using his long claws to help him balance as he made his way to Ty's hip and plopped his fluffy butt down as if he'd just staked a claim. Ty reached back and rubbed the cat's head, letting his fingers twirl the hair under his ear that Ty called his muttonchops. He knew it was Wesson just from the tenor of his purr.

"Good kitty."

"Why do you encourage them?"

"They're good kitties."

"They're your minions."

"Everyone needs a minion or two."

"You won't be so pleased when you find me ground up in their food bowl one day."

Ty chuckled, trying not to shake too much.

They waited a few minutes to see if either cat was going to attack, and when it seemed they were safe, Ty rested his hand on Zane's chest again and closed his eyes. Zane turned his head with infinite care and kissed Ty's forehead.

Wesson gave him a warning growl.

"Mine," Zane told the cat.

Ty smiled and ran his fingers through the sparse hair on Zane's chest. Wesson growled again.

"If you make him attack me, I swear to God . . ."

"I can't mind-control the cats, Zane. Who called?"

Zane reached out with the utmost care to grab his phone. He was silent as he checked the display, and Ty watched his profile with all the devotion of a lover. It wasn't hard to miss when Zane's jaw clenched and his body tensed.

"What is it?"

"It's my sister."

Ty tried to get a better look at Zane's eyes. He rarely spoke of his family, and Ty had always gotten the feeling it wasn't just the strain of living far away that kept Zane from them. He'd never pushed, though, classing Zane's family in the same category as his deceased wife or his addictions. If Zane wanted to talk about it, he'd bring it up.

"Good or bad?" Ty asked, rubbing his fingers over Zane's chest to soothe him. Smith chose that moment to come out of hiding, pouncing on his moving fingers and landing on Zane's chest. His claws sank in, turning the bed into a frenzy of cat fur, flying linens, and screaming FBI agents.

When the bloodshed was over, Zane had fled down the hall to the bathroom and shut the door to ward off any further attacks, leaving Ty to fend for himself. He laughed as he watched Smith and Wesson prowl down the hall, stalking Zane. They plopped down to stare at the bathroom door, tails twitching. It didn't matter what Zane did for them, or how many times he fed them or threw Ty in their path, they still hated him.

Maybe they *were* trying to kill him.

Ty pulled on a pair of pants and headed downstairs, stepping over the cats without being molested, laughing again as he heard Zane come out of the bathroom and yowl in pain. After a few thumps and curses, Smith and Wesson thundered down the stairs to swarm Ty's feet and wait for food.

"Good kitties," Ty whispered to them. They were both purring so loudly it was impossible to hear Zane's movements upstairs, but a few minutes later, Ty glanced up when Zane came stomping down the steps. He had his phone to his ear.

"Hey, Annie," Zane said on the phone. He met Ty's eyes and smirked as he swiped a piece of toast from one of the plates Ty was arranging. Ty swatted at him with a spatula, but missed. "No, no, it's okay, I was up. What's going on?"

Zane tensed as his sister spoke to him. Ty set the frying pan aside and watched his lover as an unsettling feeling started in his gut.

"Why the hell didn't you call me earlier?" Zane blurted. "Do I need to come out there?"

Ty held his breath, straining his ears to hear. He couldn't make out any of Annie's words, but whatever she was saying was making Zane's nostrils flare and his shoulders snap back. Classic signs that Zane was about to delve into Dark Mode.

Zane listened for a few more minutes, then bade his sister good-bye and hung up. He looked at Ty with wide eyes.

"You okay? What happened?"

Zane didn't answer immediately. When he did speak, Ty knew he was whitewashing whatever he'd just learned. "Annie said they're having trouble on the ranch. Trespassers. They think maybe it's poachers or rival breeders after the horse stock."

"Okay," Ty said, confused about why that would warrant a call to Zane. As far as he knew, Zane had little contact with his family. Even his sister, who Zane got on well with, rarely called just to chat. "So, what, you need to go down there?"

"I don't know. I mean no. No, they don't need me."

"Then why'd they call you?"

Zane waved his hand. "I don't know, Ty. I can't help, so there's no point."

"If you need to go, we can figure something out at work."

"I don't!"

Ty arched an eyebrow. "Wow."

Zane shook his head, although he looked conflicted and more than a little annoyed that Ty hadn't just let it go. "I'm sorry. If it's still a problem when the weekend hits, I'll head down there."

"You sure?"

"Yeah, can we drop it now?"

Ty nodded and watched with a frown as Zane headed back upstairs. He stopped halfway up, then turned and thumped back down.

"Forgot what I was doing," he mumbled. He snatched another piece of toast before Ty could stop him.

"Hey!"

"Shut up," Zane said as he went back up the steps, taking them two at a time.

Ty watched him go, frown in place. Despite seeming to shrug it off, he knew Zane was worried. Whatever was going on in Texas, it was so much more than a few trespassers.

🐾 ★ 🐾 ★ 🐾

Ty jumped at the sound of a file folder hitting a box on the floor. He glanced up at Special Agent Scott Alston, who ignored the file when it skidded off the top of the stack to thump to the industrial-grade carpet. Alston leaned back in his chair as he loosened his tie, and then stuck his hands behind his head and closed his eyes.

Their whole work group had been tasked with slogging through a load of files sent over from one of the other investigative teams, desperate to dredge up evidence on a case that was going colder by the day. There were literally hundreds of files, and the six of them were on their last hour before they could break for the weekend.

"Garrett, are you getting off on all this paperwork?" Alston asked.

"Zane went to the bathroom like five minutes ago, Scott," Ty said. His words were marred by the yellow highlighter between his teeth. Both hands were full of papers, held aloft as he planted his elbows on his desk.

"Oh." Alston said, running his fingers through his blond hair. Ty felt like Alston looked: exhausted, seeing double, and desperate to go home.

"Thank God it's Friday," Alston said on a deep sigh as he looked at the clock. Ty glanced at it too, out of habit. Close to quitting time.

His cell phone began to buzz at his hip, and he twisted to try to see the display. He had no free hands, and no free space on his desk to set one of the unorganized stacks down.

"Want me to get it?" Alston asked. He pushed out of his chair, and Ty nodded and stood as well, turning his hip toward Alston.

He spit the highlighter out. It clattered to the desk and rolled until it hit a stack of files too high to bounce over. Alston plucked the phone off his belt and hit the speaker button.

"Grady," Ty said as Alston put the phone on the desk and took one of the stacks of papers from his hand. "Thanks," Ty whispered.

"Ty?"

"Hey, Ma," Ty said, distracted as he and Alston tried to switch things around while still keeping the stacks in order.

"You're not still at work, are you? I can call back."

"No, I'm about done here." Ty glanced up at Alston and waved a handful of files at the shredder nearby. Alston shook his head, and Ty nodded in response, managing to start an argument without a single word.

On the other side of the pod of desks, Michelle Clancy began to giggle.

"What's going on?" Ty asked his mother as he sat down and leaned closer to the cell phone, struggling to finish up his last file and listen at the same time.

"Well, I need a favor. A few favors, actually. But they can wait 'til you get home and call me back."

Ty rolled his eyes and shook his head. Alston chuckled as he leaned against Ty's desk. "Ma, will you just get to the point, please?"

"Well, we're aiming to fix the old tin roof on the storage shed this weekend 'cause it's leaking."

"Oh God," Ty groaned. He lowered his head, files forgotten. Alston squeezed his shoulder, mockingly comforting him.

"We wouldn't need your help normally, but this morning I cut your daddy's finger off, and he says he can't hold a hammer."

Ty's head shot up. "You what?"

"Cut his finger off," Mara said again, as if she hadn't realized the news would be shocking.

The others were drifting closer, trying to hear the conversation. Ty sat silent a moment longer, his mouth agape. "On . . . purpose?"

"Well, no, it was an accident."

"Right, of course." He glanced up at his teammates to see all four of them watching and laughing.

"But it's not like he don't have four more fingers to work with. And it was only part of the little finger, and they sewed it back on. He has two hands, one of 'em can hold a hammer just fine, but no, he says he can't do it."

"Is he okay?"

"Well, yeah. Like I said, they sewed it back on. So can you come home this weekend and help out with the roof tomorrow? Deacon said he would come too, but you know how he gets with tools."

Ty shook his head, mouth still hanging open as he tried to process. Clancy leaned over to catch his eye, even waving a hand at him. "Hi, Mama Grady! Ty's checking his calendar to see if he can get away."

"Don't you lie to me, honey. He's sitting there with his mouth hanging open, ain't he?"

"Yes, ma'am!"

"Ty, if you come tonight, I'll get your daddy to tell you all about it. Your brother and Livi'll be here. It'll be fun!"

"Fun does not start with a story about how you cut Dad's finger off!" Ty said, laughing despite himself.

"It does in my book. He deserved it."

The others gave up on etiquette and laughed raucously. Ty shot them all a glare, and he finally dropped what he was doing and picked up his phone. He caught sight of Zane coming back down the hall. His partner had been sullen and distracted for the last day or two, and though he knew Zane was having issues over that call from Texas, he had his own problems to deal with now. He spun around in his chair to put his back to his coworkers, trying to turn the speaker off.

"Does it have to be this weekend?"

"Honey, if you can't come help, that's okay."

Ty rolled his eyes and rubbed a hand across his forehead. "Okay, Ma. I'll leave after work and be there . . . I don't know, a little before midnight."

"Reverse psychology," Fred Perrimore whispered.

"So that's where Ty learned it," Harry Lassiter said under his breath.

Mara either couldn't hear them over the speaker that wouldn't shut off or ignored them. "I'll have pork chops waiting! And honey, will you bring that big sharp knife of yours with you? Your daddy's is awful dull, and the whetstone went missing."

"Yes, ma'am," Ty said with trepidation.

"I'll see you tonight! Bye-bye!" Mara said, then ended the call without waiting for more.

Ty stared at the phone as the display lit up, and then he looked at the others, who were all trying to keep straight faces.

"Can we come?" Alston said, grinning widely.

"No."

"We'll help!" Clancy said.

"No!"

"Spoilsport," Perrimore muttered, and they all drifted away to leave Ty to finish his paperwork.

Zane sat against the edge of Ty's desk, in the same place Alston had occupied. He was frowning and seemed distracted, but that was nothing new. He was just close enough that Ty could have used his knee as an armrest, and though the thought hadn't crossed his mind when Alston had been sitting there, he almost did it now without thinking. He stopped himself just in time, making it look like a frustrated flop of his hand.

This wasn't the first time they'd come close to getting too friendly in front of their coworkers, and it was happening more frequently. He didn't know how to address the problem, or if he even wanted to.

"What's up?" Zane asked.

Ty stared at him for a moment, trying to decide how to answer that simple question. He was still distracted by Zane's proximity, by the way he smelled, by how easy it was becoming to slip in front of coworkers who were trained to see mistakes.

He gave Zane the bare-bones version of his call from home, and after Zane had stopped laughing, Ty tapped him on the knee.

"You heard anything about Texas? You thinking about heading down there?"

Zane shrugged, though his expression clouded over and he looked down at the carpet rather than meet Ty's eyes. "I haven't had a call back. I don't see any reason to bother."

Ty sighed. He wanted to poke at that soft spot and see why it was there, and he added that to his list of shit to do. But he had some pretty pressing problems of his own to handle first. "Want to go to West Virginia and risk life and limb with me?"

Zane smirked and gave a single nod. "Sounds like fun."

# Chapter 2

Ty shouldered his overnight bag and walked through muggy mountain air across the gravel and up the porch steps to his parents' house, stopping when he realized the rocking chair was occupied.

"Grandpa?"

"You're an observant one, ain't you, boy?" Chester Grady grumbled.

Ty smiled as he looked over his grandpa, sitting in his rocker, shovel in place over his lap. "Love you too."

"Damn fool federal agent," Chester mumbled as the screen door squeaked. "Where's your damn fool partner?"

"He's getting his damn fool bag out of the truck." Ty slipped him a smuggled cigar as he bent to hug him. "What are you still doing up? I thought you old folks went down with the sun."

Chester waved him off, grumbling and smirking. Headlights caught them as another car pulled up to the front of the house, and Chester's eyes shone with mischief.

Ty turned to watch Deuce get out of the car, squinting past the headlights.

"Hey."

"Hey," Deuce called back, sounding just as tired as Ty felt. He thumped up the steps, carrying a small overnight bag just like Ty's. He greeted Chester with a hug, then turned to give Ty one as well. Ty hugged him tight. He nodded at the black Lexus in the driveway.

"Is that a new car?"

"Like it?"

"No."

"Me either," Deuce grunted with a curl of his lip. He turned toward the door.

Ty laughed as he followed. "Where's Livi?"

"Morning sickness. We figured it was best for everyone if she stayed home."

"Good plan."

"Where's Zane?"

"Wearing his invisible suit," Zane called from the driveway. His shoes crunched on the gravel, and soon he materialized out of the darkness, joining them on the front porch with his bag.

They left Chester sitting on the porch and headed inside. Ty hadn't been home since he'd been attacked by the mountain lion last fall, and he was surprised when a jitter of nerves ran through him. He'd been sure someone would figure out that he and Zane were so much more than partners, that he was gay—a revelation he'd feared since he was seventeen. He still feared it, even though he'd started wishing he could tell his family the truth. He would have to soon, before they found out on their own. Zane was too important to him to hide anymore.

He hadn't told his mother Zane was coming, and while he wasn't surprised that Deuce had inquired about his partner's whereabouts, it did strike him as odd that Chester had done the same. Maybe they were already starting to figure things out on their own.

He took a deep breath to calm himself.

"Hello?"

They heard footsteps from the back of the house, and soon Ty's mother came around the corner and smiled brilliantly. "Come here and give your mama a hug before I have to go back outside."

Ty and Deuce moved toward her, hugging her obediently. She had to stand on her tiptoes to put her arms around their necks, and she squeezed them both tightly. Ty couldn't help but smile.

"What are you doing outside this time of night?" Deuce asked when he let her go.

"Zane," Mara demanded, ignoring Deuce's question and holding her arms out for a hug from Zane as well. Zane smiled and moved to obey. "You look better than the last time I saw you!" She pulled away from him and held him by his shoulders, looking up at him with a critical eye. "Such a handsome boy," she said as she patted his cheek. She turned her eye to Ty again. "You could use some work. Come on." She turned and headed toward the back door.

Ty huffed and followed. "What are you doing outside so late?" he repeated.

"Helping your daddy," Mara shot over her shoulder.

Zane held out a hand toward Ty. "Want me to take the bags upstairs?"

"No. Wait, what? Hey, Ma!" Ty trailed after his mother, bag still over his shoulder. "What is he doing?"

"Cutting up the four-by-fours we got for the roof."

"Oh hell," Zane said under his breath as he followed the crazy train out the back door, reaching for the strap of Ty's bag. Ty shrugged it off with a glance back at Zane, but his attention was on his mother.

They thumped down the steps in the dark and followed Mara around the corner of the house, where a pole stood in the middle of the yard. In the pool of light at its base were several stacks of tin roofing, wooden planks, crates, and Earl Grady with a large electric saw.

"Earl, the boys are here," Mara announced.

"Boys," Earl greeted without looking up.

"Hello, sir," Ty and Deuce responded at the same time.

"Dad?" Ty knelt down so he could look his father in the eye.

"It wasn't the whole finger," Earl said before Ty could even ask. He held up his hand and displayed the heavy wrapping that was keeping his reattached pinkie connected.

"It's dirty!" Mara said. "That's it. We're going inside."

"But Mara—"

"That was the deal! Inside. Now!" Mara shouted, pointing at the house.

"How did you cut off your finger?" Deuce asked.

"I didn't cut off anything," Earl answered with a look at his wife.

"He'll tell you when he gets inside."

"But Ma," Ty said, sounding almost exactly like Earl had a moment earlier.

"Inside!"

Grumbling, Ty turned, and the procession tromped into the house. They headed for the living room, and Ty threw himself onto the couch. Zane sat next to him with a little more dignity, but Ty could tell he was tense. Zane and Earl hadn't hit it off the first time they'd met.

Mara pointed for Earl to sit in the nearby recliner, and he did so without protest.

"I'll get the disinfectant and the gauze," she announced as she left the room.

Deuce sat on the table in front of Earl, and he and Ty both watched their father out of the corner of their eyes, either trying to judge his mood or waiting for him to speak.

"So, Dad," Ty finally tried, drawing the words out as he turned his shoulders toward Earl.

"It was an accident."

"I certainly hope so."

"Don't be a smartass."

"Can't help it, runs in the family. What happened?"

"Your mother cut my finger off with a set of garden shears. That's what happened," Earl answered, his tone neutral. Although, he did manage to make the word "mother" sound like a curse.

"Did you . . . deserve it?" Deuce asked shakily. Either he was afraid of asking the question, or he was trying not to laugh. Ty was inclined to think the latter.

"A little bit," Earl said. "She was out there pruning that big ol' gardenia bush, and I was trying to get the mulch under it just right as she did it."

"So, you . . ."

"She told me to wait, that I was going to lose a finger." Earl looked toward the kitchen and then back at Ty and Deuce. He snorted. "I asked her, did she think I was stupid? Then a couple snips later, whack. Off went the finger. And you know what that woman said to me? I said, 'Mara, you cut my finger off.' And your mother said to me, 'Well, Earl, who's stupid now?'"

Ty laughed out loud before he could stop himself. Deuce snorted and cleared his throat before giving up and grinning. Ty could picture the scene as if he had witnessed it himself, and he couldn't seem to stop giggling.

"It's not really all that funny," Earl said, offended. Ty's only response was to lower his head into both hands and laugh more. The more Earl protested, the harder Ty laughed. Soon he fell to his side against Zane's arm and covered his face as he cackled.

"If it makes you feel better, Dad, we *were* worried," Deuce said, though his voice wavered.

"Yeah, he looks it," Earl said. He was watching Ty with what might have been affection, though.

"He does have personal experience with finger injuries."

"That's 'cause he's a dumbass," Earl said.

Ty howled as he pointed at his father. "That must run in the family too!"

Earl eased back into his chair and shook his head as Ty finally wound down and tried to catch his breath. "Good thing it wasn't the whole hand. You'd 'a' been in hysterics."

That caused another peal of laughter. Deuce bit his lip and looked away so Earl wouldn't see him grinning, and Ty could feel Zane chuckling against him.

Mara walked into the room carrying a basket of first aid gear and frowned at them. "He told you how it happened, huh?"

"Yes, ma'am," Zane managed to say.

Ty cleared his throat and sat back up, fighting for a little decorum as he wiped at his eyes.

Mara sat down on the end of the couch near Earl and placed her basket on the floor, then gestured for Earl to give her his hand.

"Why don't you let one of the boys do that?" Earl suggested as he held his hand away from her.

"You think I can't doctor you after thirty-seven years of marriage?"

"You're the one that cut it off in the first place!"

They were all still chuckling as they headed for the kitchen to eat the late dinner Mara had promised, leaving Mara and Earl to discuss things without an audience.

🐾 ★ 🐾 ★ 🐾

The building they were here to repair had served as storage for as long as Ty could remember. It had been built into a rocky outcropping on the property, using the side of the mountain as one of its walls. Because of that, it stayed cool almost year-round, but it also had a tendency toward being dark, damp, and full of creepy-crawlies. Ty mostly stayed away from it.

The other three walls were made of two-by-fours and sheet metal, with some scrap siding and cinder blocks to give it that tetanus feeling that kept strangers away from it and its contents.

Ty licked his lips as he examined the failing roof from the front of the building. The tin was rusted through in places, jagged and reddened and full of holes where rain and runoff from the hill had eaten through it. It was possible they could replace a few sheets of the corrugated tin, but more likely they'd need to do the whole thing. The earthen portion of the building had insinuated itself into the structure over the years, and it would be a real bitch to get the tin of the roof out of the soil. It appeared they would have to dig into it.

Of course, if they were going to do it right, that's what they'd have to do. Mara and Earl had other ideas.

"I think if we just spread this tarp over it, it'll last a few more years," Mara said as she dropped the bundle of blue tarp she'd hauled out of the back of her old SUV.

"Tarp?" Deuce said with a frown.

"It's not like we live in it," Mara told him. "It'll keep it dry."

"Yeah, until the first snow," Ty said. "Then you'll be calling me and Deuce, all, 'Honey, your daddy's buried under ten feet of snow, can you bring your shovel?'"

"Yeah, I didn't drive from Philly to help you lay out a tarp."

"Oh hush, both of you," Mara said with a wave of her hand.

Earl and Chester both chuckled.

"Really, Ma, you've got all the stuff, you've got us all here to help, why not just rebuild it now?" Deuce said.

"All right, all right. Earl and Zane stay on the ground. Ty and Deacon can handle the stuff up top."

"Why does Zane get to stay on the ground?" Ty asked with an accusatory point at his able-bodied partner.

"Because he's a guest, and we don't ask guests to risk life and limb." She thrust a hammer and a plastic container full of nails into Earl's arms. Then she clapped her hands. "Get to it, boys. We're burning daylight! And when we take a break later, I've got some furniture needs moving."

Ty and Deuce both groaned as they headed for the rocky slope acting as one of the building's walls. They'd used the hill to access the roof many times in their youth, when they weren't supposed to be playing up there but had done so anyway. As Ty scrambled up the incline, it didn't seem as high as he remembered from when he was ten, but the roof looked much more foreboding.

"Ah, for the fearlessness of youth," Deuce muttered from the other side of the building. Ty snorted. They sat on the hill above the roof, fighting gravity and erosion as they tried to keep their weight off the perilous-looking tin.

"Just keep to the two-by-fours and you shouldn't fall through," Mara called up to them.

Ty and Deuce shared a look.

"Ma, we can't see where the two-by-fours are from up here," Ty shouted as he looked over the roof. They could see spots that were rusted through, and others where it looked as if a leaf landing on the metal would cause it to give in.

"They should be where the nails are," Earl called back. "Just step on the nails."

"They've got to be kidding," Deuce said under his breath.

Ty slid down the hill closer to the edge of the roof, dampness from the ground seeping into the seat of his jeans. He tapped the toe of his work boot on the nearest line of nails, testing it. "Look at it this way," he told his brother. "It's only like an eight foot drop. And any of Dad's tools that are sharp enough to impale you are in the other shed."

"You're a ray of sunshine and optimism, you know that?"

Deuce mimicked Ty's actions, testing the roof with one foot. They made their way out onto the tin, taking great care to stay on the line of nails that indicated the supporting beams below. "Speaking of optimism, how are things going with you and Zane?"

"Too good to be true," Ty said as he edged along the narrow line of safety.

"Did you bring him with you for a reason?"

"Stop psychoanalyzing me," Ty said, sing-song, as he glanced up and then back down at the roof.

"That's a yes," Deuce replied in the same tone.

"Maybe it is, but as soon as I stepped through the door, I changed my mind." Ty continued toward the edge of the building, being less careful than he should have been. "Dad was right, I'm a coward."

"Bullshit, Ty. You'll get there."

Ty glanced at his brother and nodded.

When he reached the edge, he knelt down and smiled crookedly at Zane, giving him a quick wink. Zane returned his smile. Ty almost got lost in it, but he was distracted by his father giving them orders.

"We're gonna tear the whole thing up and replace anything that's rotted," Earl said as he handed Ty a crowbar.

Ty and Deuce both groaned, but they followed with a matching, "Yes, sir." And then they got to work, yanking up the old tin roof and tossing the pieces down to the ground.

The faster they finished this disaster waiting to happen, the faster Ty could get down there to Zane and work himself up into confessing the truth to his family.

It wasn't until they were washing up for dinner that Zane was able to get Ty alone, cornering him in the tiny bathroom upstairs. The first thing Zane did was pull Ty to him and kiss him, long and hard, letting Ty's scent and the feel of him wipe away all the tension he'd built up in the past few days. He pulled Ty close, appreciating every ounce of him, letting himself be turned on by the smell of sweat and damp earth clinging to Ty's body.

When they parted, Zane's heart was pounding and Ty was trying to catch his breath.

"I've been thinking," Ty said as he pressed his nose to Zane's cheek.

"Not your strong suit."

"Oh, look who's funny," Ty said, though he was smiling against Zane's skin. He pulled back a step to meet Zane's eyes. "I'm serious. What would you think of telling my parents about us?"

Zane's heart leapt into his throat. "You want to come out to your mom and dad?"

Ty licked his lips and nodded. "I want you to be part of the family. You deserve that. We deserve it."

Zane began to smile.

"I just . . . I don't know how. I don't know if I have the guts to do it."

"Baby, I think deciding you want to is a pretty big step. We'll figure it out." He kissed Ty languidly, breathless and distracted by the heat growing between them that wouldn't be addressed soon enough. "Thank you."

"What for?"

"I know what a big deal that is. I know what you've been through. Thank you for thinking I'm worth it."

Ty stared at him for a long moment, then kissed him again, harder. They lingered over it, taking their time, letting themselves enjoy the brief moment.

"You better get cleaned up," Zane finally said as he pushed Ty away and headed for the door. He didn't look back. If he did, he and Ty would end up screwing in the shower, and that would be so very hard to explain.

He headed for the landing, meeting Deuce at the top of the stairs with a knowing grin and following him down to the kitchen. Ty wasn't far behind them. It was a glimpse into what it might have been like to grow up here, to have a family that was so close, a mother who hugged at every opportunity, a brother who was more like an accomplice than a sibling. It made Zane's stomach cramp to think of all the ways life could have been different.

Ty sat next to him at the table and held his hand as they all bowed their heads to offer thanks for the meal. Zane squeezed his fingers, wanting nothing more than to be able to hold Ty's hand whenever they wanted. The fact that Ty had broached the subject of telling his family had warmed Zane's soul in ways he hadn't known he'd needed. It might take time, but maybe they would get there sooner rather than later.

Zane dug into the delicious dinner, surrounded by warmth and laughter, feeling remarkably at home.

It was a good while later, with dessert on the table, that Mara cleared her throat and reached out to put her hand on Ty's forearm. "By the way, I told the minister and choirmaster you boys would be at the service in the morning."

Deuce and Ty groaned in unison.

"Hey, I'd get to hear you sing," Zane said, perking up. "Something besides the national anthem and the Battle Hymn."

Ty growled at him, then looked at his mother. "They have a perfectly good choir. I'm sure they don't need us."

"What's wrong with him?" Deuce asked with a jerk of his thumb at Earl. "He doesn't sing with his fingers."

Mara narrowed her eyes at them both.

"Okay, okay," Ty conceded, holding up both hands. "We'll sing."

Deuce grumbled but didn't argue. The brothers locked eyes and seemed to communicate silently, devising a way out of it. Mara was too pleased to notice.

"As long as Dad sings with us," Ty added with a shit-eating grin at his father.

Earl rolled his eyes.

"Whatever it takes," Mara said. She stood and went to the refrigerator. "All of you shitheads need Jesus so far as I'm concerned."

Zane almost choked on his tea.

"That includes you," Mara told him. She sat back down with a dish of whipped cream, and Zane waved a hand in acknowledgment as he tried to clear his throat.

Ty was laughing beside him. He patted Zane's knee under the table and squeezed, resting his hand there. Zane's eyes were watering, and his cheeks were warm with a shade of embarrassment, but it was okay. Par for the course with the Gradys.

※ ★ ※ ★ ※

After dinner, everyone gathered in the living room for coffee. Zane sat on one end of the couch, his long legs stretched out in front of him. The weather had turned drizzly toward the end of the afternoon and dropped the temperature a little low, even for late June in the mountains. The windows were open, letting in the breeze and the scent of rain.

It was a pretty scene, homey and comfortable. For all that the Gradys had bickered over the construction of the new roof and made fun during dinner, they seemed to enjoy the verbal battles, and there was no tension or malice in the air. Zane could feel weariness encroaching as the breeze and familiar scents seeped into him.

He sat slouched with one arm outstretched off the end of the couch, his fingertip brushing a little cut-glass figurine on the table. It reflected the light as he nudged it, watching it sparkle.

Ty sat on the floor, leaning back against the couch and looking exhausted. Deuce lounged on the other end of the sofa, his feet up on a stool in front of him. Earl and Mara sat on the loveseat across the room. They cuddled together, Mara curled in the crook of Earl's arm draped over the back of the loveseat. For a couple who'd been together so long and seemed to lack any sentimentality about their marriage, it was an oddly sweet thing. Zane had never seen his parents cuddling.

Deuce groaned. "Ma, what sort of pie was that?" He was rubbing his stomach.

"Bitter cherry. Lucy Hopewell had one at the potluck a week back, and I thought I might try it. It wasn't good?"

"It was good, Ma," Ty said, voice flat.

"Where do you get bitter cherries?" Deuce asked.

"Disgruntled trees," Ty said. He looked over his shoulder with a smirk.

Earl barked a laugh and Mara gave a surprised giggle. Zane studiously kept his eyes on the figurine, biting his lip as laughter shook through him.

Deuce glared at Ty, but Ty returned the look with wide-eyed innocence. "Maybe they need a shrink."

"I hate you."

Chester cackled and shook his head. He rocked in his chair, facing the couch from the other side of the fireplace, drinking from a mason jar of clear liquid that Ty had implied was some incredible moonshine. He watched the glass figurine as Zane played with it.

"I gave that to my wife on our fiftieth Christmas together," he announced, looking at the little angel with a melancholy fondness.

Zane let his head fall to the side as he watched the light play off the glass. "I bet she loved it."

"She did love a shiny thing, my Evie," Chester said with a smile.

Earl and Mara both laughed.

"We made it sixty-three years." Chester raised one gnarled finger and pointed at Zane. "Takes a whole lot of shiny things."

Zane raised an eyebrow, but smiled, and his eyes strayed to the compass pendant around Ty's neck. "Keeping anything worthwhile generally does," he agreed, looking back at the figurine, his eyes skimming over Ty along the way.

Ty wasn't looking at him, though. He was sitting with his arms around his knees to keep his balance as he rocked from side to side, staring at the rug in the middle of the floor. It was possible he'd already zoned out and wasn't listening, but Zane doubted that very much.

"Got to find the right fit," Chester continued. He waved a hand at Mara and Earl, who were watching him in bemusement. Then he looked back at Zane and pointed at him, waving his hand toward Ty to include him. "It's good you got the right fit."

Zane wasn't quite sure what that was supposed to mean, but he figured he should just be glad that he wasn't at the top of the shovel list anymore.

"Well, somebody's got to watch his back," Zane said, glancing at his partner.

"That too," Chester said as he began rocking again, hands folded in his lap.

"What are you talking about, Dad?" Earl asked Chester with a laugh.

"All's I'm saying is love's a blessing, no matter all the same."

Ty's head shot up, and he stared at his grandfather for a moment before looking over his shoulder at Deuce. Deuce shook his head and mouthed something to him, assuring him he'd never told anyone.

Zane forced himself not to move, not even to twitch as he blinked at Chester. It was an implication the old man couldn't possibly mean. Nerves started cramping his stomach.

Earl and Mara both stared at Chester, looking confused. But then, Chester probably got that look a lot. Chester rocked on for several tense moments before looking around at them all in surprise. "What?" he asked. "Y'all didn't know they was sweethearts?"

Zane was so shocked he knew it had to show as he stared at the smile on Chester's lined face. Distantly he thought he ought to be preparing something to say, but he'd gone blank. His eyes searched out Ty's.

Ty wore much the same expression as he stared at Chester. He opened his mouth to speak and looked over to the loveseat, where Earl was looking at Chester intently.

"Do what, now?" Earl asked.

"Dad," Ty said as he struggled to his feet.

Earl stood to face him, shaking off Mara's hand as she tried to tug him back down. Zane sat up straight, though he stayed on the couch. Every warning instinct in him was firing.

"Is that true?" Earl demanded, voice low and deceptively calm.

Ty put up a hand and stepped toward him. "Let's sit back down and—"

"Is it true?" Earl ground out again, not budging. Mara stood and took a tiny step closer, still looking thunderstruck.

Ty stared at his father, his lips parted. The hand at his side was trembling. Zane curled his fists in the couch cushions as he made himself sit still. He wanted desperately to go to Ty for support, to stand beside him in this moment. It tore him up to know he had to try to stay out of it.

Ty didn't look away from Earl; he swallowed hard and raised his chin. "Yes."

Zane felt Deuce shift on the sofa next to him, but no one else moved or made a sound. Mara finally raised her hand to her mouth, her eyes riveted on Ty.

Earl continued to stare at him. "How long?" he asked in the same dangerous tone. It seemed like an odd question to follow up the first with. Ty shook his head, apparently thinking the same thing and not certain how to answer. "How long have you known you were gay?" Earl shouted.

Ty flinched, but he didn't back away. He opened his mouth to answer, but couldn't.

Zane's heart ached for him. He'd never seen that look in Ty's eyes. He wanted to reach out and give Ty a hand, help him get the words out, stand between them to shield Ty from something he knew his lover had dreaded for half his life.

Ty swallowed hard and tried again. He sounded remarkably steady as he said, "Senior year."

He'd barely gotten the words out when Earl backhanded him. Zane leapt to his feet as Mara screamed, but Deuce stepped over to stop him with one arm across his chest. Mara grabbed Earl's arm to keep him from swinging it again, but Earl didn't make another move toward Ty. He actually looked surprised that he'd taken a swing at his son.

"Leave them to it," Deuce whispered as he held Zane back. He was watching them like a hawk, though, clearly ready to move in himself if things got uglier.

Ty had his head bowed to the side and his eyes closed, motionless after the slap. Then he touched the side of his thumb to the corner of his mouth and looked back at his father as he wiped at his lip.

"That's for running," Earl said, his words unsteady.

Ty stared at him, his fingers trembling. Earl had put the whole story together with remarkable speed: That Ty had joined the Marines out of high school to leave home, to run from his family and the truth. That this was the secret that had taken his son from him.

Ty let out a measured breath, nodding as he did so. His eyes never left his father's. "Yes, sir."

It was killing Zane to stand aside and watch the tension in Ty. Deuce patted his shoulder but didn't let go; he knew how Zane reacted to threats to Ty. He wasn't taking any chances on an all-out family brawl.

Earl moved again and pulled Ty into a hug, squeezing. Ty tensed, but after a second he put his chin down on his father's shoulder and closed his eyes in relief, returning the fierce embrace.

"I'm sorry, boy," Earl whispered, just loud enough for the rest of them to hear. He patted the back of Ty's head with his bandaged hand.

Deuce loosened his hold on Zane, and Zane closed his eyes for a moment. Ty had wanted to tell them the truth, but Zane doubted this was how he'd imagined it going.

When he looked up again, Earl had released Ty and was patting him on the cheek, talking to him quietly. Ty was nodding in a quick, jerky motion, his lips pressed into a thin line like they always were when he was trying to restrain emotion.

Earl had one more word for him and then stepped back. "Okay, son, now take your shot," he invited as he opened his arms.

"Earl," Mara warned.

"I got mine, Mara; now he gets his. Take your shot, Beaumont."

Before Mara could protest again, Ty reared back and hit his father with a wicked right hook that knocked Earl off his feet. Earl struck the floor hard enough to make the plate of cookies on the table rattle, and Ty immediately doubled over, holding his hand and cussing.

"Nice hook, Tyler!" Chester cried triumphantly. "Woo!"

"Jesus Christ, boy!" Earl shouted as he clutched at his nose and wallowed on the floor.

"What is your face made of, Dad, steel?" Ty cried as he held his hand. "Oh my God!"

He turned and stumbled into the kitchen.

"Should have seen that coming," Deuce muttered.

Zane cursed and followed his partner, unwilling to stay away any longer. What he *really* wanted was his own shot at Earl.

Ty was rummaging through the freezer, a bag of frozen peas already on his hand as he pulled out another bag. He let the freezer door swing shut as he stepped away and looked at Zane, his hazel eyes wide with the remnants of stark terror. He was shaking from head to toe.

"Baby," Zane said as he took a few steps toward Ty. All of his possessive and protective instincts were in overdrive, but he held himself back, reaching out to check Ty's hand instead of wrapping him up in his arms and holding him until he stopped trembling. When Ty was upset, the last thing he wanted was to be restrained in any way.

"That wasn't exactly how I saw that going," Ty said. He reached out and pulled Zane closer, wrapping his arms around his neck and holding onto him.

Zane returned the fierce hug, his heart aching for Ty. Fear of what'd just happened had been the driving force behind many of Ty's decisions and life choices. To have faced it in a moment not of his own choosing must've been terrifying. Zane held him, letting Ty hang onto him, cheek pressed to Ty's while a long minute passed.

"Well," Mara said from the doorway.

Ty pulled away and glanced sheepishly at her. She stood behind Zane, arms crossed over her chest.

"How's Dad's face?" Ty asked.

"Better than yours is going to be if I find out you been keeping any more secrets," she threatened, putting her hands on her hips. She looked from him to Zane and back. "Is it serious, the two of you?"

It took Ty a moment to answer, but when he found his voice, he said, "Very."

Mara narrowed her eyes.

"I love him," Ty said, voice firm.

Mara just nodded, looking between them again. Her expression softened and she made a disgruntled noise, then she walked up to Zane and pulled him by his shoulders into a tight hug. Though he was surprised, he let her do what she wanted. She patted his back and kissed his cheek. "Welcome to the family, Zane," she said, and the sincerity in her voice made his throat tighten. "I wish I'd known earlier, but if wishes was dollars, I'd be the Queen of Sheba."

Zane straightened and glanced at Ty, who was staring at Mara, his hazel eyes wide and his mouth hanging open.

"Thank you," Zane said. "And I'm sorry."

"No need for that." She nodded and turned to Ty, hugging him in the same manner. "You should've told us way back then," she said, her voice harsh with upset. "You didn't have to leave."

"Yes, ma'am," Ty whispered as he hugged her.

She stepped back, taking his chin in her hand and turning his head to the side. "Is that hand broke?" she asked after she'd assured herself his face was okay.

"I'm not sure."

"Well, serves you both right." She took a bag of frozen broccoli from Ty and turned to leave. "Mule-headed, the both of you."

Zane sighed and lifted the bag off Ty's hand to examine his knuckles. "Doesn't look too good," he said, lowering the bag back into place over the injury. He touched Ty's cheek, checking it for signs of redness, and tried to look at his eyes to make sure the fear was subsiding.

Ty was still shaken, but considering how terribly it could have gone, that wasn't surprising. His parents were angrier about the fact that Ty had never told them why he'd chosen to leave home right after high school, rather than the fact that he was gay. That was a promising step. A big one.

"I think I'm going to throw up," Ty groaned, closing his eyes and breathing deeply. Then he met Zane's eyes and appeared to calm. After another moment, he seemed almost back to normal. "They're right, you know. I should have done that fifteen years ago." He took Zane's hand in his. "Thank you for . . . letting it play out."

"Thank Deuce." Zane glanced over his shoulder. "I'm not sure it's a good idea I go back in there with Earl right now. I don't think you hit him hard enough."

Ty turned his face into Zane's and nodded. "Come on. We have to, sooner or later." He didn't let go of Zane's hand as he pulled him toward the living room. Zane let the mild surprise buoy him.

Chester was still rocking merrily, either pleased with himself for the commotion or oblivious to the fact that he'd caused it. Deuce was sitting on the sofa with his head in his hands. Earl was still on the floor as Mara perched on the loveseat and pressed the frozen broccoli to the side of his face.

"That is one hell of a hook, son," Earl said to Ty as soon as they appeared.

"Thank you, sir." Ty held up their linked hands as everyone in the room watched them. "Is this a problem for anyone?"

Deuce smiled, a hint of pride in his expression as he looked over at them. Mara shook her head, though her eyes seemed to be misting over. She was upset and probably would be for a while, but Zane was confident that it had nothing to do with their relationship and everything to do with the secrets Ty had been keeping and the years they'd lost because of it.

Earl took the broccoli from her and struggled to his feet, wavering. He waited a moment, and then walked over to them. He looked from Ty to Zane and shook his head. "Don't matter who you love, son," he said. "As long as you do it well." Then he held his hand out to Zane.

Zane looked at it, wondering if he could just not take it. But when Ty's hand loosened in his and let go, he reached out and shook Earl's, meeting the older man's eyes, letting his expression say what he couldn't. Earl nodded in acknowledgment of the uneasy peace. Then he moved away again, pressing the peas to his face and mumbling more about Ty's impressive right hook.

In the rocking chair, Chester began to hum. It wasn't a song yet, merely a cadence with a certain familiar ring to it. It was one of the songs Ty whistled and sometimes made up his own words to: "When Johnny Comes Marching Home."

Chester began to laugh, rocking by the fireside with his shovel in his lap.

Ty bit his lip and glanced at Zane, trying not to smile. Zane rolled his eyes. "Galloping crazies."

Ty squeezed his hand. "Well, you said you liked horses."

🐾 ★ 🐾 ★ 🐾

Ty sat on the edge of his old bed, looking down at the cast on his hand in the soft light of the bedside lamp. In all the times he'd thrown a punch in his life, he'd rarely broken one of his own bones in the process. It was a metacarpal this time, one of the bones within his hand. And it hurt like a bitch. His entire wrist had to be immobilized, hence the bright green cast on his arm.

It was a common fistfight injury, but Ty still couldn't believe his dad's jaw had broken his hand.

"Figures the old man would break my hand," he grumbled.

Zane was behind him, leaning against the headboard. "I'm going to start calling you Tytanium."

"That's clever."

"I know."

"Does it hurt that bad to hit me?" Ty asked.

"Yes."

"Good," Ty said, mollified as he looked back down at the cast and plucked at the loose cotton on the edge. He knew Zane wasn't happy, but he wasn't sure what he could do about it. He glanced over his shoulder again. "It's sort of funny."

Zane's eyes were dark and his face was expressionless, but one corner of his mouth curled up. "Why is that?"

"Oh, come on. The one time I take a swing at him, and he still comes out better than I do? There's funny in that. Like Charlie Brown with the football."

Zane smiled a little and rolled his eyes. He reached up to touch Ty, sliding his fingers along the base of his skull into his hair.

Ty leaned back into the touch, closing his eyes as relief washed over him. He couldn't shake the sense of impending doom that was always under the surface, but he'd learned to live with it. The only things that mattered were that Zane was here with him and his parents had taken the news infinitely better than he'd ever imagined.

They had every right to be pissed at him, not only for lying to them, but also for running. He turned and crawled toward Zane, stretching out to lay his head in Zane's lap.

"I always thought there'd be this huge weight lifted off my chest after they found out."

Zane's hand moved to stroke through Ty's hair. "You've been carrying that weight a long time, Ty. It'll take a while not to feel it as much."

"Maybe you're right." He looked at Zane, reaching up to touch his face. "Talk to me, darlin'."

Zane smiled. "I love the way you say that." His fingers drifted across Ty's forehead. "What do you want me to talk about?"

"Don't be dense. What do you think about all this?"

Zane looked down at the quilt for a long moment, his lips compressing. "I'm angry."

"I know you are," Ty said gently. "Talk to me about it instead of taking it out on me later."

Zane huffed, but they both knew it was valid. "I've never liked the relationship you have with your dad. It's always seemed to me he was more a gunny than a father. But it's not my place, you know? To criticize him." Zane paused. "But watching him hurt you? That's unacceptable to me. Possibly unforgivable."

Ty nodded. He knew that his relationship with his father, outwardly, hit all of Zane's hot buttons. But Earl was a good father; he had nothing but happy memories of growing up. Maybe Earl *was* more of a gunny than a dad, but it had worked. Sure, there was strain there, but he'd challenge anyone to show him a perfect relationship between father and son. Tonight had been the first time Earl had ever raised a hand to one of his boys.

"It's . . . complicated," he offered, even knowing it would sound weak to Zane's ears.

Zane's brow creased, but his anger was mixed with dismay as he spoke. "But you're afraid of him, Ty. How can that be right?"

Ty sat up, looking at Zane in surprise. "I'm not afraid of him." But there were things that made him almost ill to think of: Knowing he might have disappointed his father. Seeing shame or contempt or any number of other reactions he'd imagined when he let his father down. That all added up to making Ty tense when he thought too hard about it. All he'd ever wanted was to make Earl proud of him; he'd spent thirty years trying. "And at the same time I am terrified of him," he realized as he looked at the USMC signet ring on his finger.

Zane shrugged helplessly. "I don't know what . . . to *do*. It tears me up to see you dealing with this, and I can't help."

Ty sighed and turned to sit cross-legged on the bed beside Zane's hip. "He's my dad, Zane. I don't need you to do anything. You don't have to protect me. You don't have to defend me—or us—to him."

"I can't just not feel the need to protect you, Ty. That's not going to happen. You'd probably better not expect us to ever be much in the way of friends."

Ty smiled and patted Zane's knee. "Dad can take care of himself. You don't have to be buddies."

Zane gave an unconvincing nod.

Ty turned himself around to lay his head back in Zane's lap. "He's been angry with me for a long time. They never could understand why I left. And I could never tell them, not really."

"Sometimes telling doesn't help," Zane said. After a pause, he added, "I told Mother what a great opportunity the FBI would be for me, and to this day she just can't, or *won't*, understand why I left home."

Ty looked up at him, trying to see his eyes. "What happened with your family, Zane?"

Zane answered with a heavy sigh. "My family wasn't like yours."

"Is that why you left Texas and never looked back?"

Zane was quiet for a moment. "I wasn't willing to do the job I was born for. I wasn't wanted there unless I intended to take over the ranch."

"Zane. I doubt that's true."

"You don't know them, Ty. My sister and my dad are good people, but Mother . . . she scares me. I hate being around her."

"Why?"

"Because . . . I have a hard time finding anything I like about her, and she reminds me of me."

Ty sat up to look at him. He had his eyes closed, jaw clenched. Ty grabbed a fistful of his shirt and pulled him up to sit, then took Zane's chin in his hand and forced Zane to look at him. "Zane . . . you cannot possibly tell me that there is another one of you anywhere."

Zane gave a weak laugh and wrapped his arms around Ty. Ty turned his face into Zane's and held him close.

"I love you, Zane. Even if you are obnoxious."

"You're an ass."

Ty smirked and turned his head for a kiss. A knock at the door interrupted them, and Ty sighed. "Yeah?" he called. Zane let his arms drop so he wasn't holding Ty, but he didn't scoot away.

The door opened with a creak, and Deuce poked his head in. "Just wanted to see how you were doing. You okay?"

Ty nodded.

"I slipped some . . . surprises in the tea after y'all left. Ma and Dad should both sleep 'til noon. I might have killed Grandpa, we'll see in the morning."

Ty laughed. "Thank you, Deacon."

"Least I can do for my big brother."

"How were they after we left?" Zane asked. He and Ty had gone to the ER to get Ty's hand taken care of and hadn't seen anyone when they'd gotten back.

Deuce pursed his lips. "Ma's been crying. She kept saying if she'd only known, she'd have stopped you from leaving." He shrugged. "Dad, I can't read."

"I'm thinking Dad will be easier to handle in the long run," Ty said to Deuce, who nodded in agreement. Zane gave Ty a look that said he didn't believe it, but he didn't voice an opinion.

"Well." Deuce smiled as he moved into the room. Ty stood when he got closer. "I'm proud of you. Both of you. Even if it wasn't your doing to begin with, you did it nonetheless."

Ty nodded jerkily, surprised by his reaction to his brother's words. Emotions welled in him that he didn't think he was ready for.

Deuce wrapped him up in a hug, his eyes squeezed shut, and when he spoke to Ty in a low whisper, his voice wavered. "You'll always be my hero, Beaumont."

Ty gave a choked laugh and patted the back of Deuce's head. Deuce pulled away and cleared his throat, his eyes misting. He stepped over to give Zane a hug as well, and Ty had to turn away to wipe at his eyes with the back of his sleeve.

"How the hell did Chester come up with that?" Zane asked.

Deuce laughed and Ty just shook his head, scanning all the photos lining the walls of his old room as he wiped his eyes.

"You'll have to ask Grandpa that," Deuce told Zane. "Lord only knows what he sees when people forget he's there."

"I still think he uses that hearing aid as a listening device," Ty muttered.

Deuce laughed and smiled at them both. "You guys okay? Feels kind of heavy in here."

Ty nodded and glanced at Zane, who shrugged.

"Something happen I need to know about?" Deuce asked.

"Zane has mommy issues."

Zane reached out and thumped Ty on the arm, hard.

"Interesting," Deuce said, cocking his head at Zane. He looked like a bird of prey preparing to swoop in.

"No, it's not. I'm just coming to the realization that my mother is a bitch."

Deuce raised an eyebrow. "Interesting."

"Don't start," Zane growled.

Deuce glanced between them. "Well, I'm here if you need to talk."

"Thanks, Deuce."

"And if you need it, I've got more goodies in my doctor bag."

Ty smirked. "Deacon, go away."

"All right, Uptight. Night, you two. Sleep well," he added, then turned and shut the door behind him.

Ty sat on the edge of the bed again, his chest still tight. He'd always been the role model in his generation of Grady kids, and ever since he'd been old enough to understand what responsibility was, his greatest fear was that he'd let one of them down. To see the sincerity in his brother's eyes when he'd told him he was proud of him soothed Ty's soul in a way not many other things could.

"Your brother's a latent stoner, isn't he?" Zane asked fondly.

"I don't think there's anything latent about it."

Zane laughed and scooted down in the bed, pulling on Ty's arm as he went. "Come here."

Ty lay down with him, curling around him and settling his head on Zane's shoulder. He'd grown comfortable with the opportunities he had to do this, to lean on Zane both physically and emotionally. It had taken him a long time to come to terms with the fact that it didn't make him weak. When Zane wrapped his arms around him, it felt right.

"I'm proud of you too, Beaumont."

🐾 ★ 🐾 ★ 🐾

The next morning was a little tense, to say the least, but better than Ty had expected under the circumstances. Breakfast started out stilted and awkward, but Deuce kept a conversation going with Zane about motorcycles, and Ty eventually got Mara to start rambling about the plans for the Bluefield Fourth of July parade. Then they all moved to the living room with coffee and homemade sweet rolls. It was the general consensus that, with Earl's impressive black eye and Ty's broken hand, they could skip church.

Deuce took the seat next to Zane on the couch, so Ty sat down on the floor between their feet as the conversation strengthened on the current baseball standings. Earl and Chester both were die-hard Braves fans just like Ty, but Deuce had jumped ship and started pulling for his hometown Phillies several years back. It made for a lively discussion when Deuce started gloating.

Finally the idle talk came around to one of the many subjects Ty had been dreading. "I do have one question for you two," Earl said.

"Just one?" Ty asked, though his heart had started racing. He glanced furtively over his shoulder at Zane. His lover seemed relaxed, but Ty knew that Zane was a lit fuse beneath the surface. Zane shrugged.

"When you were here last, Zane, you were wearing a wedding band," Earl said, frowning at him.

"That's right."

Earl looked from Zane to Ty, raising an eyebrow.

"My wife died in a car accident five years before I met Ty."

Earl nodded, watching Zane with what might have passed for sympathy.

"And you still wore your ring? Our condolences, Zane dear, that must have been hard on you," Mara offered.

Zane smiled. "Yes, ma'am. It was."

Ty knew Zane would never admit how hard. Becky's death had been the catalyst that threw Zane into both alcohol and drugs, problems he would struggle with for the rest of his life.

That, coupled with the fact that Becky's memory was one of the most terrifying things Ty associated with Zane, made him shift uneasily on the floor. He would have liked to derail the conversation, but he couldn't figure out how. Zane was able to talk about Becky more easily than he used to, though it was still rare, and he was definitely more comfortable with it than Ty was. For Ty, it hit on the one major insecurity he still carried with him: you couldn't compete with a ghost any more than you could run away from one.

"Losing hits a man hard," Chester said.

Ty closed his eyes and sighed. He was going to duct tape his grandfather's mouth closed before this visit was over. He opened his eyes when he felt a soft touch on his shoulder: Zane's fingers, resting there.

"Yes, it does," Zane agreed, squeezing Ty's shoulder once before pulling away. "Ty saved me."

Ty stared at him, his heart racing.

He finally had to force himself to look away. He met his father's eyes. Earl gave an apologetic tip of his chin.

Zane's knee rapped against Ty's shoulder. When Ty looked up at Zane, Zane's eyes were focused on him. He rested his cast on Zane's leg and leaned against the couch, trying to come to terms with the fact that they no longer had to hide from his family. It was freeing, but it also felt like another shoe was preparing to drop somewhere.

"Well, I just have to say it, and I know it'll embarrass you," Mara announced, "but you two are adorable together."

Ty heard a choked laugh from behind him as he blinked at his mother. True to form, he felt himself blushing.

Earl was smiling as he leaned back on the loveseat.

"That's a word I would never have chosen to describe Ty," Zane said, practically snickering.

"Well, you didn't raise him. He was cute once. One day I'll show you the picture books."

"Ma, please," Ty begged, beginning to laugh as Deuce cackled from his spot on the other end of the couch. Ty glanced at him, narrowing his eyes. "How's Livi and the baby?"

"Oh, nicely played."

Ty shrugged.

"Livi is as happy as she can be when she's not puking her brains out. Her dad hates me, but her mom keeps sending us baby boutique catalogues."

"Have you found out if it's a boy or girl yet?" Mara asked.

Deuce shook his head.

"Are you going to?"

"Livi wants to know so we can decorate. She wants to continue the tradition of the names, though. She thinks it's the greatest thing ever."

"Really?" Ty blurted, and Deuce laughed and nodded.

"Is that just the boys?" Zane asked.

"Yeah, the first boys in the family get their maternal grandmother's maiden names, the second get their paternal grandmother's. Then it gets convoluted," Deuce said with a smirk. "Dad's first name is Antrim. Grandpa's is actually Chester."

"Fascinating," Zane said.

"So, if you have a boy, what's his name going to be?" Ty asked, trying to keep any opinion of the matter out of his voice.

"Rigsdale."

"Oh God, Deacon," Ty groaned before he could stop himself.

"I know. I'm praying for a girl."

"Good luck with that," Zane said half under his breath, then flinched and pulled his phone from his pocket to look at the display.

Ty cleared his throat. "Who wants some pie?" he asked as he pushed himself up off the floor.

"Yeah, me," Zane answered as he stood and paced toward the front door, answering the call. "Hey. Everything okay?"

Ty glanced back at him as he made his way toward the kitchen. He assumed it was Zane's sister; she was the only person Zane ever used that voice with. He slowed when Zane stopped mid-stride, hand out to open the door, shoulders snapping back. "What? Where is he?" Judging by his tone, something was very wrong. Zane listened silently, the frown on his face deepening. "And no one was with him?"

Ty watched him, pie and baby names and everything else forgotten.

"I'll be on a plane as soon as I can. I'll text you my flight information. Have Manuel pick me up at the airport." Zane slid the phone back into his pocket. When he turned back to see all the Gradys watching him, he froze.

When he didn't speak, Ty spread his hands out. "What happened?"

Zane looked at him and swallowed. "My dad's been shot."

"Oh my gracious," Mara exclaimed.

"You're going down there?"

Zane nodded.

"I'm going with you."

"Ty."

Earl was already heading for the kitchen. "I'll call Jim, see if he can get one of his boys to meet you with a Sheriff's car. Get you to the airport faster."

Zane stared at Ty, dumbstruck and distressed. He no longer even tried to hide behind that mask he'd once used.

"I'm going with you."

"How?" Zane asked, sounding defeated. "You can't get off work without telling them why."

Ty gritted his teeth, but Zane was right. He would never be given time off work for his partner's family emergency, especially since he was already pretty far into his personal days.

Zane took a deep breath. Ty reached up to hug him, and Zane rested his forehead on Ty's shoulder.

"It'll be okay."

# Chapter 3

"What interest does the FBI have in this case?"

"None," Zane answered. He was sitting in the double oven that served as the sheriff's outpost for the area ranches, fighting the urge to yank his tie off and use it to wipe away the sweat running down the center of his back. The old A/C unit in the window of the trailer wasn't doing anything to fend off the summer temperatures of Texas.

The sheriff cocked his head, and Zane leaned forward to speak in lower tones. "Harrison Garrett is my father. I'm not here in any official capacity; I'm just trying to figure out what's going on."

"You're one of *those* Garretts?" the sheriff asked, and Zane could see the man's defenses lowering.

"That's right."

Zane produced his identification again. The sheriff gave it another once over, taking his time with it. He nodded and held up a thin file, then set it in front of Zane. "That's all I got to give you."

Zane paged through the file, distraught by the lack of information.

"I can save you some time."

Zane glanced up at him and nodded.

"This is the fifth time your daddy's found evidence of trespassers on the ranch. Same place every time. We don't know what they're doing, or why they're doing it. There's nothing out there."

"Why do you think the encounter was violent this time and not ever before?" Zane asked. He pushed the file into his laptop case.

"Well, this was the first time he'd caught them in action. Before, it was always after the fact. Harrison came across them, challenged them, and they fired at him. He was hit, but managed to get away. Tied himself to the saddle in case he passed out before his horse could make it back to the big house."

Zane couldn't help but smile as he listened to the account. His dad was a hard man. Zane wouldn't want to meet up with him on the open plains, that was for sure.

"What about the scene itself?"

The sheriff winced. "Not much to it. Two days from everything. Ground's been baked harder than cement. Summer rain washed away what was left. I got some good trackers here, but there was nothing to find."

Zane nodded. He knew a pretty good tracker himself. Maybe he could convince his boss to allow Ty to come out here and help him.

He kind of doubted it.

"And there's nothing local going on? Nothing your guys have caught wind of?"

"Couple brawls between the ranch hands at the establishments. Couple boys with more money than they should have. Their names are in that file, but it's nothing a little backdoor gambling won't explain."

Zane thanked the sheriff, shaking his hand before retreating from the stifling trailer and into the open air. The sun was blazing down, making the blacktop appear to waver. But it felt cooler out here than it had in there. He hurried to the truck, one of the ranch's fleet, and fumbled to get the engine running before he burst into flames.

He sat in the cab, waiting for the air to kick in and ruminating over what he'd just learned. There was no rhyme or reason to it. He'd looked at a map of the area where his dad had encountered the trespassers, and it was near nothing but an old pump house. The underground river that had once fed the spring had long since changed its course, making the area just another barren corner of the massive ranch that served no purpose but as a riding trail for visitors.

Zane got the truck moving, heading back to the ranch and the guesthouse he had claimed as his while there. After a shower to wipe away the dust and massive, massive amounts of dried sweat, he settled at the kitchen table and pulled out his cell phone to check the time. Nine at night—still early enough to phone Ty without waking him.

He hadn't been diligent with keeping in touch, and Ty had sent text messages to check on him rather than risk calling at an inopportune time.

Zane found that he couldn't wait to hear Ty's rumbling, easy voice in his ear. He'd been in Texas three days, and he was starting to feel almost homesick. He couldn't recall feeling like that before, even as a child.

For the first time, he had a home he actually wanted to call home. The thought made him both ecstatic and melancholy.

He pulled up Ty's number and hit the button. When Ty answered, it sounded almost like a pair of plastic Solo cups cartwheeling down stairs. A moment of background noise later, Ty answered with a breathless, "This is Special Agent Grady, hang up and call 911 if this is an emergency."

Zane chuckled. Apparently, Ty hadn't even been able to look at the display to see Zane's name.

There were a few banging sounds and another tumble of plastic, then a muttered oath from Ty. Again, he spoke into the phone. "One second."

In the background was a piercing shriek, then a round of raucous laughter, and another woman's scream to top it all off. Ty, sounding far away, like he was holding the phone near his hip, shouted, "Just let me shoot it!"

A rustle, and then Ty was the one screaming. Zane remembered the last time he'd heard that sound coming from Ty.

"It can't be a mouse in the house with Smith and Wesson on duty," he said, although he knew Ty wasn't listening.

He dismissed the idea that Ty was at home after being treated to several people screaming, cursing, and banging. Some voices were overcome with laughter, some screaming bloody murder.

"Who the hell brings a ferret into a bar?" Ty shouted, and someone shouted back that all the shouting was scaring the ferret.

Zane frowned as he listened to the chaotic scene for another minute before most of the activity ceased.

When Ty returned to the phone, he was out of breath and sounding quite contrite. "This is Agent Grady."

"Hey, doll," Zane said, lips curving into a smile just at hearing Ty's voice.

"Zane? Thank God. I knew I was going to get written up for that."

Zane laughed. "Having a rough night?"

"I've had worse."

"A ferret, huh? Well, I was close."

"Not as close as I was. How's your dad?"

Zane sighed. "He's all right. They've got him in a regular room now. Talking about sending him home in a few days."

"That's good. How are you?"

Zane considered how to answer that, though the pause told more of the truth than any words he could speak. "More tired than I should be."

"I'm sorry. I wish there was something I could do," Ty said in the whispered, intimate tone Zane had been so desperate to hear.

"Got a few minutes to talk to me?"

"Yeah, give me one second." Ty said good-bye to whoever else had been involved in the business with the ferret, and a moment later Zane could hear traffic and a breeze brushing over the speaker of Ty's phone. He'd obviously been at a bar, been assaulted by a ferret, and was now walking home. It was a typical night for Ty. "I'm all yours."

Zane hummed. "That's nice to hear." He rubbed one hand over his face. "Listen, the situation down here appears to be a little more . . . complex than I first thought."

"How so?"

"They're saying that Dad getting shot was a byproduct of trespassers, but I'm not buying it. Something feels . . . weird."

"Like, 'our job' weird, or 'you're in Texas' weird?"

"Both?"

"Tell me."

"Dad says he was out riding on the far end of the property and came across trespassers near the old pump house. They took a few potshots and got lucky as they drove off."

"Jesus."

"The thing is, there's nothing near that old pump house. No reason for anyone to be there. I can't figure it out."

"So, what, you're calling in Jim Bowie and Sam Houston to clear shit up?"

Zane laughed despite the gravity of the situation. "I'm going to make some calls, yes, but I spoke with the sheriff this afternoon. He told me this isn't the first time it's happened. Dad's reported it before."

"Kind of far from the border for the usual stuff, aren't you?"

"Yeah, but that doesn't mean it couldn't make it this far. Could be drugs, could be sex trade, could be horses."

"If the next option is sex with horses, I need you to stop right there."

"We're not in that part of Texas."

"I bet you look hot in the hat though."

"Stop trying to distract me!"

"I'm sorry," Ty said, though he didn't sound sincere.

"As I was saying... Jesus, Ty, what was I saying?"

"You're not sleeping, are you?"

"No."

"You want to stay and look into it, don't you?"

"Yeah," Zane said with a sigh of relief. He should have known Ty would understand. "So that means I might be here a little while longer than I'd planned."

Ty didn't say anything to that, but the silence spoke volumes about his disappointment. Zane could imagine his broad shoulders slumping as he walked. He wanted to reach through the phone and hug his partner, who was, for all intents and purposes, a large teddy bear with a gun.

"Do you need anything from my end?" Ty finally asked.

Zane could think of plenty, first and foremost being Ty himself. He didn't say that, though, because he knew Ty couldn't take time off work for Zane's personal problems. "No, I think I've got it covered. I thought I might call and get a sanity check in the evenings."

"Call whenever you want. Mostly I've been in the office, trying to inflict a paper cut on myself serious enough to require medical leave."

Zane grinned. "Mac would just tell you to suck it up."

"Hence the many failed attempts at tripping on the rug at the entryway. The one time I managed it, I tucked and rolled and popped back up before I could think twice about it."

Zane laughed—the first real laugh he'd managed in days. It was hard to tell if Ty was serious or just playing with him, and that was one of the things Zane loved so much about him. Ty really was the type of guy who would ninja roll through the lobby of a government building and just keep walking as if nothing had happened.

A door opened and closed, and Zane heard rustling as Ty took off his jacket and moved around the house. Ty whispered to Smith and Wesson. It was a tender side to his lover no one else had seen, and it all culminated in the way he treated those damn cats.

For a brief moment, Zane was almost sick with the need to wrap Ty up in a hug.

"Are you really okay, Zane?"

"For now," Zane said, voice hoarse. He shifted to look out the window. There were no lights. Nothing on the skyline but the occasional hill or scrub tree. And stars as far as he could see, stretching on into the night. "I wish you could see this, Ty."

Ty was silent. Zane was familiar with that silence; he heard it almost every time he said something sincere to his lover and Ty tried to decide if he should respond with a joke or with something more genuine. Zane never knew what kind of response he would get, and that was half the fun of it.

"I'm sure I'll see it one day," Ty said softly.

Zane closed his eyes. He almost wished Ty had made a joke of it this time. He missed him. There was no point in lingering over it, so he moved on.

"The real problems come when Mother shows up."

"Why?"

"She's barely been to the hospital."

"Did your folks split up?"

"If they have, no one's told me. They're still both living in the same house, but it's so big they wouldn't cross paths if they didn't want to." Zane had always wondered how his dad lived with his mother every day, but to get through forty-five years of marriage, he obviously loved her on some level. "When she shows up, all she can do is tell me that none of this would have happened if I'd been here like a good son."

"You know that's bullshit, right?"

"Yeah, but . . . she's my mom." Zane dragged his hand through his damp hair. "You'd think she'd just be glad to see me, but no."

"I'm sorry, Zane. I'm not really sure how to help. Other than to tell you to quit your bitching and go buy me a Stetson."

Zane chuckled at Ty's attempt to distract him from his troubles. As usual, it was working. "I don't know. A Stetson's a real personal thing to a man. You don't just go around handing them out." He shook his head and spoke more quietly. "I'm not sure there's helping to be done. Just wish you were here."

Ty was silent for a long while—another of those silences where he tried to decide which path to take—the sound of his breathing steady and comforting. Then he cleared his throat and said, "Well, you want me to tell you about *my* night? Any story that starts out with 'There was this dude with a ferret in his beard' is bound to make you feel better, right?"

"Tell me," Zane said, smiling and relaxing back as Ty started talking. He was glad to listen to his lover ramble on in a voice as smooth as honey instead of dwelling over the trouble he was sure to find tomorrow when he started digging.

☙ ★ ☙ ★ ☙

"Suspect is on foot, agents in pursuit," the dispatcher said through Ty's earpiece. "Suspect is armed and dangerous."

Ty cut across three lanes of traffic, climbing over a Mini Cooper and then leaping over the head of a cyclist as he dove to grab for the suspect. He made contact but slid right off the man and landed hard, rolling across the sidewalk and slamming into the base of a hotdog cart. The contents tumbled and splattered all over him before he could scramble back to his feet.

He cursed and wiped relish off his arm as he sat up. He supposed he was fortunate the boiling water hadn't fallen on him, but that stroke of luck didn't make up for the fact that this was ruining what had been a nice Sunday afternoon with friends.

He could sprint and he could cover long distances, and he could fucking parkour up the side of a wall, but he wasn't built for dashing across entire cities after suspects who were part gazelle and greased up like that slimy green thing from Ghostbusters.

"I lost him," Alston panted over the earpiece. "He's like a cyborg or something."

Ty looked around as he tried to catch his breath. He and his teammates had been enjoying lunch at a sidewalk café after closing a difficult week, debating if they should order a bottle of wine or just walk a few blocks over to the nearest bar and start Sunday off early like good little heathens. And then a man had paraded up to them in a trench coat and whipped it open to reveal nothing underneath but a huge, unfortunate tiger tattoo on his chest. His nipples formed the tiger's eyes, his navel acted as the nose, and Ty hadn't allowed himself to examine it any further before he'd turned his head and spit his water all over Alston. Lassiter had jumped to his feet and knocked Perrimore's bowl of hot pasta into his lap. And Clancy had almost fallen out of her chair laughing. She'd thought it funny until the man had grabbed her, kissed her, and then run off with her sidearm.

"Maybe not having any clothes on makes him aerodynamic," Lassiter muttered, sounding just as out of breath as Alston was.

"Wouldn't the trench slow him down?" Perrimore wheezed. The man was built like a brick shithouse: good for barreling through locked doors, but not made for long-distance.

"I've got his coat," Ty said with a laugh. He was barely winded, but then, he ran every day and had for years. The hotdog cart had fared better than he had, though.

"Eyes on the suspect!" Clancy shouted, her piercing voice nearly busting Ty's eardrum. He reached up to his Bluetooth piece and turned the volume down.

"Clancy!" Alston shouted. It was a safe bet that he'd just been outdistanced by his spitfire of a partner and was now huffing and puffing to catch up to her.

Ty jogged to the end of the street, looking both ways.

"Where the fuck are you?" Ty asked.

"I got to get a treadmill," Perrimore said.

"I think . . . I think I'm outside Ty's house," Lassiter added.

"You're not, Lassie," Ty assured him. "You can't run that far."

"All these fucking houses look alike!"

"You went the wrong way, you fucktard!"

"West Lombard! Heading toward downtown," Clancy shouted.

"We might need backup with this fucker," Alston gasped. He was still on the move.

"If you say 'he's slippery,' I'm going to knock you on your ass," Ty grumbled.

"Someone, for the love of God, get ahead of him!" Alston was gasping for air. "I'm done. I'm done. I'm dying."

Ty fished his badge out of his pocket and stepped into the middle of Pratt Street, flagging down a taxi. When the man stopped, Ty went to the driver's side door and flipped his badge open. "How good are you with hairpin turns?"

They sped along the busy streets that connected the Inner Harbor with the downtown financial district, narrowly missing parked cars, pedestrians, and further hotdog vendors. Ty caught a glimpse of Clancy, her red hair and even stride unmistakable as she sprinted along the sidewalk. Just ahead of her was the streaking man with the tiger tattoo, Clancy's gun clenched in his hand, a grin in place. He had no idea what sort of pain would rain down on him when she caught him.

She wasn't gaining on him, but she wasn't losing ground either. She would catch him, eventually. In heels.

Ty tried to raise her on the conference call they had initiated, tapping his Bluetooth headset, but his phone had either died or ended the call on its own.

"Get ahead of Naked Guy," Ty told the driver as he gripped the door handle.

The taxi took a turn that almost put it up on two wheels, and it came to a screeching, jarring halt just as the streaker darted across the street. He dodged the taxi, leaping up onto the hood to try to slide across it. No doubt the guy had seen it in a movie somewhere, because no one in their right mind would try that otherwise. He hit the hood of the taxi, and the driver let out a horrified scream.

"Ball prints on my hood!" the man cried as he gripped his steering wheel and shook it.

Bare skin squealed against the windshield. The man didn't even make it halfway across the car before his own nakedness stopped him dead, and he lay splayed against the hood and windshield like a squashed bug. A big, sweaty, squashed, naked bug.

Ty got out of the car, joined by Clancy just in time to hold the man down for her as she disarmed and handcuffed him.

A crowd was gathering, laughing and pointing, applauding and booing.

Ty had to turn away from their prisoner so he wouldn't laugh when he called in the arrest. But his phone was full of mustard and pickle bits and wouldn't turn on. Alston joined them, holding his side and wincing as he pulled his phone out to make the call. Then he called Perrimore and asked him to bring one of the cars to them.

"What the hell happened to you?" Alston asked Ty as he looked him up and down.

Ty looked at his shirtfront—gray with a huge badge on it, and the words "Gravity – It's the Law" printed across the top. It was now covered with splatters of ketchup, mustard, relish, and chili.

"You smell delicious," Alston said with a smirk.

"Bite me, Scott."

"I might, Hot Dog; I didn't finish my lunch back there."

Ty couldn't help but snort.

"Hot Dog. That one might stick," Clancy said. When Ty looked at her, she snapped a picture of him with her phone.

"Really?"

"For Garrett," Clancy said, eyes wide and sincere.

"Hey, pretty lady," the streaker said to Clancy. He was oblivious to his own ridiculousness.

Ty and Alston both turned to look at him, eyebrows climbing. Whatever this guy was on, it was good stuff. The tiger on his chest was one of the worst pieces of art Ty had ever seen, and it got worse as the man moved. He was jutting his hips out, shameless, knees rocking like he was hearing music. His hair was slicked back and he had a full-blown porn 'stache, complete with gel in it to make it curl upward.

"Is that a mirror in your pocket, baby?" he said to Clancy with a goofy leer. "'Cause I can sure see myself in your pants."

Clancy rolled her eyes as she checked her weapon and stuffed it into her holster.

Ty looked the guy up and down. "Buddy, you don't have the sack to wear her pants."

"Damn straight," Clancy said.

Ty held his hand up and she gave him a high-five as she strolled away. Alston was laughing as Ty pulled a twenty out of his wallet. He handed it to the taxi driver through the window. "For the car wash."

"Lunch is on Grady!"

🐾 ★ 🐾 ★ 🐾

Zane lay awake in bed, listening to the sounds of the house settling and staring at the darkened ceiling.

He looked at his phone, sitting on the bedside table, then picked it up to check the time. Nearly three in the morning; there was no way he could call Ty and not wake him. And wanting to hear his lover's voice was not a good enough reason to wake him.

He scrolled through the photo roll, surprised at the homesickness that came over him as he looked at picture after picture of him and Ty. Most of them were taken from arm's length, with Ty in his aviators and Zane smiling like someone who hadn't been broken by life.

Some were of Ty alone, photos that Zane had taken without Ty's knowledge. Only one was of Ty without clothes. Maybe. And, of course, there was the photo Clancy had sent him this afternoon, with no explanation for why Ty was covered in condiments and looking like he'd just run a marathon. Zane had to laugh, though. He couldn't wait to hear that story. They hadn't worked today, so whatever had happened was merely a result of Ty's unspeakable ability to attract weird things.

Zane stopped flipping through the photos when he came across his absolute favorite. He and Ty had taken a weekend trip to Virginia Beach to celebrate Ty's birthday on Memorial Day weekend. They'd been standing on the beach in front of their hotel, watching a thunderstorm roll in from the sea. Everyone else had scrambled inside, and while Zane had tried to convince Ty to go in as well, Ty had chosen to stay and watch. The sky had been an impressive velvet blue, with rays of sunshine punching through as the blackness encroached. The look on Ty's face had been serene and somehow melancholy as he watched the storm whip up the tide and thrash against the shore in front of them.

Zane had snapped the picture with his phone without Ty knowing, leaving the phone near his hip and capturing Ty from below. Ty had never caught on that Zane was watching him instead of the storm, so wrapped up in whatever it was about storms out on the ocean that seemed to fascinate Ty like they did.

When the rain had hit the beach and Zane had turned to retreat to their room, Ty grabbed him instead and started a waltz in the downpour. When they finished the dance, people applauded from their balconies. It had been the first taste of what life with Ty might be like when they came out.

It had also been one of the most romantic moments of his life. He would never be able to top Ty's off-the-cuff romance with anything he planned ahead of time. He intended to spend the rest of his life trying, though.

His heart twisted as he looked at the photo, and a bittersweet feeling settled in his chest. It was still sinking in that he had a family in

West Virginia now, a family that knew he and Ty loved each other and accepted that for what it was.

And now he was back in Texas with so much uncertainty swirling around him that it made him nauseous just to think of it. His mother's constant badgering, his father injured and on the warpath, the possibility that whatever was happening on the ranch was just starting instead of ending...

And on top of all of that, Zane couldn't help imagining what it would be like to be able to bring Ty here and introduce him to his family as the love of his life.

Before he knew what he was doing, he'd clicked back over to his favorite numbers, hit Ty's picture, and pressed the call button.

It took a few rings, but Ty answered with a hoarse, "What?"

Zane smiled and closed his eyes again, breathing out a sigh of relief. He could just imagine Ty stretched out in their bed, sheets tangled around his muscular body. He'd be warm and pliant, his fingers gentle against Zane's skin as he reached out to him. He'd smell faintly of Old Spice, and his hair, which had grown, would be just long enough for Zane to twirl around his fingers and hold onto as they kissed.

"Hey," Zane whispered, voice choked on the sudden rush of sentiment and arousal.

"Zane? Are you okay? What's wrong? Is it your dad?"

"Nothing. Nothing's wrong, I just miss you."

Ty was silent, and Zane could hear his harsh breaths as he sat up in bed. "What happened?"

"Nothing, I just . . . I'm lying here in this huge bed and I can't sleep."

Ty sighed. "I miss you too, Zane."

"I'm sorry I woke you."

"It's okay. Today was a slow day, it's fine."

Zane narrowed his eyes. "I know your definition of a slow day, and I got Clancy's picture."

"Yeah, well..."

Zane heard a harsh breath and a shuffle of sheets. He suspected Ty had just stretched back out in bed, and the mental image of his lover was enough to slide his hand beneath the band of his boxers. His palm rested on his hip, fingers grazing his hardening cock.

"Are you as miserable and lonely as I am?" Ty asked, sounding pitiful.

Zane swallowed hard and looked around the bedroom of the guesthouse. He'd been living here for a full week now. The king-sized bed was far too big, the room too empty and impersonal. The television offered no company, the art and trinkets held no memories for him. Even the view out the window had grown unfamiliar.

"Yes," he said, almost choking on the word.

"Zane," Ty whispered, pulling Zane back. "I know what you're doing."

Zane found himself smiling at Ty's raspy voice, taking himself in hand to start a slow stroke. "What am I doing?"

"Same thing I am."

Zane's breath caught on an exhale. "Ty."

"Go on, Zane. Close your eyes."

Zane hit his phone's speaker button, laid it beside his head on the pillow, and closed his eyes like Ty had asked. His hand squeezed and pulled, his actions slow and sensual, mimicking the way Ty touched him when they were fooling around. His other hand dragged across his abdomen, fingers sliding over ridges of hard muscle.

With Ty's rasping voice in his ear, Zane could imagine it. His fingers dragging over Ty's body, finding the occasional ridge of a scar, digging into those incredible muscles as they tensed. He could imagine Ty's hand wrapped around his cock, thumb sliding over the head, palm massaging his balls. He could picture himself under Ty, his hand between them, stroking Ty's cock as Ty ground against him.

Zane gasped and rolled his hips, stroking faster as Ty's seductive voice whispered to him from the pillow beside his head.

"I'd give anything to see you do that," Ty said, voice hitching. "Come for me, Zane. I need to hear it."

Zane knew from the timbre of Ty's voice that he was touching himself as he lay alone in their bed. It was enough to make Zane's entire body tingle. He could picture it because Ty had done it for him several times, brought himself off as Zane watched.

He shoved the comforter and the sheets down past his hips and his boxers followed. The cold air of the room hit his skin, but he didn't care as he kicked free of everything restraining his movements.

"Baby," he ground out, pleading with Ty to keep speaking. Ty did, murmuring to him, telling him how to touch himself, what he would do to him if he were there with him, how much he loved to hear the sounds Zane made. Zane didn't try to curtail his moans and groans, letting Ty hear them, letting Ty use them to reach his own end.

"You sound so good," Ty whispered, voice deep and harsh.

The rasp of his voice covered Zane, wrapping him in warmth and pleasure. Zane pushed his hips off the mattress, his entire body going into spasms.

"Come on, Zane!" Ty yelled, sounding just as desperate as he often did when Zane was inside him.

Zane shouted and reached up to dig his fingers into the headboard as he came. His hand moved faster, then his fingers massaged his balls for an even stronger orgasm as he came all over his belly and even up onto his chest. He could hear Ty talking him through it, but he didn't register the words until his breathing had calmed.

"Zane," Ty said, his voice sounding far away.

Zane reached for the phone and turned off the speaker, then held it to his ear. The cold air hit him as he calmed, and he knew he'd have to get out of bed to at least wipe down with a damp towel before he could sleep. The stress was gone, though, and he told himself there was no reason to be lonely. Ty was out there, waiting for him, missing him.

"As good as that was, I prefer it in person," Zane said.

Ty chuckled, the sound dark and familiar. "Now go clean yourself off. Look at you, you should be ashamed."

"Ditto, you pervert," Zane grunted, smiling.

"Goodnight, Zane."

"Night, Ty."

The call ended without any further fuss or pleasantries. Zane lay awake for a while longer, shocked by how a simple call and a few minutes listening to Ty's voice could turn his outlook around.

He fell asleep with the phone still in his hand.

🐾 ★ 🐾 ★ 🐾

"Dad, what were you thinking, going out there alone?" Zane asked.

He pushed away from the railing of the big house's second-floor balcony and frowned at his father, who was sitting in one of the lounge chairs and staring out over the land.

He was shocked by the difference in the man. His hair had gone from steel gray to almost white in the last year or so. His face was thinner, bordering on gaunt, and though Zane was attributing much of it to his injuries, he was concerned by the lack of life in his father's dark eyes. The only things that hadn't changed were the impressive horseshoe mustache and the deep resonance of his voice.

"I wasn't thinking about getting shot, if that's what you're after."

Zane snorted and turned to look out over the land. "You should get some more help, you know."

"I'm doing just fine."

Zane snorted. "You're either stubborn or cheap."

"I'm lazy, there's a difference. Takes work to hire a new man I can trust."

Zane laughed, then pulled his phone out of his back pocket and checked it for the fifth time since they'd gotten home. No texts or calls.

"Still. Edges of the ranch are getting away from you."

Harrison frowned and looked out at the view of the sprawling Hill Country: acres and acres of unrelenting, rolling green, covered with prickly pear cactus and scrub trees that made passage on foot nearly impossible. It was a beautiful, foreboding landscape, and every inch they could see from their vantage point belonged to the Carter Garrett ranch. It was over five-thousand acres, and Harrison only employed two dozen or so ranch hands.

Zane leaned forward, watching his father. "Dad."

"Weren't you calling someone?" Harrison said with a wave of his hand.

Zane grunted in annoyance, but nodded. "I'll be right back, just need to check in at work."

"Take your time."

Zane paced away, heading toward the other end of the balcony as he dialed Ty. He'd tried on the way to the hospital this morning, but hadn't been able to reach his partner. He'd tried several times since bringing his father home, and each call had been kicked directly to voicemail. The phone didn't ring this time, either, just sent him to Ty's voicemail yet again. Zane hung up without leaving a message. A heavy, ominous feeling began to settle in his chest. There was no good reason Ty wouldn't answer his phone at this time of day.

He glanced back at his father, then dialed his work line.

"This is Special Agent Tyler Grady's desk," a woman answered.

"Clancy?"

"Garrett! Hey! How's your dad doing, is he okay?"

"Uh . . . yeah, he's okay. Just got home from the hospital, thanks for asking. I'm looking for Ty, is he around?"

"No, Hot Dog called in this morning and said he'd been tasked out to DC again."

Zane's stomach began to churn as that news sank in. "Tasked out to DC" was Ty's way of covering when Richard Burns needed a job done. Burns had promised Ty months ago that he wouldn't call him again for one of those jobs. Apparently, his promises had a shelf life of three months.

"Garrett? You there?" Clancy asked, sounding worried.

"Yeah, sorry. I . . . will you have him give me a call when he shows back up?"

"Sure, but you'll probably be home before he will. He said he'd be gone for up to a week on this one."

Zane nodded jerkily. "Okay. Thanks, Clancy."

"No problem. Hey, you need anything from our end, you just ask, okay? We sent flowers to the hospital. Did your dad get them?"

Zane barely heard what she was saying. "Yeah, he did. I meant to thank you." In truth, he had no idea if his father had gotten those flowers. That was the furthest thing from his mind now. "I have to run, but I'll be in touch, okay? Thanks."

He hung up as he headed back toward his dad. When he sank into the chair beside him, the phone was still in his hand and he was staring out at the land, unseeing.

"Everything okay?"

"Hmm?"

"You look like you got bad news," Harrison observed, his sharp eyes looking Zane up and down.

Zane smiled and told himself to pull it back together. "Yeah, just . . . my partner got loaned out to another agency. I can't get in touch with him."

"Is that good or bad?"

"It's dangerous, sometimes. Bad, I guess."

Harrison nodded. "You worried about your partner, Z?"

"Yeah, a little," Zane admitted.

"That's good. Last time you were here, you weren't even worried about yourself."

The echoed chime of the front door saved Zane from having to respond. That was one conversation he did not want to have.

"Sounds like someone left the gate open," Harrison said.

Every ranch in the Hill Country, big or small, had a gate. Sometimes that was all there was—just a gate on the driveway with no fence to back it up. But the Carter Garrett Ranch had fences galore.

"You better get it. Juanita's at the store."

Zane nodded and went inside. The door chimed again as he jogged down the stairs. The house around him brought back all kinds of memories, some good, some not. Parts of the house had been comfortable and homey, mostly the parts frequented by his father or Zane and the other kids, while others had been museum pieces meant for magazine shoots and society functions. He got to the door and nudged the dog out of the way so he could open it.

What he saw left him speechless.

Ty grinned. "What, it's the butler's day off?"

Zane just stared, taking in the face that had filled his dreams for nearly a week. "How are you here?"

Ty's smile softened into something more intimate, and he shrugged. "You sounded like you needed me."

It sunk in with another heartbeat, and Zane stepped forward to wrap his arms around Ty and held him tight. "Yes," he whispered. "Yes." He squeezed his eyes shut, hardly able to believe it. Ty was *here*. In *Texas*.

Ty hugged him hard, laughing.

It was a long minute before Zane could make himself step back, though he didn't pull loose of Ty's arms. Ty's tanned face and a day's worth of stubble was possibly the most beautiful thing Zane had ever laid eyes on. "How?"

"Well, see, first I took a plane. And then I rented a car. And then after getting lost twice, I found a sign that said 'Garrett,' scaled the big-ass gate down by the road, and hitched a ride on a prairie dog here." He gave a mock frown. "Those things are not as cute and cuddly as you'd think."

Zane snorted and pulled Ty inside. "Funny guy. Hell, I don't care how."

"I caught the first flight out this morning," Ty said as he stepped into the marble-tiled foyer. "Called in a favor. All my favors, actually. I explained what was going on to Dick, and he's claiming me for as long as we need to be here so I don't have to use any comp time. And Alston took the case I was working in exchange for a personal favor of unknown origin later on."

Zane hugged him again, stunned by the lengths to which Ty had gone to be with him. Ty laughed, his long fingers sliding down Zane's back. Zane had to force himself to let go. He pushed the door shut behind them and looked down at the red and white Australian Shepherd sniffing at Ty's ankles.

Ty watched it warily. "Why do they like me?" he whispered in exasperation. "It's like they smell that I was almost food once."

"Bullet likes everybody, even me." Zane leaned over to scratch the dog's ears and then shoo him away. The dog headed for the stairs, seeking out Harrison. When Zane straightened, it struck him all over again. "I can't believe you're here. And I can't believe how much I missed you."

"I missed you too. Not enough to trek my ass to Texas, but you sounded . . . I just figured I needed to be here."

Zane hugged him again. He couldn't help himself. "It's just a shitty situation," he said, glancing toward the kitchen as he released Ty. His mother was around here somewhere. Maybe upstairs in her suite, or in her office. He was surprised she hadn't come out when the doorbell rang. "But I am so glad you're here."

Ty ran his hand down Zane's arm. Then he shook himself and shrugged his bag off his shoulder, handing it to Zane. "I'll just make myself at home then."

Zane took it and dropped it on the floor next to the door. At Ty's raised eyebrow, he said, "We won't be staying here. We—"

His mother's voice rang out from upstairs. "Zane? Who was at the door?"

Zane glanced to Ty and made a rude gesture toward the stairs. "A friend of mine's here," he called back, and within a few moments,

Beverly Carter-Garrett appeared at the banister halfway around the second floor.

"A friend?" she asked, looking down at them from on high. She paused for effect, and then made her way down the polished wooden staircase, a polite smile in place.

She cut a severe figure on the spiral staircase, her graying hair dyed a harsh black, her smile not touching her blue eyes. She hadn't been expecting company today, but that hadn't stopped her from donning a designer pantsuit, high heels, and a string of pearls; her entire life was about outward appearances, and always had been.

"Ma'am," Ty said with a nod as she came down the stairs.

Beverly tipped her head to one side as she looked Ty over. He was wearing jeans and a plain white T-shirt, probably to ward off the blazing heat, and every inch of him was dusty. No way would he pass Beverly's inspection. He wasn't wearing a tie, after all. She turned her gaze to Zane as she stopped two stairs from the bottom—a tactic with which he was familiar. It put her at about his eye level. He'd gotten his height from his father and grandfather, so she'd come up with a way to compensate.

"Mother, this is Special Agent Ty Grady. Ty, my mother, Beverly Carter-Garrett."

Beverly held out her hand, like royalty. Ty took a single step forward and took the tips of her fingers in his, bowing his head in a formal greeting that, for some reason, Zane was shocked to see his partner knew how to do. By the look on his mother's face, she was both surprised and pleased.

"Hello, Mr. Grady," Beverly said, voice still polite. "How do you know Zane?"

"I'm his partner, ma'am."

The warmth and charm that seemed to exude from Ty at all times were missing. He was being gracious, but almost cool to her. It was obvious to Zane that what he'd said about his mother in the past was coloring Ty's behavior toward her, whether Ty meant for it to or not. But Beverly treated everyone like that. Zane figured she wouldn't think anything of it.

"His partner?"

"Yes, Mother. And it's Special Agent Grady, not Mr. Grady."

"Oh, I see. I wasn't aware you had a partner, Zane."

Zane just smiled, not willing to give her a chance to start an old argument. She was baiting him, pure and simple. When she didn't get the response she wanted, she turned to Ty.

"Please, come in." Beverly indicated the sitting room to her left. "Tell me what brings you to Texas, Mr. Grady."

"Well," Ty said, glancing back at Zane with a furrow of his brow. He was obviously wondering how much he should say, and probably how nice he had to be. Zane waved permissively—*go for it*. "Zane told me his father was shot."

"And that brought you all the way from Washington?" she asked, sitting primly in the armchair that faced the couch. "Just to see your coworker?"

"Mother, you know full well it's Baltimore, and Ty's not just my coworker, he's a close friend."

Beverly folded her hands in her lap. "I thought perhaps he'd brought some work for you. You do claim to be important to that place."

Ty looked between them. He cleared his throat, meeting Zane's eyes, and he pointed to the bag by the door. He held his hand against his chest, where only Zane could see it, and mimicked holding a gun. "I did bring work."

"I see," Beverly said, her voice still cool. "I was under the impression that Zane was to be at *home* with his family."

"Ma'am, I was under the impression that he's been at the *hospital* with his family. Weren't you there?"

The change that came over Beverly's face was like a storm cloud passing over a clear blue sky. For once, she'd been struck speechless. No one in the area had the nerve to say such things to her, and no one in the family bothered anymore. Zane knew she'd dig in the spurs any chance she got, but he hadn't expected Ty to shoot back. The pointed words from his partner, and the quiet way Ty was standing up for him, warmed him in a way he knew he should have been ashamed of.

But he needed to curtail it before it went further. He knew what Ty's sharp tongue was capable of, and he knew his mother. Rather than waiting for the next verbal stab, he turned Ty toward the stairs.

"Mother, I'm going to take Ty to meet Dad. We'll talk to you at dinner. Come on," he said to Ty.

Ty turned with him, pausing to nod at Beverly. "Nice to meet you, ma'am," he offered as he followed Zane to the stairs.

"Dinner is at eight o'clock sharp," Beverly called after them.

Zane didn't slow until they reached the second story landing and the small sitting alcove that led toward a set of double doors to the outside. He stopped short of opening them and turned to Ty. "That was the first time in years I've seen someone do that to her."

Ty ran his hand down Zane's arm—a gesture he reserved for when he felt Zane needed comforting. "I'm sorry. It kind of slipped out. I promise I'll be good."

"It was spectacular," Zane whispered, smiling and pulling Ty closer, palming Ty's lower back as he reveled in the kiss. He couldn't express in words how much Ty being here meant. "But yeah. Try to be good so she doesn't banish you, huh? Dad's a lot easier. And drugged to the gills on pain meds."

"Right."

Zane smiled as the rest of his mother-related tension melted away, and he led the way out to the porch. Harrison was sitting right where Zane had left him.

"Hey, Dad, I want you to meet someone."

Harrison turned his head and watched them approach. "You'll forgive me if I don't get up," he said, his gravelly voice even lower than usual. "This a friend of yours, Z?"

Ty waved his broken hand out by his hip and stepped closer. He held his left out to Harrison. "Ty Grady, sir. It's a pleasure to meet you." The difference in his tone with Harrison was night and day to his tone with Beverly.

Harrison shook Ty's hand. He glanced up at Zane and back to Ty. "Z's partner?"

"Yes, sir."

Harrison smiled. "Wondered if you'd show."

Zane blinked. "What?"

"You talk about your partner, Z. You're closer than you let on."

Zane glanced at Ty, surprised to feel himself blushing.

Harrison looked at Ty. "You're playing hooky from work to be here, aren't you, son?"

Ty smiled. "Yes, sir, I suppose I am."

"Why is that?"

"Zane's always there when I need him." He met Zane's eyes and added, "What sort of partner would I be if I weren't here now?"

Zane grinned.

"Have a seat," Harrison said, waving at two chairs in the informal grouping.

They settled in, and Zane began to relax. Ty had apparently passed his dad's inspection, and his dad seemed content to let the conversation go at that. He never had been one for idle talk.

Zane looked to Ty. "Did you eat on the way here? We've got a few hours 'til dinner."

"I had three peanuts on the airplane; I'm good," Ty said, deadpan. "It really is like surface-of-the-sun hot here, huh?"

Harrison snorted a laugh. "Why don't you two go on and get him settled in. No need to stay here until dinner." Zane opened his mouth to protest, but Harrison talked right on. "I'm well enough, Z. You've been on your feet for days now. Take him and show him the ranch. Get some peace and quiet before dinner comes around and your mother starts in on you again."

Ty looked to Zane, prepared to take his cues from Zane until he got a feel for the lay of the land. Classic Grady, studying his prey in its natural habitat before striking.

"You know what? I'm going to do that and leave you to face Mom's wrath," Zane said, standing up. "Ty put her in her place just now."

"Did you, now? Would've liked to've seen that."

Zane laid his hand on Ty's shoulder. "I'm sure you'll get another chance."

Harrison chuckled. "Go on. I'll see you at dinner."

"Okay, Dad," Zane said as he patted Harrison's good shoulder.

Ty stood and leaned over to shake Harrison's hand again. "It's a relief to see you doing well, sir."

Harrison cracked half a smile, which told Zane that he liked Ty quite a lot. "Welcome to the C and G," he said instead of good-bye.

🐾 ★ 🐾 ★ 🐾

They were driving away from the large colonial-style mansion, and Ty had just remembered to turn his phone back on when Zane spoke again.

"I can't believe you're here," Zane said, shaking his head as he guided the truck down the long dirt driveway.

"I was going to call and tell you I'd be coming, but I know you. You'd have tried to come get me at the airport and stressed about it. And I was kind of looking forward to surprising you."

Zane hit the brakes, veering off the private road onto a flat, sandy piece of land that looked just like all the other flat, sandy pieces of land surrounding them.

"What are you doing?" Ty asked, worried that he might have upset Zane by coming unannounced.

Zane jerked his seatbelt off and threw the truck into park. He left it running, though, the air conditioning blasting to ward off the blazing heat outside. Ty watched him in alarm, but then Zane leaned sideways and crawled across the bench seat to grab him and kiss him messily.

Ty flailed, a hand going out to drag down the window as he tried to keep his balance, but Zane pulled him sideways and twisted him, toppling both of them over and into the passenger side door. He grunted as his head banged against the window, but he wrapped his arms around Zane, heedless of the knock on the head or the whatever-it-was sticking into his back or the seatbelt that might strangle him if Zane pulled him again.

"You're incredible, you know that? I'm so goddamned lucky to have you," Zane said before stealing another kiss. Ty could only grunt in response.

He had to shove at Zane's chest when the kiss got too heated, holding him at bay with both hands, trapped against the door panel and looking up into those dark eyes he'd missed so much. "I refuse to let you grope me in the cab of a truck in your parents' driveway," he said, laughing as Zane began to chuckle.

Zane sat back, nodding and straightening his shirt. Ty shifted and pulled at his jeans. They'd gotten far too tight.

"So, if we're not staying in the big house, where are we staying?" he asked as Zane pulled the truck back onto the road.

"Guesthouse. It's so much smoother if I'm not under the same roof as my mother." He glanced at Ty and leered. "And no one to hear you scream."

"I'm down with that," Ty drawled, smirking as he watched Zane. He was wearing dark jeans and cowboy boots, paired with a soft blue denim shirt that hugged his slim hips and highlighted his impressive shoulders and arms. The black Stetson on the dashboard had clearly been worn. His wavy black hair had a hat impression in it.

He looked incredible. Ty could feel his heart beating faster as he looked his lover over.

"Say something else," Ty prompted.

"What?"

"Say something, tell me something else."

"Okay, that's not weird at all."

"Please?"

Zane gave him a tolerant sigh. "The closest town to us is Dripping Springs, and it's about a twenty-minute drive. The ranches out this way are all pretty massive and self-sufficient. The Carter Garrett Ranch is five thousand acres, the largest in the area. We raise horses mostly, but there's also cattle, sheep, and some llamas and emus."

"Your accent has come out," Ty said when Zane paused.

Zane glanced at him, eyebrows raised. "What?"

"It's . . . incredibly sexy."

"What?"

"Say something else."

"No, stop it," Zane said with a laugh.

Ty grinned, unable to take his eyes off Zane. "We need to go down to the front gate. I really did leave my rental there."

"I thought you were kidding."

"Nope. Climbed the big-ass fence. Impressive, by the way. It's like a castle gate and somebody forgot to build the rest of the castle."

"Yeah, well, around here people don't see your house or your yard or your front door. You have to impress them with your gate. And Mother is all for impressing people."

Ty nodded. The gate to the Carter Garrett Ranch was quite beautiful: Two towers of stacked stone on either side of the drive, with a twisted metal art piece weaving between them. A sign hung from the metal, a stylized C and G intertwined with an ampersand. A simple iron gate between the towers kept visitors out.

"I'll call and have one of the guys go fetch it," Zane promised.

"Why do you keep the gate closed? Is it to keep livestock in or people out?"

"The ranch is open three days a week to the public. We have school trips and tour buses and people can book times for riding the trails or getting riding lessons. Supplemental income for the ranch."

"Really? People just drive up at any given time?"

Zane shrugged. "Thursday through Saturday, yeah. So the other days they keep the gate closed, just in case people get the wrong day or get nosy."

Ty cleared his throat, barely able to concentrate on what Zane was saying for listening to how he was saying it. Jesus, where had *that* accent been all these months? He wondered if Zane suppressed it or if it was just something he'd lost along the way and then had fallen back into when he'd submerged himself back home.

He waved his broken hand toward the side of the road. "Can you pull over for a minute?"

Zane shot him a concerned glance and pulled the truck to the side of the gravel driveway, putting it in park.

Ty unbuckled his seatbelt and crawled toward him. The only thing preventing him from climbing right into Zane's lap was the steering wheel. Zane grabbed at him, laughing as they kissed again, over and over. Ty unbuckled Zane's seatbelt, pulling at him and leaning backward, and Zane wriggled out of the seatbelt and followed, laying Ty down on the bench seat. Ty propped his foot on the door and held on as Zane dug his hands into Ty's hair.

"Christ, why'd you have to start this?" Zane grumbled. Ty could feel his body responding, and his jeans were going to be impossible to unzip in a few minutes if this kept up. "We're five fucking seconds from the house."

"I missed you." Zane felt solid against his fingers, and after a week of closing his eyes and imagining it was Zane's touch in place of his own, Zane's weight felt incredible against him.

"I'm not going to fuck you here," Zane said through gritted teeth, though he appeared to be trying to convince himself and not Ty.

Ty shook his head and hummed, but he pushed his hips up against Zane's and closed his eyes as sensation swept through him. "Does anyone else stay at this guesthouse?" he asked, voice going lower.

"No," Zane growled. He bent to kiss Ty's chin, and then kissed and nipped along his jawline until he reached Ty's neck and began to suck. "We'll have the whole place to ourselves."

Ty groaned, squirming under him. "Are there washing machines at this guesthouse?"

"Yeah, why?" Zane whispered against Ty's ear.

Ty answered by delving into a messy, hungry kiss. He thrust up against Zane, rubbing their cocks together through the thick denim of their jeans.

"Jesus, Ty," Zane ground out. He shoved his hand under Ty, dragging his fingers against Ty's shoulder blades as he pushed their hips together. Ty gasped, thrust back, desire flowing between them in a feedback loop of desperate need.

Zane lapped at his lips, forcing his way in to lick and suck at Ty's as the kisses got messier and harder. They didn't even bother trying to unbutton their jeans, just rutted against each other. Ty rolled his hips to increase the friction. They were like teenagers necking, stealing a moment that couldn't be put off one second longer.

Zane shouted his name, clamping down on him so hard that Ty bowed his back to keep from being hurt. When he realized Zane was coming against him, he let go of the last vestiges of his pride and self-control as well, clutching at Zane and gritting his teeth against a moan as he came in his jeans.

🐾 ★ 🐾 ★ 🐾

It was a good mile before they hit a curve around a copse of trees that brought a group of buildings into view. Ty had seen the turn-off when he'd walked up the driveway, but he hadn't paid it much attention at the time.

Zane stopped in front of the house, though he didn't cut the engine. "This is the guesthouse."

Ty nodded and looked around. There was a garage made to look like a barn, and a storage shed built like a carriage house. The house itself was a cabin, the bucolic façade broken only by solar panels on the roof and a satellite bolted to the side. Ty glanced over at Zane, unsure of what to say now. He'd known Zane and his family had money, but he hadn't realized until setting foot on the ranch that they were downright loaded. It took serious coin to keep a ranch like this running.

Zane glanced over at him but didn't press for a comment. "I hope you'll consider it home for a while."

Ty enjoyed it when Zane got a little on the sentimental side. He was so sweet and vulnerable, it was hard not to love him. "I'll do that."

Zane nodded, smiling.

Ty pointed at him sternly. "As long as I get a hat. And boots. Red ones. And I want a belt buckle bigger than my hand," he added as he held up his broken hand.

Zane was laughing as Ty rattled on. "I can handle the hat and the boots," he said. "But I draw the line at the belt buckle." He grabbed the keys and unfastened his seatbelt.

"But why?"

Zane reached over and dug his fingers into the front of Ty's jeans, which were still a mess from their foray into illicit groping. "I'm not breaking my hand when I want to get into your pants."

Ty snorted. "Fair enough. But don't be grabby, it's rude." He smacked at Zane's hand. "And wash your hands." Grinning, Zane let him loose, then opened his door and climbed out of the truck.

Ty hopped out and reached into the bed of the truck to retrieve his bags, looking around at the house and trying to ignore how uncomfortable his jeans were. He liked the place. It was small and almost quaint, with hints of modern luxuries hidden behind the rustic details. He followed Zane through the little gate and up to the door. Zane didn't get out his keys; the door was unlocked.

Most of the inside was open up to the two-story pitched roof, with only a bedroom loft to break the space, and the back of the house was all glass, looking out to rolling hills and pasture. A huge stone fireplace dominated one wall, and a couple of comfortable-looking leather couches faced it. The furniture was minimal but functional.

Zane walked through the main room to open a sliding door that led out to a wraparound deck. A cross-breeze started up that was almost cool. Then he turned and looked at Ty. "How about we just lose the truck keys and stay awhile?"

"Will we have to barricade the door?"

Zane sniffed. "Nah. Although, as soon as Annie learns you're here, she'll barge in like a Tasmanian devil and demand to meet you."

Ty barked a laugh. Zane crossed the room back to Ty, pulling off his denim shirt and tossing it on a chair nearby.

"What'd you do with the cats?"

"I asked Alston to feed them every night on his way home."

"Alston?" Zane said, his voice going alarmingly high. "What if he goes upstairs? What if he sees all my shit in the closet?"

"It's okay, Zane."

"Ty!"

"He's scared of Smith and Wesson. And I told them not to let him past the first step."

"Ty," Zane said in exasperation.

Ty knew it made Zane nervous, but that was half the fun of it. He just raised an eyebrow and smiled.

Zane sighed and returned the smile, looking almost unwilling. "Thank you for coming." He stepped forward and pulled Ty into a kiss.

Ty returned it with something like relief. After so long apart, it was wonderful to get that kiss without the added urgency of needing to get off. Zane stepped back just long enough to unbutton his jeans and then Ty's, pushing them down so they could both kick out of them. Ty's boxer briefs went next, falling alongside Zane's. Then Zane slid his arms around Ty's waist so he could hold him close, drawing the kiss out. Ty hummed as he dragged both hands up Zane's arms and started to tug on his undershirt, but just as things were really starting to get interesting, the phone in the pocket of his jeans began to vibrate, followed by a loud sound that could only be described as an old car horn.

Ty grunted in annoyance as Zane stepped back.

"What the hell was that?"

Ty snorted. "I had to get a new phone. Got one like yours."

The phone honked at them again, and Ty bent to find it.

"What happened to your other one?"

"Relish. Long story." Ty rummaged through the pockets of his jeans. He held up his cast. "Had to get a new cast, too. Everything got . . . I was covered in condiments."

"Uh-huh."

He'd have to spill that story soon, because Zane rarely let things like that go for long, but he didn't offer to tell it right now. He sighed as he finally found his phone and looked at the display. It was a text message, one of the dozens he received every day. He shook his head and stood.

"It's from Nick," he said, knowing his old friend was a sore spot for Zane, and with good reason. But he was always honest with Zane whenever he spoke to Nick, even if it grated on the man. Hiding it would be a mistake, and Ty's conscience wouldn't condone it.

Zane wrinkled his nose but didn't seem annoyed, which was a vast improvement from the way he'd initially felt about Nick. "What's he say?"

Ty shrugged and looked down at the phone again. "He's working a weird case. I asked him to text me every now and then to let me know he's alive." He read the text with a frown. "He says Canadians are scary." He looked up at Zane. "I don't know what that means."

Zane pulled him closer and kissed him again before bending to gather their pile of clothes. "You deal with that, then. I'm going to go throw these in the wash. There's a shower and a bed in the loft upstairs if you want to get some rest before dinner."

He headed for the kitchen and what was presumably a washer and dryer near the back door.

"Will it be bad?" Ty called after him.

"So very bad."

# Chapter 4

Ty dozed on the couch, trying to recuperate from his trek to Texas, while Zane did whatever the hell it was Zane did when Ty wasn't paying attention.

He was vaguely aware of his surroundings, not quite comfortable with the unfamiliar sounds just yet. The ceiling fan high above, the dryer whirring in the kitchen, Zane's occasional footsteps on the creaking hardwood floors. A tiny, quiet breath.

Ty cracked open an eye.

Just inches from his nose was a pair of large Hershey brown eyes. They were accompanied by long dark lashes and ringlet curls that framed a cherub's face. Said cherub was wearing a yellow sundress, red bows in her hair, and red shoes. She stared at him, her hands clasped behind her back as she turned her shoulders back and forth.

Ty looked at her for another moment, disconcerted. "Hi," he said, voice still hoarse with sleep.

She gave him a frown that looked familiar. Zane's niece was three or four, if Ty remembered correctly. "You're a stranger."

"You're right." Ty unfolded his arms where he'd had them wrapped around his chest and let his broken hand extend toward her. "I'm Ty. Are you Sadie?"

She nodded, still mistrustful.

"It's nice to meet you."

"I'm a princess."

"Is that right?"

She stepped closer and leaned on him, pushing her sharp elbows against his chest. He gasped. She was so close that he almost had to go cross-eyed to look at her.

"I'm a princess and I got a pony."

"Oh yeah?" Ty looked around the room, trying to find an adult who might be responsible for the little girl—aside from himself. There was no one. He looked back at Zane's niece, bewildered by her sudden appearance. How long had he been asleep? "What color is your pony?"

A scowl appeared on her face. "It's a *pink* pony." She started twirling a curl around a finger.

"A pink pony? Are you sure?"

"I turned it pink with my wand."

"Oh, I see."

"Do you know how to ride a pony?"

"No. Do *you* know how to ride a pony?"

"I do!"

Ty looked toward the bank of windows and beyond at the deck, trying to find Zane. And there his partner stood, leaning on the banister and grinning at him through the window. Alongside Zane was a slim female of Zane-like origin, matching grin and all.

"Want to see?"

Ty returned his attention to Sadie. "Not really, no." He dropped his voice to a confidential whisper. "I'm scared of ponies."

Her eyes went wide. "Scared of ponies?"

"Very scared."

"It'll be okay, don't be scared." She petted his face, her sharp little fingers barely missing his eye. He couldn't fend her off, so he just squeezed his eyes shut to protect them. Suddenly, she grabbed his face between two tiny hands and pulled until they were nose to nose. "Do you want to play with me?" she asked, her voice full of hope and her eyes wide.

"Sadie, remember we're just here visiting," the woman called out as she stepped through one of the open French doors. Ty recognized her voice: it was Zane's sister, Annie. "Leave Ty alone and come give Uncle Z a hug. It's time for us to go see Granddaddy."

"But Mommy, Ty is going to play with me!"

"If you can convince him to play, then that's just fine. After dinner."

Sadie hugged Ty's head closer. "But I want to play now!"

"Sadie."

"I'm not a Sadie, I'm a princess!"

"Fine, you're a princess," Annie said as she came closer. "You're Princess Doesn't Listen. Hand out the hugs and let's go."

Sadie looked back at Ty, batting those long lashes at him. She put her hands together under her chin. "Please, will you play with me?"

"Oh Lord," Ty laughed. "Sweetheart, I'll do whatever you want me to after dinner."

"Yay!" She jumped up and down, then lunged at him and wrapped her arms around his neck. Ty gasped in surprise, and then she was gone, darting over to the deck doors to throw herself into Zane's arms for a hasty embrace. He laughed as he picked her up, hugging her close even as she struggled to get down again.

Ty sat up and watched them, smiling faintly. He'd rarely seen Zane interact with a child, and Zane was always uncomfortable when he did. He didn't appear to be now, though, and it was an odd feeling to watch him with the little girl.

Annie smiled and walked over to Ty, offering her hand. "Welcome to the C and G. It's great to meet you in person."

Ty stood to shake her hand. It was hard with just the tips of his fingers poking out of the plaster cast, and he kept forgetting to offer his left hand when he was surprised with a handshake. He felt like an idiot giving the weak finger shake, but what could he do?

"You sure pulled out all the stops with the welcoming committee," he said, gesturing toward her daughter.

"If it makes you feel better, she's like that with everyone."

"She's a little sparkplug," Ty drawled. He looked at Zane again. He had Sadie propped on his hip, watching her with a smile as she chattered about her pony that she insisted was pink.

Annie laughed. "You have no idea."

"Mama, I want to see my pony," Sadie announced.

"What's your pony's name?" Zane asked as he set her down.

"Pink Pony!"

Annie laughed at the expression on Zane's face. Ty glanced at her, but found his eyes going back to Zane.

Zane shook his head and kissed Sadie's cheek. "She's your pony. I guess you can name her what you want."

"Uncle Z had a pony named Tortilla," Annie told them.

"That's a silly name for a pony," Sadie said with a frown.

Zane shot Annie a look before glancing at Ty. Ty smiled warmly when their eyes met. Zane looked back at Sadie. "All right. Go see Pink Pony, and I'll see you for dinner at Granddaddy's house, okay?"

"Okay!" she answered, hugging Zane around the leg before running for the door.

"Did you say good-bye to Ty?" Annie called after her.

She didn't stop running, merely blew him a kiss over her shoulder and followed it with a trailing, "Bye!"

"See you guys later," Annie said with a wave before jogging after her runaway.

When they were gone, peace and quiet again descended. Ty watched the door for a minute longer, and then looked at Zane with a raised eyebrow. "Wow."

"Sorry she woke you." Zane moved close and slid his arms around Ty's waist. "She promised to stay quiet."

"Yeah, I've seen that type before. She'll never be quiet again."

Zane laughed.

Ty put his hands on Zane's shoulders. "It's okay, I love the creepy feeling of waking up to someone staring at me."

"Did you get any rest?"

"Some. You?" He gave Zane a tug and started backing toward the couch.

Zane went along, keeping his arms around Ty. "I sat and stared at you while you slept."

"Look who thinks he's funny."

"I'm so glad you're here," Zane said as he held tight to Ty and rested his chin on Ty's shoulder.

"I just came to get a hat."

Zane laughed and kissed him, bending him backward just enough to force him to hold onto Zane so he wouldn't fall. It made the butterflies start churning in his chest. He loved when Zane did that to him.

"Then you're in luck," Zane said against his lips. "I know just the place to find one."

"How far away from dinner are we?" Ty asked roughly.

"Formal dinner's at eight. Drinks beforehand. So we've got about thirty minutes. What have you got in mind?"

"I was just wondering if anyone else would be stopping by to look through those big-ass windows or if I could ride you down here on the couch," Ty said, forcing his voice to sound nonchalant. Zane's breath caught on a sharp exhale, and Ty plucked at one of the buttons of Zane's shirt. "Too bad I don't have a hat, though. Can't ride without a hat."

Zane caught Ty's good hand and placed it on his chest. "Sure you can."

Ty tried not to smile as he met Zane's eyes. "Better safe than sorry, huh?"

"No one else will come by," Zane growled. Then he shrugged and added, "And if they do..."

The invitation tugged at Ty, and he took a deep breath as he mulled it over. He didn't want Zane to come out to his family by being caught in a reverse cowboy on the couch, but the idea had its merits all the same.

Ty's body was responding, anyway.

He exhaled to calm himself, kissing Zane again as Zane finally straightened up and loosened his hold. They both knew thirty minutes wasn't enough time.

"Zane?" Ty said, voice more serious. "What do you plan to tell your family about us?"

Zane stared out the bank of windows for a few moments before looking back at Ty. "I'd like to tell them the truth. Can I rent Chester, do you think?"

Ty laughed and pushed his fingers through Zane's hair, fighting against the bout of nerves that fluttered through him.

"I'd like to tell Annie, for sure. She already knows about me; it's just telling her about you. I think... I hope Dad would be okay with it. He's pretty laid back." Zane rubbed his cheek against Ty's shoulder like he could burrow deeper. "If I had a choice, I wouldn't tell Mother."

"I'll follow your lead. I don't mind telling them we're just partners if it makes your life easier."

"I know," Zane whispered. "But I'm tired of easy. Like you said, we deserve better."

Ty kissed the side of his mouth, then ducked his head for more.

Zane's grip tightened on Ty's hips until it was almost painful. "I love you, Ty. More than anything." He took a deep breath, as if steadying himself. "But it'd be smarter to wait until things have settled down here."

"Whatever you think is best."

Zane nodded, looking drawn and worried. Ty slid his fingers down his lover's face. He knew where the stress was coming from.

Zane rested his head on Ty's shoulder and Ty rubbed a hand down his back. "Let's go get ready."

Zane held on tight. "Not letting go," he whispered.

"Okay." Ty drew out the word with a frown. "But that's going to make dinner awkward."

᠃ ★ ᠃ ★ ᠃

They drove down the private road that serviced the Carter Garrett Ranch, arms hanging out the windows. The land was wide open on both sides, surprisingly green with those strange, knobby little hills and scrub trees, dotted with cactus flats and brush. It seemed tame, but Ty could see just how difficult it would be to traverse, either on foot or in a vehicle.

The land wavered with heat, even as the sun descended. Summer evenings in Texas were apparently blazing hot right up until the sun went down, when they became merely uncomfortably warm.

Zane was so quiet that the silence started getting to Ty, who fidgeted and squirmed more and more. He took his baseball hat off and messed with the bill, then put it back on and removed his sunglasses, wiping them clean before putting them back on and finding something else to mess with. He moved the air vents around and fiddled with the radio buttons, flipping through station after station of static before turning it off altogether.

"Aren't I supposed to be the nervous one here?" Zane asked.

"I'm afraid I'm going to say something that screws things up for you," Ty admitted as he slouched down in his seat and propped his booted foot on the dashboard.

"You? Say something untoward? You would *never*!"

"Okay, smartass, make fun of me."

"Just be yourself, Ty," Zane said, glancing over and offering him a warm smile. "I don't care what you say to Mother and neither will anyone else."

"What's your mom's deal?" Ty took his sunglasses off again and frowned down at them. They had scratches he hadn't noticed before.

Zane snorted. "She's just . . . very determined."

"So are you, but you aren't a frigid bitch. Usually," Ty added as he slid his sunglasses back on and scrunched up his nose when they wouldn't fit right. The frames seemed to be bent.

"Ugh." Zane shook his head and slowed the truck to pass over a burbling creek. The wheels hit a metal grate in the road, jarring the vehicle. It wasn't the first grate Ty had seen; they were all over the main roads too. And while he'd been walking up the driveway he'd stopped to stand on one and look down into it, thinking they all might be over water or something. There was nothing under most of them.

"What are those?"

"Texas gates."

"What?"

"They're cattle guards. They keep the livestock from passing over them. We call them Texas gates."

"Cows won't cross those?" Ty glanced over his shoulder to look at the receding grate. It went from one side of the road to the other, met on both sides by the creek bed. Most were flanked by barbed wire fencing.

"Cows won't even cross bridges. But nothing else will cross the cattle guards either. Sheep, goats, pigs. The grates are far enough apart that their feet go through."

"So you use them instead of gates you have to open and close. Smart." Ty glanced over at Zane and plucked a wad of cotton out of the end of the bright green cast on his arm. "So, wait, do those ring the property? Is that how the trespassers are gaining access?"

"Probably. Stop messing with it." Zane said as he swatted at Ty's hands. "I don't want to take you back to the damn emergency room to have another put on."

"You realize I'll be cutting this thing off with my Strider in about two more days, right?"

"You cut that thing off, Grady, I will break your other hand."

"You can try, Hoss."

Zane was quiet a long moment as he stared out the windshield.

Soon enough, Ty was drumming his fingers against his leg. The truck topped a small rise and the main ranch sprawled in front of them. Three massive barns, two corrals, miles of white fencing leading off over the hills, and the three-story white colonial-style house that towered over the spread. Ty hadn't taken the time to look around when he'd arrived this morning, too concerned with seeing Zane and finding air conditioning to think of anything else. It was an impressive sight.

He began whistling "Home on the Range."

Zane shot him a glare and reached out to thump his chest. "Asshole," he said as he steered into the drive.

"Ow!" As soon as Zane put the truck in park, a man walked out of the barn. "Is that your dad?"

"What the hell is he doing out here?" Zane opened the door and headed toward the barn, and Ty trailed along behind him at a safe enough distance to give them privacy if they needed it.

"Dad. You're supposed to be resting."

"I am resting."

Zane motioned with his hands, reminiscent of the way Ty would flail sometimes. Ty bit his lip to keep from smiling. Every once in a while he noticed something like that: evidence that they were beginning to pick up characteristics from each other.

"I needed to get out of the house," Harrison said, aiming a pointed look at the beautiful mansion.

"Oh." Zane glanced at Ty, uneasy.

Harrison nodded and reached into his pocket for a pouch of tobacco and rolling papers. "She's planning the Steers and Stripes fundraiser. On the warpath."

"You're fucking kidding me. She's still having it here? What part of 'trespassers with guns' does she not get?"

"Appearances are everything. And watch your language," Harrison added, shooting a tired smile Ty's way.

Ty frowned and moved closer. "What's going on?"

"Every Fourth of July we hold a barbeque fundraiser. We should cancel it after what happened, but my wife refuses."

He began packing a cigarette with experienced fingers. Ty opened his mouth to say something, but then closed it again with a frown.

"Until we learn more about what's going on, there's no way that party should happen," Zane spat.

Ty reached out and set his hand on Zane's shoulder. "Calm down."

Zane looked back at him, fuming.

Ty squeezed his shoulder. "We'll sit down and take a look at the problem, see what we can do. The fourth is like a week away; this might not even be an issue by then. And if it is, holding a big party here might turn out to be helpful."

"How do you figure?" Zane asked. Any good the last few hours may have done him was gone; he'd turned edgy and combative in what seemed like the blink of an eye. Zane's mother must have been a real piece of work for the mere mention of one of her ideas to have this effect on Ty's normally stoic partner.

Ty glanced at the bright red front door of the mansion and then met Zane's eyes with a small smile. "It'll be okay," he said, voice soft and calm.

Zane stared at him for a long moment, then rolled his shoulders and began to relax again. "You're right. No need to get worked up. Yet."

Harrison whistled and drew Ty's attention from Zane. "That's impressive, son," he said to Ty as he watched Zane. He put a hand around Ty's shoulder and pulled him close. "You ever tried to break a horse? I bet you'd be real good at it."

Zane laughed on his way to the truck, but Ty wasn't quite sure he understood the joke. He shook his head and glanced at Zane's father. "I'm not all that fond of horses, sir."

Harrison looked amused. "We don't stand on ceremony here, Ty. Call me Harrison." He patted Ty's shoulder and released him. "Besides, Z already told me you could be a real son of a bitch."

Ty narrowed his eyes at Zane. "Real son of a bitch, huh, Z?"

Zane's eyes widened as he came closer, carrying a box he'd retrieved from the truck bed. He obviously hadn't heard what had preceded his nickname. "What?"

"Jackass," Ty said to him. Harrison laughed.

"What'd I do?"

Ty gave him a wink.

Zane rolled his eyes. "I got you something in Austin. I was going to bring it home, but since you're here . . ." He handed Ty the box.

Ty took it with a quirked eyebrow at Zane and a sideways glance at Harrison. But Zane wouldn't have given it to him here if it were something . . . dubious.

He pulled the top off the box and peered inside to find a felt cowboy hat, light brown with a black band. On the front of the band was a beautiful silver and turquoise concho.

Ty laughed and pulled the hat out. "Thanks, Zane."

Zane plucked off Ty's baseball cap, then took the hat out of his hands and set it on top of his head. Zane fussed with it, making sure it fit right, and Ty stared at him from under the brim of the hat, watching Zane's dark eyes go darker.

"Looks good," Zane said with a curt nod, the undercurrent in his voice unmistakable. It must have looked pretty damn good.

Ty gave him a jaunty grin. "Thank you."

"You wear that like you're from Texas," Harrison said, nodding his approval.

They heard a shout from inside the house: Beverly on the phone in her study, where an open window let in the evening breeze.

"Oh, kill me now."

"It can't be that bad, right?" Ty asked, looking between Zane and his father.

"Optimists are so cute," Harrison said around his cigarette.

Ty did a double-take, and Zane grunted. "God help the poor party planner she's dealing with." He sighed and jerked his hand. "But better her than me."

"She's your mother," Ty said, voice low. "Next time she gets on your case, you do what all good sons do and lie to make her happy."

Zane looked up sharply, blinking. Harrison threw his head back and laughed again. Ty merely raised an eyebrow at Zane. His hat shifted with the motion.

Harrison patted Ty's shoulder, shaking him with surprising vigor for a man who'd just been released from the hospital with a bullet hole in his arm. "I like this one, Z."

Zane smiled gamely.

"You boys don't tarry, now. Dinner'll be on soon," Harrison said, then made his way back toward the house, sliding what was left of his rolled cigarette into his pocket.

They waited until he was out of earshot, and then Zane stepped closer. "You got any idea what she gets on my case for?"

"Tell me."

Zane stared at him for a long moment. "She wants me back here, running the ranch, married again, with kids. Like a good Texan boy. And to hell with what I want." He took another step, until their chests brushed together. Ty had to tilt his head back to keep the brim of his hat from poking one of Zane's eyes out. "I've got other ideas of what I want," Zane said quietly.

Ty nodded, glancing around the yard out of habit, then looking at Zane with an odd rush of nerves.

Zane tipped his head to one side, studying him. "I think you might be able to see the problem."

"I see it," Ty whispered. He sniffed as he looked around the yard again. "What is that smell?"

Zane shook his head. "What smell?"

"Smells like horse."

Zane snorted, and Ty turned to move toward the front porch. Zane chuckled. "It's a ranch, Ty. Dad's got whole barns full of horses. Better check your boots, buddy boy."

"You'll find one up your ass soon enough," Ty promised as he walked away. Zane's laughter followed him across the yard.

They got halfway through dinner before Beverly brought up the topic Zane was desperately wishing she'd avoid.

"Zane, when are you going to come back here and settle down? Surely you've gotten this government nonsense out of your blood by now," she said as she passed the gravy to Annie, like it was an everyday conversation.

"Now, Beverly, you know Z's worked hard to get where he is. He can't just drop it," Harrison said.

"I can't just up and leave my assignment, Mother."

"Surely you can request a transfer or retirement." Beverly turned her eyes on Zane's silent partner sitting across the table from Zane. "Can you do that, Mr. Grady?"

"Oh, look," Ty said, as if he'd just discovered something wonderful. "Biscuits!" He tore off a piece of bread and stuffed it into his mouth.

Annie snickered, and Zane kept his eyes on his plate as he tried not to smile. Even Sadie began giggling, looking around the table with eyes that shone. She was sitting next to Ty, mimicking his actions. Ty looked sideways at her and winked.

Beverly drew a breath to continue, but Harrison spoke first. "So what is it you're doing now, Z? You must like it pretty well."

Zane looked at Ty before speaking. "We do a lot of investigative work. Research and field work, stuff like that."

"Research," Beverly sneered.

"Mother, not right now, okay? We can talk about it later."

Ty pressed his lips into a thin line and kept his eyes on his plate, obviously trying to keep from saying anything. But then he glanced up at Zane's mother, brow furrowed, and then at Zane. He was probably tying his tongue in knots trying to restrain himself from weighing in.

The whole thing made Zane angry. And then there was Ty, here to support him and being forced to sit through Beverly's cutting remarks. She had yet to address him by any of the titles he'd earned, instead calling him Mr. Grady. Zane glanced up and met his partner's eyes.

Ty raised one eyebrow pointedly. "Lie," he mouthed.

Zane's jaw clenched. "I'd been thinking about it."

Silverware clattered as both Annie and Harrison looked at him in surprise, and Beverly broke into a smile. "Well, you merely had to say so, Zane. We can talk all about it sometime this week. Now, Juanita, what do we have for dessert?"

The matronly little woman hovering nearby bustled off toward the kitchen, and Beverly surveyed the dinner table with a smile.

Eyes wide, Zane stared at her and then Ty in disbelief.

Ty pressed his lips together again, clearly trying not to laugh as he ducked his head and tightened his grip on his fork. Zane kicked Ty's shin under the table, and Ty gave a muffled grunt and jerked before he could stop himself, clanging his fork and plate together.

Harrison looked up, his lips twitching. "Okay there, Ty?"

"Yes, sir," Ty answered with a grimace. "Bad leg. Old football injury. Tripped over the water boy. There was Gatorade everywhere, it was horrible."

Annie began giggling again, and even Zane grinned as Juanita came back in with a tray of churros and bowls of sweet dips.

As Sadie dove into the desserts with all the enthusiasm of a three-year-old, Beverly placed her napkin on the table at her elbow, leaning forward and watching Ty. Ty seemed to sense the attention and he looked up, meeting Beverly's eyes.

Zane's stomach flipped. His likened his mother to a wild animal sometimes; if you made eye contact, it was like a challenge. But Ty always made eye contact, and he didn't back down from challenges. Watching his mother and his lover stare at each other was the proverbial irresistible force meeting an immovable object.

"So, Mr. Grady, how did you find yourself in the FBI?"

"It's *Agent* Grady, Mother."

Ty gave her a charming smile. "The Marines didn't want me, and it's hard to find a job where you can shoot things without getting arrested."

Zane actually groaned.

Beverly was struck speechless for a moment, and Ty took advantage to change the subject. He looked around the table, addressing Harrison and the others.

"So, what exactly has been going on? Can someone fill me in?"

"Well," Harrison started.

"Do we really need to talk about such nasty business at dinner?" Beverly asked. She still sounded flustered, and Zane couldn't decide if it was unsettling or amusing. His mother didn't like it when things were out of her control; that was where their similarities began.

"Your husband was shot on your own property. Doesn't that make you a little angry?" Ty asked.

"Made *me* angry," Harrison mumbled as he sipped at his water.

"Of course it's upsetting," Beverly snapped. She straightened and cleared her throat daintily, then looked to Harrison. "Don't you believe we should wait until Mark is here to discuss it?"

"Mark won't be here until tomorrow, Mother," Annie said.

"Still. I believe we should wait for him. He does have a military background, after all. And don't we need someone with a mind for this sort of thing before we go off half-cocked?"

"Mother, really. Zane and Ty do this for a living."

Zane opened his mouth to tell her about Ty's background, but he felt the tip of Ty's foot at his shin. Ty shook his head and smiled.

"Harrison?" Beverly said, ostensibly deferring the decision to Zane's father, despite her warning tone.

Harrison sighed and nodded. "Problem's been going on for a good while now. I think we can afford one night to give Ty here a chance to rest before we put him to work for us."

Zane smiled, impressed with his father's quiet diplomacy. He looked at his partner and found Ty watching Harrison, head cocked. Ty nodded. "I appreciate that, sir, thank you."

Harrison smirked knowingly.

Beverly wasn't as impressed with her husband's decision as Zane was, but she let it go at that. It was like watching a shark release its hold, and something in Zane began to relax.

She placed her napkin on the table and stood. "Now if you'll excuse me, I have plans to attend to in the study."

She left the formal dining room, and Zane watched the doorway for a long moment. He reminded himself it would just be a few more days, and then they'd be out of here.

"Well, that went well," Ty finally said, sounding far too chipper about it.

"Lie to her, Zane, it'll help," Zane grumbled in a high-pitched mockery of Ty's drawl.

Ty chuckled.

"Speaking of lying," Harrison said, leaning both elbows on the table. "You two care to come clean now, while your mother's out of earshot?"

"What?" Zane asked, panic settling heavy in his stomach.

"I don't know what it is you're both hiding, but I can smell it."

Zane swallowed hard and glanced at Ty. Ty raised an eyebrow, nodding. He looked calm, but there was no telling what was going on beneath the surface. Zane licked his lips and was surprised to find his mouth dry.

"Ty and I . . ." He looked at his father, the fear and uncertainty skittering through him. "We . . ."

Out of the corner of his eye, Zane saw the compass rose around Ty's neck. He'd worn it almost every day since Zane had given it to him. He would do anything for Zane, and he deserved the same. Ty bit his lip and looked down at the table as Zane hesitated, and though Zane caught only the briefest glimpse of his lover's expression, he recognized it: disappointment. It burned its way through his body and settled uncomfortably in the pit of his stomach, pushing him toward the words.

"Ty and I . . . we've been dating for about a year now."

Ty's head shot up, and Annie glanced between them, eyebrows climbing so high her bangs hid them.

"Dating?" Harrison echoed.

Zane met and held Ty's gaze. "Ty isn't just my partner at work. He's my boyfriend. I love him."

"Oh." Harrison sounded thoughtful. "Well, that explains it." He went back to cutting the churro on Sadie's plate, and Zane and Ty both stared at him, incredulous.

"That's it?" Ty blurted.

Harrison shrugged and chewed a piece of the sweet bread Sadie had stuffed into his mouth. "Had a gay bull I had to sell last year. That was a damn nuisance. Gay son? That don't cost me nothing."

Ty laughed before he could stop himself. He had one of those boyish, infectious laughs that made the people around him giggle too no matter why. Soon they were all laughing raucously, the sound ringing through the massive house like bells in a cathedral.

✿ ★ ✿ ★ ✿

Ty stood in the foyer, looking up at an oil painting tucked away in one corner of the grand entryway. He'd seen the painting before dinner, a fascinating vista of browns, oranges, and pinks that made up a surreal look at the Hill Country outside the door.

It was pleasing to the eye, and the colors were well-suited to the décor, so Ty couldn't understand why it had been shoved into this alcove where no one would see it unless they made a concerted effort to do so.

He cocked his head and took a sip from the wine he was trying to finish before Zane came back from talking with his father and sister.

"You like it?" Annie asked as she came up behind him.

Ty turned and gave her a confused smile. "It seems familiar to me and I'm not sure why."

"Are you a connoisseur of art?"

"Hardly. I'm more a photograph person, if anything." He cocked his head the other way, examining the colors and brush strokes. There was an element of profiling to looking at a painting if you knew enough about art, but Ty didn't.

"You're familiar with the artist." Annie stopped at his side and looked at the painting with a smile.

"No, really, I can only name like five painters."

"I bet you can name this one."

Ty looked at her sharply, and then turned his eyes back to the painting. He pointed with one of the fingers holding his wine glass. "Zane painted this?"

Annie nodded.

"You're shitting me!"

She laughed, and Ty looked around with a wince as his words echoed off the marble floors.

"That's incredible," he added, quieter. He studied the painting again. Careful strokes, meticulous details that still somehow formed a sloppy likeness of the sun setting over the desert. There was calm beneath the vibrant surface, like Zane in reverse.

"You didn't know Zane could paint?"

Ty shook his head, still gazing at the brush strokes.

"He's quite a talented artist. His charcoal sketches were heartbreakingly beautiful."

"I never knew he could do that."

"Even so. You recognized this as his." She patted his shoulder and Ty felt her move away. He licked his lips and set his wine glass down, eyes still riveted to the painting. He had to force himself to look away and followed her to the front door.

Annie slipped her hand into the crook of his arm. They strolled through the yard, the temperature surprisingly comfortable. It was still hot, but there was a breeze that seemed to be apologizing for the sun trying to melt them all day. Ahead of them, Zane and Harrison were trailing along behind Sadie, who was fluttering like a butterfly, chasing lightning bugs.

"Why do you tease him like you do?" Annie asked.

"You want the real answer or the one I'd give his sister?"

"The real one."

"Fair enough. Because I enjoy it," he said with a sideways glance. "And so does he."

"So... foreplay."

Ty barked a laugh.

"And the answer you'd give his sister?"

"I don't know, I'd have had to stall to come up with one. Probably would have tripped you or something."

Annie laughed. "Well, Ty Grady, I bet he has his hands full with you."

"God, I hope so."

"I'm glad he has someone. I worried about him for so long."

Ty nodded, his mood turning more somber. They walked in silence a moment, and Zane and Harrison slowed their pace until he and Annie came abreast of them. Harrison was moving well, but seemed to tire quickly. He had his hand on Zane's arm, and when they caught up he took Annie's arm instead, freeing Zane to fall in next to Ty. Sadie was a few dozen yards away, dancing, twirling, and skipping around the yard.

They ambled along, content in the silence. Ty stopped and stared as the sun melted into the ground ahead of them.

"That's spectacular."

"Everything's bigger in Texas," Zane whispered, a smile in his voice.

"Oh God."

Zane laid his chin on Ty's shoulder to watch the sunset. His familiar scent and his comforting presence were wonderful, and Ty turned his head to touch his cheek to Zane's. He was aware of how close they were in front of Zane's family, and though he was enjoying the moment, he could feel his shoulders tensing.

Harrison cleared his throat. "Now, I believe we need to discuss this situation a little more seriously," he said as the landscaping lights began to flicker on around them.

"You mean, should we tell Mother that Ty and I are screwing?" Zane asked, voice flat.

"Oh, look," Ty said. "Horses." He took a step and made to escape.

Zane reached out and grabbed him by the back of the neck, and he flailed and stumbled as Zane's fingers snagged his collar.

"No wandering off, Grady. This is your problem now too."

"Do you have to tell her at all?" Annie asked. She looked genuinely concerned. Ty wondered how many members of Zane's family would give a damn if Zane was gay. It seemed the real problem on everyone's mind was what Beverly would do. Ty was beginning to think that perhaps all this family money was hers. If not the money, then definitely the power.

"She'll find out through the grapevine soon enough," Zane said as Ty tried to shake him off.

"Well, yes, I suppose she will," Annie said, wincing.

Harrison lit the cigarette he'd rolled before dinner, and Ty gave one last swat with his cast before he stopped struggling against Zane's fingers.

"You prepared for what might happen when you mother finds out?" Harrison eyed Zane's grip on Ty's collar, shook his head and smiled. "Let your friend go, Z."

Zane released Ty's shirt collar, and Ty squared his shoulders and straightened his shirt, giving Zane a glare. Zane smiled serenely when he met Ty's eyes.

"I say let her find out when she finds out," Zane said. "I told the important people."

"If that's the way you want to play it," Harrison said. "But I do have one question."

"Okay . . ." Zane said.

"Not for you." Harrison nodded at Ty instead.

Ty raised his chin and braced himself for whatever Zane's father could throw at him. After facing down his own father, he didn't think anything could scare him now.

"You know anything about horses, son?"

Ty raised an eyebrow and leaned closer, not sure if he'd heard right. "Not much, sir," he answered. "I know how to get on one, and I know how to fall off one."

Annie snickered and Harrison nodded. "Well, then. I guess we can't all be perfect."

Ty narrowed his eyes at Harrison. "I have a question."

"Fair enough."

"How in the hell do you do that with your mustache?"

Harrison gave him a grin and wink as he turned away.

🐾 ★ 🐾 ★ 🐾

Zane and Annie watched in total exasperation as Ty spent most of the evening teaching Sadie how to jab a pressure point with two fingers, and where the most effective pressure points were located.

Zane could only laugh as Sadie jabbed at Ty's carotid and Ty sprawled in the grass, complete with his tongue hanging out for effect. Sadie was enjoying it a little too much. But then, so was Ty.

It was well past dark when they returned to the guesthouse and Zane finally had Ty to himself. As soon as they walked in, Zane pulled Ty toward him and kissed him, taking his time, drawing it out.

Ty grinned against his lips. "How does it feel?"

"Damn good," Zane growled as he squeezed Ty's ass.

"That's not what I meant."

Zane laughed. He didn't let Ty go, but he nodded. "It feels good. I can't believe my dad took it like that."

"Your dad is pretty epic, Zane."

Zane laughed again, harder this time. He met Ty's eyes, taking in the whole package. The hat brought out the hazel, making them sharper, shadowing them and giving Ty that mysterious cowboy aura that so many people tried and failed to achieve. Ty could almost pull off the hat better than he could and Ty'd only had it for a few hours. The way Ty had handled himself tonight, the way he'd charmed Annie and Harrison and even little Sadie, and held his own with Beverly, made Zane proud.

Having someone to be proud of was an indescribable feeling.

"I love you," Zane said as he gazed into Ty's eyes, reveling in the truth behind the words. Every step they took as a couple felt so damn good.

Ty smiled, eyes bright. Then his expression fell and he smacked Zane's chest. "Why didn't I know you can draw?"

"What?"

"I saw your painting. And Annie said you do charcoal sketches."

"I—"

"You are going to draw me something, and you're going to do it tonight."

Zane laughed. "What?"

"You should draw me a tattoo!"

Zane raised an eyebrow, arrested by the thought. He hadn't drawn in years, hadn't even thought of it, but the idea of using Ty's skin as a canvas was appealing in so many ways. "I might have to do that," he rasped.

Ty nodded. Zane pulled the hat off Ty's head and stepped in close to kiss at the corner of his mouth. Ty reached to tug him closer, but stopped when his cast got in the way. He couldn't grip Zane's arm, couldn't drag his hand over Zane's back, couldn't even work at any of Zane's buttons. Zane huffed in annoyance and started on his own shirt buttons.

Ty grunted and turned his hand over.

"How much longer are you in that thing?"

"Couple more weeks, at least."

"That's really going to cause some chafing if you're not careful."

"Zane, come on, that's just mean." Ty didn't sound too amused, but then, a broken hand had to drive a man like Ty nuts. Especially since it was his dominant hand.

Zane looked from Ty's eyes to the cast with a sinking feeling. He knew what Ty was thinking.

Sure enough, Ty bent and extracted the Strider at his ankle.

Zane squared his shoulders and pointed. "Tyler Grady, don't you dare cut that cast off."

Ty put the blade to the edge of the plaster, eyes wide and innocent, as if he were hurt that Zane would think he'd do such a thing.

"I'll take it from you, Ty."

Ty narrowed his eyes, then turned and took a few steps away. "Try it, Lone Star," he said as he shoved the knife under the padding and started sawing at it. He hunched his shoulders when Zane took a step toward him.

"Ty! Do not cut that cast off!"

"It itches!"

Zane grabbed his hand, pulling it and the knife away from the cast.

Ty slithered away and held the knife out to the side, blade pointed away from Zane. "Quit it!" he said, holding out his hurt hand as if to keep Zane at bay. He stayed there for a second, a standoff as they stared at each other, then took a quick step back and began to saw at the cast again.

Zane darted close, grasped Ty's cast, and yanked it to the side, away from the knife. Ty held the knife out again, stepping closer to Zane to hinder his movements rather than trying to pull away from him. He couldn't get the cast out of Zane's grasp, though.

"Just let me cut it off!" Ty begged as he tried and failed to twist it free.

"No!" Zane grabbed at the knife, fully aware of—and turned on by—how their bodies aligned when they grappled. Just like the first fight they'd ever had, a real one, where he'd found himself with a raging hard-on as he'd pinned Ty to a wall in an alley in New York City.

Ty shot Zane his best seductive smile. "I'll do fun things to you if you let me cut it off."

"You'll do fun things to me anyway."

"Dammit!"

"You cut it off, you'll start using it. You start using it, you'll fuck it up again."

"That's the fun of life," Ty insisted. Then he hooked his foot behind Zane's ankle and pulled his leg forward.

Zane swore as he stumbled and pitched backward toward the floor, but managed to snake an arm around Ty to pull him down with him. They both hit hard, and Zane rolled over and scrabbled at Ty's good wrist, trying to get the knife.

Ty stretched his arm as far as he could while wrapping his legs around Zane's waist and clamping down, putting the knife just out of Zane's reach. So Zane grasped Ty's arm and started beating it against the floor to dislodge the knife.

Ty struggled briefly, but then gave a plaintive, "Ow! Dammit!" and the knife clattered to the plank floor. He yanked his hurt hand away from Zane and whacked him in the arm with the hard plaster cast.

"Ow! Ty!" Zane shouted. He pushed down on both Ty's shoulders, pinning him to the floor. "Give it up."

"Have you ever known that to work with me?" Ty asked wryly, attempting to roll onto his stomach even with Zane's weight pressed against him.

Zane kissed him, letting it go hot and messy, but he didn't loosen his hold. If anything, his hands gripped tighter and his knees closed against Ty's sides. Ty pulled him closer, wrapping him up, letting Zane feel his cock hardening against him.

"That's an illegal move," Ty panted. He closed his eyes and rested his head on the floor.

Zane chuckled and lowered himself to his elbows, rubbing his nose along Ty's jaw. "Since when is any move illegal with you?"

Ty pressed his mouth to Zane's. "When it gives you the advantage." His words rumbled against Zane's lips as they kissed, and Zane moved one hand to touch Ty's face.

Ty arched his back, stretching his arms out above him on the floor. "Ah ah ah," Zane said as he slid his hands up Ty's arms to pull them back down. Ty twisted and Zane struggled to get him under him again. God, how he wanted him now! If Ty would cooperate, they could be fucking in a matter of minutes. "Just stop it. You're not taking that cast off! And you're driving me fucking crazy!"

"There's a short trip!"

Zane pushed to his knees and hauled Ty up against him so he could straddle Ty's lap. He grabbed his chin and kissed him. "For God's sake, shut the fuck up," he said, breathless, before kissing him again.

Ty snickered.

Zane kissed him harder. "You feel like putting that hat back on and saddling up?"

Ty's breath hitched, eyes dark and cheeks flushed. "Oh yeah. But if you utter the words 'ride 'em cowboy,' I'm done."

Zane grinned. Ty slid both hands up Zane's side, but stopped when his cast met resistance. Zane flinched as something poked him in the side.

They both shifted enough to look at Ty's arm.

The tip of the Strider had found its way into the plaster of Ty's cast, cutting through the edge, and both tip and handle were sticking out at opposite angles. It had gone completely through.

"Shit," Ty whispered as he stared at his cast, now complete with movie-prop knife sticking through it.

Zane blinked at the knife in horror and released Ty, who flopped onto his back. "Son of a bitch, Ty."

Ty began to laugh again, holding his arm to the side, which was a pretty good indication that the knife hadn't actually cut him. Zane rolled his eyes, grabbed the Strider, and yanked it out. Ty howled in protest, but he was far too late. He lay there with wide eyes, looking at Zane incredulously as Zane flipped it around and around before brandishing it over Ty, not in the least bit amused.

"What if it was in my arm, you toolbag?"

"Then you would be bleeding."

"You didn't know I wasn't bleeding, you can't see the wound!"

"I made an educated guess."

"Ha! Now I have to take it off! I could be injured."

Zane snapped the knife over and over in his hand with simple flicks of his wrist. "I'll give you injured."

Ty grinned crookedly and shifted a little under Zane. "Bring it."

A smile pulled at Zane's lips, and without answering, he threw the knife to jam into the wooden door of the bathroom. Then he curled his fingers into Ty's shirt and drew Ty up toward him, the muscles in his arm straining.

"Nice toss," Ty said, but he was staring up into Zane's eyes, his expression torn between arousal and annoyance.

"Thanks."

Ty grabbed Zane with his good hand, yanking him toward the floor as they kissed. Zane went willingly and settled on top of Ty, who spread his knees wider so Zane could sink between them, making him hotter and harder as he rutted against Ty's body. He grabbed Ty behind the neck and crushed their mouths together, his tongue invading Ty's in a messy kiss. Then he pulled back.

"The cast isn't coming off."

"Dammit!"

Zane climbed to his feet with an annoyed grunt and stalked over to the bathroom, where he jerked the Strider out of the door. "And I'll be holding onto this for safekeeping."

"No, no, no!" Ty scrambled to his feet. "I need to be armed, Zane. What if the horses revolt?"

"You can put that sharp wit of yours to use."

"Clever use of wordplay, I approve. Penalty points subtracted."

"I'll give it back in the morning. Or after I've been laid at least three times. Whichever one comes first."

Ty sighed and flopped his hands, as if the thought of having sex with Zane in return for his knife would be such a hassle.

Zane raised an eyebrow, smiling as Ty stalked closer. He jabbed the knife into the doorway again, then met Ty halfway, wrapping him up in a slow, passionate kiss.

"I knew you'd come around," Zane murmured.

"Just shut up and undo some of these buttons."

Zane couldn't help but laugh. He did as requested, undoing the buttons of his own shirt and popping the ones on his and Ty's jeans. He let his hand settle on Ty's torso, appreciating the toned muscles under his fingers, loving the way Ty raised his arms and settled his hands on Zane's shoulders just because he knew it would make Zane tighten his hold and kiss him.

Zane loved little things like that. They'd grown so familiar with each other they could give and take such cues and rarely even realize they were doing it. He occasionally found himself talking with his hands like Ty did, and once or twice he'd noticed Ty sitting idly by as their coworkers argued, too mellow to involve himself.

They were good for each other in so many ways, even if foreplay did sometimes include a Strider and a sucker punch to the midsection.

"Zane," Ty gasped as he broke the kiss. "Come back."

"What?" Zane asked, confused and turned on and distracted by his tangent.

"Whatever you're thinking about right now, drop it and come back." Ty emphasized the request by pushing Zane's pants down his hips.

Zane started laughing, surprised by just how funny it struck him. Ty's fingers were on his skin, sliding his boxers to his thighs, and it warmed every inch of Zane's body as he gazed into Ty's eyes.

"I was just musing over how perfect you are for me."

Ty's lips twitched into a smile. He didn't appear to have anything clever to say. His rough hand dragged across Zane's chest and he began backing toward the door where he'd left his bags earlier in the day.

Zane followed him, kicking out of the remainder of his clothes. It was rare that Ty had nothing to say, no witty rejoinder, no snappy remark. It intrigued Zane, his body tingling with growing anticipation. The last time Ty had pulled the silent game was before they'd left for the cruise ship last Christmas, when Ty had wanted to practice being a mind-blowingly sexy submissive. Zane's cock jumped at the mere memory of that evening.

He watched Ty saunter across the room, taking his fill of Ty's naked body, tempted to sit on the couch and touch himself to see what Ty would do. He would much rather Ty be the one touching, though.

Ty rummaged through his bag, no doubt searching for lube. Zane took a deep breath, trying to calm himself. He loved that the prospect of having sex with Ty could still make his stomach flutter like a schoolboy's and his body react like a man twenty years younger.

When Ty stood up, he had a bottle in hand. But instead of coming toward Zane, he stuck his bare foot into the cowboy hat on the ground and kicked it into the air. He caught it with his good hand and turned a mischievous grin on Zane. He didn't say anything, merely held the hat out as if displaying it. Then he flipped it and turned it around his hand, rolled it up his arm, and set it on his head with a flourish.

Zane grinned from ear to ear, not sure whether to be impressed or turned on. He was both, at this point.

He took a step back, letting his heel hit the couch behind him. He sank down onto it, slouching and spreading his legs wide as he wrapped long fingers around his cock. Ty was advancing on him, and that crooked grin from beneath the brim of that cowboy hat should have been illegal in most states.

The hat, the compass rose pendant, and the grin were the only things Ty wore now. Zane's breath came in shallow bursts as Ty climbed into his lap.

"Ty," he whispered as he looked up into his partner's eyes.

"You told me if I ever came to Texas you'd teach me how to ride," Ty drawled. The low gravel of his seductive voice never failed to hit all of Zane's happy places.

"I did."

Ty kissed him, long and hard, forced to turn his head so the brim of his hat wouldn't interfere. Zane tried to push his hips up, but Ty wasn't sitting in his lap; he was hovering, the muscles of his thighs straining. Zane grabbed them and squeezed, enjoying the feel of Ty's hard muscles at work. Ty's hand was on him, slathering him in lube, squeezing and pulling, teasing. Zane moaned, close to blissful as Ty handled him.

He pulled Ty closer by his thighs, forcing his body to contort until he could no longer manage the kiss, and Ty's cock brushed Zane's chest as Ty arched his back and sighed. Zane scanned up his body, eyes following the smooth lines of hard muscles, a six-pack he had once licked whipped cream from, and the edge of Ty's jaw as he tilted his head back.

He was, without a doubt, the most beautiful thing Zane had ever laid eyes on.

Ty looked down at him, his eyes in shadow. Zane hadn't expected to find the hat sexy, but the way Ty looked in it and nothing else was indescribably so.

Ty didn't say a word. He just shifted, his hard cock brushing Zane's chest, his hips moving under Zane's hands, his muscles flexing.

"Ty," Zane groaned as his lover turned in his lap. He slid his hands over Ty's ass, squeezing hard and spreading him apart with his thumbs as he massaged the muscles with his fingers. He kept his hands there as Ty straddled his lap backward and lowered himself; Zane flexed his hips, guiding him down, trying to help.

Ty didn't just lower himself, though. He rolled his hips and arched his back, rubbing his ass against the head of Zane's cock but always missing the entry, making a show of it. He flexed his shoulders, twisting from side to side so that Zane had to work hard to force him down.

Zane found himself both turned on and frustrated by the teasing lap dance.

"Jackass," he said through gritted teeth.

Ty laughed.

Zane reached up to grip Ty's shoulder with one hand, exerting enough force to pull him down while his other hand kept Ty from wriggling his hips away. Ty gasped as the head of Zane's cock shoved into him.

"Fuck, yeah," Zane groaned.

Ty squeezed him, and Zane watched the play of muscles as Ty rolled his hips and forced Zane further into him. Zane's hand dragged down Ty's back, sliding around his ribs to his belly. There wasn't a wasted pound on Ty, and every inch of him was hard when his body was tense. He was so much fun to fuck.

"Come on, doll," Zane begged. He flexed his hips up, but Ty merely rode the motion, not allowing Zane to go deeper.

Ty looked over his shoulder, a smirk playing at his lips, his eyes shining. He reached up to pull the brim of his hat lower like some villain in an old western. Zane grinned. Oh yeah, he was in for a wild ride.

Ty rolled his hips, and Zane followed the sensual movement with his fingertips. His cock slid deeper into Ty with every roll, and he hastily reached to spread Ty apart so he could watch his thick cock plunging into his lover.

Ty moaned as Zane sank deep. It wasn't a short gasp or a surprised groan like the sounds he usually forced out of Ty when they fucked. This was a sultry, intentional sound that made all the remaining blood in Zane's body rush to his cock.

"Jesus, Ty, what are you doing to me?"

Ty reached back to drag his fingers over Zane's ribs. "I'm using you to get off."

Zane moaned as Ty started to roll his hips in circles, reaching up to find somewhere to hold. He settled one hand on a hip so he could feel Ty's intoxicating movements. The other hand he dragged up and down

Ty's back as his cock plunged deep, massaged by Ty's tight muscles, surrounded by slick heat. Ty would tighten those muscles and Zane would cry out and drag his fingernails down Ty's side as he tried to buck his hips.

It was a slow build, like embers kindled deep in his belly.

Then Ty rose up, sliding those tight muscles along the shaft of Zane's cock.

"Yes, baby. Oh God, yes," Zane stuttered. He reached around to grip Ty's thighs, pressing his chest to Ty's back.

Ty sank down just as he'd risen, shimmying his hips from side to side. His back dragged against Zane's chest.

"Oh, God! Please, Ty! Christ, I'm begging you, go faster."

When Ty turned his head, Zane could see he was biting his lip. "I thought I was supposed to be learning some sort of lesson."

Zane groaned and tried to shove himself deeper, but Ty anticipated him and rose to his knees again. Zane growled in frustration. "I'll teach you a goddamn lesson."

He wrapped his arms under Ty's, pulling him back by his chest as he sank his teeth into the side of Ty's neck. Then he thrust his hips up without letting go, and Ty shouted as he shoved in deep.

"Ride me now or get fucked face-first on the floor."

Ty laughed breathlessly, rolled his hips, then pushed forward and began to ride Zane's cock faster.

"That's it, doll," Zane gasped. He gripped Ty's hips and tried to urge him to go faster, but Ty rose again, pulling Zane's cock almost completely out of him.

Zane called out and scrabbled for Ty's shoulder to keep him from going farther. The head of his cock pushed at the stubborn muscles of Ty's entrance, spreading him apart, forcing those muscles back with its girth. Ty threw his head back and moaned again. He rolled his hips around, forcing Zane's cockhead to massage him.

Zane watched with his mouth wide open, tongue touching the back of his top teeth, gasping for breath. Ty was blatant about using Zane to pleasure himself, and Zane loved every minute of it.

Then Ty sank down again, crying out as he hit his prostate. He reached back to grab at Zane, who caught his hands, sliding their fingers together, gripping him hard as Ty shimmied his hips. The sounds coming from him were debauched and downright wicked, and not one of those was calculated.

Then he started riding again, faster this time, fast enough to draw a gasp and a curse from Zane's lips. Zane still held both of Ty's hands, and he pulled Ty's arms behind his back, holding him there as if his wrists were tied together. Ty continued to ride him, moaning in approval of Zane's newest idea.

Zane pushed his hips up, bringing both of them off the couch. Ty moaned again—that decadent, sinful sound Zane knew he was making on purpose. Zane's groin growing heavy and tight, pleasure spreading as Ty rode him harder and faster. His ass slapped against Zane's lap. Zane's cock slammed into him over and over.

Zane's grip on Ty's wrists tightened, and he pulled until Ty's back was arched at an awkward angle. He shoved his cock up into his lover, grinning when Ty called out his name and turned his head to try for a kiss. Zane curled and managed to meet his lips, reaching around Ty's body, gripping his cock and stroking him. How was Ty still riding him with his body so contorted? Zane was going to come inside him any second if Ty didn't hold still.

He reached up and took the hat off Ty's head, tossing it over the back of the couch, then grabbed Ty's hair, yanking his head back so he could whisper in his ear. "I'm going to come in you so hard you'll be tasting it."

Ty's entire body shuddered against him. "Yeah. Please, yes."

"I want to see you first."

"Zane."

"Shoot your load for me and I'll throw you down on that floor and fuck you. Hard and messy, just like you want it."

Ty gave another decadent groan. Zane smacked his ass to get him to go faster, and the sound of his palm slapping skin and Ty's desperate cry nearly sent him over the edge. He forgot about the hand job he'd started for Ty, and he pushed Ty to sit up straight again, gripping his hips hard.

"Yeah," Ty whispered, sounding relieved at Zane's loss of control.

"Yeah, what?" Zane growled in his ear.

"I'm not calling you sir during sex."

Zane grabbed a handful of hair. "Ride me, Ty!" he shouted, his harsh voice echoing off the high ceiling. "Come on!"

Ty bent forward, riding Zane with those sinuous movements of his hips, faster and faster until sparkles started to form on the edges of Zane's vision.

He grabbed Ty in a one-armed bear hug and pulled him back against his chest, restraining Ty's movements as he fought off his orgasm. Ty was breathing hard, biting his lip as he tried desperately to roll his hips. Ty leaked all over Zane's hand when Zane slid his fingers over his cock.

Zane started to stroke him with one hand, yanking that handful of Ty's hair with his other as he whispered into Ty's ear. "You better come without moving too damn much."

Ty's lips parted, but no sound came out. His head rested on Zane's shoulder, and the faster Zane stroked him, the tighter Zane's grip on his hair became. Ty's body began to contort, his breathing growing erratic and labored. Every inch of him was straining to remain still, and the restraint and the tortured look on his lover's face drove Zane's hand faster and faster.

"Zane!"

"Don't fucking move!"

Ty's head thrashed from side to side, fighting Zane's grip as he writhed on Zane's straining cock. He finally managed to press his mouth to Zane's, and Zane returned the kiss with all the hunger and lust of a man fighting his own orgasm.

As their tongues fought for dominance, Ty thrust his hips up into Zane's hand, and he called out into Zane's mouth as he started to come. It hit both their chests and even spattered up onto their chins as Zane pumped Ty's cock.

Ty licked a drop of cum off the corner of Zane's mouth, and Zane's control snapped.

He released Ty only to grip Ty's hips hard, fucking Ty at his own brutal pace. His movements were so powerful and out of control that he nearly tossed Ty to the floor. Then he grabbed Ty and did shove him to the floor. They both hit hard, Ty's hands still trapped between them, and Zane lined up quickly and pushed his cock past those tight muscles without giving Ty a moment to recuperate. Ty bucked under him, fighting back against the hard fucking in a way he knew would drive Zane insane. Ty's cries and shouts and curses turned into begging. Begging Zane to take him harder, begging Zane to come all over him, begging him for more of everything.

Zane went at him harder and faster, pulling completely out and then forcing himself back in. When Zane started to come, the first spurt spilled out over Ty's ass before Zane could shove back into him. He continued like that, coming inside him and all over him at the same time, pulling out only to shove past a pool of his own cum, watching himself shoot against Ty's ass and knowing he was filling him up inside, too.

Zane's shout, primal and wordless, echoed off the high ceiling. Ty kept moving, his muscles sliding under Zane's hands, moaning as Zane made a mess of it.

When Zane's body finally gave in, he collapsed against Ty's back and pressed his face against him, licking at the sweaty skin.

Ty hummed, his hands still trapped between them like he really was restrained that way. He craned his neck for a kiss and Zane was more than happy to oblige: he took Ty's hands in his, pinned them to the floor, then leaned over him for a languid kiss. Ty's ass pushed against him as Ty contorted, his body asking for more.

It didn't happen often, but sometimes Ty sank into this submissive mindset, and Zane took advantage when he could. It shocked him how good Ty was at playing the submissive when he was so dominant at other times.

Just the thought of Ty being in one of those moods had Zane wanting to fuck him all over again. Snugged up against Ty's ass, surrounded by his own cum, didn't hurt the urge either. Zane flexed his hips, wondering how long they could stay like this until he was ready to go again.

"What's gotten into you?" Zane asked, whispering in Ty's ear.

Ty gasped and shuddered beneath him. "Besides you?"

Zane ran his hands over Ty's hard muscles, the smell of sweat and sex and Old Spice helping to convince his body that it could indeed take Ty at least one more time tonight.

"Besides me."

Ty grinned, rolling his hips to spur Zane along. "Must be the Stetson."

## Chapter 5

"I wonder where Dad went."

"Probably got tired of the horse smell," Ty grumbled. He was watching Zane work from his perch on the edge of one of the stalls, his feet dangling. Zane was having a hard time keeping his eyes off him.

He'd missed the routine of the ranch, and he was enjoying getting his hands dirty again. Brushing down the horses certainly beat loitering inside under Beverly's watchful eye until Mark arrived.

"Uncomfortable?" Zane asked, smirking.

Ty darted a glance at the horse Zane was brushing. "They keep . . . looking at me."

Zane looked at Ty for a long moment, trying not to laugh. "Looking at you," he managed to say.

Ty gave the horse a wave. "Look at him! It's like he knows something."

Zane snickered, and the horse mimicked him with a whicker, which just made Zane laugh harder.

"That shit's not funny, Zane."

"Agree to disagree," Zane crooned.

"Hello the barn!" The call echoed from somewhere behind them.

Ty perked up like a hunting dog on a new scent, and Zane straightened from brushing the horse and peered down the barn's center aisle. "In here!"

A lean man in a cowboy hat was walking toward them. The sun shone into the barn behind him, turning him into a faceless silhouette.

Ty tensed and looked over his shoulder to watch the man approach. He was always on edge in unfamiliar territory.

"Hey, I'm looking for—" The man stopped several feet away, where his face came into view. "Z? Damn, I thought you were your daddy."

Zane stepped toward the stall door. "Mark. Been a while."

Mark Masterson pulled off his hat. His blond hair underneath was shorn almost into a crew cut, and his goatee was neatly trimmed. He gave Zane a hug and then stepped back, blue eyes shining. Zane waited, apprehensive. Mark wasn't exactly an open-minded individual, though he was a decent enough guy. Annie hadn't been certain how he'd take the news that Zane was involved with a man, but they'd decided to tell him up front and let the chips fall where they may.

"Annie, uh ... told me about what I missed at dinner."

Zane straightened, squaring his shoulders.

Mark turned his head to look Ty up and down. Ty stared at him, unmoving, until Mark met Zane's eyes and nodded. "I'm just glad to see you happy again, Z. We were worried for a long while it wouldn't happen."

Zane exhaled the breath he'd been holding. "Thanks."

Mark looked at Ty and nodded, offering his hand. "Mark Masterson."

Ty shook with his left hand, still wary.

"Ty, this is Annie's husband. Mark, this is my partner, Ty Grady."

Ty looked Mark up and down. Zane had seen him do it many times, but he always enjoyed watching Ty's gears turn. "Semper fi," he said to Mark with a small smile.

Zane's brow jumped. "How'd you know he was a Marine?" he blurted.

Ty grinned enigmatically at him, and Mark laughed. "You wouldn't understand, Z," Mark said. He nodded at Ty again. "Welcome to Carter Garrett Ranch, Ty Grady."

"Thanks."

"Are you *the* Ty Grady? From Camp Lejeune?"

At that, Ty grew even more tense and quiet. It was unlike Ty in so many ways. What was this undercurrent between them about? And it was astonishing that Zane's brother-in-law had heard of Ty before. What kind of badass Marine had Ty been to have his name known by people he'd never met?

Ty nodded. "That's right."

"I knew that name sounded familiar. I remember hearing it quite a bit."

"I'm sure you did," Ty said with a small, mirthless laugh.

"You were Second Recon, right?"

"I was."

Mark nodded sharply, then glanced sideways at Zane. "Recon squads at Lejeune when I was there were a crazy bunch."

"We had our moments," Ty said, voice low and careful. It sent a chill up Zane's spine, the type that often preceded wanting to be pinned to the ground and fucked to within an inch of his life. Somewhere along the line, he'd come to terms with the fact that the more dangerous Ty seemed, the hotter he was. Zane had no regrets.

Mark nodded. "Well, it's a pleasure to meet you. Will y'all be staying awhile?"

"Until we get something settled with Dad's attackers. We'll be around. We were waiting for you to show before we gathered on it."

"All right, then. Hey, a couple of us are heading to the roadhouse later tonight. You two game?"

Zane cast a glance at Ty, who nodded. "Yeah, sounds fun."

"Just, uh . . . fair warning. Word's already got around the C and G about you two. Won't be long before it gets out. Hope you're ready for that."

Zane fought against the butterflies. "Really? That was faster than I expected."

"Yeah, well. The last remaining Garrett starts doing a guy, it makes the rounds."

Zane laughed despite himself. He hadn't thought of it that way, but he supposed it *would* cause a stir, considering he had no kids and was therefore the last Garrett in a long line of them.

Mark turned to go. "We're ready when you are."

Zane nodded, but he was watching Ty.

"Ty?" he said after a few seconds.

Ty tore his eyes away from Mark and met Zane's eyes. "Hmm?"

"You okay?"

Ty nodded curtly. "Just wasn't expecting to be recognized."

Zane wanted to ask why it bothered Ty, but he'd save it for later. "You ready to head inside?"

Ty pushed off the gate and landed light as a cat in the dirt. "Was that true, what he said? Are you the last Garrett?"

"Yeah, why?"

"He's right, that's going to cause a stir."

"I don't care. Do you?"

Ty shook his head. Then he gave the horse one last mistrustful glance. "Let's do this," he said with a huff. He turned toward the barn doors. "It's about damn time I hear what's been going on."

They walked side by side toward the house. Zane slid his hand into Ty's back pocket. "Yeah, I'm sorry for keeping you in the dark, but I figured the less I told you, the better you'd be able to look at it through new eyes. I want to see if you can find an angle all of us are missing."

Ty rolled his eyes. "No pressure."

🐾 ★ 🐾 ★ 🐾

They gathered in the drawing room to brainstorm and fill Ty in on the details. Ty and Zane sat on the edge of Beverly's desk, their shoulders brushing.

"Have you had any land grabs in the area? Redistricting? Minerals, oil? Any reason to try to run you off your ranch?"

"No, nothing like that," Harrison answered.

"The land is the only thing I can think of that makes sense," Ty said, casting a troubled look at Zane.

"You want to take a look at it?" Zane asked.

Ty nodded, so Zane retrieved a map of the area from a bookcase along the wall and laid it out on the desk, smoothing it as they all gathered around it. The family knew it by heart, but Ty bent over the map and studied it closely. He pointed at a square in the middle. "This is the big house, right?"

"We don't call it that," Beverly snapped. She'd made it abundantly clear that she thought this was all a waste of time.

"The large structure in which you live, then?" Ty said, one eyebrow raised. Zane had to look away so Beverly wouldn't see him smile, and Annie and Mark both coughed as they examined the carpet.

Zane cleared his throat and picked up a pen. He drew a circle around the house, then several other spots on the map. "This is the main house. The guesthouse where we're staying is here, and this is the entrance off the main road."

"Okay. Where did your dad get shot?"

"It was out near the old pump house," Harrison answered.

Zane traced his finger along the line of the map and found the general area where the old shed was that housed the ancient spring and pump. He marked it with an X. What was Ty seeing, looking at it from a fresh angle? Zane could trace the lines and ridges of the property with his eyes closed, but that wasn't always the best way to find something you were missing.

"Pump house? Is there still water there?"

"No," Mark said. "The underwater river that fed it has moved on."

"Did it leave behind caverns? Pockets of open space or caves?"

Mark and Annie shared a glance. "Something like Hamilton Pool?" Annie asked.

"What's that?"

"It's a swimming hole," Zane said. "Huge collapsed cavern from an old underground river. Dripping Springs, the town I told you about? There are water features all over the place."

"So it's possible there's something out there under the map, somewhere dark and cold."

Zane met Ty's eyes with a hint of pride and nodded. "Perfect for temporary storage in the Texas heat."

Ty nodded. "Do you have a bigger map? One that shows the surrounding areas and the water?"

"I'll get it," Mark offered. He went to the bookshelves and came back with a topo map that he laid on top of the first one.

Ty bent over it, staring at it long enough for the group to grow restless.

"What is this green area here, on the edge of the map?" Ty finally asked, brushing his finger over the spot. "It passes within a few miles of where he was shot. Is it state land? A national park or something?"

Zane sucked air through his teeth and clucked his tongue. "You're not going to like it."

Ty eyeballed him, then the others. "Why, what is it?"

"That's the animal sanctuary," Beverly said with a sniff. She'd never been a fan of the place.

"It's the what?" Ty asked.

"It's a big cat sanctuary," Annie said. She edged closer and looked at the map. "It's been there for about fifteen years."

"Big cat?" Ty repeated, his voice going flat.

Zane was torn between wanting to laugh and wrap Ty up in a hug.

"Yeah. They take in exotic animals that have been abused or abandoned or rescued. Most of them are big cats, though I think they take in other types when they can."

Ty stared at her, his jaw tightening. "Why?"

"The big cat population in the states almost outnumbers those in the wild. They need somewhere to go. There are dozens of sanctuaries all across the country, a lot of them right here in Texas."

"Why so many here?"

"Well, because Texas laws about exotic animals are very loose. For the most part, they're awful, but it means the sanctuaries can move freely where they can't in other states. The cats need all the help they can get."

Ty glared at Annie for a minute, then looked back at the map. "I hate Texas."

Annie leaned toward Ty. "Sorry?"

"Nothing. So, all this green on the map here is the second circle of hell?"

"What?"

"Fur and ... stripes and ... teeth."

"Yes," Zane managed to answer without laughing.

Ty frowned hard. "Doesn't make any sense."

"What doesn't?"

"Well, I was assuming your land was being used either as a storage dump or a delivery highway, and if someone found a cavern down there, it's perfect. But it's so damn out of the way, it reads more like a point of origin than anything. If this section that abutted it was park land or some other sort of protected area, that's where I'd think the factory would be."

"Factory?" Beverly asked, mouth twisted as if she hated to be curious but was anyway.

"He means if it was drugs," Zane said. "A protected place like a national park would be a good place to manufacture them."

"Yes," Ty said, eyes still glued to the map. "The same goes for human trafficking."

"We're a bit far from the border for that," Zane said.

"It doesn't work, either. There's no reason to use your ranch to make anything, and certainly not to stash live bodies en route. It's too remote, too far from the trade routes, and too well-utilized."

"Trade routes. You're talking like this is some sort of seafaring business."

"It pretty much is," Ty said to Beverly. "Trucks are like ships, taking cargo all over the country. Very profitable. But they take the same routes because they know the ins and outs. They don't stray to new territory often. It's too risky."

"That's horrid."

"That's what Zane deals with, Mother," Annie said, her voice cold.

Beverly cast a glance at her daughter before brushing off the admonition. "If it is neither drugs nor this... human trafficking, as you call it, and you believe it wasn't a mere case of trespassing, then what do you propose it is?"

Ty chewed on his lip and looked back down at the map.

"Ty? You have an idea?" Zane placed his hand on the small of Ty's back, trying to urge him to speak.

"I'm not really sure if I do."

"Try us."

Ty shrugged. "Annie, you said exotic animal laws in Texas were different than most. How so?"

"What does that have to do with this?"

"Humor him," Zane said.

"Well, Texas law allows for the ownership, sale, and breeding of exotic animals. Like I said, it's hardly regulated. It's barbaric."

"And other states do regulate it?"

"Most, yes."

"That makes exotic animals a commodity."

"I guess you could call it that."

"Is it big money?" Ty asked. "Exotic animals?"

"Yeah, I guess so," Annie said. "People will pay thousands for a tiger or lion, especially on the black market, but legally as well. They're kept as a sort of status symbol. And they're used for income. Circuses, traveling entertainment, private zoos. Not to mention their pelts being worth thousands."

Ty nodded and glanced at Zane. Zane raised an eyebrow. "What, you think this is about exotic animals instead of drugs or sex trade?"

"I think... maybe someone should pay a visit to that place and see if any of their animals are missing."

Zane studied the map. The sanctuary abutted the ranch and passed within two miles of the pump house. He smiled ruefully and shook his head. He never would have even considered it.

"Makes more sense than anything we've come up with yet," he said, and he reached for the corner of the map to begin folding it back up.

"You kids go on, then," Harrison said. "Check out that place."

"Oh, hell no," Ty blurted. "I mean, no, sir. Hell no, sir."

Zane chuckled. "Come on, Ty."

"What? No. Not me."

"Chicken," Zane whispered.

"Yeah, that's what they think I taste like."

Zane laughed harder.

"I don't do big cats, Zane."

Annie held up a hand. "I'm sorry, why aren't you going to the sanctuary?"

"He has an unnatural aversion to large felines," Zane told her.

"It's not unnatural, Zane. It would be unnatural if I *weren't* afraid of something that tried to eat me."

Annie smiled gently. "They're nothing to be afraid of. Big cats rarely attack humans."

Ty turned his glare on her, but before he could speak, Mark barked a laugh. "And here I thought the famous Tyler Grady wasn't afraid of anything."

Ty glared at Mark for a moment, then at Zane, crossing his arms over his chest. "Screw you all, I'm not going."

🐾 ★ 🐾 ★ 🐾

Zane and Annie stepped into the lobby of the big cat preserve, but Ty balked, freezing on the welcome mat. It had a black and orange Bengal tiger face on it.

"It smells like death in here."

Annie took his arm and smiled. "I'm sure that's just the bleach they use on their habitats. Come on."

She dragged him over the threshold, and Zane followed with Mark, trying not to laugh.

A woman in khaki pants and a "Save the Kitties" T-shirt met them in the lobby and shook their hands.

"You must be the ones who called earlier. I'm Tish."

Ty offered his left hand to shake, and when she took it, she immediately gripped it with both hands and pulled it to her face to look closer.

Ty stumbled and watched her with wide eyes, too dumbstruck to say or do anything.

"What was this, *puma concolor*?" she asked as she examined the scar on his hand.

"What?"

"A mountain lion? A cougar?"

"Uh."

"This is stunning. Cougars are more closely linked to smaller felines than to large jungle cats, most people don't realize that," Tish rambled as she turned Ty's hand over and over to look at the faded, jagged scars.

Zane often found his own fingers tracing the tooth marks and surgery scars on Ty's hand when they were lying in bed. The pattern was hypnotic, in a way, and one more reminder that Ty was a fighter of the highest order. The only reason he'd lived through that attack was because he was too stubborn to die.

"They don't usually attack humans. Were you feeding her at the time?" Tish asked.

"I was . . . trying not to," Ty said. He gaped at Zane, silently asking him to *do something*.

Zane patted his shoulder. "We think he got too close to her babies or she was defending her territory."

"Yeah, or he just wasn't hungry cause he'd already eaten a dude right before me."

Tish practically bounced. "This is just awesome, we don't see many bite marks that nicely preserved. I mean, not on living things. You were lucky she was just playing with you."

"You were actually bitten by a cougar?" Mark asked.

Ty grunted, and Zane squeezed his shoulder to keep him from saying anything more.

Tish let his hand go and smiled. "Anyway! How can we help you? Were you here for a tour? It's a little unorthodox on a weekday on such short notice, but it can be arranged, especially for neighbors who've been so kind to us."

Zane smiled and shook his head as he pulled out his badge and showed it to her. Ty did the same, although more grudgingly. "Actually, we're here in an official capacity. We were wondering if you've had any break-ins. Any animals go missing recently?"

Her eyes widened as she looked at the badges, and she nodded. "We have. Two residents are unaccounted for. Have you found them? We've been worried sick about them."

"I'm sorry, no. Were they reported?"

"Oh, of course. We reported them to the local animal registration agency and local law enforcement, as per the state statute—"

"Okay," Ty interrupted. "How do you know they're missing?"

"Well, they're not in their enclosures anymore."

"That's . . . really?" Ty asked.

"What my partner means is, um . . . do you tag them in any way? So you can track them?"

"No, the residents are never intended to be off the property. Tagging them would be costly, traumatic, and redundant."

"So, they're in cages, you said? How does a lion or tiger get out of its cage?" Ty asked.

"We call them habitats or enclosures. Each one has a double gate, where we can lock the cat in one section and clean the other safely. We believe one of the interns may have improperly latched the gates after cleaning or feeding, but . . . we take such precautions, I just don't see how that could have happened. I mean, both gates?"

Ty and Zane shared a look. It was looking more like Ty's theory might be correct. Ty's eyes strayed past Zane to the wall behind him, and he began to drift toward it to look at a large, colorful map of the preserve grounds.

"The preserve has a perimeter fence?"

"It does. A backup measure for this very thing. We searched for days, but we have over one-hundred acres. I'm sure the tigers are still on grounds; we simply don't have the manpower for a concerted search. We're still looking."

"Ma'am, we don't believe that to be the case," Zane said.

"I don't understand."

"A week ago, the owner of the C and G, the ranch that borders the preserve, was shot just a mile or two from one of your boundaries."

"Oh, dear!"

"We think he witnessed a catnapping." Ty managed to say that with a straight face. Zane had to fight back a snicker.

"You think someone came in and stole our cats?"

"Have you found any perimeter breaches?" Ty asked.

"No." Tish brought a hand to her neck. "Really, we just thought they'd come home once they got hungry. We've all been on the alert."

"Yeah, 'cause tigers are completely helpless when they want food," Ty muttered as he looked back at the map.

"How tight is your security?" Zane asked.

"Well... our security is more for the safety and containment of the animals, not to keep people out. The border fences are electrified. Each habitat has a lock on it that requires a key."

"What about this building?"

"A standard alarm system."

"Are there any night guards? Caretakers for the animals?"

"There are six to eight interns on staff throughout the year. They all stay in the dormitory area. I can show you. Someone took the cats, didn't they? To sell them? Oh my God." Tish clapped her hands to her face, looking so distraught that Zane wished he had better news for her.

Annie patted her shoulder. "If anyone can find them, it's my brother."

Zane's breath caught at the flow of surprise and warmth filtering through him. Ty brushed his elbow, a discreet showing of pride or support.

"Can you tell us what species are missing?" Ty asked.

"Of course." Tish swiped a hand over her forehead. "They were two white Bengal tigers."

"Bengal tigers?" Ty repeated.

"Yes. A male and female. Hansel and Gretel."

Ty leaned in to whisper to Zane. "Those are the big-ass ones, Zane."

Zane nodded.

"Actually, the Siberian tiger is bigger," Tish said, babbling faster and wringing her hands. "Most people think white tigers are Siberians, but they're usually a mixture of the two. The white gene comes from the Bengal, but they do tend to grow bigger than the orange ones."

"So, very large tigers," Zane said. Tish nodded and smiled weakly.

"I fucking *hate* Texas," Ty hissed in Zane's ear before turning back to Tish with a charming, fake smile.

Tish led them through the grounds, between large holding pens filled with every imaginable species of big cat and the trappings of keeping them healthy and happy. There were over forty habitats. Most were at least fifty feet square, with soaring cages that went over twenty feet high. They had inside and outside areas, with platforms as high as thirteen feet up, built around trees and hills. There were plastic playhouses and igloos, fake ponds with burbling waterfalls, tires on the ground and hanging from the trees, and debris that had probably once been rubber toys.

Leopards, cheetahs, lynx, tigers, cougars, bobcats, servals, and lions occupied the habitats, along with one small raccoon-like creature that lay curled protectively inside a hollow log, as if it smelled the fact that it was the only omnivore in the place.

Zane kept an eye on Ty as they moved through the facility. He felt sorry for his partner, sort of, but he was also amused. Ty seemed to have developed an extra nervous twitch the closer they got to the animals. Not that Zane could blame him.

When they passed a mountain lion named Duke, Ty skirted around the cage, putting Mark between the chain link and him. He didn't look at the cat, and Zane grew concerned when he saw Ty shifting his weight from side to side, like he might be ready to bolt. His fingers constantly played with his USMC signet ring, and several times Zane saw his hand drift toward the gun in his holster. Zane frowned. Maybe he'd pushed too far, forcing Ty to come with them. He put his arm around Ty's shoulders and squeezed.

"I'm sorry I made you come."

Ty took a deep breath and nodded. "I'm okay."

They followed Tish as she told them about each occupant in loving detail. Each cat had a tragic beginning, and Zane found himself lingering over the plaques that displayed their names and how they'd been rescued.

They walked past a pair of large jaguars up a tree, one black, one spotted. Green eyes tracked them from on high as sinuous tails flicked through the air.

Zane was beginning to feel more and more sympathy for Ty as the hairs on the back of his neck stood on end.

They continued on, through winding pathways and up shady hills until they topped out on a plateau. The habitats were larger here, and further back sat sheds that housed equipment. The first enclosure they came upon on the plateau held a spectacular creature, one of the most beautiful Zane had ever seen up close: a white tiger.

"Baihu is a cross between a Bengal and a Siberian," Trish said, slowing as they crossed in front of the new enclosure. "White tigers are prized among collectors, but they're not at all rare like people think. Most are inbred for the recessive white gene and have certain health issues. If you look closely, you'll see that Baihu is cross-eyed. And I must warn you, he's quite aggressive, so when you pass by you may want to give him a wide berth."

Ty muttered under his breath as they walked between Baihu's fence and the fence of a small lynx named Zelda. Zane watched him closely, so focused on Ty that he was only dimly aware of a movement to his side. By the time he was able to turn his head, all he could see was the massive white tiger rushing at them, teeth bared. It leaped, hitting the fence with a growl. The chain rattled. Teeth gnashed at the chain link and claws hooked through it as the weight of the tiger's massive body swung the fence back and forth.

Annie screamed and ducked behind Mark, grabbing him as he flinched away. Zane stumbled back, throwing his arms up and ducking. The urge to flee was instinctive, even knowing the fence would protect them.

Tish was laughing, obviously accustomed to seeing that reaction when Baihu charged.

Zane sought out Ty as he tried to force his heart to settle. Ty stood several yards away, staring at the tiger as the animal clung to the chain link fence. He was covered in dirt like he had rolled away from the attack, and he had his gun in his hand.

"Ty," Zane yelled, "don't shoot the tiger!"

"He started it." Ty continued to stare at the tiger, and the tiger at him.

Zane pointed at him in warning. If Ty went bonkers in this place, Zane was leaving him here.

Ty glared at him, but then handed over his weapon without Zane having to ask for it. Zane shoved it into his pocket.

"Way to leave the rest of us hanging, there, Grady," Mark said as they moved on.

"Mark," Annie hissed.

Ty grunted. "Guy with a gun, I'm your man. Big white tiger with teeth, it's every steak for himself."

Zane ran his hand down Ty's back, trying to comfort him.

The next enclosure held two orange Bengal tigers roughhousing in a playground of ponds, tires, and large blue barrels.

"This is Barnum and Bailey," Tish said, a hint of pride in her voice.

They gathered at the fence to look in, and Tish gave a short whistle. The two tigers looked up and started barreling toward them. These two weren't attacking, however, but cavorting. They threw themselves against the fences, gnawing on the chain link, grunting and making sounds that seemed pretty happy to Zane's ear.

"That noise they're making is called a chuff," Tish said. "Only tigers can make it; it's sort of like their version of a purr. Barnum and Bailey are brothers. Inseparable. They came to us earlier this year. Barnum is the one with the limp ear. We rescued them from a—"

"Circus," Ty said. Surprisingly, he stepped toward the fence, as if drawn toward the two animals.

"Yes! How did you know? They've been around people since they were young and they're quite friendly. They love to roughhouse—just don't let one of them get behind you or they'll think you're playing tag." Tish put her hand out and let one of the tigers lick her fingers through the fence. "And you do not want to play tag with a tiger."

Zane glanced at Annie and Mark, then met Ty's eyes. Ty shook his head. There was no way they were getting him to stick his fingers in that fence. Annie stepped closer, though, putting a tentative hand out. The tigers grew still, watching her approach, and then sniffed at her cautiously. Bailey gave her fingers a nudge with his nose, but neither animal seemed thrilled by her.

She backed away. Mark took a hesitant step forward, and Barnum made a sound in the back of his throat that nearly triggered Zane's most primal instinct to turn and run.

"Then again, maybe not," Mark mumbled. He stepped behind Annie and hid there.

"Try it, Zane," Annie whispered.

Zane reluctantly moved forward, holding his hand out. The tigers reacted much as they had to Annie, sniffing him and staring. Not the type of reaction that would inspire him to jump in there and wrestle with them.

Barnum began to stalk along the fence, toward where Ty was trying to hide.

"Oh God, why did I come here?" Ty whispered as he took a step back. The tiger leaned its heavy body against the fence, and the entire cage rattled with his weight. He rubbed his face against the chain link, looking at Ty as if inviting him to rub him.

"Special Agent Grady, you have a real way with animals," Tish said. "Look, he likes you!"

"Yeah, so did the last one," Ty said under his breath. He reached out his hand, though, tentatively as if forcing himself, and pressed it to the fence with a shiver. The tiger rubbed his nose against Ty's palm, trying to edge around so Ty would rub his ear. Ty stared at the tiger for a moment, but then pushed his fingers through the fence to scratch at the bottom of Barnum's floppy ear. Barnum plopped down and threw his head back, basking in the attention. He started chuffing again, purring on every exhale.

Tish laughed and clapped her hands. "Usually it's Bailey who makes friends. Barnum rarely warms so quickly."

"Really," Zane said, eyes on his partner.

"Yes. I've never seen Barnum react that way! Perhaps you could come back and spend some time with him. We love to give the animals human contact when we can."

"Wrong tree to bark up," Zane said, though he watched his lover with a fond smile.

Ty was scratching under Barnum's chin, a half-smile on his face. He finally withdrew his fingers, and they moved on. Barnum followed them, eyes on Ty, making a variety of sounds, like he was trying to talk to them. When they passed the end of his enclosure, the tiger stood on his back feet and propped himself on the fence, grasping at the chain link as he watched them walk away. Ty glanced back at him, and Zane knew the look in his partner's eyes. He had a feeling they might be back here after all.

"Go on," Ty said to the tiger, waving a hand at it.

The tiger made a grunting sound and dropped back to all fours, then sat and watched them walk away.

When they reached the final pen, where Hansel and Gretel had been housed, Ty and Zane circled the exterior once, looking for any evidence of a break-in. But the hard-packed dirt was so full of footprints and wheel tracks it was impossible even for Ty to follow their story.

Zane shivered as a lion roared in the distance.

Ty knelt to examine the lock on the door. "It hasn't been picked."

Zane turned to Tish. "How many people have access to the keys to these cages?"

"Oh, every staff member and intern has a master key. In case of emergencies, of course."

"Interns stay on the premises?"

"Yes."

"How long are they here?" Ty asked.

"Six-month stints. Most of them go on to work at zoos. Some stay here."

Ty dragged his fingers through the dirt, then stood. "What sort of preparation do they need for the internship?"

"Most are getting their Master's degrees."

"So, not an easy thing."

"No."

"When did this batch get here?"

"Last month. Why?"

Ty and Zane shared a look. That was when the problems had started.

"We're going to need a list of all your employees," Ty said. "Especially the interns."

Tish pressed her hand to her chest. "You don't think someone who worked here would do this, do you?"

"Anything's possible," Zane said. At this point, even she was a suspect.

Ty peered off toward the east. "How far are we from the perimeter?"

"Oh, roughly half a mile. We try to pad the cages with some acreage, just in case."

Ty smiled gamely and nodded.

"What are these numbers at the bottom of all the plaques?" Annie asked, pointing at the plaque for Hansel and Gretel.

"Those are the costs of keeping them healthy and happy. The first number is monthly, the second yearly, and the last is a lifetime estimate based on a twenty-year lifespan. We rely heavily on donations. You can even adopt one of the animals to ensure it's taken care of."

"Admirable," Zane said. He watched his sister, who was not only a veterinarian but also an animal activist. She was heavily involved with the local humane societies, and her home was full of adopted strays.

"I'd love some information on your programs," Annie said as she and Tish headed back toward the main facility.

Mark followed them, shaking his head.

Ty stood next to Zane, looking around with narrowed eyes.

"What?"

"I just... if I'm busting in here to catnap two tigers, I'm going to be prepared, you know?"

"Of course."

"Plaques say these two tigers topped out over four-hundred pounds each. And you know they had to be tranquilized. They're not just going to waltz out of here on a leash."

Zane sighed. "We'll get the details on all the tranquilizers in the facility. Stuff like that is heavily monitored. If any is missing, it's a solid lead. And if there's not any missing, we might be able to canvas the local vets and suppliers."

Ty made a clicking sound with his tongue, his hands on his hips as he watched the others walk off. "And we'll track down any SUVs or trucks the facility has on site. We also need to locate every key in the place and vet all the employees."

"We have absolutely no jurisdiction here," Zane warned. "If anyone kicks up a fuss, we're done."

Ty nodded. "We'll cross that cattle guard when we get there," he said, then headed off after the others.

"You'll have to ride a horse to do it."

"Shut up."

Zane hung back, watching his partner go. Something about the way Ty moved—the roll of his shoulders, his easy gait—had always reminded him of a large cat in the wild. Ty fit in here more than he'd probably want to admit. Zane smiled and hurried to catch up.

When they walked past Barnum and Bailey's cage, Barnum shadowed Ty the entire way. Ty let his fingers slide against the chain link, stopping to rub the tiger's ear as he went. Barnum chuffed and threw his heavy body against the fence.

Zane smirked. Either Ty was taking a page out of Deuce's book and trying some exposure therapy, or he had just fallen hard for a tiger.

# Chapter 6

"I don't understand what any of this has to do with tigers," Beverly said as they sat around the dinner table. "And I certainly don't understand why Mr. Grady needs to be here to offer wild theories."

"Mother . . ." Zane scowled. He'd known she'd be rude, but he hadn't expected it to embarrass him. He met Ty's eyes, and Ty smiled and winked at him.

"Mother, you should have come with us today," Annie said. "The sanctuary is beautiful. And Ty and Zane were like real FBI agents, flashing their badges and asking questions."

"We *are* real FBI agents," Zane told her with a smirk.

"You say potato . . ."

Zane rolled his eyes.

"So, two of their tigers are missing," Harrison said as he cut into his steak. "And you think what I saw was someone stealing them."

"Yes, sir," Ty and Zane said in unison.

"Huh."

"Ridiculous," Beverly hissed.

Zane met Ty's eyes across the table. It was an odd theory, but well within the realm of possibility. Exotic animals were a big trade.

Ty nodded and gave Zane another smile. He seemed to have sensed that Zane was uncomfortable and embarrassed, and he kept trying to reassure him. He held Zane's gaze for another few seconds, then looked down at his own plate. The cut of steak he'd been given was at least twenty-four ounces. It filled almost his entire plate.

Ty pointed his knife at it. "You Texans really take your steak seriously, huh?"

Everyone at the table stopped eating to stare at him. He glanced around and cleared his throat, smiling that self-conscious half-smile that made Zane want to do unseemly things to him.

Ty poked his steak with his knife. "Did this one have a name, or . . . ?"

"Ty, shut up and eat your steak," Zane said with a smirk.

Ty nodded and started in on it. After their initial burst of conversational effort, they ate the majority of the meal in silence. It wasn't a comfortable one like the dinners in West Virginia.

When most of their plates were empty, Mark put down his fork and asked, "So, what do we do?"

"About what?" Zane asked through a mouthful of food.

"About the cat thing. How do we handle it?"

"Well, we could take it to the local authorities." Ty shook his head, so Zane added, "But they'll probably laugh at us at this point."

"We need more," Ty agreed. "I'd like to go out to the spot and look around, see if we can get something solid. Check the ground for cave entrances."

Zane nodded.

"What do cave entrances have to do with tigers?" Mark asked.

"Not a damn thing."

Mark raised an eyebrow at Ty.

"We'll gather the boys and head out there tomorrow," Harrison said.

Beverly's fork clattered to her plate. "Harrison, I forbid all of you to go rampaging over the ranch, wasting time that should be spent in more lucrative endeavors."

"Rein it in, Beverly," Harrison said, calm as ever. He didn't even look up, just kept eating.

Beverly inhaled noisily and glanced at Ty as if it was all somehow his fault. Ty either didn't see it, or he ignored it. The urge to defend his lover was getting stronger, but Zane pushed it down.

"It won't take but a few hours to ride out that way," Harrison said. "We'll take it easy."

"I'm sorry." Ty looked up from what remained of his food. "Did you say 'ride'?"

Harrison nodded.

"On a horse?"

"What other kinds of things do you ride?" Zane asked.

Ty glared at him. He licked his lips, and Zane had to look away before his body could react any further.

Harrison either missed the double entendre, or he was ignoring it. "We'll give you a trail horse, Ty, you'll never know she's there."

"Great."

"Well, I think Ty and I need to call it a night if we intend to ride tomorrow," Zane said. He pulled his napkin out of his lap and set it on the table.

Harrison nodded between bites of mashed potatoes. "Meet here for breakfast," he said.

"Don't y'all want to go out with us tonight, Z?" Annie asked. Her eyes were shining like she knew Zane was counting the seconds before he could get Ty in bed. "Cody and Joe are coming, and I think Marissa and Jill said something about wanting to see you."

Zane glanced to Ty, willing his partner to decline the invitation with something creative and convincing.

"Can I wear my hat?" Ty asked.

Zane rolled his eyes, smiling despite the wave of irritation. "Yeah, you can wear your damn hat."

---

Zane looked a lot more relaxed now that they'd escaped the big house and his mother's cutting commentary, but he still shot Ty an annoyed glance as he drove.

"You couldn't have just said you wanted to be dragged back to the house and fucked, huh?"

"I didn't know that was an option!"

Zane laughed and returned his attention to driving.

They idled as Mark got out and opened up the impressive gate, but they didn't wait once they hit the main road. The truck following them stopped, and either Cody or Joe got out to close the gate before continuing on. They cruised with the windows down, the night air still warm and smelling of dirt and grass. It was a peaceful drive until Zane steered the truck into a gravel lot packed with vehicles.

Before them stood a large, two-story clapboard building lit with neon beer signs in every window. Strings of red chili pepper lights lined a porch crowded with tables and patrons. In the back lot, half visible from their parking spot, sat a handful of battered, vintage Airstream trailers of various sizes that gave the whole thing a very North Texas, you're-about-to-be-abducted-by-aliens vibe. A banner hanging on the front of the building proclaimed half-price drinks for members of the armed services. A vintage porcelain sign near the road advertised cold beer and air conditioning.

Ty could see how that would be a commodity in Texas in the summer.

Zane found a parking spot, and when he turned off the engine, they could hear the music blaring out of the honky-tonk. Zane grinned. "This is more my speed."

Ty looked out the window at the garish décor. "You and me both, darlin'."

The flickering and flashing lights reflected in the mirrors and windows, splashing shards of color across Zane's face. He pulled the keys out of the ignition, pocketing them before turning to dig behind the bench seat of the pickup. He leaned back with a sharp-looking black Stetson that he settled on his head.

Ty burst out laughing, clapped a hand over his mouth, and snorted loudly as he tried to stop himself. Zane just grinned and winked, obviously not surprised by Ty's reaction.

"Oh, Jesus," Ty mumbled behind his fingers. "I'm sorry, I still can't get used to it."

"It goes with the boots."

Ty shook his head, hand still over his mouth. Zane glared at him. The hat settled well on his head and shaded his eyes from the light. "Watch it, Grady."

"Or what, Sheriff? Showdown at high noon?" He lost his hold on his composure and laughed harder.

Zane grinned, lowering his head until the hat shaded his eyes. Ty had to admit, the man could pull off a cowboy hat. He chuckled and shook his head, reaching out to cock the hat and give Zane a more rakish air.

"Where's yours?" Zane asked, still smiling from under the brim of the hat.

"I left it at the house."

"You were so determined to wear it, and you left it behind?"

"I'm not Yosemite Sam; I'm not used to grabbing my hat every time I go out the door!"

Zane rolled his eyes, then held up his index finger in a "wait" sign and turned to reach behind the seat again. He pulled out a straw bullrider hat and offered it to Ty.

Ty laughed and took the hat, turning it over to inspect it.

"No, wait. That's just like yours at home. Here," Zane said, and then he pulled the Stetson off his own head and set it on Ty's with a flourish.

Ty went cross-eyed as he looked up at the brim of the hat. Zane was staring at him, teeth worrying his lower lip, eyes dark and liquid.

"I think the black suits you more than the brown did."

"Oh yeah?"

"Brings out your eyes."

"Is that what you look for in cowboy hats?"

"Maybe. You know, in high school, if a girl got a guy to give her his Stetson, it was a sure thing they were going steady," Zane said, his voice heated and smug.

Zane's attempts at flirting were a never-ending source of amusement. And damn him, they were starting to work. "You saying I'd make a great Texan girl?"

"I'm saying you look damn good in my hat," Zane growled. He cupped Ty's chin with one hand and leaned over in the shadowed truck cab to kiss him.

Ty had to give him points for effortlessly ducking under the brim. He smiled into the kiss, giving Zane more points for the ability to kindle that low-grade heat of anticipation with just a single look or kiss. Ty didn't have a smart-ass reply for that.

The languorous kiss went on for long minutes, and when Zane finally pulled back, he ran his thumb along the corner of Ty's lips. "Ready to honky-tonk, baby?" he drawled, voice husky with arousal.

"Depends on what that's code for in Texas," Ty replied, voice just as thick.

Zane's laugh sent a shiver up Ty's spine. "Every little dirty thing you're thinking and more."

"Then let's get started." Ty grinned crookedly; he enjoyed nothing more than when Zane was in this kind of mood. It usually ended up messy. With bruises. And holes in the drywall. It was a good thing they had somewhere private to return to tonight.

Zane slid the bullrider on and pulled it down low over his eyes. His hair was long enough that it curled under the brim. Ty couldn't keep his eyes off him as they climbed out of the truck. He would stay in Texas forever, as long as Zane promised to wear a hat all the time.

Their boots crunched on the gravel. Zane reached out and slid his fingers into the palm of Ty's hand. Ty looked over at him, finding it suddenly hard to breathe. He squeezed Zane's hand and Zane smiled as he sauntered toward the door.

There were fifty or more people sitting out on the patio, waiting to get a table inside. Where the hell had they all came from?

"Z! Over here!"

Zane stopped on the rough wooden steps to find the origin of the voice, and then he smiled and waved. He turned to Ty and took his elbow. "They're waiting for us," he said, nodding to the door as the others disappeared inside.

Ty grunted, gesturing for Zane to lead on. It was fascinating to see Zane with people who'd known him before, like watching a wildlife show—prairie dogs in their natural habitat.

In short order, they arrived at a set of tables with three other couples, one of them Annie and Mark, who gave Ty a bright smile and a sardonic salute, respectively. Annie threw him off his game by introducing him as Zane's boyfriend. Word *had* gotten around, because no one even blinked at that. They merely shook his hand and told him their names.

"Okay, who's driving?" one of the women asked, raising her voice over the music. She jingled her keys in front of her.

"That's me." Zane doffed the bullrider and held it out over the table, waggling it.

"I don't want to see any scratches on my baby, Z," Joe said in a slow drawl that seemed as stereotypically cowboy as his handlebar mustache and lanky, bow-legged frame.

"You drive a puke-green Chevy, Joe," Cody said. He was Joe's exact opposite: dark hair, dark eyes, clean-shaven, and beefy shoulders. "1980 with the floorboards rusted out."

"But the engine is cherry!" Everyone laughed, and Zane waved the hat, now weighted down with other sets of keys, in front of him.

Ty's eyes were stuck on Zane, on the crow's feet that formed when he smiled and the light in his eyes. It was so rare to see him relaxed and having fun.

Keys stashed in his pockets, Zane sat down next to Ty and sprawled back in his chair as the ladies started suggesting drinks. Ty settled his hand on Zane's knee, something he'd rarely been able to do in Baltimore.

"How about margaritas?" one woman suggested. Jill, maybe? He hadn't quite been able to hear.

"Beer," Cody said.

"Mojitos?" That one was Marissa. Or Melissa.

"Beer," Joe said, voice flat.

"Jack Daniels!" Annie cried.

"Beer," Mark insisted.

Then six sets of eyes turned on him and Zane.

Ty looked around the table with a raised eyebrow. "I hear beer is good."

The guys all crowded in agreement, and Zane gave him a tolerant look of amusement. "Sure you don't want a peach bellini?" Zane teased.

"Hey, those things were pretty good. And they kicked my ass."

The laughter carried around the table as Zane related the peach bellini story to the others. It was an odd feeling, being able to share experiences like that with other people. Ty was determined to enjoy it while he could.

No sooner had Zane ordered a pitcher of iced tea, than Jill jumped up and pulled on Zane's arm.

"C'mon! No one else will line dance with me."

Ty shook his head and reached for the basket of peanuts in the center of the table. Zane could line dance all he wanted as long as they didn't drag him out there too.

"And you ask so politely, Ms. Marshall," Zane said as he crossed his arms and shook his head.

"Oh come on, Garrett," Ty said over the thumping music.

"Shut up, Grady."

"You dance, I sing. Nothing to be ashamed of," Ty needled, smirking and tossing a sidelong glance at Zane.

Zane allowed Jill to pull him to his feet, but before she dragged him out to the crowded dance floor, he leaned over and poked Ty's arm. "Turnabout's fair play, you know. They do karaoke every night at ten."

"They *what?*"

Zane didn't answer. Ty watched him head off into the crowd, then looked at his watch. It read 9:15.

Drinks arrived a moment later, and Mark pushed the bucket of iced-down beers toward Ty. "Drink up, Marine."

Cody and Joe lifted their bottles in silent toast.

Ty reached for a bottle and toasted along with them, his eyes seeking Zane out in the crowd. It didn't take but a minute of watching Zane dance—the way his hips and shoulders moved, his long, lean body, his thumbs hooked into the pockets of his jeans, the smile on his handsome face—to convince Ty that he couldn't watch Zane dance in public.

"So, Grady. How long you and Zane been screwing?" Joe asked.

Ty almost choked on his beer.

"Joe, come on!" Marissa said with a wave of her beer bottle.

"What?"

"There's got to be a better way to ask than that."

"No, it's okay," Ty said, still trying not to choke. He put the back of his hand to his mouth. "Just caught me off-guard."

"Do you take a lot of shit from people?" Marissa asked.

"Not really. But people we work with don't know, so . . ."

"You might take some shit around here," Mark told him.

Ty nodded and shrugged. "I kind of expect that."

Annie looked troubled by it, but said nothing. The conversation turned toward how good Zane looked compared to the last time he'd visited. Despite Ty's better judgment, his eyes strayed to Zane on the dance floor. He was the tallest man out there, easy to spot because he wore no hat. His thin western-style shirt hugged his slim torso and highlighted his impressive muscles, and his dark jeans were just tight enough to make him look even longer and taller.

He was a good-looking man, that was for damn sure.

Ty felt eyes on him and forced himself to stop staring at his lover and return his attention to the others at the table.

"This is one hell of a place," he said.

"This is the only bar within easy driving distance of the surrounding ranches," Annie said, pointing to a prominent picture on the far wall of several men in 1970s fashion, breaking ground. "The ranch owners all went in together and built the place to keep the ranch hands from driving all the way into Austin and getting in trouble. It was Dad's idea. Now people drive from Austin just to come here."

"Nice."

"Dancing, singing, drinking, whatever. They even have the trailers out back you can rent if you can't get home."

"I just come here to drink beer," Mark announced.

"You come here to watch the blondes in the short shorts," Annie teased.

"I can *watch*."

Laughter rippled around the table again as Annie swatted at the back of his head.

When the conversation ebbed, Ty put a hand out in front of him, as if asking them to slow down. "But I won't have to sing, right?"

Annie leaned forward over the table. "Z's got the keys."

"Yeah?"

"That's the tradeoff," Joe said with a sigh. "Z will make you sing or dance. Believe me, I've had to pay worse for a ride home."

"I'd pay Z more than one song for a ride," Marissa said, waggling her eyebrows and making the others laugh.

"Save it for the bull," Mark advised. "Z's not interested. But Ty might be able to get away without singing."

Mark smacked Ty on the back, laughing. Ty wasn't sure why it felt odd that everyone at the table knew he and Zane were a couple, but it did. He liked it, but it was still weird. Being out was definitely going to take some getting used to.

★ ★ ★ ★ ★

Zane begged off three songs later, claiming he was ignoring his guest, and escaped the floor by edging along the lines of dancers. He came out a quarter-turn around the room from their table, and it gave him the opportunity to watch Ty unobserved.

Ty seemed to be enjoying himself, using his unique brand of charm to fit in with the group. He held a half-empty beer bottle in his uncasted hand, but he was using both hands to gesture as he related a story the others were laughing and shaking their heads at. Zane had long ago become convinced that if Ty's hands were tied behind his back, he wouldn't be able to string together a single sentence.

Ty seemed at home in Zane's black Stetson, which he hadn't taken off since Zane had placed it on his head. It looked damn good on him.

Zane hummed and started moving again. He weaved through the tables and arrived at his chair, thumping against Ty as a gaggle of girls passing by almost knocked him into Ty's lap.

Ty reached out to help catch him with one hand, holding the beer bottle way out to the side with his broken hand so it wouldn't spill. "Whoa, Lone Star," he said, laughing as he looked Zane up and down with a critical eye. "You'll have to buy me dinner before you get that far."

"I already bought you dinner," Zane pointed out as he righted himself and sat down.

"And he's already gotten that far!" Mark added.

Ty shook his head, but he was still watching Zane from under the brim of his black hat.

"You call him Lone Star?" Annie asked, snickering.

"He calls me a lot of things."

"We need to order wings. And poppers," Mark said, thumping his bottle on the table. Marissa stood and started waving her hand, trying to flag down a server.

Zane snorted and glanced at Ty. Ty was watching him with that crooked half-smile Zane loved so much. It took more willpower than Zane expected to quash the urge to sit up, lean over, and kiss him right there.

"Z, you're undressing him with your eyes. Take it out back if you have to," Mark said, voice droll. Zane kicked at him under the table, and Mark kicked back a few times as they tried to get at each other.

Ty seemed content to let them rag each other without adding his own comments. He sat back and finished the bottle he'd been nursing. Zane could feel his eyes on him, though.

The conversation veered into current events around the ranches, and since Zane hadn't kept up with anyone, he didn't have anything to add. It freed his attention to turn back to Ty.

"So, Grady," Zane said, keeping his voice down. "Thought about what you're going to sing?"

Ty groaned and reached for the bucket of beers in the middle of the table. "I guess I'll take requests if I really have to do it."

"God, don't do that. They'll pick something off the list of shame."

"Then you pick one for me," Ty invited in a voice just loud enough to carry to Zane.

The thought of Ty singing something just for him was arresting. Ty didn't sing often, and when he did it was either because he was being forced to or had been drinking. Zane looked back to Ty and felt that *urge* again, this time with the visual of yanking Ty up out of that chair and laying him out on the table, which made all thoughts of possible song choices scatter.

He leaned forward until he was close enough to smell Ty, close enough to imagine he could taste the sweat on Ty's neck.

Jesus, waiting until they got home was going to kill him.

"Will you sing something for me?" he asked, low and intimate.

Ty swallowed hard, and their eyes locked as Ty licked his lips. "Anything you want to hear."

Zane's heart rate ratcheted up. He set his glass down and stood. "Time for a quick break," he said under his breath. He needed to cool off.

Ty nodded, frowning as Zane moved away. He excused himself from the table, and a moment later he was at Zane's side, fingers sliding around Zane's arm. "You okay?"

Zane cleared his throat and managed a laugh. Having Ty so close wasn't helping him calm down enough for public consumption. He shifted his weight and met Ty's eyes. The crowded bar seemed to slow around them, fading into the background as Zane's world narrowed to the man in front of him.

"Zane?"

Zane nodded. They didn't have to stay in public, and Zane wanted him badly. A few minutes away wouldn't be a problem. "Come on."

Ty frowned in confusion, but after a glance back at the table, he followed Zane without questioning him again. Zane headed for the back of the honky-tonk, where there were tiny bathrooms and lines a mile long. It would be quieter there away from the music, and they could talk. Or not talk.

They were in the back hallway, at the end of the line for the ladies' room, when Zane spotted a utility room door open. He stopped and turned to Ty. Ty gave him a wary look, as if he knew Zane was about to do something stupid. Zane could hardly believe he was considering this, but he figured they'd done worse.

He gave Ty a grin, grabbed his wrist, and pulled him into the utility closet. Ty flailed but didn't make a sound as Zane yanked him, and as soon as the door shut, he grunted in surprise and annoyance. With their eyes not yet adjusted, it was impossible for them to see each other. Zane groped for the lock, and turned it with a muffled click.

"What the hell, man?" Ty asked as he found Zane's shoulder with his fingers.

Zane chuckled, found the light switch and flipped it, illuminating a single, bare, low-wattage bulb above them. "I needed a break."

"In the broom closet?" Ty leaned against the door and met Zane's eyes, smiling and shaking his head.

Zane moved in close, placing a palm flat on the door on each side of Ty's shoulders, caging him in. "A little more private than a bathroom stall."

Ty raised his head, making his hat hit the door and slide up away from his eyes. "*That* kind of break," he said, a hint of playful sarcasm to his words. "It's the hat, isn't it? Just can't help yourself."

"The hat just makes it worse," Zane growled. He pressed his body to Ty's, touching from chest to knee.

"Want me to take it off?"

Zane had had enough teasing, and he decided to shut Ty up in the only way that ever consistently worked: he leaned in to capture Ty's full lips in a voracious kiss.

Ty's arms snaked around him, fingers digging at Zane's shoulders. He hummed against the kiss, and when Zane pulled back, Ty panted, "I've been wanting you to do that all night."

Zane dragged his hands down Ty's sides. "I've been wanting to do that all night."

Ty arched, fingers gliding under Zane's belt at the small of his back. "Do it again," he said with a nod of encouragement and a lopsided grin.

"Bossy," Zane teased, but he did lower his head to indulge in another hard kiss.

Ty's hands found their way under his shirt, yanking at it to untuck it and slide his warm hands up Zane's back. "We've really got to stop doing this out in public," Ty mumbled, sounding insincere as he continued to work Zane's shirt loose and drag his hands against Zane's bare skin.

Zane abandoned the thin pretext of just making out and shifted to straddle Ty's thigh. He bit at Ty's neck as he ground against him hard, thumping Ty back against the door. "You look so fucking hot tonight," he growled.

Ty laughed breathlessly. Zane could feel Ty's heart hammering, his pulse picking up. Ty's quiet, furtive breaths against Zane's skin were intoxicating and heady. Zane pulled Ty's shirt from his waistband before reaching for Ty's belt buckle, all the while licking at Ty's lips and kissing him again, hard and messy. He didn't bother to swallow the soft groans he might normally have worried about someone overhearing. The music was so loud in the bar that someone could stand right at the door to this closet and not hear a peep.

"Fuck, Zane," Ty gasped, sounding both exasperated and turned on. He grasped at Zane's belt, at his sides, his shoulders, anywhere he could touch. But he seemed content to let Zane have his way. And right now, Zane was of a mind to have it hard and fast.

He slid his hand under Ty's briefs to squeeze Ty's cock. "I should make you get on your knees," he whispered, lips moving against Ty's ear. Ty shuddered against him, obviously liking the idea. "Then again, maybe I'll just fuck you right up against this door."

Ty huffed out a breath and bit his lip against a smile. "That could probably be arranged." Lord knew they'd both had a number of backroom encounters like this in their lives. Just never with each other.

Zane's reply came out a rumble as he claimed another kiss. He pushed Ty's jeans and briefs down to his thighs, groping as he went. He knew Ty was humoring him—about the locale if nothing else—and he planned to enjoy it to the hilt. Literally. He pulled one hand away and reached into his back pocket, where he'd stashed a single-use packet of lubricant when he'd changed clothes.

Ty burst out laughing when he saw it. "Is that a travel pack of lube? I didn't even know they made those."

Zane grinned. "Where the hell have you been buying your lube?"

"You've been buying it, Zane."

Zane slapped Ty's hip just hard enough to sting. "You hold still," he instructed, and in one smooth motion, he went down on his knees and sucked Ty's cock between his lips.

He heard Ty's head bang against the door behind him. The hat dropped at his side, either tossed to the ground or knocked off. Ty's hand tangled in Zane's hair, and he pushed his hips forward.

The times Zane had done this, he'd been slow and careful and thorough. Tonight he sucked hard and fast and messy, taking Ty in over and over.

"Fuck, Zane!" Ty gritted out. He tugged at Zane's hair, and his hips pushed away from the door, thrusting into Zane's mouth without the care he usually took.

Zane managed to take a balancing hand off Ty long enough to tear open the lube packet and squeeze some out, and then he reached around Ty to slide the tip of his finger inside him and rub as he kept sucking. He was burning up inside; all he wanted was to hear Ty yell as he fucked him wild.

"Christ, you were serious," Ty stuttered. He turned his shoulder, as if struggling to remain motionless and let Zane do what he was doing.

Zane pulled his mouth free and wrapped his fingers around Ty to pump his cock. "Fuck, yeah, I'm serious," he growled, pushing the tip of his thumb into Ty.

Ty groaned wantonly, arching his back away from the door. Zane felt the steady beat of the music in the floor and the walls, heard the commotion of people just on the other side of the flimsy wooden door. None of it mattered. He pushed his thumb as far as it would go and shuttled it in and out as he licked around the head of Ty's cock. He focused on Ty's face, watching the pleasure there, letting it fan his own desire.

"Baby," Ty gasped, closing his eyes as his hand tightened painfully in Zane's hair. His entire body was taut, just one breath away from snapping. And Zane knew that voice. If he didn't want it down his throat, he had to stop right now.

He thought twice about it, wondering what it would be like, if it would turn him on half as much as he thought it would. He'd almost convinced himself to try it once or twice, chickening out at the last moment and letting Ty come on his lips or his chin instead, which had been hot enough on its own.

He didn't want to risk losing his nerve again and getting come all over his shirt, though.

So he lurched to his feet and turned Ty around, thumping his chest against the door. He used the rest of the lube on himself, letting his cock push against Ty's ass as he stroked himself. He was so hard and hot, even the warm air in this little closet felt cool to him, and he wasted no time widening his stance and shoving into Ty.

Ty cried out, splayed his fingers against the door, and threw his head back, resting it on Zane's shoulder. He shouted again, almost like he was in pain, as Zane pushed past those tight muscles, then turned his head into a desperate kiss and Zane bit at his lip and shoved his cock in harder.

Zane grunted and started to thrust as their mouths bumped and slid. He could feel the scrape of his jeans on his inner thighs, taste the beer on Ty's tongue, hear women laughing outside the door. It all just heightened the sensations of fucking the hottest man in the bar in a messy back-room encounter.

Ty felt so fucking incredible against him. Zane dragged his hands up and down tight muscles and slammed Ty against the door again. Ty had to stand on his tiptoes as Zane fucked him.

Zane growled and gave himself over to the hunger, dropping any pretense of self-control. Ty was keeping up a litany of curses, and the occasional gasp tore from him with Zane's more brutal thrusts. He pushed against the door for leverage, back into Zane, grinding their bodies together and making it more violent and messy than it already was.

"Come on," Zane taunted with a sharp thrust. He dug his fingers into Ty's hips, trying for any small bit of control he could get. "Paint the door for me, and you'll be feeling my cum drip out of you the rest of the night."

Ty growled back, moving one hand between himself and the door. Zane could imagine what that hand was doing, and it made his groin cramp. Then Ty's head was on his shoulder again, and Ty was crying out his name as his body tightened and pulsed around Zane's cock.

Zane hunched over, grabbing Ty's ass and spreading him apart as he fucked him brutally for five or six thrusts, nailing him to the door. He let out a long moan, and his hips stuttered as he began to come.

For all the frantic violence of the coupling, his climax spun out slow and scorching, and it left him dizzy, almost staggering as it went on and on. He could feel the cum slipping out of Ty, dripping down his cock, and yet it continued.

Ty reached back and clutched Zane's hip, and Zane dragged his teeth against Ty's shoulder, still thrusting, still coming. Ty rested his head against the door, panting. Zane leaned forward and pressed his forehead to Ty's shoulder as he gasped for breath, moaning as he pulled out of his lover.

"Jesus fucking Christ," Ty gasped, so low that it probably wasn't meant for Zane's ears.

Zane huffed a short laugh and wrapped his arms around Ty from behind, hugging him close. "Love you," he whispered against Ty's ear.

Ty laughed, nodding as his body relaxed. Zane smiled and nuzzled his cheek, kissing him. The gentle caress was a wild contrast, especially since his pulse was still thundering.

Ty turned his head, grinning as he tried to catch his breath. "Certain parts of me are going to cramp if you don't let me go."

Zane grunted. He released Ty and stepped back, then glanced around the room and grabbed a roll of paper towels off a shelf.

Ty leaned against the door, watching Zane from under lowered brows and smirking. After wiping off, Zane offered Ty the roll and smirked right back.

"You know I have to ask."

Zane finished tucking himself in and zipping up. Instead of answering right away, he leaned over and picked up the Stetson, dusted it off, and placed it back on Ty's head. "Ask?"

"I mean . . . what the hell?" Ty laughed. "What brought this on?"

Zane sighed in satisfaction, stepped close, and kissed Ty soundly. "Must be the Old Spice."

Ty smiled, his gaze softening "I love you too," he said. "Now let me pull my pants up, huh? You can't wear a hat with your junk hanging out."

Zane laughed raucously. "They're probably wondering where we are."

Ty pulled his jeans up and buckled his belt. His eyes crossed as he looked up at the brim of the Stetson. "There's no cum on this hat, is there?" he asked, deadpan.

"No." Zane unlocked the door, then paused and gave Ty a smug look. "You look like you've been totally fucked over."

Ty rolled his eyes and peered down at himself, fixing the buttons of his shirt and smoothing his hands over the material. Zane chuckled as he opened the door just a bit to check the hallway. And flinched in surprise. Annie was leaning against the wall opposite the closet door, arms crossed, waiting in line for the bathroom. She looked up when the door opened, and her expression swiftly morphed into an evil smile.

"Aw, hell," Zane muttered.

He felt Ty move, ducking behind the door.

"Well, that explains your disappearance," Annie said. Her lips compressed like she was trying not to laugh. "Is this what they mean when they talk about coming out of the closet?"

Zane glared at her, and she gave up and laughed.

"God, she's as bad with the puns as you are," Ty said from behind the door.

Zane pulled it the rest of the way open, still glaring at her. "You're just all kinds of clever, aren't you?"

Ty pointed at Zane as he looked at Annie. "His fault."

Annie raised one eyebrow at Zane. All he could do was shrug. She grinned again and turned her gaze on Ty.

Ty brushed past Zane, a hand on Zane's lower back as he did so. He tipped his hat to Annie and stepped out into the hall. "I'm too sober for this conversation," he said, and turned with the clear intention of making a quick escape. But Zane saw it coming, and caught Ty by the waistband of his jeans.

"Oh no, you don't."

Ty swiped at Zane's hand, trying to free himself. Zane and Annie both laughed as Ty turned in a complete circle, grunting as he finally managed to make Zane let go of his jeans. He straightened his shirt again and squared his shoulders, as if he could salvage some dignity.

Annie grinned as the line moved and she took a few steps away. "Looks like you got out of singing for your ride."

Ty cursed under his breath, blushing even in the garish neon light.

Zane chuckled. "She's right. I think you paid for your ride, doll."

"You know, you'd probably get laid more often if you didn't call me a whore so much."

"Stop your bitching," Zane said. He waved a hand toward the end of the hall. "I'll buy you a fresh beer."

Ty grumbled and made his way down the hall toward the chaotic bar room. Zane turned to follow.

Annie called out from behind him. "You gave yourself away, you know. To everyone in the bar."

Zane stopped in place and turned to stare at her. "What? How?"

Annie grinned and nodded toward Ty. "He's wearing your Stetson."

* * *

Zane had a hard time keeping his eyes off Ty, and the lingering scent of Old Spice on his clothes and skin helped to combat any urge to drink that cropped up as the night carried on. Ty made it so very easy for him to stay on the straight and narrow.

By midnight, the place had calmed. No one was dancing, and though plenty of people were still drinking and eating, it was an older crowd. Ty and Zane sat at a table, talking with the others about everything from how they had met on their first assignment to theories of what was going on at the ranch.

"I still think it's drugs," Cody said as he sipped at his last beer.

"A valid theory," Ty said. "What about rustlers? Does that even happen?"

Joe nodded. "It does, but not much, and not around here. There's just nowhere to take the livestock and no way to get it there after you've rustled it."

"Rustled?" Cody asked.

"It's a thing."

"If you say so."

Ty smiled, and Zane chuckled at them. Joe and Cody were two of Harrison's best hands. They'd been around since high school, and they were the only two of the dozen ranch hands who'd been invited to meet Ty who had actually come.

Annie slid back onto her stool, carrying a new bucket of beers. Marissa and Jill had called it an early night, both claiming they had to be at work in the morning. Marissa worked with Annie at her veterinary practice, and since Annie rarely saw Zane, Marissa had drawn the short end of the stick. Annie would get to call in hung over for work the next morning, while Marissa opened up.

Ty reached for another beer as Annie told them about her practice and her tentative plans for helping the sanctuary. He opened the bottle on the edge of the table, then stuffed the cap into his pocket. "So, did you want to be a vet, or was that something you got steered toward for the benefit of the ranch?"

Annie blinked. "Wow. You are good."

"Ty was briefly trained as a profiler," Zane told them. "I hate it." They all laughed at him.

"Just a lucky guess," Ty told Annie, modest as ever when it came to his more impressive skills.

"Mother thought it would be good to have a veterinarian in the family. Turns out she was right, and I do love it, so . . . I didn't fight it. Not like Z did."

Ty glanced at Zane, his smile softening. He wasn't drunk, but he was just buzzed enough to be sweet and affectionate without being self-conscious. "Zane *is* a fighter."

Zane rewarded him with a fond smile.

Ty threw back the last gulp of his beer and set the empty bottle on the table in front of him. A shadow fell across their table, and Zane started at the sight of four men standing behind Ty.

"You're Garrett, right?" one of them said, voice hard and almost slurring.

"That's right."

The man looked at the back of Ty's head. Ty was looking down at the table, face expressionless and shoulders relaxed. If being approached from behind was making him nervous, he wasn't showing it. But Zane knew he was looking down so he could see with his peripheral vision and be ready if anything happened.

"That makes you the queer, huh?" The man reached out and poked Ty in the arm.

"Hey!" Annie shouted. Mark put a hand on her shoulder to calm her.

Ty remained seated, but he looked up to meet Zane's eyes. He still appeared calm, which was shocking, because Zane was roiling with anger. Thinking these men were coming at him hadn't bothered him, but to see them go at Ty was too much.

Ty lifted his broken arm, his fingers raised toward Zane in a calming gesture.

"I'm talking to you, faggot," the man sneered as he poked Ty harder.

Ty reached for his new beer. "Yeah, I heard you." He took a drink and met Zane's eyes again. Zane wanted to bash the man's skull open;

he had no idea why his usually short-tempered partner hadn't already done so.

"Why don't you just go away, Stuart? We're not looking for trouble tonight," Mark said, as unruffled as Ty. Zane attributed it to their Marine training. It wasn't easy to prod a seasoned Marine into a bar fight.

Stuart laughed, and his buddies all chuckled. "We ain't looking for trouble. We just come over here to meet the queer."

Ty stroked his chin, looking thoughtful as he gazed at the wall above Zane's head. What was he waiting for? Zane wanted to see him beat the pulp out of these assholes. He knew Ty could do it, even with one arm in a cast.

Stuart shoved Ty again, hard enough to tip him and his stool sideways. Ty managed to save his beer and avoid whacking his broken arm on anything, but the stool fell out from under him and clattered to the ground.

The noise of the bar faded as the patrons noticed what was going on. The people at the table adjacent to them got up and moved away.

Ty turned to look at Stuart, straightening to his full height. He was taller and wider than any of the four men heckling him, and they all seemed a little surprised at his size and stature. One man took a step back.

Stuart puffed out his chest and sneered at Ty. "You gonna fight me, faggot?"

Ty looked him up and down, then glanced at the men behind him. He shook his head. "Not until you make it a fair fight. Go get more friends. I'll wait."

People around them laughed nervously. Ty hooked his foot on the bar stool and popped it back up. Then he righted it and sat down again, putting his back to them.

"He thinks he's fucking funny. Funny ain't gonna help you here, boy."

When it didn't appear that Ty was going to do anything but ignore them and let himself be shoved around, Zane pushed his stool back and stood. Stuart and the other three turned to face him, crooked smiles on their faces.

Ty slid off his stool and stepped between them, putting a hand on Zane's chest and shaking his head. "Not worth it, Zane," he whispered.

"Ty—"

"Leave it," Ty hissed.

Zane looked into his lover's eyes, and then at the men trying to pick a fight. He'd been lured right into it: poked and prodded with words and insults until he was ready to throw the first punch in front of a saloon full of witnesses.

Ty patted his chest, waiting until he was sure Zane was calm before turning around to face Stuart and his posse. He raised both hands. "You gentlemen done?"

"Why, you got somewhere to be?"

"Yeah, we do," Annie said. She got off her stool and tugged at Mark's arm. "We're leaving."

The others moved away from the table, giving them a wide berth. But Ty and Zane were hemmed in, unable to step away unless the men moved or they went through them.

"What's the matter, Garrett? You such a big man you got to hide behind your sissy boyfriend?"

"I can't wait until he shows you what 'sissy' means in his vocabulary," Zane growled.

Ty glanced over his shoulder, silently asking Zane what they should do. They could go through these four men with little effort.

"All right, break it up over here!" a man shouted as he stormed over from the bar. He was carrying a shotgun and waving his beefy hand as if shooing a pack of dogs off his lawn.

Stuart raised his hand, giving the proprietor an insolent smile. "No problems here, Bobby. We's just making friends."

They backed away, staring at Ty and Zane with smirks that made Zane want to shoot each of them in the face. It was a good thing Ty had remained calm enough for both of them, or Zane would have been on his way to a jail cell somewhere.

As soon as the door swung shut on the last man, Zane put a hand on each of Ty's shoulders and squeezed hard. "Thanks," he whispered.

Ty nodded and looked over his shoulder, his jaw set in a hard line, his hazel eyes flashing green. He was not as calm as he had seemed when facing the other men.

Annie skirted around the table. "Are y'all okay?" She looked just as angry as Zane felt.

"Fine," Zane said through gritted teeth. "If stupidity was the worst thing we dealt with every day, we'd be golden."

Ty was still staring at the doorway, jaw set. Annie put her hand on his arm. "Ty?"

He glanced at her and nodded, then looked back at the door. "Who were they? They work on a ranch close by?"

"Yeah, they're hands over at the Cactus Creek Ranch," Joe answered.

Ty nodded. "Word usually travel that fast around here?"

"Depends," Cody said. "Big news can, but not usually. They must have been talking to someone who works on the C and G."

Ty glanced at Zane and nodded, but Zane wasn't sure what he was thinking. He put his arm around Ty instead of commenting on it. "Can't believe you didn't knock him on his ass," he said as they filed out of the building into the pleasant night air.

"Would have been rude," Ty said, and he sounded serious. Mark laughed, but Zane felt like he wasn't quite getting the joke.

Mark helped Annie into the cab of Zane's truck. Zane hung back with Ty, holding his hand to keep him there. "I'm sorry about—"

"Zane, don't." Ty looked around the parking lot and then at Zane. "Don't apologize for shit you have no control over."

Zane stared at him, enjoying the feeling of his racing heart and the butterflies in his stomach as he realized, all over again, just how much he loved the man in front of him.

Ty smiled. "Do I get to ride in the back of the truck?" he asked, a little too eager.

Zane laughed and glanced over as Cody and Joe climbed into the bed of the truck. They were making a mess of it, just drunk enough to be clumsy and not care. Joe tumbled over the edge into the bed and laughed. All they could see was one boot sticking up in the air.

Zane grinned. "Yeah, go ahead."

Ty gave him an impulsive kiss and headed for the tailgate. Zane pulled himself into the driver's side in time to watch Ty climb over the tailgate and plop himself down next to Cody. The man held his fist up, and Ty touched his knuckles to Cody's as he settled in.

Zane shook his head, still smiling. How in the hell did Ty worm his way into a little niche wherever he went? It was amazing. By the time they were on the road home, Zane could hear Cody and Joe teaching Ty how to perform a proper yee-haw.

Annie and Mark were laughing, and soon Zane joined them. It was a clear, free sound—the kind of laugh he was only just recently remembering he could have.

"Zane," Annie said with a hand on his shoulder. "Go find a state that allows it, and marry that man."

# Chapter 7

Harrison Garrett wasn't doing any hard labor as he strolled through the barns. His body wasn't up to it yet. But he loved the smell of the barns: the hay and the leather, the horses and the wood. It brought him peace in a world that had gone crazy. Men were trying to kill him, lions and tigers lived next door, his wife was on the warpath, and his son had brought home a man he loved.

When he reached the far end of the stalls, he stumbled across Ty and Zane just outside the barn door. Ty was perched on a hitching post as he watched Zane rope the horn of a saddle set on a fence rail ten feet away.

Zane tossed the rope, landing it around the saddle horn time and time again. He was trying to teach Ty the proper technique, but Ty wasn't watching his hands or his posture, or even the rope as it sailed through the air. He was watching Zane's face.

"You ready to give it a try?" Zane asked, unaware that they had an audience.

"No, show me one more time."

Zane gave him a tolerant sigh and nodded. Harrison snorted, luckily not loud enough to draw their attention. This Ty Grady had Zane wrapped around his finger. It was almost sweet. And Harrison had rarely seen a man who could go toe to toe with Beverly and come out alive, much less on top and smiling. The more he saw of the man who'd caught his son's heart, the more he liked him. And the more he saw of his son, the more he realized how close they'd come to losing Zane altogether. Even before his wife had passed, Zane had been a cold and rather distant man. He'd been so much like Beverly. Now, though, there was warmth in Zane that Harrison had never thought he'd see.

It could have been a coincidence that Zane had found new life and Ty at the same time, but Harrison didn't put much stock in coincidences.

Ty was smoking a thin cigar, holding it in his left hand. He put it in his mouth and knocked on his cast in frustration. "Show me one more time, then I'll try it lefty. Unless you'd like to cut this off."

Zane looked him up and down and started to speak, but he stopped himself. Then he rolled his eyes. "You're stalling."

"I'm not stalling. I'm learning."

"You're bullshitting."

"Don't they call it horseshitting down here?"

"Come on, if you're not going to try this, I'll show you how to saddle the horse instead."

Ty pointed his good hand at the doors to the barn, where Harrison stood. "I'm not going back in there with that horse."

Zane flopped the rope against his thigh. "Ty, the horses are not conspiring against you."

Ty crossed his arms and shook his head. "He looks at me. And he talks to me! And he knows I don't know what he's saying!"

Zane squinted at him. "Okay. I think you've been out in the sun a little too long."

Harrison cleared his throat, unable to keep from laughing.

Ty flinched and straightened, pushing off the hitching post. "Hello, sir," he said as he put out his cheroot on the denim of his jeans.

Harrison smirked. Zane had managed to go off to New York City and find someone who would have fit in on the ranch almost seamlessly. And it was obvious, even if they were trying to be subtle, that the two of them were very much in love. Harrison had never known the feeling, but he'd seen it often enough to recognize it.

Zane came over, reaching out to offer an arm. "Dad. How are you feeling?"

"Winded," Harrison admitted. He took Zane's arm and leaned on him. "What are you boys up to?"

"Zane was showing off for me," Ty said with a smile.

"I was trying to teach him how to rope."

"I can't imagine he'll learn much, way he was staring at you."

Ty looked away, but even the hot summer sun couldn't mask the blush creeping over the man.

Harrison smiled. "Take a walk with me, huh?"

"Sure," Zane said as he tossed his heavy rope toward the saddle on the fence.

"I'll just, uh . . . I'll be inside." Ty jerked his thumb toward the barn door. "Talking to the horse."

"No, you too."

Ty raised an eyebrow but moved closer. "Of course, sir."

"I hear you boys had a little rough-and-tumble at the bar last night."

Zane sneered. "Yeah, some jackass tried to pick a fight."

"I hear you two didn't entertain it. I'm glad. People been talking good about you today."

"Really?" Zane glanced at Ty, eyebrows climbing higher.

Harrison nodded. "Ty, tell me something. Do your mama and daddy know about you and my son?"

Ty blinked at him and looked down at his feet. "Yes, sir, they do."

"And what do they think of it?"

"Well... they were upset that I misled them for so long. I should've told them years ago."

"What are you getting at, Dad?"

"Ty, here, he has impressive manners. I think I'd like to meet the people who taught him. I was just trying to see if they reacted like Beverly is sure to and stormed out when you told them, or if they'd want to meet me too."

Harrison reached out to take Ty's arm for some extra support. Ty's shoulders were tense, and Harrison couldn't read his expression until he gave a half-smile. "I'm sure they'd be happy to meet you."

Harrison nodded, and was about to respond when Ty stopped walking. Harrison slowed, and Zane came around to look back at Ty. The man was staring into the darkened doorway of one of the outbuildings.

"Ty?" Zane whispered, hand going to his gun. Apparently, Zane acted on such cues from his partner a lot, treating him like a well-trained hunting dog.

Ty held out one hand. "Sir, may I go in there?"

Harrison glanced at the shed with a raised brow and nodded. "Sure."

Ty advanced on the doorway. Inside was a stack of junk, old parts and rows of rusted tools spread around a ratty canvas tarp. The shape of the bulk beneath the tarp was barely discernible, but Harrison knew what was in there. From the looks of him, Ty Grady knew as well.

Ty edged up to the front of the tarp and put a gentle hand on it, bending until his eyes were level with the expanse of canvas. He looked back at Harrison and Zane, hazel eyes shining. "Do you know what's under here?"

Zane shook his head, though he appeared more interested in Ty's reaction than he had ever been in the storage sheds.

Harrison smirked. "Why don't you tell us what it is?"

"If I'm not mistaken," Ty said, a hint of anticipation in his voice, "this is an early model Mustang GT. Look at the lines and the curve of the hood there."

Harrison laughed, surprised by Ty's accuracy. "Lift it up, son."

Zane moved to help, and he and Ty rolled the canvas tarp back, revealing the rusted-out carcass of the old classic beneath.

Harrison watched, fascinated. The car had fallen into disrepair and had been sitting in the old shed for three decades, waiting for someone to come along and see the beauty in her. No one in the family had ever possessed the time, inclination, or skill to see her for what she was. Harrison had known; he'd just never been able to raise a hand for her.

The original paint had been blasted away, leaving a dull gray primer. She had no wheels, no insignia, and no interior. The hood scoop had mice nesting in it. The grill was full of straw.

Ty fell to a knee and put both hands on the grill. "She's a '67 fastback, Zane," he said, his voice a reverent whisper. "Oh my God, she's beautiful."

Zane laughed as he looked over the old heap. "If you say so, doll."

Ty ran his hands over the body, as gentle as if he were stroking a baby's cheek. "A little bit of time and effort, and she would be." He got back to his feet and disappeared into the darkness of the shed, pulling the tarp off the rest of the car.

Zane came to stand beside Harrison, smiling and shaking his head.

"Oh my God, she's a Shelby!" Ty called from somewhere in the dark.

Zane began to laugh, smile lines streaking his handsome face. His eyes filled with joy and warmth, and his frame relaxed. Harrison hadn't seen his son like this since he'd been a boy.

Harrison peered back into the darkness. "Ty, come on back out here," he called.

Ty edged his way out to them, looking chastised and letting his fingers slide along the car's rough exterior as he moved. "Sorry," he offered when he reached them. His eyes were still alight, though, and he was gazing at the car with sincere admiration.

Zane put a hand on Ty's shoulder. "Ty enjoys bringing old things back to life."

Harrison narrowed his eyes. "Ty."

Ty ripped his gaze away from the Mustang. "Sir?"

"I want you to have that car."

"Excuse me?"

"She's been sitting here for thirty years. A piece of work like that deserves someone who loves it. Someone who sees it as special even when it looks like that."

He looked from the car to his son. The expression on Zane's face was both hopeful and heartbreaking. He was holding his breath. Harrison met Ty's eyes. Ty was holding his breath too.

"I can see you're a man who looks beneath the surface. And if you can do for that car what you did for my son, well . . . it'll be in good hands." Harrison glanced from him to the Mustang, and then gave Zane a sly smile. "Consider her a . . . welcome-to-the-family gift."

Zane put a hand on Harrison's shoulder. "Dad? Really?"

Harrison nodded, and Zane gave him a fierce hug, barely remembering to be careful of his injury.

"Thank you, sir," Ty said, clearly stunned.

Harrison held out a hand to him. "You brought my son back and turned him into a beautiful thing. I expect you'll take the same care with that ol' Hoss."

"Yes, sir," Ty choked out as he shook Harrison's hand.

"I'll call this afternoon and arrange for delivery to Baltimore." Harrison clapped him on the shoulder, then turned and patted Zane on the chest before walking away. "Breakfast is in a few minutes. Annie and Mark are riding out with us."

"Ty's skipping breakfast," Zane called back. "He's heading back to the cat place to play with his tiger."

"Interview the interns," Ty corrected.

"Have fun with your tiger, Ty," Harrison called.

Ty's shoulders slumped. "Thank you, sir."

Harrison chuckled. When he looked again, Ty had Zane by the hand and was dragging him toward the old Mustang. Zane only managed to stop Ty's excited ramblings by grabbing his face and kissing him.

Harrison had never seen Zane happier or more at home than he was with Ty's arms wrapped around him. Even when he'd been with Becky, he'd never lit up quite like he did now.

Harrison nodded and turned away. That was enough for his peace of mind.

Ty sat on the front steps, waiting for everything to be prepared so they could ride the freaking horses out to where Harrison had been shot.

He didn't know anything about horses, and he only had one good hand, so he couldn't help much. He just sat and observed as he finished the cheroot he'd been smoking before breakfast. It fended off the horse smell.

Harrison stopped outside the stable to exchange a few words with Zane, something that made Zane smile. Ty blew a ring of smoke into the air, watching it float away and enlarge to frame Zane and his father in the distance. Harrison waved a hand and headed into the barn. Zane turned and walked toward Ty. No, he *sauntered*. Ty loved what Texas was doing to Zane.

Zane grinned when he saw Ty watching him, but Ty sneered back. He loved Zane, but he hated horses. He hated smelling horses. He hated looking at horses. He hated riding horses. He hated falling off horses.

"You sure you don't want to just hog-tie me and drag me behind you? I might enjoy it more."

"I don't know, that's awfully tempting." Zane stopped in front of him, his hands in his pockets. "But I'm betting either way, your ass is toast."

"Don't you have some sort of motorized ... dune buggy thing?" Ty asked. "Or I could walk."

"Ty, is there some past history with horses here that I don't know about? Like with motorcycles?"

"No." Ty lowered his head as a wave of embarrassment passed through him. Zane arched an eyebrow and waited. Ty shifted uncomfortably. "I just ... really don't like horses."

"Good. Then I can torture you without feeling bad."

Ty crushed what was left of his cheroot on the heel of his boot. "Jackass."

"What'd you find out at the Sanctuary?"

Ty shrugged. "All the interns were scared shitless of me. They also smelled like granola. None of them struck me as the type to be part of this. Three of them were crying by the time I was done asking questions."

"Ty."

"I was nice, I swear! They don't even know they're suspects; they were upset about the tigers."

"But it screams inside job."

Ty shrugged. "A volunteer, maybe? I don't know. It's not exactly Fort Knox over there."

Zane nodded and sighed. Then he smirked and looked at Ty over his sunglasses. "Did you get to see your tiger?"

Ty couldn't help but laugh. "They're tame, Zane. It's amazing. I mean, I wouldn't want to meet one on a dark mountaintop, but when they're in their enclosure and feel safe, they're like big kittens. Barnum even stood on his hind legs and hugged me."

Zane shook his head. "I refuse to live with any more evil cats. It's him or me."

Ty made a show of thinking it over. Zane kicked dust at him and Ty laughed as he ducked away.

"How is it that you can love cats so much and hate all other forms of animal?"

Ty frowned. "I don't hate all other animals."

"Horses. Dogs. Chipmunks."

"They're twitchy, Zane. And chipmunks have shifty eyes."

"Moths?"

"They have erratic flight patterns!"

Zane doubled over, laughing so hard he couldn't catch his breath.

Ty glared at him. "I'm glad my phobias amuse you."

"Just the fact that someone like you *has* a chipmunk phobia amuses me," Zane gasped.

"What'd you find out from your dad's guys?" Ty asked, raising his voice to get Zane's attention.

Zane wiped at his eyes, still chuckling. "Nothing. A couple of them said they'd heard rumors of weird things about Cactus Creek hands, but that was it. They're pretty reticent to talk when they know I'm the law."

"Yeah, Big Iron," Ty said with a grin.

"Shut up. I thought maybe you could work your magic as we ride, see if you can get anything from them."

Ty stood and stretched. "I'll give it a go." He smiled slyly and added, "Let's get this dog and pony show on the road then."

"Oh, come on," Zane grunted. "I thought you hated puns."

"Not when I'm the one making them."

"How many horse jokes do you have stored up?"

"So many."

"Christ." Zane scrubbed one hand through his hair before turning to look down the dirt road that led up to the house and barns.

"You make me ride a horse, you get unbridled puns."

"That's clever, I approve."

"Thank you." Ty said. He realized Zane was distracted, though, so he shielded his eyes to look in the same direction.

Dust started billowing up the road. Zane turned his head toward the barn. "Dad, they're here!" he yelled out as a truck drove into view, followed by two others.

"Who's what now?" Ty asked.

"Dad told me while you were gone. He asked some of the family to go riding with us as well as some of the boys from the ranch." He shifted his weight as the trucks parked around the front yard. It was a nervous habit he showed occasionally, and it made Ty anxious too.

"Who?"

"I'm not sure. If there are problems, I'll let you know."

"Yeah, send up a smoke signal."

"Give me one of those cigars and I will."

"You want one?"

"Yeah, I do."

Ty patted his pockets like he was looking for another, then shook his head sadly. "Aw, I'm all out."

"You're an ass," Zane whispered, though the words were uttered fondly.

Car doors opened and closed, and then several men ambled up to them, giving Zane hugs and handshakes.

"This is my partner, Ty Grady," Zane said to the group of ranch hands and family. "I'm not even going to try to individually introduce you; you'll have to do it yourselves."

The others gave Ty sporadic greetings. He didn't catch many of their names, but he saw Cody and Joe and nodded at them.

Ty caught wisps of the conversation as they asked Zane questions. He rubbed his fingers over his mouth, looking away so no one would notice him smiling. They were asking about research and desk work. These people had no idea who or what Zane was.

"C'mon, buddy," Joe said as he broke away from the little group and came toward Ty, slinging an arm over his shoulders. "Let's find us some horses."

Ty muttered as he was dragged along.

"How long have you been with Z, Ty?" a ranch hand named Ronnie asked as they all walked toward the barn.

"Going on about nine or ten months now."

"Well, you won't know him much, then," Ronnie said. "So we can tell you all the stories he wouldn't want you to hear."

Zane's head snapped around. "Now, now, be nice."

"Oh, yeah," a man named Jamie said, thumping Zane's right arm. Ty thought he'd heard that this was Zane's only cousin. "We can share the dirt."

"That won't be necessary," Ty said, voice flat. "My opinion of Zane can't get much lower if he makes me ride a horse."

Zane glared at him before turning to lead the way through the barn, where several horses were saddled and ready to go.

"'Bout time," Harrison said. He and an older gentleman were already astride their horses.

"Sorry, Uncle Harrison, we were just getting reacquainted with Z," Jamie said.

Ty gave them a distraught glance. "Is there anything I can do to get out of riding this animal?"

Harrison rode up beside him and clapped him on the back like he thought he was joking.

Zane peered at him over the back of one of the horses. "You're the best tracker we have, Ty. We need you."

Ty grunted and looked at the horse he'd be saddled with for the afternoon. It was a large bay gelding, which for Ty translated to "big-ass brown horse." The horse eyed him back. They were heading out to the site of the shooting, hoping to find some clue as to what had happened. And Zane was right, as usual. They needed a tracker.

"What do you mean, *he's* the best tracker?" Ronnie asked. "He's a city boy, can't even ride a horse."

Zane shook his head, grinning. "You won't be singing that same tune in a few hours. Ty can track anything, anywhere."

Ty couldn't help but smile. The pride in Zane's voice filled him with emotions he didn't normally allow himself to linger on for fear of growing overly cocky.

"Isn't there access from the road?" Ty asked in a last-ditch effort to save his ass.

"This way's cleaner on the crime scene."

"Dammit."

Zane chuckled.

"You sure you're not going to break that horse, Garrett?" Ty asked his evil partner. They were large horses, obviously good stock, but Ty couldn't imagine anything but an elephant carrying a man of Zane's size over long distances without just snapping in two. Zane was 6'5", 225 pounds. Ty almost felt sorry for his horse.

Zane grinned, and his answer was pitched low. "He's a big boy, he can take it. Can you?"

Ty clucked his tongue and narrowed his eyes, trying to decide if Zane was propositioning him or insulting him. Possibly both.

Annie and Mark joined them as they were checking their supplies. They formed a formidable group: ten riders, all well-armed. The others mounted around them, but Zane held back as the rest moved away from the stables.

"You okay to mount?" he asked Ty.

"Next time you ask me that, you better be naked." Ty gripped the pommel of the saddle with his good hand and pulled himself up in the stirrup. The animal took a few steps to the side, and Ty cussed as he held on for dear life. As soon as he was able, he pulled himself into the saddle and wrapped the reins around his palm, then slid his cast between the buttons of his shirt to keep himself from trying to use his broken hand.

He looked down at Zane and shook his head. "I want you to put 'He didn't want to ride the damn horse' on my tombstone."

"Noted," Zane said with a grin. "You did okay."

Ty nodded. He and his family had sometimes ridden horses along the mountain trails back home when he'd been younger. He'd been shitty at it then, too. He just hated them. Hated them as much as they hated him. And horses meant for mountain trails were small and hardy, easier to handle. Nothing like these monsters. These were American Quarter Horses, strong and stocky, built for working on ranches. This one was about sixty-four inches at his withers, where the neck met the back.

Ty looked down at the ground. "It's getting off the damn thing that might get interesting."

Zane patted his thigh. "You'll do fine." Then he moved to his own horse and swung fluidly into the saddle. Ty wasn't afraid to admire him. "Goddamn, Zane."

"What?"

"How is Texas making you so freaking hot?"

Zane laughed heartily. "Must be the horse smell."

Ty grunted. Zane winked at him. "Here we go—the rocky expanse, salt flats, and rattlesnakes, dead ahead."

Ty urged his horse to follow Zane's. "What could I have possibly been thinking, never visiting Texas before now?"

"The stars at night are big and bright, deep in the heart of Texas," Zane sang.

"I will knock you off that glue stick."

Zane chuckled, then sang under his breath, "I've been through the desert on a horse with no name..."

"Garrett," Ty growled.

Zane smiled fondly. "You should sing for us. I can teach you a trail song."

"I wouldn't mind doing that if I were riding an ATV." Ty shifted in the saddle. It was an odd feeling, and a precarious one, not being able to guide or hold on with both hands. But he didn't trust his hurt fingers to have any strength in them. So he was forced to use his knees, which he thought was the way it was done anyway. Still, he was not liking it.

His horse sidestepped and snorted. "Yeah? Well, the feeling's mutual," Ty said loudly.

"The horse doesn't like you because you won't relax."

"You know why it doesn't like me? Because horses never like me." Ty took his hat off and set it on the horn, then pulled a red buff out of his back pocket and fixed it onto his head, arranging it like a balaclava to protect his neck and face from the elements. Then he set his hat on top of it, pulling at the brim with the tips of his sore fingers so it would shade more of his face.

He almost lost his balance before he was able to grab the horn again. The horse tossed his head, whinnying.

"He's laughing at me, Zane."

"He's not the only one."

"Shut up." Ty nodded at the riders ahead of them. "You want to catch up to them?"

"Yeah, we should. Jamie will rag the hell out of me if he thinks I can't ride anymore."

"Blame it on me," Ty offered. He clucked his tongue at the horse and urged it into a canter.

"I blame everything on you."

Their horses slowed as they came alongside the others, and Harrison turned to look over his shoulder at them. "You okay back there, Ty?"

"Yes, sir," Ty said, withholding the smart-ass remark he'd been about to add. He grumbled and pushed his broken hand farther under his shirt as he fought the urge to use it.

Zane grinned crookedly at him.

"You don't look too happy to be here," Cody said, leaning to catch Ty's attention.

"I can think of at least ten things I'd rather die doing."

Cody grinned.

"You really as good a tracker as Zane thinks?" Ronnie asked from Ty's other side.

"I guess we'll see." Ty loved that Zane had bragged about his skills, but he also hated it. He would much rather be underestimated. He pushed his sunglasses back up his nose. "Come on, Elmer," he said to his horse. "Let's find a nice prickly cactus you can toss me into."

🐾 ★ 🐾 ★ 🐾

The group rode an hour through the flats and dry hills, admiring the scenery and talking. Zane sensed an undercurrent of tension, though. Everyone had a rifle strapped to their saddle, and Zane and Ty weren't the only ones carrying knives and pistols.

When Harrison called a halt for a brief lunch, Zane was more relieved than he would've cared to admit. It had been too long since he'd ridden. He dismounted and watched Joe, Cody, and Ty bring up the rear to join them. Ty's horse was shying to the side, and Ty was cursing emphatically. For years Zane had dreaded coming to Texas so much that he'd forgotten all the things he loved about it. Ty was somehow reminding him with every word of complaint and unfortunate accident.

He walked over and caught the reins on Ty's horse. "You doing okay?"

Ty leaned over the horn, wincing and shaking his head.

Zane offered his hand, trying not to laugh. "Need help?"

"Kiss my ass, Garrett."

The dust wafted up around them when Ty's feet hit the ground. Even behind the sunglasses, Zane knew Ty was glaring at him. He would have given anything to be able to drag Ty behind a tree.

Instead, he slid his hand over Ty's hip and into his back pocket, pulling him closer. He had to take his hat off to steal a kiss.

Ty smiled against his lips, though when he pulled away, Ty was glaring at him over the top of his sunglasses. "My ass hurts, Garrett."

"Didn't we have this conversation when we first met?"

"Have we had the 'I hate you' conversation lately? I'd like to have that one again. Real soon."

"Play nice, boys," Harrison said as he stopped by to take the reins.

"We're not fighting," Zane said.

"Yes, we are," Ty sing-songed.

"I swear, you two..." Harrison pulled the soft cooler off the side of the saddle. "Here you go, son. Don't want to forget your lunch."

"Yeah," Zane said darkly, eyes on Ty. "Don't want you swooning from hunger later."

"I'll show you swooning."

Harrison took the reins and led the horses away. Zane brushed against Ty's arm, pausing to whisper, "My ass hurts, too."

"Good."

Zane popped him in the chest with his knuckles and kept walking, cooler dangling from his hand. At least Ty seemed in decent humor. But then, Zane had noticed that Ty was often in his best moods in the face of adversity, whether physical discomfort or outright danger. He complained, sure, but often in a way that was amusing and managed to keep up the morale of others. No wonder he had thrived on a Recon team.

As Ty strolled away, the backdrop of the Hill Country offered a glimpse of Afghanistan behind a Marine. Zane's active imagination could see it, and it brought up questions he'd been spending the last few months trying not to ask.

Why had Ty left the Marines? He'd admitted to receiving a substantial payoff, but he hadn't offered to explain and Zane had decided it wasn't worth the fight to find out then. Every time he'd thought about asking since, he'd found himself thinking of Ty in his dress blues, the hint of melancholy behind his eyes when he wore them, and he let it go.

There were some sore points you just didn't poke. Ty stayed away from Zane's, and Zane gave him the same courtesy. He couldn't help feeling that Ty's secrets were darker than Ty let on.

The other guys had taken up seats on some low rocks under the shade of a copse of trees and started unpacking their lunches, and Ty wandered over to sit between Joe and Cody, making a show of being sore and stiff. Zane knew he was trying to glean more information from the ranch hands, so he let him go alone. They laughed at him as he flopped down.

He was dusty and growing more and more tanned by the minute, and he wore that hat like he'd been made for it. It was enough to hold Zane's attention as Jamie, Mark, and Annie sat around him, unpacking their lunches.

"Hey, Z. He seems like a good guy," Jamie said.

Zane chuckled and turned to look at his cousin. "He is. But you haven't even talked to him; how would you know?"

Jamie shrugged, glancing at Ty as if he was truly considering the question.

"What do you know about your partner, Z?" Mark asked after a few moments of silent shuffling with their coolers.

Something about that question made the hair on the back of Zane's neck rise. "Excuse me?"

Mark glanced over his shoulder at Ty and the others, then leaned closer. "What do you know about him?" he asked softly. "Like, do you know anything about his past?"

Zane was tempted to tell Mark how inappropriate that question was, especially when asked in front of others. But it was so odd for Mark to bring up the issue at all that Zane was curious to find out what he was getting at. "We don't talk a lot about the past," he admitted. "Why?"

"I knew him when he was still in service." Mark frowned. "Or, I knew *about* him. He was a big deal where I was. Lots of respect, lots of fear."

Zane didn't doubt that, not one bit. That was true even now. People respected Ty for his abilities, and feared him because of his attitude. Zane knew he was just a big marshmallow under all the gruff sarcasm and badassery, but no one else did.

"I know he was awarded the Bronze Star and a few Purple Hearts," Zane said with a hint of pride.

Mark nodded. "He was an excellent Marine, no doubt about that. But there was a lot of talk too. He seems like a nice guy, so the rumors might have been just that, but . . . stories I heard about him and his team make me worry a little, is all."

"Mark, what the hell are you talking about?" Annie asked, her voice hushed.

Mark cleared his throat and shook his head. "Guess it's not the best time to discuss it."

"Oh, it's too late for that," Zane snapped. He could feel an accusation coming, and he was already growing defensive about it.

"It's just . . . out here with him and everyone armed like we are, I realized it was making me a little nervous," Mark admitted.

"What is?"

"Him."

"What? Why?"

"Because . . . word was, around the Corps, that your boy was crazy as hell."

Zane couldn't help it when the laugh popped out, and he had to swallow hard against more. "Mark, that's not news to me."

Mark didn't crack a smile, though. "Like, *Full Metal Jacket* crazy. People said he was unbalanced, he was a hard-ass. And he was dangerous."

Zane nodded. None of that was news to him or to anyone who worked with Ty.

"And there at the end, folks were afraid to work with him. They said he'd throw you to the wolves to save his own skin."

"*Bullshit*," Zane said.

Mark raised both hands to fend off Zane's anger. "Hey, I'm just the messenger."

"It's bullshit. Ty took a bullet for his last partner."

"Okay," Mark said with a nod.

Zane gritted his teeth. It wasn't the first time someone had warned Zane that Ty might turn on him to save his own skin. Serena Scott had said the same thing when they'd worked their first case together in New York City. Despite being used as a paintball shield once during a training mission, Zane saw nothing like that in Ty's personality. If anything, he was loyal to a fault, and willing to risk himself for a stranger's safety. Why the hell did people keep telling him to watch his back around his partner?

"He tell you why he left the Corps?" Mark asked.

Zane's breath caught, and he found himself looking over Mark's shoulder at Ty to see if he was paying attention to them. He wasn't. He was eating his sandwich and smiling as Joe and Cody talked with him.

Zane shook his head. "No, he never told me. Do you know why?"

Mark glanced around again and slid closer to Zane, leaning in and lowering his voice. "We had our guesses. 'Round about when I was sent to Lejeune, Grady and his Recon boys were there, too. At that time, Marine Recon wasn't considered Special Ops. They wanted all Marines to be elite, you see? So they didn't class any of them as different. But Recon was missing out on the special assignments."

They were all leaning in, giving their little group a conspiratorial look. Zane was hyper-aware of the others, praying Ty wouldn't take notice of them. He hated that he was listening to gossip about Ty's past, but he just couldn't seem to pass up the opportunity to learn something without having to ask Ty again.

Mark paused to take a drink as Zane's stomach churned with nerves.

"So around then, the Corps put Recon into the Special Ops ring. A few months after I got there, Grady's group came home from a float. Two of them were real beat up. I mean beat all to hell. Grady was one of them."

Zane swallowed hard. This must have been right after Ty and Nick O'Flaherty had been captured and tortured. He felt ill as he imagined the shape the two of them must have been in when they'd returned home.

"The story was they'd got into some sort of brawl in Spain and spent time in jail, but bar brawls don't cause the damage I saw, and neither does a Spanish prison. There were rumors they'd actually been taken prisoner on a black ops mission and escaped. Now *that*, I believed. I remember running into Grady in the mess hall one night after he got back. He was ahead of me in line. He had this . . . vacant look, like he was lost in his own head. Wouldn't meet anyone's eyes, just looked right through them. Marines call it the thousand-yard stare. I remember it being pretty eerie to look at him. Lot of guys avoided him and his buddies."

"Is that why Ty was discharged?" Jamie asked, frowning. "Battle trauma?"

Mark shook his head. "He and his buddy both recovered pretty fast. But one of the other men in Grady's secondary group, he went . . . he was stark raving mad. I mean real, certifiable crazy."

Zane raised an eyebrow at that, but it didn't surprise him. From what he knew of Ty, all Recon boys were certifiable to varying degrees. "That's . . . kind of sad. But what does that have to do with Ty?"

Mark shook his head. "This guy started causing problems, on base and off. Word was a couple of them caught him trying to rape some girl in town, stopped him, and dragged him back to the brig before he could. Guys that saw him said he was beaten to a damn pulp. Rumor was Ty had done it."

"Jesus," Annie said. "I'm sorry, but what does that have to do with him being dangerous? He caught someone trying to rape a girl and beat him up. Good for him."

"I know. But the Brass didn't want it getting around that Recon assignments were literally driving Marines nuts, so they had to sweep it under the rug. Word around the camp was they called Grady and this other guy—Sanchez, I think?—in for a talk. A week later, twelve of them went out on a training mission. Eleven came back."

For some reason, the implication went right over Zane's head at first. But when he reviewed what Mark said, he couldn't keep from frowning. Was he actually accusing Ty and his Recon group of murder?

"They said he jumped off a cliff," Mark said with a snort. "I was transferred shortly after that, so I never heard what happened. But Ty said the Marines didn't want him anymore. I have to wonder if that was why."

"What's your point, Mark?" Zane asked. The upset was roiling in his gut again, but he wasn't sure why he was angry. Perhaps it was because he couldn't say with conviction that Ty would never do that. In fact, Zane knew that if Ty perceived someone as a threat to him or something he loved, he'd definitely push that person off a cliff.

"My point is . . . he might have violent tendencies. And he follows orders above all else. You should know, and I think you should be careful," Mark said, looking as if he hated the fact that he was saying it. "You know. Wary of his . . . mental state."

"That's ridiculous," Annie grumbled. She went back to her sandwich. "People at Lejeune also said Blackbeard haunted the rescue helicopter."

Mark shrugged. "I just . . . I wouldn't want Z getting hurt." He glanced over his shoulder to look at Ty one last time.

It hit Zane hard. Mark was unnerved by Ty—a fellow Marine—and he was concerned for Zane's safety. Ty had saved Zane's life many times over, in many different ways, and yet Mark was concerned for *Zane's* safety. The harsh dichotomy almost made Zane sick. It wasn't fair that people looked at Ty like that, not after all he'd been through and all he'd sacrificed.

"All right," he managed to get out, though the words tried to stick in his throat. "Consider me warned."

Mark nodded, then took another long drink of his water. All three of them sat watching Zane.

"I gotta admit, I was expecting more of a reaction," Mark said.

Zane stared at him, unmoving even when Mark shifted uncomfortably. Finally, he said, "I don't know. I know what Ty's capable of, and I know he battles a few demons. Hell, we've even exchanged a few blows in the past. But I also know he loves me and I love him, and I think he'd die before he'd hurt me. So I guess I'll take my chances."

"Fair enough," Mark said.

"We've missed you, Z," Jamie said instead of commenting on it. "We're glad you're here. And most of us are glad to meet Ty, too."

Zane considered him for a long moment. "I need to stay in touch better."

Jamie grinned. "Absolutely. Even if your boyfriend *is* nuttier than squirrel shit." Then he looked across the grass to where the other guys were sprawled. "So, you love him?"

Zane's lips quirked. "Yes. I love him."

"Then he's a good guy," Jamie said with a glance at Mark. "I can't see you loving someone who's not a good person."

Zane almost choked on his sandwich. He turned an incredulous glance on his cousin.

"Well?" Jamie said, gesturing toward Ty and the others. Mark rolled his eyes and started massaging the bridge of his nose.

"He's also really hot," Annie added.

"Hey," Mark grumbled.

"Hot is hot, baby."

Zane laughed, and the uncertainty that had settled on his shoulders began to dissipate as his gaze shifted to Ty. His partner was leaning against a rock, eating and talking with the men around him. Cody and Joe had immediately taken a liking to Ty, and Ty to them. Zane smiled.

Annie whistled and Jamie broke out in a laugh. "He's that good, huh?"

"You have no idea."

"Thank God for small favors."

The conversation turned to the past, Zane reminiscing about their childhood adventures with his sister and cousin. Soon Harrison was moving them back toward the horses.

Zane met Ty at his horse. "Learn anything?"

"Cody and Marissa are having a thing. What were y'all talking about over there?"

Zane licked his lips and shrugged. "Mark thinks you're crazy and dangerous."

"Oh," Ty said evenly, though his eyes gleamed with amusement. "He tell you about the time we killed one of our teammates by shoving him off a cliff?"

Zane blinked and nodded.

Ty laughed as he slid his sunglasses back on. "Yeah, good times." He put one foot in the stirrup. The horse took a step, causing him to hop with it to keep from falling down. Then it took another, playing with him. "Hold on now, Elmer," Ty growled as he pulled himself into the saddle.

Zane put a hand on Ty's thigh and peered up at him. "Is it true?"

Ty stared at him for a moment, his expression hidden behind his sunglasses and the shade of his hat. He finally gave a curt nod. "He fell off a cliff, that's for sure. But the only thing that pushed him was the ghost of Blackbeard."

Zane shook his head, smiling. "I love you. Even if you are a crazy, cold-blooded murderer of your coworkers."

Ty grinned and reached down to run his fingers through Zane's hair. As soon as he let go of the reins, the horse danced sideways, taking Ty with him. Zane laughed as Ty cursed the horse and his lineage, trying to regain control.

He was still laughing as he headed for his own mount, investigating the feelings of the last half hour. Even if what Mark had said about Ty was true, Zane didn't care. That in itself was kind of scary.

"Come on, Elmer. Let's go find a glue factory," Ty said to his horse, who tossed its head and snorted as if in argument. "Uh-huh, you know why? Opposable thumbs, bitch!"

"Man's crazy," Zane's uncle said to Harrison.

Zane grinned.

Harrison nodded and they watched Ty argue with the horse. "Seems to work for him."

"That's why I'm up here, and you're the one wearing the saddle," Ty told his horse as they headed off.

When they reached the pump house, Ty dismounted with a grateful groan, then cursed the animal up and down. The guys surrounding him cackled as they swung down with no problems.

Zane was still chuckling as he joined Ty, though they were both moving stiffly. Zane put an arm around his shoulders and squeezed. Ty was still getting used to being able to do it without fear of being seen.

The pump house was simply an old adobe and wood shack, patched and patched again over the years, there to mark the ancient spring well and to show tour groups that came through.

Harrison took them through the events of the morning he'd been shot. It had been just past dawn and he'd been riding, as he said, to check the problem area at the problem time.

He'd seen a vehicle parked beside the pump house and gone closer to investigate. They weren't far from a main road, and since he suspected most of the trespassing was just kids messing around, he'd assumed someone had been off-roading and gotten stuck, broken down, or possibly even hit the old building and been hurt.

When he'd gotten closer, however, he'd seen that the truck was idling, a large tarp covering the back roll bars. And then the driver had fired at him.

He'd been lucky to get away with just the one bullet hole in him, and he'd lashed himself to his saddle before passing out from loss of blood. The horse had carried him home.

Ty was unspeakably impressed with Zane's father. Now he knew where Zane got it from.

By the time anyone had come back out here, whoever had done it was long gone. The place had since been trampled with police vehicles, horses, and footprints. Ty surveyed the scene, shaking his head. It was daunting. Now he *really* wished Zane hadn't bragged about his tracking skills.

"What do you think?" Zane asked, voice low. "Think you can unearth anything?"

"I don't know, Zane. I mean . . . it's been baking in the sun for two weeks. The scene's been disturbed by all kinds of things. I'm not sure I could recreate what happened, even knowing how it went down from your dad's statement."

Zane caught his hand and ducked his head so Ty would meet his eyes. "Will you try? Please."

Ty stared at him, held captive. Zane so rarely busted out the cartoon bunny eyes, it worked on Ty every time he did it. Damn him.

"Of course, Zane," he whispered. He squeezed Zane's hand. "Just . . . don't get your hopes up, okay?"

Zane nodded, looking pleased as he let go of Ty's hand.

Ty huffed at him. He headed for the pump house first, taking his time as the sun beat down on his shoulders and waves of heat shimmered in the distance. He shed his shirt, leaving the paper-thin Henley underneath to protect him from the sun.

It took him nearly half an hour to traverse the entire scene. He was aware of the others getting restless, spreading out, finding shade, grumbling, napping. He pushed all that away, trying to focus on the tidbits of evidence he could find in the sand and shrubs.

Finally, the others lost patience with him.

"What's the news, Grady?" Joe called out.

Ty winced and wiped at the back of his neck with the buff he wore. "A car was parked here, by the pump house. It had been here for a few hours." He bent with a plastic bag in his hand and picked up a husk of a cigarette with it. There were several nearby, telling the tale of someone waiting there. "It was a four-wheel drive vehicle, a truck or possibly an SUV."

"Yeah, thanks Sherlock, we know that from what Harry said," Ronnie grumbled.

Ty nodded, unperturbed. "There were three men, and after they parked, two headed that way, toward the perimeter fence." He pointed toward the large, artfully camouflaged fence that abutted the Carter Garrett Ranch and the Roaring Springs Sanctuary.

Everyone in the group squinted off into the distance. The fence was about two miles away, across rolling hills and deceptive flats. No wonder the shooters had parked so far away if their goal was the sanctuary; the land wasn't passable by vehicle from here.

"When they returned, there were five of them. That's six perps total. They were carrying something heavy, and they made two trips."

"How do you know that?" Annie asked, sounding impressed.

"Their footprints are deeper on the return," Ty answered. He held up a different plastic bag that contained a shell he'd found in the rubble next to the adobe pump house. "They scrambled when they saw Harrison, fired from a .44. You're lucky, sir, that they had rifles and not small arms."

"Impressive," Harrison said with a nod.

Ty turned where he stood and cocked his head at the fence in the distance. "That's a long-ass way to drag a drugged tiger."

Zane came up to stand beside him, placed a hand on his shoulder and squeezed. It was basically a "good boy" pat on the head. Ty bit his lip to keep from grinning like an idiot.

"Maybe they thought there was security?" Zane suggested. "They parked next to the only structure in the area, on the side that would hide them from the preserve."

"Everything points to an inside job, so they wouldn't be worried about security. They parked here because they couldn't get their truck any closer."

"And they returned with more men than they went in with? You're sure?"

"I'm betting someone went in through the front, bypassed the security, nabbed a key since none of them were missing, and just waltzed on out."

"I'd hate to carry a tiger in a cage over two miles across this terrain," Zane said.

"I'd hate to carry a tiger at all."

Zane hummed and narrowed his eyes, then glanced around at the others. Harrison was scratching his head. "Dad, is it possible what you saw under those tarps was animal cages?"

"They could have been alien spaceships for all the look I got at them." Harrison rubbed at his arm, obviously sore.

Ty glanced up at the sky. They had many hours of daylight left. "You should send your dad home," he whispered to Zane.

"Good luck with that," Zane said, then turned away and headed back to the group.

Ty watched him walk away, then returned his attention to the ground. He continued to look around the old pump house, scanning the area for anything he might have missed. The boot treads were all worn to nothing, no way to tell shoe sizes or height and weight, nothing but their numbers.

He stepped up to the crumbling doorway of the pump house and peered in, not sure if the structure was sound. Shafts of light filtered through the broken roof. The walls were so thin in places that he could see shadows moving through them. The interior was empty, save for a few faded beer cans and trapped tumbleweeds. He shook his head. This was no drug runners' stronghold.

He knelt and plucked a stone from the ground, and was arrested by how cool it was. He placed his palm on the ground in the shadow of the building.

"What are you doing?" someone asked from behind him.

Ty looked over his shoulder to find Mark standing there. He hesitated, paying more attention to the feeling of unease settling in his gut. Something wasn't right, but he couldn't decide why.

Jamie and Zane joined them, both frowning down at Ty.

"What is it?" Zane asked.

Ty looked from Zane to the others and stood, holding up the rock and trying to put a smirk on his face. "Souvenir," he said as he slid the rock into his pocket and stepped away.

Jamie and Mark shared a glance, then both shrugged. Zane, however, hadn't been fooled. His eyes followed Ty.

Annie's cell phone began to ring as they returned to their horses, the sound out of place in the middle of nowhere. She fumbled in her saddlebag for it, finding it and answering with a professional greeting.

Her face immediately lost its composure. "What?" she exclaimed, looking at Mark and then Zane with wide eyes. "When? Okay, we're out in the hills right now. No, I promise you, my brother will do everything he can. Hello? You there?" She pulled the phone away and looked at it.

They were all waiting as she put the phone away.

"My stupid battery died!"

"Who was it?" Zane asked in exasperation.

"It was Tish. From the preserve. She said two more of their tigers are missing."

"What?" Ty asked, his heart sinking. "Is it Barnum and Bailey?"

"Yeah, how'd you know?"

Ty swallowed hard. "Their enclosure was the next closest to the perimeter. Easiest targets."

Zane looked from Annie to Ty. "Means someone's got your tiger, Ty."

"Goddammit!" Ty spat.

Harrison turned his horse. "Okay," he said. He looked at Zane's uncle, who Ty had decided must have been Beverly's brother and not Harrison's, since everyone talked about Zane being the last Garrett around. "Stan, you go with a few of them and head back for the house. I want you to stay there until you hear from us." He glanced at Joe and Cody. "Got it? These people find out we're after them, I want the house covered."

"Yes, sir," the men said in unison.

Stan was nodding, gathering the reins to his horse. "We'll lock her up tight. Alert the authorities."

"Annie, you go with them," Harrison added.

Annie put her hand on the black bag that was strapped behind her on the saddle. "No, I'm coming with you."

"Annie," Mark started, but she cut him off.

"I'm the only one with medical training here. And you might need me if the tigers are out there and you're able to retrieve them."

No one seemed to like it, but they couldn't argue with that logic. Ty chuckled. "Next thing you know, you women folk will be wanting to vote and everything," he joked as he pulled himself into his saddle.

Annie tossed a bandana at him, which he caught and waved like a prize. He winked at her as the others parted from them, heading back to the ranch as they'd been ordered.

"Did the woman from the cat place say when Barnum and Bailey went missing?" Ty asked as her horse drifted closer to his. He handed her the bandana.

Annie shook her head, grunting a thank-you as she stuffed the bandana into her pocket. "She said they found them gone when they went to feed them."

Zane exhaled noisily. "If we assume they did it the same time as the last job, that means we're as much as six hours behind them."

"Let's see if we can find where they entered. It's got to be close," Mark said.

They headed off toward the fence, weaving through narrow gullies and over odd-shaped hills. Ty was surprised at how distracted he was at the thought of Barnum and Bailey in danger.

"What do they do with these tigers, do you think?"

"They won't hurt them, not on purpose," Annie assured him. "They're either breeding them or selling them as commodities. A live and healthy tiger is far more valuable than a dead or injured one."

Ty let out a relieved breath. He'd grown attached to Barnum. Something about the way the tiger looked at him with those golden eyes, one ear flopped to the side. He'd felt an instant connection to the animal. When he'd gone back to visit, he'd seen more of the tiger's personality and he'd been hooked. Now that Barnum might be in danger, it felt personal.

"You lurve the tiger," Zane crooned.

"Shut up, Zane."

"Oh come on, admit it. You're a big bad tough guy who fell in love with an itty bitty kitty."

Ty barked a laugh, then tried to glare at Zane and failed. "Are you done?"

"Not nearly," Zane practically giggled. "You just like things that can maul and maim you."

"Explains my affinity for you, Hoss."

"Meow Mix."

Ty rolled his eyes.

"Why do you call him that?" Harrison asked.

"When we went hiking last October, he was attacked by a mountain lion."

"Seriously?" Jamie asked, voice going higher.

Ty raised his left hand to show the scars.

"He has a paw print on each shoulder too," Zane told them, sounding almost proud of the fact.

"You're both wrong in the head."

Ty remained quiet as they came upon the fence that ran along the perimeter of the sanctuary. Zane could tell his partner was pissed off and worried, and it struck him as sweet that a man like Ty was concerned over the welfare of a pair of tigers. He also knew whatever Ty had found at the pump house, he'd kept to himself. It worried him—not that Ty was keeping secrets, but why. He knew better than to ask about it now. It would have to wait until they were alone.

They dismounted, leaving the horses with Annie a few dozen yards away, and spread out, trying to find a sign on the ground or a path through the fence. Zane wasn't exactly a master tracker, but he could find footprints in sand, and that was what they were seeing.

It took them roughly ten minutes, but Harrison stumbled over the entrance, links of the chain fence and the shrubbery that grew along it all cut by a bolt cutter so it would open and close like a door. When they'd visited the sanctuary the day before, Tish had told them that no one had checked the perimeter fences from inside yet. But Zane wasn't sure they would have seen the opening even if they had. It was only obvious because of the tracks leading to it.

They gathered around Harrison as Annie kept the horses back, trying to preserve the tracks on the ground. The fence had been cut almost seven feet off the ground, and when Ty sliced off a piece of cactus and tossed it at the fence, no current was running through it.

"Means an inside job again, don't you think?" Zane whispered.

Ty was nodding. "Someone killed the security measures to make it safe to cut the fence."

"If it's someone working at the preserve, why not just open the front door and cart the tigers out that way?" Mark asked.

Zane shrugged. That was a good question. "Could be someone with limited access. Could be a convoluted way to cover their tracks. Hell, it might even have been easier to go this way. All those hills and trails inside? We need to look closer at their security to know for sure."

"I think it's safe to call in the local LEOs now, though," Ty said.

"The local what?" Jamie asked.

"LEO. It's short for law enforcement officer," Mark answered.

"Oh."

Zane nodded again. They had enough evidence of a crime to bring in the local authorities. Which meant Ty and Zane could head home soon. The thought excited Zane, but it also made him sad. This was the first visit home he'd truly enjoyed since he'd left for college. Ty and the truth were both powerful sources of happiness.

He glanced at Ty as his lover paced back and forth, head down, body tense, like a prize hound on a scent. Zane grinned. He wondered if Ty would be open to coming back here regularly.

They continued to snoop around, trying to glean more information before they called it in. Ty told them what he was seeing: evidence of three men going in, and six coming out, carrying a heavy load. There were small tire tracks this time, like a hand truck or cart had been used. And they were fresh, less than an hour old.

Ty bent and examined something on the ground, and when Zane came closer, he saw that Ty was holding a tranquilizer dart.

Annie shouted from where she was keeping the horses at bay. "It's probably a mixture of azaperone and sufentanil. Or maybe carfentanil. A combination of dopamine antagonist and analgesic that would be appropriate for such large animals."

"What'd she say?" Ty asked.

"She said don't stick yourself with it."

"Oh."

Annie drew closer to look at the dart. She left the horses, their reins draped over scrub brush to keep them from wandering. "When the dart hits, there's a steel ball that pushes forward and injects the medication. It's collared to keep it from falling out. The barbs on that dart haven't been replaced properly, meaning it was either yanked out or it fell out."

"Why would that happen?" Zane asked. Ty twirled the dart between his thumb and forefinger.

"They could have hit bone with it instead of muscle. That means that the animal they were trying to sedate didn't get nearly enough of the medication to be out."

"I hope he eats them," Ty growled.

Zane patted his partner's shoulder, torn between amusement at Ty's vehemence and worry for the animals.

Ty got up and began wandering north along the fence, away from the tracks.

"We've got tire tracks, clear as day. I say we follow them," Mark called out as he examined the tracks that led south, toward the nearest roads. The poachers had obviously found a more direct path to the fence this time.

Zane nodded. He headed over to peer down at the tracks. They were so clear that even he could have followed them. They'd had a rare summer rain several days ago, making the earth just moist enough to retain the heavy impressions. He glanced up, seeking either his father or Ty for their opinions. Harrison was nodding, but Ty had wandered away from them. Annie had managed to wrangle in the other horses, but Ty's horse was following behind him, unbeknownst to Ty, of course, or he would have been throwing a shit fit about it obscuring evidence.

Zane almost laughed as he watched the animal plod along. What was it that made Ty a target for such undying loyalty? He seemed to inspire it in everyone he dealt with, including animals he hated.

Ty was studying the ground, good hand at his mouth, the casted one stuffed into his pocket.

"Ty!" Zane called out.

Ty glanced up and turned, saw the horse standing right there behind him, and stumbled back with a surprised shout. He almost tripped over a cactus behind him, but he caught himself and bent over, holding his hand to his chest.

"Don't do that!" he yelled at the horse. The animal whinnied happily and butted its nose against his shoulder.

The rest of them laughed, not even trying to spare Ty's pride.

When Ty finally pushed the horse's head away, he looked over at Zane, but then returned his attention to the ground. "I think I have cat tracks here."

"Tiger tracks?" Annie asked.

"It sure as hell ain't Tom and Jerry." Ty knelt to touch the dust near his feet. "I've never tracked a tiger before, but this is definitely feline and not canine. Can somebody come get this stupid horse!"

"We thinking one of the tigers got away?" Harrison asked, clearly concerned. He had thousands of acres of horses, sheep, cattle, and other livestock out here, not to mention the daily busloads of greenhorns who came to ride the trails. The last thing they wanted was a large predator on the loose.

"He definitely got away. These are running strides."

Zane smiled as he watched his partner. The confidence with which he could say that was indescribably sexy, and Zane wasn't ashamed to admit that he was proud of Ty.

Ty's aviators glinted in the sunlight, and his jeans and thin white Henley were soaked through with dirt and sweat. Zane wanted to tackle him to the ground and lick him all over.

"I think we follow the truck," Mark said. "Finding the tiger doesn't get us any closer to catching these guys."

"Agreed," Ty said immediately. Zane looked over in surprise. "But if the tiger's hurt he won't last long. There's also the possibility he'll be attracted to the main house and barns. To the livestock, or even one of your trail rides."

"Ty's right. We at least need to notify the authorities, let them know there may be an exotic on the loose," Harrison said.

"I think we should follow the tiger," Annie said, tossing a pleading look at Zane and Mark. "He might be hurt. You know he's scared."

"Annie. Honey. He's a *tiger*. He's top of the food chain."

"We could split up," Jamie suggested. "We'll follow the tire tracks and see where it's getting access to the property. Ty and Zane can track the tiger, and Annie can head back to the house and alert the animal control people."

"Or hell, walk into the preserve and use their phone," Zane said with a wave at the fence.

"No, no one goes anywhere alone right now. That tiger can take down a horse and rider, sure as the world," Harrison said. "Damn, I should have kept the boys with us."

"No, it was the right call to send them back to the house," Ty assured him.

Harrison nodded, frowning. He glanced at Zane. "I'm sure the sanctuary people called the authorities."

"But they won't know the tiger is loose, and —"

"Zane," Harrison said in a voice that stopped Zane dead in his verbal tracks. "We need a badge to follow after that truck, just in case they're still around and we actually catch up to them. And Ty's the only one can track that cat. He needs a vet if he's going."

"Wait a minute," Mark said, voice going higher. "You want Ty and Annie to go after that tiger alone?"

Harrison nodded. His gnarled fingers rolled a cigarette as he spoke.

"Sir!"

Harrison shot a look at his son-in-law that immediately silenced him.

"I have the tranquilizer darts," Annie said with a hopeful look at Ty.

Ty shrugged. He took his hat off and ran his hand through his hair before replacing it. Zane found himself staring again. He met Ty's eyes, wincing as the sun flashed off his sunglasses.

"I don't like it, but it makes the most sense," Ty said.

They laid down a few more logistics, then separated. Zane sat high in his saddle and watched as Ty led his horse away on foot, picking up the trail of the lost tiger. He mounted a few moments later, Annie following a few feet behind him.

"He'll take care of her, right?" Mark asked, eyes on Annie.

Zane nodded. "With his life."

Ty estimated they rode for roughly three miles before the tiger tracks started to get too faint to see from horseback. He dismounted and continued to follow the trail for another half a mile before he lost it completely.

Annie sat and watched him pace back and forth. He was going grid by grid, trying to pick the trail up again. While he performed the methodical search, Annie told him what she knew about tigers. Like many other predators, he'd studied them back when he'd been trying to learn everything there was to know about how to kill, but he listened anyway, recognizing her rambling knowledge dump as a sign of her nerves.

She told him that a tiger could hit a top speed of thirty-five miles per hour, but could only maintain it in short bursts. If the tiger caught the drop on them, it would take down a horse before they could outrun it. If they were alert, though, and stayed away from areas of easy ambush, the horses would be able to outrun and outdistance the big cat.

The problem with that was that out here, almost everywhere was an easy ambush for a tiger.

Ty found himself glancing around every few seconds. The fact that they usually hunted at night didn't comfort him much, nor did the fact that Barnum and Bailey were tame and used to humans. A life in the circus being petted by kids didn't mean they weren't still tigers with the survival instincts of wild animals. He wasn't fooling himself into thinking they weren't in danger.

"Have you lost him?" Annie asked after a few minutes.

"I think so, yeah," Ty admitted. They were atop one of the odd, knobby hills that peppered the land, sun-baked and windswept. It was nearly impossible to find a sign. Hopefully, he'd pick up the trail again on the descent, but he had to find the route the tiger had taken in order to do that.

The sun beat down, searing through Ty's shirt and reminding him of the many days he'd spent on Recon missions, wishing he were in a pool.

"It's impressive, what you're doing," Annie said.

Ty shrugged and continued his careful search. "My dad taught me to track in the mountains. It's easier there—lots of underbrush to hold sign, and the ground is usually moist enough to retain a track. I picked up more in the military, learned new terrain. The desert is tricky. Hard-packed dirt is near impossible sometimes."

"Yeah. I wasn't talking about the tracking. Although I am impressed," Annie added, a smile in her voice.

Ty peered at her, raising a hand to shield his eyes from the sun.

"The last time I saw my brother, he was... not my brother. Broken. Drinking and torn apart and hopeless. No one could reach him. His eyes were dead and I just knew he would be too, soon. But here he is."

Ty smiled, but he shook his head. "What makes you think I'm responsible?"

"I've never seen Zane as happy as he is right now. Even when he was with Becky. You've been good to him, and you've been good for him. And no matter what Mother or anyone else has to say about it, or what Mark says about your past, I want you to know that I thank you from the bottom of my heart for giving my brother a reason to live again."

Ty swallowed, surprised to find his throat tightening. "Well. He did the same for me."

Annie smiled. "You're not nearly the hard-ass you want everyone to believe."

Ty rolled his eyes and waved at her. "Might as well get down, take a little rest. This might take me a while," he said, voice still hoarse as he tried to stop thinking about Zane and start thinking about the tiger on the loose again.

Annie dismounted and stood beside him as he gazed out over the rolling terrain, mind churning. He glanced at Annie. "I love him very much."

She smiled. "Good. I—"

Ty held up a hand, shushing her, and cocked his head at an odd buzzing sound in the air. He had the sense it'd been building for a while, but his conscious mind had only now taken notice. It was far off and echoing, so there was no way to tell where it was coming from. He peered out over the endless hills, and after a moment, he realized what it was.

"Engine."

"You think it's them?" Annie asked, looking around too.

Ty nodded. There was no way an animal control vehicle would have been dispatched this quickly, not this far out. It had to be the poachers, out looking for their escapee. Ty took a deep breath. If they came across a vehicle with three to six armed men in it, he was outgunned by a long sight. There wasn't much he could do about it, and though they could hear the engine, it gave little warning to the vehicle's presence because of the odd distortion of sound in the hills. It could be two miles away, or two hills away.

"The tigers liked you, Ty; try calling out for them."

Ty hesitated, wondering if it would be imprudent to call out since they obviously weren't alone out here. He decided it was worth the risk, though. He cupped his hands around his mouth and shouted the names of both tigers as loud as he could, and then stood listening to the echo fade across the hills. He strained to see movement, but there was too much real estate to cover.

He sighed and went back to his survey of the ground. He could find no trace of the tiger's passing. It was as if the cat had mounted the hill and taken flight. It was frustrating, and not a little embarrassing after Zane had made such a fuss about his tracking skills. It also crossed his mind that they were too late. That engine may have been carrying both tigers away as they stood here.

He was on the verge of giving up when he found a divot in the earth, tiny trails where a few small pebbles had rolled from the edges of the depression. And on the lip of the innocuous circle was a tell-tale gouge. A claw.

"Got him!"

Annie came rushing over. She patted him on the back excitedly and then looked out over the land in the direction Ty was indicating. The hills made it hard to see far, and it made him uneasy that something as large and vicious as a tiger could be lurking behind the next knoll.

They picked their way down the hill, trailing their horses behind them. It would have been easier to let the horses find the way down, but Ty wanted to be certain he had the trail. They bottomed out into a wide arroyo, the first flat ground he'd seen that was longer than a football field since they'd left the preserve fence behind.

He stood and breathed out, trying to think. His horse jerked at his reins, then sidestepped and whinnied. Out of the corner of his eye, he saw a flash of vibrant color amidst the tan and green of the land.

He whipped his head around to see the tiger speeding toward them.

"Oh shit," Annie gasped. She turned toward the panicking horses and fumbled in her saddlebag for the case of tranquilizer darts, and managed to jerk it out before the horses broke and fled back up the hill.

Ty's hand was on his sidearm, but it was a last resort. They were here to save the cat, not kill him.

The tiger bounded over cacti and scrub brush, and every time he leaped into the air and came back down, the skin of his face would lift and reveal razor-sharp teeth. His deadly claws dug into the earth for traction.

Annie handed Ty the dart gun, her fingers trembling.

Ty was surprised he wasn't flashing back to the last big cat who had charged him: the cougar in the mountains of West Virginia. But it had been dark then, and he hadn't seen the cat coming. Now, he stood frozen, waiting for the tiger to come within range of the darts. He was oddly calm, his body not yet recognizing the danger.

It was unusual for the tiger to charge over open ground, in daylight no less, but Ty couldn't guess at the behavior of an animal who'd been held captive all its life. He lifted the dart gun, his fingers less steady than they had been a moment before. Annie ducked behind him.

A gunning engine rent the silence, and the tiger made a sharp turn, retreating from the 4x4 tearing through the open end of the arroyo. The 4x4 careened to a stop, and a man hanging off the roll bar in the bed of the truck pointed a long-barreled rifle at the fleeing tiger.

The 4x4 displayed no markings. The men within it were armed, their faces covered. This was definitely not an official vehicle.

Ty dropped the tranquilizer gun and reached for his sidearm, drawing and firing with practiced speed. He hit the side of the truck, sending sparks flying. The shooter in the 4x4 shouted and turned his rifle on them.

"Shit," Ty muttered as the other three men in the truck, all of them bristling with weapons, took notice of them. "Annie! Get down!"

Behind him, Annie screamed. Ty grabbed her and pulled, stepping in front of her to take the shot from the first man's rifle.

It hit him in the chest, the shock of the impact knocking him backward into Annie. She caught him under his arms with another scream, but they both went tumbling backward.

Ty looked down at the dart in his chest. He grabbed it and yanked it out, surprised at how much it hurt. "Run. Go," he panted, words harsh as he pushed himself to his knees and began firing. He felt Annie turn and run, hopefully after the fleeing horses where she could make a clean escape. His vision was already beginning to go dark, but he continued firing. He hit one man and saw him go sailing into the bed of the truck, rattling two large cages. Then he hit the windshield, and next a tire. He fired until his clip went empty and he sank back into the scrub grass. The world around him was turning a grayish purple.

He was distantly aware of the sound of retreating horse hooves and the truck's engine idling. Several men stalked toward him. He fumbled for his other clip, but his fingers were numb.

"Used all my damn darts," one man snarled as he pulled a gun. He sounded garbled, like he was speaking through a synthesizer.

"What do we do with him?"

"Take him. When he wakes up we'll make him track down that damn tiger for us. Then we'll use him as kitty chow."

They drew near, one of them carrying what looked like a burlap sack. Someone knelt next to Ty, and though his face wavered and morphed, Ty didn't have to see his expression to know he was in trouble. He pulled his knife from his boot—his last-ditch resort—and jammed it into the man's thigh.

The man screamed.

A sound somewhere near them echoed it, a scream of anger and agony. Something primal in Ty knew what that was: the roar of an enraged predator. The men all stopped, looking up and around in a panic before turning and running back toward the safety of their vehicle, dragging the man Ty had wounded behind them.

And suddenly Ty's vision was blue. It took him a moment to realize he'd fallen over and was on his back, staring at the cloudless sky. He couldn't move. Not even his fingers would twitch. He was paralyzed, losing consciousness, in the middle of the desert. Alone.

He blinked, barely able to force his eyes open again.

From somewhere, a horse neighed, and hope rose in his chest. Perhaps Annie had seen the poachers retreat and had come back for him.

A blur of color entered his field of vision. For a moment he thought he was hallucinating, but then the figure made another chuffing sound, mimicking the neigh of a horse almost perfectly. Ty realized that he wasn't hallucinating, and he wasn't alone. He was merely staring into the black and orange face of a Bengal tiger with one floppy ear.

⁂

Zane was surprised when the trail they were following made an almost 180-degree turn. The truck had circled around, heading farther into the ranch and not off it, picking its way through the nearly flat gullies between the hills. The longer they tracked it, the more they began to realize that the truck hadn't fled the scene, but rather had gone off searching for a passable route into the hills to follow the escaped tiger.

"Jesus, Ty and Annie are out there," Mark said as they passed over one of the horse trails that crisscrossed the ranch. "Three to six men. How much ammo has he got?"

"As far as I know, just a knife, his service weapon, and an extra clip. It's what he carries standard. Then they each have a rifle on their saddle and that dart gun."

Mark wiped at his forehead, unable to sit still in his saddle as he grumbled and worried about his wife. Zane was worried too. But he had more faith in Ty than Mark did.

They kept following the tire tracks until Harrison paused, quieting the clopping of the horses' hooves to listen. From the distance came an echo of gunfire and, not long after, the distinct roar of a tiger. The sound registered low, and the hairs on Zane's arms rose with a prehistoric fear.

"Jesus."

They waited, tense and on edge, but there was nothing more. Mark was growing restless and Zane desperately wanted to head off over the hills in search of the source of the gunfire, but the desert made it impossible to locate. They could do nothing but keep to the trail they were following.

Zane soon realized he could hear a buzzing sound over the clopping of the horses, and he hissed for everyone to halt again. It swelled until they all heard it: the distant growling of a car engine far to the east. Soon, it grew fainter.

"Shit." Harrison stood in his stirrups and tried to peer off into the distance with his binoculars. "Sounds like they got what they came for."

"Or they got run off," Jamie added.

"We have to find Annie," Mark said, growing more and more agitated.

They continued on, still following the tire tracks for lack of anything better to guide them. It wasn't long before they heard the unmistakable sound of a galloping horse.

Annie topped a knoll and called out to them, her voice a panicked shout across the dancing heat waves. She urged her horse down the ridge toward them. Mark headed off after her, and he dismounted when he got close, pulling her off the horse to hug her.

Zane watched the ridge, his heart in his throat. A moment later, Ty's horse topped the hill and picked its way down. It was riderless.

"Where's Ty?" Zane demanded as soon as he came up on them.

Annie shook her head. Tears streaked her dirty face. "They shot him with a dart. He shielded me from it and told me to run." She gasped out a sob. "I left him there."

"Shot him?" Zane asked. His entire body had gone cold.

"It was a tranquilizer," Jamie said. "Means he could still be alive."

"No, you don't understand." Annie had told them that animal tranquilizers weren't meant for humans, and some could kill in minutes. And then . . . this was Ty they were talking about. "He's allergic to all kinds of medication, there's no telling how he'll react to animal tranquilizers. We have to find him."

Annie gulped in air and shook her head. "The tranqs won't matter, Zane. The tiger . . ."

"What?"

"We found the tiger right before they attacked us. They shot Ty, and I think he drove them away with his handgun. But . . . I left him out there with the tiger."

• ★ • ★ •

They backtracked Annie's trail, Harrison in the lead. Zane's mind would not stop spitting out all sorts of scenarios, every one of which ended with Ty dying alone in the desert—the desert he dreamed about, the desert he screamed about in his sleep. Reacting to the tranquilizers and suffocating or having a heart attack or a seizure. Mauled by an angry tiger, shot by exotic animal smugglers as he tried to save Zane's sister.

Several times, Zane almost had to stop to throw up, but he kept himself together. He could lose his mind after they'd found Ty, if he needed to.

Harrison halted on top of a high knoll and pulled his binoculars out again, scanning the land. He stopped and tensed, sitting up straighter. "Found him."

Zane urged his horse forward. "Where? Is he okay? Let me see."

Harrison lowered the binoculars and shook his head, giving Zane a look that made Zane's heart leap into his throat. "I can't let you see, son."

"Why not?"

Harrison hesitated, glancing at the others before he choked out, "The tiger found him too."

Zane's stomach turned and his vision started to narrow. "No. Let me see."

"No, son."

Zane spurred his horse up the hill, reaching across the horn of his father's saddle to snatch the binoculars from him. He aimed them in the direction Harrison had been looking. It took his trembling hand a moment to find the splash of color, but when he did, the bile rose in his throat.

The tiger lay recumbent in the middle of an arroyo, protected on all sides by low hills. He could see Ty lying nearly under the big cat. The red buff on his head was hard to miss, as was the lime green cast on his arm. The tiger was licking and gnawing on his hand like a kitten playing with a ball of yarn. Zane could see no blood, though. No carnage. He focused in closer, desperate to spot a sign of life from his lover.

The tiger rolled onto his back, powerful legs stretching out to the side. Ty's cast was in his mouth between gleaming white teeth. He rested his head on Ty's outstretched arm as he chewed.

Zane frowned. Then he caught it, the barest of movement from Ty. The fingers of his right hand curled in a come-hither motion.

"He's moving."

"Probably muscle spasms, Zane," Mark said, voice gentle and careful. "I'm sorry, but . . . that's a goddamn tiger down there."

"He's alive. He's . . ." Zane held his breath, hardly daring to hope. "I think he's rubbing the tiger's nose."

"What?" Annie asked through a quiet sob.

"He's goddamn petting the tiger."

"*Petting* the tiger?"

"I'm going down there."

"Zane, wait!" Annie cried as Zane urged his horse down into the arroyo.

At the sound of her shout, the tiger sat up in a rush and focused on him. His horse balked, dancing sideways at it caught wind of the big cat's scent. The tiger lunged to his feet, letting out a roar that froze the very marrow in Zane's bones.

Zane was peripherally aware of the horses panicking. Ty's bay broke away from Jamie and ran. It took all of Zane's skill to get his own animal under control again.

Zane stopped his horse from going closer, but the damage was done. The tiger bent and took Ty's arm in its mouth, pulling him by his wrist across the arroyo bottom. Ty didn't move, didn't struggle. Zane's stomach knotted, and he had to fight the urge to retch as he watched Ty's limp body being dragged across the ground, at the mercy of one of the largest, most dangerous predators on earth.

Annie joined him on foot, breathless and pale. "Tigers are territorial, Zane. Either Ty is his meal, or Ty is his friend. Either way, he sees us as a threat. We have to drive him off or tranquilize him before we get anywhere near Ty. And I lost the dart gun."

Zane nodded, dizzy and ill. Annie reached for his saddle, pulling the rifle out of its scabbard and pointing it into the air. She fired.

The tiger jolted away, bounding a few yards before hesitating and looking back at Ty's limp body. He seemed confused and intimidated by their aggressive behavior. Annie fired again and again, each time driving the tiger further away. Zane urged his agitated horse forward, and the animal just seemed glad to be getting away from the gunshots as it barreled down the hill. Annie fired the last round in the rifle as Zane's horse charged, and the tiger turned and ran, disappearing into the hills.

Zane dismounted while his horse was still moving, hitting the ground running and then sliding to his knees in the scrub brush next to Ty. Ty's eyes were open and unblinking, his body contorted in the position the tiger had left him.

"Baby?" Zane said through a broken sob as he reached for Ty's face.

Ty closed his eyes, a painfully slow gesture, and when he opened them again he was staring at Zane.

"Oh Jesus, Ty. Are you okay?"

Ty closed his eyes again. He tried to speak, lips barely moving.

"What?" Zane asked as he leaned closer.

"I hate Texas."

# Chapter 8

Zane held Ty's limp body in the saddle. It wasn't comfortable, but Ty seemed to have no control over his limbs and little awareness of where he was or even who he was. Zane couldn't allow him to be strapped to a saddle like a dead man, so he rode with Ty in front of him.

Joe and Cody greeted them when they trotted into the main yard, running to help get Ty off the horse when they realized he wasn't conscious. Ty's horse had beaten them there, tipping the others off that something had gone wrong. A police vehicle and an ambulance were already on the way, even though Joe confessed they'd all just thought Ty had fallen off his horse.

Ty was a dead weight in their hands, and they had to carry him into the house together. Annie ran to her truck and retrieved the well-stocked bag she took with her on calls, and then she followed them in.

Zane stood in the yard, stunned and staring at the open front door.

"Z?"

He turned to his father.

"You fall apart later, you hear me? Your man saved my little girl today. You go in there and be strong for him."

Zane blinked at him, and then nodded. He headed for the house, putting one foot in front of the other. It was the only way he could manage to function.

The boys had placed Ty on one of the sofas in the den. Annie was checking his pulse and blood pressure.

"I don't understand why he was even conscious," she said to Zane when she realized he was there. "That dart should have dropped him before he could get off a shot, much less empty his clip. And he's still partially responsive, even now. I don't understand."

Zane nodded and ran his hand over Ty's forehead, then leaned down to kiss it. "He has strange reactions. Two Tylenol will wire him up just like one of those five-hour energy shots. Benadryl makes him sick. Vicodin makes him stop breathing."

"Christ, there's no telling what he's going to do with this! I know he pulled the dart out; maybe he didn't get a full dose. Maybe it hit bone. Get his shirt open, let's see where it hit him."

Zane pulled out his knife and put the blade to the collar of Ty's Henley.

Ty reached up and grabbed his wrist. Annie screamed and dropped her stethoscope.

"Don't cut the shirt."

"Jesus, Ty, are you awake?" Zane tossed the knife to the floor and dropped to his knees beside Ty.

"I hate Texas," Ty said without opening his eyes.

"Why does he keep saying that?" Mark asked from the doorway where he stood watching.

"Obviously, he hates Texas!" Zane snapped. "Why shouldn't he? It keeps trying to kill him!"

Ty's head lolled to the side.

"Ty?" Annie asked as she leaned closer to him. "Can you hear us?"

Ty groaned.

"Baby?" Zane whispered. He rested his chin on the couch, letting his nose touch Ty's. He closed his eyes and put his hand against Ty's cheek. "Are you in there?"

"I feel weird, Zane."

Zane fought back a sob of laughter and ran his hand through Ty's hair.

"What in the world is going on in here?" Beverly demanded as she came into the room. She saw Ty on the sofa and put her hands over her mouth. "Oh my God!"

"He got shot with a tranquilizer dart," Mark told her. He and the others were staying out of the way, watching from the doorway.

"Will he live?"

"We think so," Annie answered as she checked his heartbeat again.

"Oh my. We have guests coming, is he bleeding on the upholstery?"

Zane raised his head, meeting Annie's wide eyes. Zane pushed to his feet and rounded on his mother, fire boiling through his veins.

"You bitch," he growled, sounding stunned even to his own ears.

Her eyes widened and her jaw dropped.

Joe turned and ran for the door, yelling, "Harrison!"

"How dare you talk to me like that!" Beverly shouted.

Zane felt Annie's hand on his arm, pulling at him and trying to calm him. He shook her off. "The only thing you give a damn about is your reputation and that goddamned party. You have a man who could be dying on your couch and you're bitching about the upholstery?"

"You said he wasn't dying!"

"Not the point, Mother! Jesus Christ!"

"It's his job to risk his life for law and order, and that is precisely what he's doing."

"He's not here because it's his job! He's here because he loves me!"

Beverly's eyes widened and she shook her head, looking from Ty, lying half-conscious on the couch, and back to Zane. "Well, the young man is obviously confused, Zane. Shame on you for taking advantage. As soon as he wakes, I expect him to be on the first flight home." Then she turned and stormed out of the room.

Zane shouted in frustration and ran both hands through his hair.

"Zane," Annie whispered.

Zane glared at the threshold, peripherally aware of Mark and Cody watching him, and of Joe and Harrison coming through the front door.

"Zane," Annie said again, more insistent.

Zane turned to look down at her and Ty. She was perched on the edge of the couch near his hip, her hand on Ty's chest. Ty's fingers grazed the oriental carpet. His head had lolled to the side, and his eyes were closed.

Zane swallowed hard and went to kneel by his side again.

"He's gone," Annie whispered.

Zane looked up at her with wide eyes.

She gasped and put out her hand. "I mean he's unconscious! Not gone! Just unconscious." She winced and gave the others a helpless shrug as she put her hand over her mouth.

Zane studied Ty's face. "I love you, Ty," he whispered.

He got no response. Annie was feeling for Ty's pulse again. She nodded, but she still looked concerned. "The ambulance is on the way.

They can monitor him in the hospital. I suspect he's going to be out for a while. He fought it. He fought it hard."

Zane ran his fingers through Ty's hair, letting his thumb graze over Ty's cheek.

"That's what he does."

---

"I don't understand why you're keeping him around. Why not send him home? He obviously can't handle himself in such a rough environment," Beverly said as they sat at the dinner table.

Zane had been seething ever since they'd loaded Ty's limp body into the ambulance and he'd come back into the house to find one of the maids hard at work, scrubbing the dust and dirt off the upholstery.

He'd gone to the hospital, but as soon as visiting hours were over, he'd been forced to leave. He wasn't family, and though he'd tried to argue that Ty might be disoriented when he awoke, maybe even destructive if someone familiar wasn't with him, the officials at the hospital had heard none of it. To add insult to injury, now he was being forced to sit through his mother's opinions at dinner.

"He's . . . actually quite capable, Mother," Mark said, and Zane could see his brother-in-law's feathers ruffling too.

"God knows what would have happened had he not been with me," Annie tried.

"You wouldn't have been there in the first place," Beverly said. "I'll have Manuel drive him to the airport when he's discharged."

"Mother, stop," Zane said through gritted teeth.

"And it's quite uncouth of him to just drop out of the sky, uninvited, and expect you to play host, Zane." Beverly spread her salad across her plate, unaware of how angry Zane was getting.

"That's it," Zane ground out. He glanced at the others before turning his attention to his mother. "I was hoping to avoid this, Mother, but you really leave me no choice."

"Oh, Z, slow down," Harrison said.

Beverly's eyes widened before she regained control and cocked her head at Zane.

"Ty's not just my partner and he's not just my friend. And he's certainly not uninvited or unwelcome. He's my boyfriend, we've been together for almost a year now, and he's not leaving."

Beverly stared at him, not blinking, not even twitching. "Boyfriend?"

"Yes. We've been living together for months. And I've been seriously thinking about asking him to marry me."

Annie gave a little golf clap before she could get control of herself, and she bit her lip.

"That is... scandalous! Zane!" Beverly stood. "How dare you come into my home and say such things!"

Zane stood as well, refusing to let her feel superior with higher ground.

"Is it really so much worse than letting me kill myself with drink and drugs? He's the only reason I'm still here!"

Beverly's eyes hardened, her nostrils flaring. "You're still here because of him? Not because your family needed you?"

"He's my family too, Mother. He's in that hospital alone because he sacrificed himself for *my* family. And because everyone else thinks just like you, I can't even go and be with him!"

Beverly took a deep breath and looked around the table. Zane could feel all their eyes on him, but he didn't look away from his mother. Rage boiled deep inside him, and whether she deserved it or not, she had become the target.

She schooled her features, putting on a painfully familiar mask. It almost sickened him, recognizing himself in her, seeing what his future might have held. An emotionless, tactical assault on the world. Not even Becky had been able to steer Zane off the path he'd started on, rising in the ranks to power, taking the world by both horns and bending it to his will.

Ty was the only one who'd ever been able to break him out of what his mother had taught him, to show him what a life well-lived and hard-felt could be like.

Before he could allow himself to dwell on it anymore, or to say anything to his mother he might regret, he turned and walked away, leaving his family in stunned silence behind him.

He almost barreled over Sadie as he left the room.

"Uncle Z, will you play with me?" she asked, tiny voice full of hope, completely oblivious to the drama around her.

Zane forced himself to exhale and knelt in front of her. "Of course, sweetheart." He tried a smile. She climbed onto his knee and he gave her a hug as he stood. "You want to go call and check on Ty first?"

"Will he play with me?"

"Probably not, baby doll. He's asleep."

"Then no. Let's go play!"

Zane couldn't help but laugh as he obediently carried her to the stairs. So much for Ty's ability to inspire undying devotion in every creature he encountered.

🐾 ★ 🐾 ★ 🐾

Zane sat on the front steps, eyes unseeing, thinking of Ty and worrying. The screen door behind him creaked and shut with a snap, and heels on the wooden planks approached.

From somewhere in the distance, a tiger roared.

Zane stood to stare into the night, shivering at the sound.

"Oh my," his mother whispered.

Zane tore his eyes from the moonlit landscape to look at her. She seemed nervous. Why had she come out here? He could count on one hand the number of heart-to-hearts they'd shared over the years, and before every one, she'd looked like that.

"That's an unpleasant sound."

Zane nodded. "It's because the roar hits a frequency so low we can't hear it. It's called infrasound. Causes a sense of terror. A roaring tiger can actually paralyze with fear."

"How do you know that, Zane?"

"Ty told me."

She sighed and looked out over the darkened vista of the ranch. Zane studied her profile. "Was it true, what you said?" she asked finally. "Are you going to ask him to marry you?"

"It's true. I think."

She swallowed hard. "I don't know that I can live with it, Zane."

Zane stared at her, chest tightening. The tiger roared again, and he tore his eyes away from her to look into the darkness. They had secured all the animals, locking the horses safely away in the barns and putting all the hands to work at wrangling in the other livestock. They were still exposed in pens, but they were closer to the house. His spine tingled as the tiger continued to roar. "He's getting closer."

"It's quite unsettling. What's being done about it?"

"They've got animal control people coming from Austin to hunt him. So far, the locals aren't having any luck. Probably because they're still looking way out near the preserve."

"We should call them and inform them he's come this way."

"Annie's on it. She thinks he followed us here. That he tracked Ty's scent here."

"Goodness."

Zane nodded. Of course the tiger would track Ty across miles and miles of desert. It was Ty. He attracted death and disaster and undying loyalty like nobody else.

"Did Mr. Grady truly save Annabelle's life?"

Zane nodded. "And mine. Many times over."

Beverly sighed. "Desperate times call for unusual allies," she said. She glanced at him. "I phoned the hospital and explained the situation to them. They said you were welcome to stay with him until he wakes."

Zane whipped his head around. "Really?"

She nodded, though she didn't look pleased with herself. Zane lunged toward her and hugged her, picking her up off the ground. She gasped and made a gurgling noise, and when Zane set her down, she put a hand to her hair. "My goodness, Zane."

He took her by her shoulders. "Thank you!"

He hopped off the porch and ran to his truck, leaving her looking bewildered.

🐾 ★ 🐾 ★ 🐾

Hours later, Zane was sitting by Ty's bed. Ty had shown signs of waking, but after a night of lying in the hospital as Zane paced beside him, he was still unconscious.

They had run all kinds of tests and discovered exactly what type of dart had been used. They'd given Ty the appropriate human antidote, and Zane had set the local law enforcement on a hunt for any of the same that were missing from area vets.

Then he'd called their boss, Dan McCoy, who'd been supremely pissed to learn that Ty was unconscious in Texas and not in DC doing whatever lie he'd told to get out of work.

They'd done all they could for Ty, and though the doctors seemed concerned that he was still unconscious after receiving the antidote, Zane kept telling himself that with the way Ty reacted to medications, he merely needed to sleep it off. The antidote had made him restless briefly, but it hadn't woken him.

Zane found his eyes drifting shut and his head drooping. He jerked awake and looked around, surprised.

"Zane."

Zane surged forward, kneeling on the edge of the bed to look down at Ty, but Ty's eyes were closed and he wasn't moving. There was no indication that he'd spoken at all.

Zane suspected he was beginning to imagine things. "Baby?"

Ty's eyes fluttered open for the briefest of seconds before closing again.

"I know you're in there," Zane whispered. He leaned closer, brushing his lips against Ty's cheek, then stretched out next to Ty and laid his head down. He stared at Ty's profile, willing him to move, praying to see another flutter of his eyelashes.

Ty finally parted his lips, taking in a deep breath. He said Zane's name, a mere puff of air. Zane pushed up and looked down at him, brushing his hand over Ty's face and then sliding his finger over Ty's lower lip, just like Ty did to him when he was asleep. Ty's eyes opened again, staring past Zane at the ceiling.

"Ty?"

"Did we get hit?"

"No, Ty, no. You aren't there. You're here with me. You're safe."

Ty reached for him, gripping him with alarming strength. His eyes closed, and he started speaking in Farsi.

"What? Ty, I don't understand."

Ty opened his eyes to look up into Zane's. He spoke again, sounding desperate and almost scared.

Zane had heard his lover speaking Farsi before, oftentimes in his sleep. But never in a waking dream, never while Ty was looking into his eyes and trying to communicate with him. He licked his lips and reached to the bedside table for Ty's phone. He wasn't too proud to call for help.

Only after Nick O'Flaherty answered, sounding sleepy and sullen, did Zane realize it was the middle of the night. He winced, but he was too worried to apologize.

"It's Garrett, I need your help."

"Yeah, what's wrong?"

"Ty's speaking in Farsi and I need you to translate."

"What?"

"Just . . . I'll explain later, I'm afraid he's going to fall asleep again." Zane pushed the speaker button and held the phone out.

"You people get into the weirdest trouble," Nick said.

"What's he saying?"

Nick was silent as Ty mumbled. After a few moments, he said, "Well first of all, that's not Farsi. It's Dari."

"Does it matter?"

"It does if you don't speak Dari."

"Do you speak Dari?"

"Yeah. Just expect a little more accuracy from the likes of you."

"O'Flaherty, come on."

"He's saying he's thirsty. And he's asking if you can help him. 'I'm U.S. military, can you direct me to the nearest base?' Garrett, this sounds a lot like what we were both saying after they picked us up in the desert. I asked for directions in my sleep for months after. Is he drugged? Hurt?"

"Animal tranquilizers."

Nick was silent. "Of course. That should have been my first guess. He's also saying the ground is cold, if that means anything."

"No," Zane said with a sigh.

Ty spoke again, the words slurring. Nick started laughing.

"What? What'd he say?"

"He said his hovercraft is full of eels."

"What? Is that code for something?"

"No." Nick still sounded amused. "He's just muttering, Garrett. He's high. Lost."

Zane inhaled deeply and nodded, almost disappointed that Ty hadn't been trying to communicate something more than his need for water and a blanket.

"Hey," Nick added solemnly. "He's okay until he starts speaking Russian."

"Russian? Since when does Ty know Russian?"

"He doesn't. You guys need help? Where are you, what's going on?"

"No, no. We're okay. Just a dustup in Texas."

"With animal tranquilizers."

"He'll fill you in later."

"If you're sure."

"I am. You sound hungover."

"It's Canada Day."

"So?"

"So, I'm in Canada."

"Why?"

"Because it's Canada Day! Come on, Garrett!"

Zane snorted.

"Call me when he wakes up, okay? Tell him I said to take it easy on the hard stuff."

Zane huffed and set the phone down, then reached for the glass of water by the bed. He offered it to Ty, helping him raise his head. After a few swallows, Ty was calm again, his eyes closed, his face relaxed and serene as Zane laid his head back on the pillow.

Zane studied him like the unsolved mystery he was. He remembered overhearing Julian Cross ask how Ty knew Russian Sambo after Ty had taken him down in a scuffle. He knew Ty had been paid off to keep his silence about the way he'd been discharged from the military. And Mark had alleged a murder on Ty's part when he had been in the service.

But he had no doubt that he knew who Ty was now, inside and out. He knew every one of Ty's quirks and weak spots and favorite things. He knew what Ty found funny and what annoyed him. He knew what would break his heart. He knew how to touch him to drive him wild, and when to back off when Ty was having a bad day. He knew that Ty was kind and loyal and funny, that he had a deep sense of honor and righteousness. He knew that Ty would die to save a stranger, and kill to save a friend. That was the type of man he was.

He knew who Ty was now. But he suspected that the Ty he knew was a different man from the one Ty had been. The man who'd once made hardened Marines uneasy. He reached out and put his hand on Ty's forehead. "Who were you, Ty?"

Ty responded with his name, rank, and serial number. The words were mumbled, but with an undercurrent of defiance and threat. The last person who'd received those answers from Ty hadn't lived through the interrogation. A chill ran down Zane's spine. He didn't ask another question, merely laid his head down beside Ty's to sleep.

🐾 ★ 🐾 ★ 🐾

Ty woke disoriented, just as Zane had known he would. But he was able to answer the questions two determined nurses asked—with the assistance of some creative hand signals from Zane as he stood behind them—and he was grudgingly released. He fell asleep with his head in Zane's lap on the way home, and Zane needed three others to help him carry Ty into the house and to a bed upstairs.

Zane was still asleep, curled up next to Ty, when he heard the doorbell ring. He raised his head, confused about where he was for a few seconds. It was his old bedroom, but everything about it had long ago changed. Not even the bed was the same. The ceiling still had that same crack in it, though, the one Zane had often traced with his eyes when he couldn't sleep.

He heard voices from downstairs. It was Thursday, and the ranch was open for business. But no one ever came into the house unless they were very special or very rich, and Zane couldn't imagine Joe or Cody letting anyone get this far without guiding them toward the barn where they were supposed to be.

Zane looked down at Ty, running his hand over his face. Ty didn't move, didn't even twitch. Zane checked his pulse. Everything was as it should have been, and his pulse was strong. A man of Ty's size should have been able to shake off the tranquilizers by now, but there was never any guessing how Ty would respond to such things.

Zane rolled out of bed with a heavy feeling. There was nothing he could do for his partner right now, and he hated it.

He slid his feet into his shoes and rubbed at his eyes as he headed for the door. He didn't even bother looking in a mirror. He just ran his hands through his unruly hair as he thumped down the stairs.

He stopped short when he saw four men sitting in the formal living room. His mother was there, standing by the doorway, and his father was seated as he talked with the visitors.

Zane approached carefully, listening to the conversation.

"... figured we'd come by and see how he was."

"That's right neighborly of you," Harrison said, though his voice was cool.

Beverly turned to see Zane standing there, and she reached out and patted him on the shoulder, moving him until he was leaning against the wall, out of sight. She let him go and turned back to her visitors.

A tingle of apprehension ran through Zane. His mother obviously thought something was wrong and wanted him to listen without being seen.

"Well, when you hear a man got mauled by a tiger on the next ranch over, it does cause some concern."

Zane knew the voice. It was Stuart, the asshole from the bar.

"He hasn't woken yet," Beverly said, her voice cold. "He's still at the hospital. We don't know what happened."

"So he ain't told anyone the details?" Stuart asked.

Beverly didn't answer, and Harrison cleared his throat. "We can't say what happened. Won't know 'til he wakes."

"If he wakes at all," Beverly interjected.

Zane turned his head sharply, trying to see his mother's face.

"That bad, huh?" Stuart asked. The other three visitors began to murmur their apologies.

"He's in quite bad shape," Beverly said with a nod.

"That's a shame." Stuart sighed, like he was standing.

Beverly put her hand behind the wall and waved at Zane urgently, shooing him away. Zane retreated to the alcove that used to be a butler's nook when the house was first built, and flattened himself there.

"We'll just be heading on, then. Our regards to the rest of your family," Stuart said, and soon the four men were filing out.

Zane recognized them all as the men from the honky-tonk, Stuart and his fellow ranch hands from Cactus Creek. They were dusty and dressed in their work clothes. It looked as if they'd come here directly from their ranch. Stuart was limping, trying not to drag his foot. Harrison walked them out, and as soon as the door was shut, Zane stepped out of the alcove. Harrison and Beverly both turned to look at him.

"I'm sorry to have excluded you, Zane, but I felt you would prefer to hear and not be seen," Beverly said. She smoothed her hands down her suit in a rare gesture of discomfort.

"Thank you, Mother," Zane said, surprised by her awareness.

"I felt they weren't here under honest pretenses."

"They sure as sin weren't," Harrison growled. "Trying to figure out how much Ty told us about what happened and whether he was like to wake up again."

Zane nodded. He'd gathered as much from the snippets he'd heard.

"What'd you tell them?"

"Told them we found him unconscious being eaten by a tiger."

Zane couldn't help but laugh.

"They didn't even take pause at that, like that was normal," Beverly huffed.

"They kept digging to see if anybody saw anything besides the tiger," Harrison told Zane.

"Awfully suspicious," Zane grumbled. "Did you see him limping?"

"Yeah? That mean something to you?" Harrison asked.

Zane nodded. "Ty's knife was gone. I'd bet anything he put it in that man's leg."

Harrison nodded, looking both impressed and worried. "You think your boy can identify them?"

Zane shrugged. Ty had once been able to look at a poker table full of people and tell Zane each player's tell, down to the type of cuff links one man liked to play with when he was nervous. But there was no telling what details he'd been able to notice after being struck with a dart, alone and under fire. "I don't know."

"Well. Soon as he comes to, we'll call the sheriff. I'm going to get Mark and Annie to come here and hole up, where we can be sure they're safe."

Zane nodded, and he looked at his mother again as Harrison left the foyer. Beverly met his eyes, then gave him a nod. Her expression was a mixture of concern and pride, something Zane could honestly say he'd never seen on her before. Was it possible that she was just now realizing that what he'd done with his life was both dangerous and worthwhile? Or was she merely circling the wagons, protecting the family and the ranch like always?

She walked away without saying anything, and Zane put his hand to his chest to rub at his sternum, trying to dispel the tightness there.

Maybe there was hope yet.

🐾 ★ 🐾 ★ 🐾

They were all gathered for dinner when they heard the shuffling of feet coming down the grand staircase. Zane pushed out of his chair and darted into the foyer, where Ty was staring at the front door as if he was trying to figure out where he was. He turned and met Zane's eyes for a long moment. There wasn't much recognition there, and his face was expressionless.

"Ty?" Zane said carefully as the rest of the family joined him.

Ty's gaze took them all in before landing on Zane again. "I didn't know they had elephants in Texas."

"What?" Zane asked. Had Ty simply lost his tenuous grip on reality in the twenty-plus hours he'd been unconscious?

"I feel like one sat on me." Ty rubbed at his chest and swallowed with difficulty. He sniffed at the air. "Is that steak?"

Zane laughed and went to hug him. Ty rested his chin on Zane's shoulder and hugged him back. Every muscle in him that was usually hard and tense felt relaxed when Zane touched him.

"Are you okay?"

Ty nodded. "How long was I out?"

"Almost a whole day."

Ty closed his eyes. "Like the worst acid trip ever."

Zane laughed and hugged him harder, just because he could.

"You told me your hovercraft was full of eels."

"What?"

"In Dari."

"That's stupid," Ty said.

"Well," Beverly said, prim and proper as ever. "As glad as we all are that Mr. Grady is well, we don't want dinner to go cold, now, do we?" She gave a little clap and turned on her heel to head back to the dining room.

Sadie went skipping after her grandmother, but the rest of them ignored her and gathered to greet Ty. Annie hugged him fiercely, thanking him and almost tearing up when she apologized for leaving him to be eaten by the tiger. Mark gripped his hand and met his eyes, giving him a mere nod that Ty returned. It must have been a Marine thing, because that was the only exchange they shared.

Harrison gave his shoulder a squeeze as he shook his hand, telling him he was glad to see him up and around.

Beverly called from the dining room, sounding tense.

They all shuffled off after her, grumbling mutinously. Ty watched them go. "I think your mom would do really well with a tranq to the ass," he said flatly.

Zane couldn't help but smile.

"A nice parting shot from me to her. What do you think?"

"I think you need food. And then a shower."

They'd cleaned him up after making sure he'd live, taking great pains to make sure they hadn't missed any injuries. Zane had put fresh clothes on him, borrowed from Harrison, so he'd at least be clean when they put him to bed. But he'd still been dragged across the ground by a tiger and not showered afterward.

Ty slipped his arm around Zane's waist. "How'd you know what I said if it was in Dari?"

Zane grinned, relieved that Ty's mind was working well enough to ask that. "Called O'Flaherty, had him translate. I was afraid you were trying to tell me something important."

"Great."

"I called McCoy too, told him what was going on."

Ty winced.

"He asked if you were catatonic," Zane said, voice trembling as he tried not to laugh.

"That's not funny."

"It kind of is."

"I'll never hear the end of this shit."

Zane laughed and squeezed him close. Ty patted his arm and stopped walking. To Zane's surprise, Ty was grinning.

"Stars and stripes, Zane."

"What?"

"It's the Fourth of July. I saw stars, and then I saw stripes." He began to laugh like it was the most hilarious thing he'd ever heard, doubling over and grabbing Zane's arm to hold himself up as he cackled. Though Zane knew it was the lingering effects of the drugs on Ty's system, he couldn't help but laugh too. Whether he was laughing with Ty or at him, he wasn't sure.

"Come on, you stoner," Zane whispered. He pulled Ty, still giggling, into the dining room. Ty calmed and cleared his throat, attempting a little decorum.

Beverly was quick to greet them with a disapproving glare. "Mr. Grady, I suppose we all owe you a debt of gratitude," she said, sounding like she was trying to chew a light bulb.

Ty sat in the chair Zane pulled out for him, and he nodded, still too sedate to engage her.

Zane wondered if they couldn't just pack up and go home now. They'd gotten enough of a lead to give to the local authorities, and Ty didn't deserve the abuse he was putting up with for Zane's sake. Not from those yahoos in the bar, not from the elements, and not from Beverly Carter-Garrett.

"I do hope we'll leave this to the real authorities now, though?"

Zane glared down the table at her.

"What real authorities?" Annie asked, her tone acerbic. "The sheriff is overrun, and animal control are chasing their asses around a hot potato because people are reporting loose tigers from here to Austin. It's caused a panic."

"That is none of our concern."

"It will be when that tiger gets hungry enough. We all know he's still on the C and G."

"Annie."

Annie shrugged, but went back to her meal without provoking Beverly further.

Beverly looked around the table. "We don't want any more incidents drawing unwanted attention to us."

Out of the corner of his eye, Zane saw Ty reach for the wine in front of him and toss back the entire glass in one gulp. Zane winced. That wasn't going to react with those tranquilizers well.

"Mother, we can't let this drop now. Ty's life is in danger. You saw that this morning when they came here fishing."

"Who went fishing?" Ty asked.

"Forgive me for being callous, but if he'd leave, he wouldn't be in danger anymore. As it is, he's attracting trouble to our ranch."

"And I smell like tiger breath," Ty muttered.

"Now Beverly, none of this is Ty's fault," Harrison said, voice calm as he handed Ty his own wine glass. Ty whispered a thank you and downed that as well. Zane almost said something, but the conversation distracted him from his disapproval.

"They'll keep coming back until there's nothing to come back for," Mark interjected. "Annie was out there too, and if she saw them, they may have seen her. They'll know it was her, and she's in danger too."

"We need Zane and Ty here, Beverly," Harrison said. "Circling the wagons."

"Yes, I can see how much use *that* particular wagon is going to do us," Beverly said, nodding toward Ty.

Ty stared at her, and Zane could see it coming from a mile away. He had two, maybe three seconds to stop his partner from tearing his mother's head off.

He sat back and crossed his arms instead.

Ty's eyes drifted from Beverly, who sat stiff and proper, waiting for his retort, and landed on Sadie instead. She smiled shyly at him and stuck a piece of chicken in her mouth. Zane watched in fascination as Ty gave her a half-smile and returned his attention to the tabletop.

Everyone else noticed it too. They all looked at Sadie, who was still grinning and chewing.

Ty cleared his throat. "If you want me to leave because you think I'm putting your family in danger, then I will." He met Beverly's eyes, then looked at Sadie again. "But I would like to stay and help protect your family."

The table was silent, but for the sounds of Sadie eating. The emotionless mask on Beverly's face was back, but Zane could see her struggling with her response. Ty had realized that trading barbs with her was not the way to handle it—that a direct, sincere approach was much more likely to throw her off her game. It was a little unnerving sometimes, watching Ty manipulate others. Zane couldn't help but wonder how many times Ty had done that to him without him realizing it.

Beverly finally exhaled and gave a curt nod, blinking rapidly. "If you believe yourself fit enough for the job, Mr. Grady, then so be it."

Everyone was silent, letting the tension settle over the table. Soon enough, Harrison picked up his fork and knife and began to cut into his steak.

As they ate, the tension slowly broke, and they filled Ty in on what he'd missed. He sat with a frown, listening and offering little in response. When they were done, Ty sat in silence, still nodding his head, staring at the table.

"Ty?"

Ty looked up as if Zane had splashed him with cold water. "I don't think this is about tigers."

"What?"

Ty glanced around and gave a small shrug. "I don't think the tigers are the target."

"But we caught them in the act. We saw them poaching the tigers," Mark insisted.

"Just give it a little time," Zane said more gently. "Let your mind catch up to the tranquilizers, okay?"

Ty eyes flickered to Mark, but he nodded. "Right."

"Well. You all will excuse me. I have business to attend to." Beverly stood without waiting for a reply and made her way out of the room.

Zane sat back, watching Ty, a sense of foreboding creeping over him despite everything. Ty knew something he wasn't sharing, and Zane intended to find out what it was tonight.

🐾 ★ 🐾 ★ 🐾

Ty sat with his booted feet propped on the railing of the large porch, rocking himself in a wooden chair. He held one last glass of wine in one hand and a slim cheroot in the other, secure in the knowledge that he deserved to indulge in both vices. The sheriff had come and gone, taking his statement without even a raised eyebrow.

The voices of Zane's family filtered through the dry evening air, but he had no urge to join them. He was feeling decidedly unsociable. He had a lingering headache he would almost have called a hangover, but it hadn't been nearly as fun to earn.

The sunset over the rolling Texas landscape was astonishing, though. Nothing like the rising sun burning away the mists on the mountaintops of West Virginia or the moon glowing down on the beaches near Kaneohe Bay in Hawaii, but still beautiful in its own way.

He'd been to a lot of places in his life, places most men never got to see. Places most people had never even thought about. The dry tropics of Somalia. The jungles of Colombia. The hard rock mountains of Afghanistan and the desert of Kuwait. But he had rarely stopped to appreciate them until after the fact. It was hard to appreciate the beauty of a place when the scenery was being used to try to kill you.

The occasional roar of Barnum in the distance added a surreal feel to the whole thing. Ty smiled grimly. "I hear you, buddy."

The cell phone in his pocket began to ring, startling him. He had yet to set his new phone to any of his usual rings, so he had no idea who it was or whether it was worth digging the phone out to answer.

He groaned and shifted forward as he struggled to pull his phone out of his jeans pocket. He couldn't get his cast past the denim, though, and he couldn't hold both the cigar and the glass in his broken hand to use the other one. Finally, he had to stand up, and by that time he was cursing and looking around for somewhere to put his drink down.

When he turned to glance behind him, he was surprised to find that he wasn't alone. Sadie stood there watching him, a doll in one hand and a smile on her face. Ty stared at her for a second and then handed her his wine glass. "Hold this."

She giggled and took the glass, clutching it and her doll to her chest with both hands as she watched him twist and struggle to fish his phone out of his pocket with his opposite hand.

"Don't drink it, okay?" She nodded.

When he got the phone out, he sat down and answered it with a distracted, "Grady here." He reached for the glass, but when Sadie returned it, she also crawled into his lap and curled into the crook of his arm. He put his cigarillo out on the denim of his jeans and let it drop to the floor beside his chair so any lingering smoke wouldn't be near her.

"Ty," Dan McCoy said over the phone. "I hear the fuck-up fairy has visited you two again."

Ty stared at the horizon as he tried to work out how to answer. There really wasn't a short version. Barnum roared somewhere in the hills. "Uh..."

McCoy groaned as if he were in pain. "What have you done now?"

"Nothing. I just . . . nothing is really going to plan down here."

"You had a plan?" McCoy asked in genuine shock.

Ty pursed his lips. "Not really," he answered after a moment. "But if I had, I'm pretty sure this is not the way it would have gone."

McCoy sighed. Ty could imagine him rubbing his forehead.

"You talked to Zane?" Ty asked with an expectant wince.

"He called and said you'd been tranquilized by exotic animal smugglers in Texas," McCoy said with an almost audible frown. "I prefer when *you* lie to me, it's more of a challenge trying to decide if it's true. Garrett's not very good at it."

Ty laughed and closed his eyes. "You're right, he's not. He's telling the truth, though."

McCoy was silent. "Why, Ty? Why do you do this to me? One day I'm told you're being loaned out to Richard Burns, the next I hear you're playing footsy with Tony the Tiger in Texas to help out Garrett's family ranch!"

Ty smiled and watched as Sadie's tiny fingers played with the broken pieces of plaster on his cast. "Mac. Do me a favor, okay?" McCoy grunted, not willing to commit. "Tony the Tiger in Texas. Say it three times."

"Stop it, Grady. Do you two need backup down there or is this just par for the course when you go off the grid?"

"No, Zane handed it over to the locals this morning. Animal control is all over it, they've got it under control."

"He said you'd been lying in a puddle of your own drool for almost a day, there was a tiger loose on his family's ranch, and no one has any idea who's behind it, how they're doing it, or what's going on."

"Yeah?"

"That's 'under control'?"

"Don't judge me, Mac."

"I don't mind sending in the cavalry down there if it'll hurry things along. I can make a call to the San Antonio division. Burns says I can't call you back unless Baltimore is burning."

"Is Baltimore burning?"

"No."

"Then I'll talk to you after the Fourth, Mac. Have a good night." Ty hung up the phone with a grin. He slid it into his shirt pocket, thinking it would be easier to get it out next time, and tilted his head to look at Sadie.

Her eyelids were growing heavy as he rocked, her head resting on his shoulder as she stared at the setting sun. Ty drank down the last of his wine before putting his glass on the floor, then pulled her closer. He adjusted her until they could both be comfortable.

"Did you got eated by a tiger?" she asked as she poked her finger into one of the tooth marks in his cast.

"I guess I did. He was a good tiger, though."

"Did he bite you?"

"Yeah, a little."

"Then he was a bad tiger."

"You think so?"

"Biting is bad," Sadie said with a nod.

"I guess you're right."

She yawned, struggling to open her eyes again. "Will the tiger bite me?"

"No, sweet pea," Ty said. He rested his chin on her head.

"Daddy will keep me safe."

Ty stared off into the sunset, pushing at the floorboards with his toes to keep the chair rocking. He nodded and pulled her closer, rocking and holding the little girl to him to keep her bare arms and legs warm as the night grew cooler. If his suspicions about Mark were correct, Sadie's daddy might not be around to keep her safe for a good long while.

🐾 ★ 🐾 ★ 🐾

"Have you seen Sadie?" Annie asked as she came into the den where Zane was sitting with his dad. "We can't find her anywhere."

Zane and Harrison stood to help look, Zane's mind going immediately to the tiger on the loose. He pushed back the instinctive panic and chastised himself. It was a valid concern that the tiger would be attracted to the activity of the ranch. They'd been hearing his roars for two nights now. But Barnum was not going to start plucking the people Zane loved out of the house no matter how bad Zane's luck was.

He found Ty and Sadie on the porch, and stopped short when he saw them. He hissed for Annie, who was walking through the foyer, and then moved closer.

Sadie was curled in Ty's arms, sleeping peacefully, her long lashes dark against her cheeks. Her fingers were tangled in his hair where she'd been twirling it. She was tucked up under Ty's chin, and he was resting his head on top of hers. He was sound asleep too. Zane wasn't surprised; those tranquilizers would take a while to flush out of his system, and he'd consumed a good deal of wine at dinner to combat the stress. Zane was surprised, however, to see his lover snuggled up with the little girl.

He smiled and leaned against the porch railing.

"Oh my goodness, that is precious. Where's my camera?" Annie whispered. When she went to look for it, Zane took his phone out of his pocket and snapped a picture for himself. Whether he'd use it as blackmail or frame it when they got home was up for debate. Maybe both.

One thing was for sure, though. After being in Texas with him, Zane could see Ty as part of his family, and more importantly, he'd seen that most of his family would accept Ty for what he was: a quirky, brazen, possibly crazy, integral part of Zane's life. The idea of "forever" with Ty was becoming more and more certain.

Ty opened one eye and looked up at Zane.

"Time to go," Zane whispered.

Ty moved his arms until he was cradling Sadie and stood up carefully. His wide shoulders made her look tiny, but he was just as gentle with her as Zane knew Ty was with all fragile things. Her hand fell out of his hair and dragged down his face, over his nose and lips, to tuck up under her chin with her other hand. Zane watched in silence, trying not to laugh as Ty merely closed his eyes and let it happen.

Ty handed Sadie off to her daddy a few minutes later, and they said good-bye to Mark and Annie as they headed upstairs to bed.

Harrison stood with them on the porch, then bid Ty and Zane a good night and turned to go inside.

"Sir, I'm sorry for causing problems," Ty said. He sounded sincere, one of his rare apologies. Harrison stopped at the door and looked him up and down.

"Son, there's not a problem here that's your fault." Harrison nodded to both of them and went back inside.

### 🐾 ★ 🐾 ★ 🐾

Ty could tell that something was weighing on Zane's mind as they headed to the guesthouse, but he waited for Zane to speak up.

Zane didn't. Ty lasted until after he'd showered and they were both up in the loft bedroom, getting ready for bed, before he lost his patience.

"What's on your mind, darlin'?" he asked, drawling the affectionate name with a smirk because he knew that Zane loved to hear him say it.

Zane snorted and glanced at him as he folded the shirt he'd been wearing. "What makes you think something's on my mind?"

"Because you're Zane Garrett. And Zane Garrett always has something on his mind." Ty stepped up to Zane and slid his hands onto his hips. Zane smiled at him, though Ty could tell he still wanted to talk about something. He didn't, though, just wrapped his arms around Ty's neck and started to move. It turned into a slow dance as Zane's smile grew wider, and Ty kissed him and slid his hands up Zane's back.

"I was so damn worried about you," Zane said. "I promised myself I'd get a dance when you woke up."

Ty smiled and hugged him tighter. "I've decided if I can't get eaten by a tiger or killed by an animal tranquilizer, then I must be invincible."

Zane laughed and kissed him again before resting his chin on Ty's shoulder. "Tytanium."

"Hovercraft is full of eels, huh?"

"That's what you said."

"I think you're bullshitting."

"God's honest truth."

Ty's smile softened and he buried his nose in Zane's neck. "You know you can get a dance anytime."

"I know," Zane whispered against his ear. "I wish we could have done this at the bar."

Ty nodded, wondering if that was what Zane was thinking so hard over. He'd been told how Beverly had reacted to Zane's news, but that she'd later softened and helped Zane spend the night with him at the hospital. And though Ty was angry and frustrated over the lack of acceptance, he suspected there were added layers.

"Next time we will, if you want to."

Zane hummed. "I don't know. I might be embarrassed for everyone to see how bad a dancer you are."

Ty grunted and pushed his snickering lover away.

"Oh, don't be like that," Zane crooned as he reached for Ty again.

Ty turned Zane around in a simple box step to put him in front of the bed, then gave him a push to make him sit.

Zane huffed as he thumped down on the mattress. "What do you know that I don't?" he demanded.

"So much," Ty said with smirk as he sat beside Zane.

"Ty, come on. What did you find at the pump house? I know you were hiding something."

Ty nodded. "Why would Mark tell you about what happened at LeJeune when he did?"

"What does that have to do with anything?"

"Think, Zane. Why would he tell you something meant to make you suspicious of your partner right before we're riding out to look for evidence? It was a preemptive strike, like he was trying to give you a reason to doubt what I found when we got there."

Zane frowned harder. It was obvious that the thought hadn't crossed his mind.

"Why would he do that unless he was afraid of what I'd find?"

Zane shook his head. "What did you find?"

"The ground was cold."

"What?"

"It was cold. The pebble I picked up, the ground under it. It was cool. There's something under there."

Zane stared at him, then stood up to pace. "You tried to tell me that at the hospital."

"In Dari?"

"Uh-huh. We need to go back out there."

Ty waved at himself, looking offended. "Does this look like it's going on a horse again?"

Zane stopped pacing and barked a laugh. He stalked closer and climbed into Ty's lap, brushing his nose against Ty's. "My apologies."

"I know how you can make it up to me."

"I'll bet you do." Zane pushed Ty onto his back. "Annie says you're handsome."

"Of course she does. Have you seen me?" Ty grinned crookedly, laughed and put his hands behind his head, lounging under Zane.

"You were sweet tonight, with Sadie."

"It's easy to be sweet with a cute kid in your lap."

"Sadie's way too pretty for my peace of mind. I'm glad I'm not her daddy."

"She already knows how to wield the batting eyelashes. Teach her to handle a gun, give her a classic muscle car, she'll take over the world."

Zane chuckled. "At least you're true to type. If she's raised like I was, she'll have at least two guns before she's a teenager. More likely a truck than a muscle car, though."

"Shame."

"My uncle taught me to shoot."

Ty ran his fingers down Zane's cheek. "You could teach her, you know."

Furrows appeared on Zane's brow. "If we end up putting her daddy in jail, there might be some strain there."

Ty nodded. He didn't like suspecting Mark any more than Zane did, but there was a lot that wasn't adding up.

"Run it through for me, okay?"

Ty nodded again. He held up his hand and pointed a finger to count. "He knew Stuart's name in the bar. He tried to throw you off the scent by telling you about LeJeune. He dogged my steps out there, tried to convince you and I to go after the tiger instead of the poachers, and he'd have access to the kind of information and type of tranqs he needed through Annie's vet practice."

Zane looked at Ty's hand, now displaying all five fingers with the points he'd listed. "Jesus, Ty," he said, and he ran his hand through his hair.

"I've been wrong before."

Zane shook his head. "How are we going to explain to Sadie that her daddy's in jail because Uncle Z put him there?"

"She'd have you, Zane."

Zane met his eyes and took in a deep, shaky breath. "I don't know. I've never really been around kids. I'm not sure I'd know what to do."

"They're just little people. They can be charmed like anyone else. Be a little silly, let them know what they're saying is the most important thing in the world, teach them right from wrong. You'd be fine."

Zane met his eyes, thoughtful. "You like kids, don't you?"

"Some of them, yeah," Ty answered with a shrug. "I love the little ones, when they still look at the world with stars."

Zane smiled wistfully at the sentiment. "I've seen you with Elaina. And now with Sadie. She's an outgoing kid, but she took to you like glue. You're really good with them."

Ty just nodded, wondering why Zane was lingering over it.

Zane glanced away, then back to meet his eyes. "Did you think about having kids?" He paused a moment before adding, "With Ava?"

Ty blinked at him. Ava Gaudet had been a near-miss of Ty's while undercover in New Orleans. Probably the last serious relationship he'd had before Zane. He was glad Zane had asked, though. There was too much between them they still kept hidden, either on purpose or subconsciously. It was high time they started asking each other questions any normal couple would ask.

Ty nodded. "She wanted kids. Not when we were together, but eventually. It was never really an option for us, though."

"Well, you were still undercover. And hadn't told her about it."

Ty winced and looked past Zane's shoulder to the ceiling. "That didn't really factor in."

Zane frowned. "I don't follow."

"When I was younger, I took a bullet in the wrong place."

"Is there a right place to take a bullet?" Zane asked with a smirk.

"No, but for the purposes of having kids, there is definitely a wrong one." Ty pulled the hem of his shirt up and pushed his pants down to show Zane a faded white scar, right at the juncture of his hip, that he knew Zane had seen before. Hell, Zane had licked it before. "Even if I wanted kids . . ." He shook his head and put his hands under his head again. "The doctor that did the surgery said nothing doing."

Zane's eyes widened before his expression settled into something sadder. "Tytanium," he whispered as he ran his fingertip across the scar. "You can't tell me that doesn't bother you."

Ty shrugged. "It did for a while, at first. I mean hell, I was twenty-two. But I never lived the life of someone who could be a good daddy. It was never in my cards."

"I guess that's true," Zane said before turning his gaze toward the windows.

"Tell me what you're thinking, Zane."

Zane inhaled deeply and let it out in a soft sigh. "Becky and I never talked about having kids," he said. "Not real seriously. We were both working a lot. I was a rising star, she was doing charity work."

"Did you want them?"

"That's what I was just thinking about. I don't know. We never really did see ourselves as parents." He shrugged and met Ty's eyes. "And then she was gone, and I didn't have any reason to think about it anymore."

Ty pursed his lips and laid his hand across Zane's where it rested on his chest.

"You'd make a great dad, you know," Zane said, his voice quiet and melancholy. Ty glanced up, eyebrows climbing high. "I think I'd almost like to see it."

"Are you saying you might want kids one day?"

"I don't know. Tonight was literally the first time I truly thought I might."

Ty gaped, at a loss for words. Was *this* what Zane had been thinking about all night?

Zane remained quiet, watching him for several breaths before echoing, "Tell me what you're thinking, Ty."

"Uh... I'm thinking... I love you. And I'm glad things didn't go to plan when we were both younger."

Zane slid his fingertips across Ty's lips. With a blink, his expression changed, and he was gazing at Ty with such longing and love that he might as well have screamed it at the top of his lungs. "I wouldn't change it," he rasped. "Any of it."

He leaned his hands on both of Ty's shoulders, right on top of the cougar scars, and bent down to kiss him.

Ty hummed and let the warmth of Zane's demanding hands spread through him. Zane's lips gave against his. He moved one hand to tug Ty's T-shirt up, and then slid it under to smooth across Ty's side and lower back. Ty winced when Zane's fingers dragged over the scrapes and bruises he'd earned from being keelhauled by a goddamned tiger, but it didn't stop him from grabbing a handful of Zane's hair as they kissed.

Ty smiled against his lips. Zane hadn't finished changing yet, and Ty let his fingers dig into and linger over Zane's bare skin. He ran his hands down Zane's sides, irritated that the cast was getting in his way. It also had sharp pieces now, both from where the knife had gone through it and the tooth marks.

For the first time, they were actually discussing their future in concrete terms. They'd both known, on some level, that they intended to spend the rest of their lives together. It felt like a solid force now, though, something as real as the hands that pressed into his back or the lips that met his over and over as they made love.

# Chapter 9

"I think we need to go to San Antonio," Zane said. They were sitting at the little breakfast table in the guesthouse, eating cereal and watching the sunrise through the bank of windows.

"What? Why?"

"We can drop in on the field office, see if we can put a bug in someone's ear."

Ty stared at him, chewing his Rice Krispies.

Zane shifted under Ty's attention. "What?"

Ty waved his spoon through the air. "Go on."

Zane rolled his eyes and sighed. "Okay, fine. I want to take a page out of your book and use us as bait. See if anyone follows. And I figured you'd go nuts over the Alamo and I wanted to walk down the Riverwalk with you. We could spend a night there, maybe. Enjoy Texas a little before Mother's big party on Sunday."

They'd be heading home after the Fourth of July. They'd done all they could here without stepping on jurisdictional toes, and though there were still poachers out there, and Ty's tiger was still on the loose, they did have jobs back in Baltimore to get to. It just wasn't their case to work. Zane thought a side trip to San Antonio before they left was well-deserved after what they'd been through.

"So? What do you think?"

Ty smiled, one of his rare smiles that showed his dimples. They drove Zane crazy. "I'd like that," Ty drawled in a way that sent shivers up Zane's spine.

"We'll head up to the house, let Dad know what we're doing, and then we can head down there."

"How long's the drive?"

"An hour or two, depending on traffic and the shape of the back roads."

Ty nodded, looking down at his cereal bowl. Zane had lived for his job for so long it was odd to think he might want something different, but he could imagine that, in ten or twenty years, they'd be able to do this every morning. Get up late, fix breakfast together, and plan their day as they ate. The thought of retirement came to him more often now.

What he'd said to his family at dinner the other night was true. The thought of asking Ty to marry him was appealing. There were obvious problems, first and foremost being that they'd have to go to another state or country to do it. But the more Zane thought of it, the more he liked the idea. He knew beyond a shadow of a doubt that he'd spend the rest of his life with Ty. And after last night, he could even picture himself and Ty with kids. Not soon, because he wanted Ty to himself for a while. But it was something solid in their future.

"You're thinking kind of hard," Ty said. He sat back and cocked his head.

Zane took in a deep breath. He didn't want to tell Ty what he was thinking; he wanted it to be a complete surprise when he finally did it. Ty narrowed his eyes, but Zane gave him an enigmatic grin and stood to tidy the dishes.

"Fine, keep your mysteries, Garrett. They make you fun."

Zane laughed. That pretty much summed up how Ty saw life. He glanced over his shoulder. "This party is going to be a bitch, you know."

"We can always abscond in the night."

Zane pointed at Ty. "You get to face Mother after that, buddy boy."

"See, we need to go over your definition of abscond."

Zane turned and threw the dishrag at Ty's head. They both laughed. "Go pack and we'll head on."

"I love it when you get all bossy," Ty said with relish as he headed for the stairs.

He sauntered away. He was barefoot, had no shirt on, and his sweatpants were barely staying on his hips. How could he be so damn sexy and in such a good mood after almost getting eaten by a tiger and being in a tranquilizer-induced coma for a day? Zane couldn't help himself; he called out, "Hey, Ty?"

"Yes, my darling?" Ty responded sarcastically from halfway up the staircase.

"I love you."

Ty grinned and started up the steps again. "I like what Texas does to you, Zane."

★ ★ ★ ★ ★

"I don't care what you say, Harrison, or what *he* says, that man is taking advantage of our son and I will not stand for it!"

Harrison sat in his recliner with yesterday's newspaper in his lap, unread. He was massaging the bridge of his nose and seriously considering taking a few of the painkillers the doctor had given him for his shoulder, just so he could have an excuse to go hide on his porch. Anything to get away from his wife. Their marriage had never been about love. It had all but been arranged for them, to solidify the wealth of the two families. When it had turned from convenient to intolerable, he couldn't quite identify.

Harrison just wanted to do good by his horses and his family, and he was a happy man. But Beverly had always been driven by power, money, and status. At one time he'd seen vestiges of that same drive in his son, and he'd resigned himself to never being able to understand either of them. But something had reached inside Zane, something had changed him, and Harrison was damn sure that something had involved Ty.

"Beverly, Zane is his own man, and he's a smart one at that. And if you'd take a minute to get to know Ty, you'd find that he's a good man too."

"How can you approve of them? Does it not bother you that your son, your only son, the very last male to carry the Garrett name, goes home from work every night to another man? That doesn't offend your sensibilities?"

"Not one bit," Harrison said. He picked up his newspaper again. "At least he looks forward to going home."

She grabbed the top of his newspaper and yanked it down. Her eyes were flashing and her nostrils flared.

"Mind your blood pressure, Beverly."

"What if they go off and get married? You know they allow that in some states? That . . . that *hooligan* could be entitled to half the estate!"

"You can't take it with you. What do you care? As I see it, they're happy. Zane has every right to be happy, and I for one would rather see him more than once a year. If welcoming Ty into the family with open arms is what it takes, then I find that quite agreeable."

"He will *never* be part of my family, Harrison. I won't allow it. He can stay here and fight the good fight all he wants, but I won't allow my only son to be brainwashed like this."

Harrison scratched at his chin, pursing his lips thoughtfully. "If that's the way you want it."

"It most certainly is," Beverly snarled. She spun on her heel and stomped off.

Harrison pursed his lips and finally nodded. "What do you think, Bullet?" he grumbled to the Australian Shepherd at his feet. "Think you can dig us a hole deep enough nobody'd find her?"

The dog answered with a wiggle of its docked tail. Harrison grinned and rubbed the dog's head.

There was a knock on the doorframe, and Zane stepped into the room, smirking. Harrison put his paper aside.

"Don't get up," Zane said quickly. "We're not staying long."

Ty leaned against the doorframe and didn't come farther. He was wearing a pair of aviator sunglasses, and the way he held himself made it look like he was being careful with how he moved.

"Morning, Ty."

"Good morning, sir."

"How you feeling?" Harrison asked as he eased back down.

"Still a little hungover, to be honest."

Harrison laughed and nodded. "And sore?"

"That too."

"What are you two up to today?"

"Oh, I just figured I'd show Ty some more of Texas. Head down to San Antonio and visit the Bureau office there," Zane said. He shot a sideways look at Ty. "Maybe spend a night in Beaumont."

Ty smacked his forehead and turned his head away.

"Not much in Beaumont to see," Harrison said with a frown.

Zane grinned. "Even so, we're going to try to get it in."

Ty had his hand over his mouth, his head down. He was either going to throw up or he was laughing. Harrison felt he'd missed a joke, but he thought maybe he didn't want to know.

"You planning to miss the barbeque?" he asked Zane.

"No, sir. We'll be here."

"I know what you're doing, Z. It ain't a good idea."

Zane just raised an eyebrow.

"You two are traipsing down to San Antonio seeing if anything comes out of the woodwork to follow."

Zane just laughed. "It kind of crossed my mind. Spread the word around that we're leaving, huh? Call me if anything happens."

Harrison nodded. "You boys have fun."

Ty smacked Zane in the arm as they walked out of sight, Zane's laughter echoing off the marble hall in the foyer.

Harrison nodded. It was soothing to his soul to see his son happy again, and to know that he might come back more often now that he'd gotten so much off his chest.

If Beverly wouldn't allow Ty to be part of her family, then she might just need to find herself a new one.

★ ★ ★ ★ ★

They checked into the Hyatt on the Riverwalk in San Antonio. Ty realized that he had revealed one of his hidden passions to Zane, and Zane was exploiting his love of history for everything he was worth. Just like the battlefield at Gettysburg months ago, Ty went completely crazy over the Alamo.

They spent a solid hour exploring the tiny footprint of the famous mission, and then they strolled along the Riverwalk hand-in-hand. They finished their foray with a candlelit dinner, and as Ty gazed across the flickering flame at his lover, he could tell there was something Zane wanted to say. It was almost fun to watch him try to work up to it and then chicken out and back down. Ty was curious, but he'd found that sometimes it was better to let Zane make his own way though his mind. How long would it take him to finally get it out?

Dinner ended with Zane in an atrociously good mood and Ty just buzzed enough to be malleable as they wove through a celebratory crowd on the edges of the Alamo. Zane had Ty's hand in his, leading him somewhere. They found their way into the Alamo Gardens amidst a few dozen other people. The crowd had a feeling to it, like everyone was waiting for something to begin.

"What's going on?"

Zane gave a shrug, but turned to look back at Ty with a half-smirk. Ty narrowed his eyes.

"I know a good spot," Zane told him.

"For what?"

"You're not triggered by fireworks, are you?"

"What?"

"Fireworks. Do they... trigger flashbacks or anything?"

Ty shrugged. "Only happened once. It was right after I got home, though."

"Good." Zane's hand tightened in Ty's and Ty had to laugh as he dodged a low-lying oak branch and tramped along in the moonlight and flickering light of the lanterns that lined the Alamo. It wasn't hard to see, but it was hard to keep up with Zane and his excitement.

Ty couldn't help but smile as Zane led him toward the massive, sprawling oak tree that stood as the centerpiece of the gardens. Ty had marveled at it when they'd visited earlier. They passed by it, heading for another of the trees near the perimeter of the walled courtyard. A low branch hung out over the grass, and beneath it, a blanket had been laid out.

"You sneaky bastard," Ty said as Zane laughed.

"If you tip high enough, the concierge will do just about anything for you. I figured we could watch the fireworks from here."

"When you go for romantic, you go all out, don't you?"

"Only way to go." Zane knelt and crawled onto the blanket, straightened the edges out where they'd blown over, then turned around, still on one knee, and held his hand out. Ty took it, meeting Zane's eyes in the flickering light. Zane hesitated, looking up at him with brown eyes that seemed to have gone liquid in the low light. Time seemed to slow.

Ty found himself short of breath, and he had no idea why.

Zane bent his head to kiss Ty's fingers, breaking the little spell he'd cast, and then he tugged Ty down to join him on the blanket.

They stretched out on their backs, looking up at the velvet sky and holding hands.

"Thank you, Ty," Zane whispered.

Ty turned his head to look at Zane's profile. "For what?"

"Everything."

Zane pushed up onto his side. His face was shadowed, but Ty knew every inch of it by heart. He saw those eyes in his sleep. He reached to slide the tips of his fingers against Zane's lips, and Zane bent to kiss him, his hands tucking under Ty's body.

The first pop of pre-emptive Fourth of July fireworks over the Alamo made them both jump, and Zane turned so they could watch the fire rain down from the sky through the branches of their oak tree. Another shot soared into the air, bursting into flickering flames of red, white, and blue. People began to hoot and holler. No one was paying them any attention.

Zane looked down at Ty, and Ty grinned. This was nothing special for Ty. In his world, every time Zane's lips touched his, something somewhere caught fire.

Zane rolled onto his back again, resting his head on Ty's stomach as they watched the show. It was impressive and loud, with each burst of color and flame followed by whoops and shouts from the people gathered around the Alamo and in the streets of San Antonio.

Ty carded his fingers through Zane's hair. The moment felt heavy. As if it were fated for something of great importance, like there was something they should have been doing but weren't. It wasn't necessarily a bad feeling, just something they were letting pass them by.

"Ty?" Zane said after the last of the fireworks had faded into trails of smoke in the sky.

"Yeah?"

"Would you be willing to come back here with me? To the ranch, I mean, if we came back for Thanksgiving, or . . ."

"I'd go anywhere you wanted me to."

Zane sat up and turned until he was resting on his elbows and looking down at Ty. "Will you tell me something if I ask?"

Ty frowned at the odd way the question was posed. He had a feeling he knew where Zane was going, and though it made him uncomfortable and tense, he nodded.

"What happened to you in the Marines?"

Ty's stomach flip-flopped and he swallowed hard. It was a question Zane had every right to ask, and it was one Ty had hoped he never would.

Ty licked his lips, his mind racing. "I can't . . . I can't tell you all of it."

"What *can* you tell me?"

Ty swallowed hard, hesitating as he stared into Zane's eyes. "I . . . I was taken prisoner on a Recon mission in Afghanistan. The op is still classified and we were never officially prisoners of war. But I guess it's something you should know. Classified or not."

Zane nodded and took one of Ty's hands. "You and Nick, right?"

Ty stared at him, mouth hanging open. "You're not surprised. Do I hide it that poorly?"

"No. But I'd suspected that before. I overheard you and Nick talking when he came to visit that first time. I've been sleeping with you for the better part of a year. You speak in Farsi. I try to wake you when the dreams are the worst."

Ty nodded. They both had nightmares. It wasn't something they discussed often.

Zane finally glanced up to meet Ty's eyes. "And then Nick told me, when we were on his boat."

Ty's eyes widened. "He *told* you?"

Zane nodded, wincing.

"How much?"

"All of it."

Ty reached up and put a hand over his mouth, feeling sick.

"Ty?" Zane whispered. He ran his hand over Ty's face.

Ty had to try twice before he got the words out. "I've just never dealt with anyone knowing about it."

"I'm sorry."

Ty shook his head, trying to shrug it off. "You should know. You should know all of it."

"Will you tell me?"

Ty peered deep into the sincerity and worry, the love and devotion shining in Zane's eyes. "Yeah. I can't . . . I'll tell you more than I should."

Zane smiled a smile so brilliant it rivaled the fireworks. Ty slid his hand over Zane's chest and up his shoulders. Then his fingers were dragging over Zane's neck, his thumb digging in near Zane's ear as he pulled him closer and kissed him.

Zane scooted over to rest half on top of him, and Ty lifted a knee to let Zane settle between his legs. The longer they kissed, the less urgent the past seemed.

Zane finally pulled back with a low growl. "Do you feel lucky enough to be fucked in a National Landmark without getting arrested?"

Ty barked a laugh. "You've lost your damn mind."

Zane's head felt heavy as he and Ty tromped up the front steps. They'd spent a solid two days traipsing across Texas, and the only attention they'd attracted was from an overly flirtatious denizen of San Antonio who Ty had almost decked before Zane could drag him away.

They were home with just hours to spare, and Zane's mother had requested his presence, citing something of great importance she wanted to discuss before the Steers and Stripes Barbeque began.

"Any ideas?" Ty asked.

"No, but I am ever the optimist," Zane grumbled as he led the way into the big house. They could hear the others in the kitchen, gathering supplies and making preparations. "Go ahead. I'll see what Mother wants and be there in a bit."

Ty nodded distractedly as he took his gun and checked it. It'd become a habit of his every time he entered or exited the house, and like every new quirk Zane noticed Ty developing, it fascinated him. He turned to head for the drawing room, but he stopped in the doorway and peered in before entering.

Beverly was sitting at her desk, papers spread out around her.

Zane walked into the richly decorated room. "You wanted to see me, Mother?"

Beverly looked up, surprised. Zane glanced around the room, the same sense of foreboding assaulting him as when he'd been little and gotten in trouble. This time, it seemed, Beverly was nervous too.

She offered him a weak smile and stood. She was dressed in one of her pristine white suits and had her hair pulled back in a chignon. Surprisingly, a few red and blue ribbons were woven into her hair, a delicate touch of whimsy for the party on an otherwise staid and severe visage.

"I've been having a crisis of conscience, Zane."

Only Zane's years of practice at hiding his emotions let him cover any outward reaction. Inside, he went cold. He'd gotten that ability from his mother.

He knew what this was about, and he prayed he'd misjudged her. He swallowed hard. "Excuse me?"

"You're my only son, Zane, and I have loved you in the only way I know how. I have tried to hold my tongue when you made your decisions. I prayed that you would come home to us, in one piece, and find solace in your family. But I've seen these past days that you've chosen to get your comfort elsewhere. And it is one place I cannot in good conscience allow you to go."

"Mother," Zane said, surprised when his voice came out hoarse and tight.

"You are the last Garrett in a long line, Zane. This family needs you in more ways than you can imagine."

Her words were like ice, biting and sharp, and each one cut Zane deeper. How could she not care one iota that he was happy now? He tried to stay calm as he spoke. "Mother, we've beaten this horse to rawhide. I'm not coming back to Texas, much less to anything else you seem to think is my duty. I certainly won't marry some woman I don't love just to produce another generation of miserable Garretts."

"You seem to have no problem flaunting your... your what? Friend? I don't even know what to call him," Beverly said, her lips twisted into an ugly frown as she stalked around her desk.

"His name is Ty. You can call him my partner. Or my boyfriend. How about prospective son-in-law?"

"Zane Zachary Garrett!" Beverly slapped her hand on the desktop, cheeks flushing. "I will not stand for it! I will not ruin this family's name by having a son who thinks he's gay simply because he's got an easy screw on hand!"

Zane's eyes widened, and the anger he'd been trying to hold back broke free. "You are totally out of line."

"As are you," Beverly snapped. "He is after your money, pure and simple."

"You don't even know him. You've said all of three words to him, all of them cruel."

"I know his type, and they're all the same no matter what parts they have."

"I guarantee you've never met *his* type before."

"Zane."

"I love him, Mother. And he loves me. It has nothing to do with money."

"Did he tell you he loved you before or after you mentioned your family was wealthy?"

Her proposition was patently ridiculous, but his analytical mind was forced to stop and a take a moment to consider the answer anyway. It had been after, in fact, but it didn't matter.

His pause made Beverly close her eyes and sigh deeply. She seemed truly tortured by the revelation, and for a brief moment her defenses dropped and Zane could see the war behind her mask. She was torn between love of her son and prejudices and preconceptions she had held all her life.

Zane stepped forward, desperate to use that torment to his advantage. "Mother. Please, just give him a chance. You said you have only one son, but you could have two if you'd just see him for what he is."

She pressed her lips into a thin line, fighting not to show any more emotion than she had. She knew it was a weakness Zane would exploit, and she made an effort to bury it away again, right in front of his eyes.

Zane understood suddenly, the realization hitting him like a blast of cold water, what Ty had seen him do so many times.

He was stunned into silence by how badly it hurt.

Beverly took a deep breath. She put her hand on his chest, and when she spoke, her voice wavered. "Have I ever told you how proud I am of you?"

The pain dug deep inside him, and Zane had to choke on a breath to fight back tears. "No, ma'am."

She pursed her trembling lips and gave a jerky nod. A tear broke free as she stepped closer and hugged him. Her head barely came to his chest. Zane realized he was crying as he hugged her. She felt old and fragile, so very fragile in his hands.

She pushed away and turned, wiping her eyes as she paced away. "I simply can't, Zane," she said, her voice ragged but gaining conviction. She shook her head. "You can't have it both ways."

"Both ways?"

"You can have your family, Zane. Or you can have him."

Zane took a step back before he realized he'd given ground. While they had always argued over these things, never had his mother been so cold, so ruthless, and he couldn't even absorb it as he stared at her. His stomach was roiling.

"What the hell are you talking about?"

"Zane," she said with an almost-sympathetic tilt of her head. "It's my job to protect this family at all costs. You're my son. But you're also a drunk and an addict, you've got a worthless job with no future, and you're a widower who's taken up with another man."

"I—"

"He's not interested in you, Zane, merely your family's fortune. Can't you see that? He's no more than a whore who works on credit!"

"That's too far," Zane whispered.

"I will not have you running off and marrying that man to give him access to the family's money."

"Mother."

"If you choose him, I will draw up a statement of disavowment, Zane." Her voice was shaking, but she clearly meant it. "You will be cut off from the family's fortune to protect it."

Zane thought he might throw up right there on the carpet. She actually believed this would put him in his place.

"It's really very simple," Beverly said. She took a step toward him and put her hands on his arm. "You don't even have to go back to Baltimore. All you have to do is call in to start the retirement paperwork. We love you, Zane. You need to be at home."

The bile rising in his throat kept him from answering. There was roaring in his ears, and he wanted to roar along with it and rail at her, but he couldn't find the words. She'd never had a chance, despite what she thought.

"You're talking about my partner. The man I *love*."

"Zane. Blood is thicker than water."

Zane's body went cold. "Mother, he's shed more blood for me than you ever will."

He turned and headed for the door.

"I'm not bluffing, Zane!" she called after him. "At least think about it!"

Zane rushed out of the house, blinded by rage so intense he thought he might injure himself if he didn't dispel it somehow. He shoved the front door open and began to pace on the front porch, dragging his hand through his hair.

The floorboards creaked behind him and he whirled to give his mother another piece of his mind. He drew up short when he found Ty standing there.

"You okay?" Ty asked, his voice gentle.

Zane struggled for a breath and realized he was about to start hyperventilating. He was definitely not okay.

The next thing he knew, Ty was beside him and pulling him into a tight embrace. He squeezed his eyes shut and clutched at Ty's shirt, hurting so much he couldn't imagine standing at all if it weren't for Ty holding him up. Ty's hand came to rest on the back of Zane's head.

"It's okay," he whispered. "Breathe."

Zane was shaking, falling apart. His own *mother*. "Ty, she—"

"I know, I heard." The anger in Ty's voice was masked by layers of warmth and support as he murmured into Zane's ear. "Family ain't all about blood, Zane. It'll be okay."

The soft West Virginia twang was more comforting than Zane would have expected, but he still buried his face in the crook of Ty's neck. He just needed another minute to let the pain peak. He could understand why she didn't like that he was with Ty. Prejudices ran deep, as did the desire to continue the Garrett name, and to Beverly Carter-Garrett, appearances were everything. But couldn't she just be pleased to have him happy, like a real mother? Why the hell couldn't she give Ty a chance?

Zane gritted his teeth and tried to get himself under control. The tears weren't cooperating.

Ty stood and held him close for long minutes, long enough for Zane to pull himself together. He took a deep breath and stepped back.

Ty took his face in both hands and looked him in the eyes. "Feel better?"

Zane nodded and covered Ty's hands with his own. "I don't understand."

Ty's rough palm brushed over his cheek. "She's lashing out the only way she knows how. Give it time."

Zane closed his eyes as he pressed his cheek against Ty's hand. "I've given it more than forty years," he said, and it came out more harshly than he'd planned. "I'm not giving it any more. I hope you're not too fond of Texas. I think I'd rather steer clear for a while."

"Steer clear?" Ty asked drily. "Is that a cow joke?"

Zane choked on a laugh and whacked his knuckles against Ty's chest. Ty reached out and hugged him again, and Zane held him close, thanking God that he'd found him. It didn't matter what happened or what they went through, Ty always seemed to know how to make it better.

Zane frowned as he twisted a pink balloon around and around, forming it into what would ultimately look like a wiener dog with a huge nose. He tied off the last twist and held it up for Sadie.

"That doesn't look like a pony, Uncle Z," she said, scowling.

"But it's pink."

She narrowed her eyes, and after a long moment she petted his knee with a sigh. "It's okay. You'll do better next time." Then she snatched the wiener pony out of his hand and went running.

Zane coughed against a laugh and glanced across the table at the others. Annie and Mark were laughing, their eyes on Sadie as she caroused. Zane's gaze fell upon Ty. He was lounging and hiding a smile behind his hand, watching Zane.

"Shut up," Zane grumbled, but he couldn't take his eyes off Ty.

"I didn't say anything."

"You try it next time."

Ty chuckled and winked at him. He'd already regaled a group of the younger kids with magic, making a coin disappear and then pulling it out of Sadie's ear, amongst other tricks. The only thing Zane could do that didn't involve a knife was make a balloon animal. He'd made swords or those nebulous four-legged animals for each child. Now they were all swashbuckling and pretending to be tigers with their balloons.

There was a loud pop from somewhere nearby, and Zane cleared his throat and shifted in his chair, hoping no one had noticed him staring at his lover. No one was paying any attention to him, though.

The annual Carter Garrett Steers and Stripes Barbeque was in full swing.

Hundreds of people were in attendance, laughing, dancing, eating, and drinking. Kids roamed the crowd in packs. The sheriff and his men were here, as were several animal control officers.

Amidst the festivities was an undercurrent of tension. Barnum the Bengal tiger was still out there somewhere, and there was a high possibility he'd fixated on Ty's scent as something familiar. The poachers were still free and running around, probably even at the party. And the news of Beverly's ultimatum had spread through the family, the ranch hands, and the guests. Soon it would be all the way to Austin, and that seemed to be the biggest news of all. Zane was surprised to find that while some seemed to approve of Beverly's "tough love" approach, most were appalled. She was being snubbed by a few individuals that shocked even Zane. But then, so was he.

"Donations for the trick shooting contest are about to close, ladies and gentlemen," Harrison called out from the flatbed trailer they'd turned into a flag-festooned stage. "All proceeds this year will be donated to local animal shelters and the Roaring Springs Big Cat Sanctuary. You can sponsor a shooter for two hundred dollars. Let's have a few more contestants."

"You two ought to shoot, Z," Annie said, looking across the round table at Ty and Zane.

Mark narrowed his eyes at Ty. "I suppose Grady would give a good showing. From what I remember, you were pretty good at the competitions."

Ty shrugged, a mixture of humility and nonchalance. Zane was still trying to shake the nagging feeling that they would be putting Mark in handcuffs soon. With that and the ultimatum from his mother, he was having a hard time concentrating on what was going on around them.

He tore his eyes away from Ty and adjusted his hat.

"What do you think, Ty?" Annie asked. "Are you two good enough to compete?"

Zane tried not to smile too much as he glanced at his partner. They had no idea what he and Ty were capable of. Zane almost wanted to see Ty show them all what he could do.

"I don't know, we do okay," Ty answered with a careless shrug. He took another drink of his beer, then glanced over at the large area they'd cleared for the shooting gallery. "Trick shots don't usually have much to do with how good a shot you are."

Marissa leaned forward. She was sitting on Cody's lap, and they'd been whispering and flirting for most of the day. "Why do you say that? I've been watching this stuff all my life, and it's always the best shots who win."

Ty shook his head. "It doesn't just take shooting straight. It takes practice. It's kind of like playing mini golf; they're more like puzzles than pure tests of ability. Same guy who can hit a moving target at a hundred yards can't always hit a penny on a fence post with a mirror. And a dude who can shoot the fluffy part off a toothpick at thirty yards while he's hanging upside down by his balls might not hit a moving truck if it was trying to run him over."

That drew a round of laughs, and Zane shook his head as he drank from his water bottle. It was hot, hotter than he remembered from his youth. He could feel the sweat making its way through his shirt. Ty had one of his Buffs around his forehead, sitting under his hat, and another around his wrist that he used periodically to wipe the sweat away from anywhere that needed. Zane imagined it was a system he'd created while in the Corps.

"You get a lot of target practice working for the FBI?" Cody asked. "I didn't even think to ask if you carry normally or if it's just been since you came to Texas."

"Not exactly target practice," Zane said under his breath. He ran his water bottle over his forehead.

Ty shot him a grin and emptied his beer. "Nothing too exciting," he answered, tongue-in-cheek. "But yeah, we carry all the time."

Cody nodded.

"I think you should enter, Z. Someone from the family should," Annie said.

"Since when is Mark not family?" Zane asked.

"Jackass," Mark said with a snort. "You know she means a blood relative."

"You'll have to talk to Mother about that," Zane said, trying not to sound bitter and failing.

"Come on, Zane," Annie whispered. Zane shrugged.

"How about it, Grady?" Mark said. "We'll all enter, see who's held onto their skills."

Zane glanced between them, not sure why Mark would warn him about Ty being unstable and dangerous and then try to get Ty to enter a *shooting* contest. Perhaps it was just a little too much testosterone for his brother-in-law to handle. Or maybe Mark was trying to find a reason to have a loaded gun pointed at Ty's head.

Ty glanced at Zane and gave a lazy shrug. "I got three beers in me, no way I should be trick shooting."

Mark laughed and threw back the rest of his beer.

The sheriff walked up to their table as they talked, tipping his hat when they all looked at him.

"Sheriff Barnes," Zane with a smile. "Any news for us?"

"Some," the man said, as unflappable and unreadable as ever. "We found the vet practice the tranquilizers were stolen from."

"That's great!" Annie said. She sat forward in her chair.

"Yes, ma'am. Unfortunately, it was yours."

"What?" Her smile morphed into a horrified gape.

Zane glanced at his sister, then he met Ty's eyes. Ty was looking at the table, probably trying to observe Mark's reaction without being noticed. There was another point against him.

"I reported it missing the other night when I was taking stock of everything," Marissa admitted, looking mortified.

"Why didn't you tell me?" Annie asked.

"I thought it was drug seekers, not tiger poachers!"

"We'll flag 'em down," the sheriff said. He tipped his hat. "Y'all enjoy the party."

He sauntered away, leaving a pall over their little gathering.

"What does that mean?" Annie finally asked.

Ty and Zane shared a look, but neither was willing to answer.

"Oh no," Annie said.

Zane glanced up, but Annie was peering past his shoulder at someone else approaching. Zane turned to find Stuart walking toward them.

"Garrett," Stuart said. He touched the brim of his hat with a finger and Zane stood to meet him. "I come to apologize to you and . . . your friend."

Zane couldn't help it when his eyebrows climbed high.

"Well, that's... decent of you," Zane said.

Stuart held out his hand, but Zane hesitated before taking it. After the things this man had said to him, and more importantly, to Ty, Zane wasn't feeling overly friendly. He also had pretty solid suspicions that Stuart and his buddies were behind the tiger poaching, and one of them had probably shot his father. Still, he didn't want to tip his cards yet, so he took the hand Stuart offered.

Stuart turned to Ty, offering to shake. Ty didn't stand; he merely drank his beer, one foot on the edge of the table in front of him, leaning back in his chair.

"It's Grady, right?" Stuart asked. "Staff Sergeant Grady?"

Ty looked at the man's hand, then at him. Zane glanced between them, wondering how the hell anyone had learned Ty had been a Staff Sergeant. He glanced at Mark as another wave of suspicion went through him.

It was impossible to see Ty's expression between the aviators and the Stetson. "Nice limp."

"Accidents happen when you work on a ranch."

Ty cocked his head, examining the man's leg. Zane knew his partner was seeing what no one else was.

"You're not going to shake my hand?" Stuart demanded.

Ty waited another few heartbeats, long enough to make the man even more uncomfortable. Then he slid to his feet. He was several inches taller, and when he stood, his proximity forced Stuart to take a step back. Ty offered his left hand, and Stuart was obligated to give him an awkward, backwards handshake. For whatever reason, it pissed the man off. He didn't say anything else, just turned on his heel and walked away. He was indeed limping, and it seemed more pronounced than it had several days ago.

"That was weird," Mark said, frowning hard.

Zane nodded.

Ty took a long drink of his beer. "Is he one of the shooters?" he asked, voice filled with cruel anticipation that sent a shiver of pleasure up Zane's spine.

"I believe he is," Joe answered, smiling. "He and his buddy damn near beat Jamie and Mark last year."

Ty nodded. "I'm in."

The others let out whoops and started banging on the table, and Zane couldn't help but laugh. He set down his drink. "I guess we ought to pay in, then."

The others chattered as Zane and Mark walked over to the stage to make the donations. When he returned to the table, Zane stopped at Ty's side and looked down at him. "All these boys are good. You better bring your A-game, Grady."

Ty just smiled and stood, reaching out to grab the three bottle caps he'd collected and slide them into his pocket. "Ladies," he drawled as they left the table.

Ty's shoulder bumped Zane's as they walked, and it was harder than Zane expected to keep from wrapping his arm around his partner. He talked to distract himself.

"There's several events, and they tally scores for individuals and teams as we go along." They made their way to the shooting gallery, set up in a nearby corral. No one was allowed in before the contest started, to avoid any unfair advantages.

"Okay," Ty said. He rolled up the sleeves of his thin linen shirt and wiped at his forehead with the buff on his wrist. They came up to the main table and surveyed the gear laid out. "Rifles, pistols, knives." Ty began to laugh. "The things you get me into."

Zane grinned. "Texas," he said, since that was the answer to everything. "What are you up to, Ty?"

Ty just hummed as he wandered off toward the end of the table. Zane had no idea why Ty had offered to enter the contest, other than for the chance to stand close to one or more armed men they knew wanted Ty out of the picture.

They wouldn't know what shots they were taking until they were unveiled during the contest, so they wouldn't know if there was a possibility of danger either.

If anyone was going to take a shot at Ty, though, this would be when they did it. Zane followed along, checking out the competition. He recognized a few of the men. Stuart and one of his asshole companions were there. Several hands from another neighboring ranch had signed up, as had Cody and Joe. Mark and Jamie made up the fifth team, and he and Ty would be the sixth. Zane shook his head as butterflies fluttered.

He didn't have anything to prove here. It was for charity, and he didn't care what the others thought about him. What he was really looking forward to was Ty showing them all up. Or arresting them in the middle of it.

"Zane, are you entering the competition?"

Zane looked up to see his mother and two of her friends approaching. "Yes, Mother. Along with Ty."

Beverly looked him over. "Well. Good luck," she said. She lingered a moment, looking torn, but then moved away without saying anything more.

Ty chose that moment to come sauntering back to Zane's side. He'd managed to grab another bottle of beer from somewhere, like he was producing them out of his ass. "That's not awkward at all."

Zane shook his head.

Ty met his eyes, still grinning. "You really want to go into this thing with me after I've been drinking and baking in the sun all day?"

Ty's smile and his shining eyes were enough to make Zane forget all about his mother. "Absolutely. Let's kick some ass."

"Or shoot some." Ty shoved his shoulder into Zane's and they made their way toward the gathering of shooters awaiting instructions.

Ty and Zane were deemed Yellow Team. Judges directed them to stations set up through the corral and around the barn, and partygoers began gathering with them, bringing their cocktails along. The bleachers began to fill. Looking around, Zane wondered if he was the only sober person here. The thought was wildly funny for some reason.

He was catching snippets of conversation from people around him, their words traveling in the heat in unpredictable ways.

"Is that guy drinking?"

"Is that the Garrett boy's gentleman friend?"

"He's not anything like I thought he'd look. He's quite strapping."

"Zane looks good, doesn't he?"

Zane shook his head and turned his attention to their first challenge as all the teams gathered. It was a gallery of ten weighted ropes hung in a row, all different lengths and with varying sizes of weight attached. The idea was to shoot through the rope and make the weight drop. They would have a limited number of shots. He glanced to the judge approaching with a rifle.

"Preference?" he asked Ty.

Ty leaned back to look at the gun, then eyed the ropes with a growing smirk. "I kick ass with a rifle," he whispered, then took a slow sip of his beer.

"Then by all means," Zane drawled, sweeping one hand toward the judge.

"Gentlemen, pick your shooters. The rest of the team members, if you will please join the crowd."

Zane waited until Ty was passing by to whisper, "I'd kiss you for luck, but it would probably cause a ruckus."

"So will your shooting," Ty told him, and he smacked Zane on the hip for good measure, then handed him his beer bottle. "Hold this."

Zane took the bottle with a good-natured snort. With Ty in his line of sight, the beer in his hand wasn't even a temptation.

Zane scanned the crowd. He found Harrison standing over to the side, talking to some of the judges. When Harrison looked up, Zane caught his eye and nodded. To Zane's delight, Harrison mimed a pistol with his finger and thumb to shoot at him.

Zane turned to watch the competition, feeling much lighter all of a sudden. It still shocked him how much his parents' approval meant to him. He knew he would never gain his mother's, but Ty had been right about his father; he was epic.

The first shooter was given the rifle and told where to stand as the others moved to a safe observation point. They weren't wearing earplugs or safety glasses like they should have been. Ty glanced around and pulled his aviators out of his shirt pocket to slide them on. He looked in Zane's direction as the first man took aim and fired at his first weighted rope.

Ty didn't flinch away, holding Zane's gaze with each rifle blast. Just because he could, Zane gave Ty a quick wink.

Ty smiled, the same evil smirk Zane knew so well. Whether they won the whole thing or lost every single contest, Zane knew he was getting laid later. It almost made him want to ditch the entire day and take Ty somewhere secluded.

Ty finally turned his attention back to the shooting. The first contestant had hit four of the ropes but only snapped three. He'd also hit one of the weighted bags, and sand was gushing out of the holes. His score of three was chalked up on a large board on the side of the gallery, and the rifle was reloaded and new ropes tied up. There was a smattering of distracted applause as the next shooter, Stuart's teammate, went up. He didn't fare much better. The ropes were tough and thick, and though they snapped when nicked with the heavier weights, the lighter weights weren't enough to pull a missed shot.

Annie appeared at Zane's elbow. "What do you think?"

"I think your husband is in for some stiff competition."

"I think you're blinded by love."

Zane nodded, acknowledging the truth in that. He looked over the other competitors standing with Ty. They were all capable ranch hands, and Mark had been a Marine. But like Ty had said, this sort of competition was as much a puzzle as it was a test of skill. What he was really concerned about was Stuart, and the idea that Mark was the mastermind behind their trouble.

"Mark keep up with the rifle range?" Zane asked.

"Like clockwork," Annie replied.

As new ropes were hung up and the rifle reloaded, Ty stepped away from the others and began fiddling with his shirtsleeve again. Apparently it was his turn. Zane watched him, recognizing some of the quirky mannerisms, but not others. He didn't seem to be paying much attention to what was going on, or he was drunk, and he seemed supremely distracted by the cuff of his shirt. It wouldn't roll up like he wanted it to.

"Is he okay to shoot?" Annie asked.

Zane covered a laugh by clearing his throat. "Yeah, he's fine. Superstitious, you know? Never steps on home base before a game, that kind of thing."

Annie hummed but she didn't say anything else, and Zane gave her a regretful glance. He prayed they were wrong about Mark.

Finally, Ty stepped closer to Mark and said something, to which Mark gave him a tolerant look and reached out to fix his shirt cuff for him. Ty thanked him with a smack on his shoulder that sent Mark stumbling sideways, and Ty sauntered up to the judge holding the rifle and took it with an easy grin.

He looked the rifle over and hefted it. "That's nice," he said, loud enough for the crowd to hear. "What is it, Marlin .44 Special?"

The judge nodded, frowning.

"That's real nice," Ty said. He cradled the rifle in the crook of his arm, the muzzle aimed carelessly toward where Stuart stood. Stuart flinched as the barrel swung his way.

"Watch where you aim that damn thing!" Stuart shouted. A round of laughter followed.

"I'm watching," Ty said, his tone lazy but his words heavy. He rested the rifle in the crook of his arm, using his other hand to discreetly keep the barrel aimed at Stuart as he moved forward to stand on the X marked in the sand.

Stuart sidestepped but couldn't get out from under Ty's aim. He flushed in the hot sun. Zane read his lips as he called Ty all kinds of unsavory names.

Annie turned a look of disbelief on Zane, who had to cover his mouth to muffle the laugh. He knew Ty; there was no way he'd pick up that rifle while drunk unless he or someone he loved was threatened. Ty was playing it up. He was also sending Stuart a clear message: they had him in their sights.

"Shooter ready?" the judge called, and Ty brought the six-pound rifle up to snug it against his shoulder. His stance was wide and even, and something about the way his shoulders rounded was incredibly fun to watch. But he was having a hard time gripping the rifle. A ripple of laughter went through the crowd; they expected him to make a fool of himself.

"Zane, I told you we should have cut off this cast," Ty called out.

He had a point. He couldn't just switch up and shoot lefty with a rifle. The cartridges were made to eject to the right of the shooter, and if he fired with his left hand, the hot cartridge would eject right into his face after every round.

"Hope he shoots better than he fights," Stuart said loudly, and another round of laughter followed.

The first shot of the .44 kicked Ty back, but his aim was true and the bullet snapped through the rope just an inch above the weight. A murmur of surprise went through the crowd. He rattled off six more shots in rapid succession, his long fingers cocking the rifle with practiced speed and ease despite the cumbersome cast. Each shot drew more sounds from the crowd, until many were hooting and whistling every time he dropped a target. It was an impressive show.

And then he missed. The eighth rope twisted as the bullet grazed it. A groan ran through the crowd. Ty shrugged his shoulders and looked up from the sights of the rifle. He grumbled something. He tried the next rope and missed again, fraying the rope but not enough to make the lighter weight drop. He graced the crowd with a distinctive curse, held up his broken right hand and waved it, then aimed at the last rope.

The weight dropped with an anticlimactic plop in the sand, followed by a round of rowdy calls.

Ty handed the rifle off, then threw his hands up and took a cheeky bow for the crowd. They ate it up, and Zane had to shake his head. His lover was a born entertainer who liked to kill things. How he wasn't in a psychiatric ward or on a Most Wanted list somewhere was anyone's guess.

Zane tore his eyes away from Ty to glance at Stuart. The man looked a little green now, and even Mark was shifting his weight nervously.

"Huh," Annie said, turning to Zane with a suspicious look.

"What?"

Annie rolled her eyes. "You brought in a ringer."

Zane's lips twitched. "No. Although his lethality is a hell of a benefit."

Annie smacked his arm once, then again, and Zane shoved at her hand, rubbing his arm and laughing. "Hey, I've got to shoot. Stop it!"

Annie poked him in the chest. "I have to go home with Mark! You know what kind of mood he'll be in if you beat him?"

"You're the one who pushed us to enter!"

"Yeah, well, I thought you'd bomb!"

Zane wrapped his arm around her shoulders and pulled her close. It hurt to think he'd have to be the one to tell her that her husband was the bad guy, and he hoped Ty was wrong this time. He looked up to see Ty walking—no, *swaggering*—over to the other shooters waiting their turn. He hugged Annie tighter.

Ty stopped in front of Mark first, smirking, and held out his arm. "Luck must have rubbed off on me," he said as he swiped at his shirtsleeve. "Want it back?"

"Oh Lord." Annie shoved at Zane's chest and walked away. Zane smiled sadly. Annie still thought this was a friendly shooting competition.

Ty came to stand beside Zane, valiantly trying to restrain his grin. Zane glanced at him, snorted, and pressed his lips together hard to stave off the laugh. "You're such a showboat."

Ty turned to him, the sun reflecting off his sunglasses as a smile flitted across his lips. He pushed his hat back. "You telling me you didn't enjoy that?"

"Oh, I enjoyed it a little too much. One down, several to go." Zane grinned. "And at least you look good."

Ty clucked his tongue. "Damn good."

Zane couldn't stop himself from sliding his hand against Ty's back. Mark took up his spot and readied to shoot.

"Watch this," Ty said, almost laughing.

"What'd you do?"

The crowd fell quiet. After a few heartbeats, Mark pulled the trigger. His shot grazed the rope but merely frayed it. He had missed the first and easiest shot.

Zane cleared his throat and stared at his boots for a long moment, trying not to tip their hand with his expression. "What'd you do?" he asked Ty under his breath.

"Got in his head, stole his luck," Ty said. Mark turned to glare at them, and Ty pointedly wiped his imaginary luck off his shirt cuff, still grinning.

Mark rolled his eyes and set up again. He made the next shot, and the next. Ty was still laughing, obviously enjoying the mental game as well as the physical one. This was the same part of Ty that enjoyed profiling.

Mark ended up scoring one less than Ty, and although he looked like he was shaking it off, Zane didn't miss his narrowed eyes as Mark walked off the range.

"I don't care if we win," Zane said as he watched Mark and Annie talk. "But I'd really like to beat him. And Stuart."

Ty hummed. "Cut my cast off."

"You know I don't want to do that. You're taking advantage of the situation," Zane grumbled, though there wasn't any heat behind it. Would it be horrible of him to consider re-injuring Ty's hand if it meant beating Mark and that asshole Stuart in this stupid competition?

Ty looked over his sunglasses at Zane. "Okay. But I can't promise a win with only one hand. And what if all hell breaks loose? I'll need both hands then."

"Tell me now, no shit, that your hand's okay."

Ty laughed incredulously. "It's broken. Of course it's not okay."

Zane glanced toward Mark and back. "No," he said, setting his fingers on Ty's cast. It was the most pitiful excuse for a cast he'd ever seen, covered with signatures, phone numbers, a knife wound, several places where Ty had tried to saw at it, and tiger bites. Dirty beyond all reason, and it didn't smell like the most wonderful thing in the world. It was probably uncomfortable, too.

"It's not worth it," he said, trying to tell himself that as much as Ty. "Besides, if we win anyway, it's that much worse for him to know he got beaten by a man with a broken hand."

"If you say so, Quickdraw."

Zane turned to look at him, watching him raptly as Ty took a step forward and waved a hand when they were announced as the winning team for that challenge.

As a group they moved on to the next round, Ty hummed under his breath, his elbow brushing Zane's. Zane soon made out the Battle Hymn in the hum, and he groaned.

At the next station, a bowl of fruit sat on the table, and the same Marlin .44 Special was being reloaded. The judge began telling the shooters what they were supposed to be doing, and the instructions made it clear that Zane would be the one trying his hand at this one. The shooter would take three oranges from the bowl, toss them in the air, and shoot as many as he could before they hit the ground.

Ty leaned over to whisper in Zane's ear. "That rifle weighs six pounds. No way I can swing it with my hand. This one's all you, big boy." He smacked Zane's ass and turned to head for the crowd.

"Ty," Zane hissed. Ty turned to look at him. "Make yourself scarce, huh? This is the perfect shot to claim a misfire into the crowd, know what I mean?"

Ty nodded, but then he sauntered over to stand shoulder to shoulder with Stuart's teammate in the front row.

"Great," Zane said under his breath. He headed up to the table with the other competitors. He was a good shot with a rifle, that wasn't his concern. But he'd have preferred a practice run with this shot. He just hoped he didn't drop the rifle.

He stopped at the table with the others, and someone bumped his shoulder. He looked up to see Mark grinning at him.

"I didn't figure he'd be able to do this one with that cast," Mark said. "When was the last time you fired a rifle?"

"It's been a while."

Mark clapped Zane's shoulder, hard enough that Zane had to take a step to keep his balance. "Buck up, brother. Time for a lesson from the master."

Zane glanced at Ty. This was a bad idea. He knew the game Ty was playing with their quarry, and he shouldn't have encouraged it. Ty raised his chin and gave Zane a languid smile. He didn't look worried.

Mark volunteered to go first. Zane couldn't shake the tension as he waited, praying he was wrong about his brother-in-law. He knew what kind of shot Mark was. If he missed one of those oranges and it went anywhere near the crowd, it was a warning shot, loud and clear.

Mark chose three oranges from the bowl, picked up the firearm, and moved into place. When the judge blew the whistle, Mark tossed, flipped the rifle up from the crook of his arm, and took the shots, quickly pulling the lever between each one. Juice flew through the air as all three rotten oranges exploded.

Zane released a pent-up breath, but he couldn't relax. Just because Mark had yet to make a move didn't mean he wasn't going to. The next two shooters hit two each, one man missed all three, and Stuart caught all three even though he tossed them a little too close to the edge of the crowd for Zane's comfort. Then it was Zane's turn. He resisted the urge to look over his shoulder at Ty, but he imagined he could feel Ty's eyes on him.

"Nothing like taking shots at a couple fruits, huh Garrett?" Stuart hissed as he passed by him.

Zane narrowed his eyes, refusing to rise to the bait.

He settled the rifle in the crook of his arm, nodded to the judge, and chose his oranges. They gave under his fingers, enough that he almost laughed, and it helped dispel the nerves. Determined not to dwell on what he was doing as he headed toward the mark in the sand, Zane took a deep breath, exhaled, and tossed the fruit, pulling up the rifle and shooting.

Two oranges disintegrated in the air, and the third exploded just before it was about to hit the ground.

Zane blinked in shock as the crowd applauded. He handed the rifle back to the judge before walking over to Ty with a shrug.

"You sure as hell showed those oranges who was boss," Ty said, though the pride in his voice was easy for Zane to hear.

Zane chuckled, relaxing even more. "Never mind that it's been a few months since I even touched a rifle."

"You're so getting laid tonight."

"Lucky me."

The contests continued, each event getting more outlandish and difficult, each rife with an undercurrent of antagonism and threats. Ty had to fire a Colt revolver over his shoulder using a mirror, holding it with his left hand, to shoot the ace of spades out of a playing card. He was the only shooter to even nick the card, much less the spade, and he came in first. Zane did both knife-tossing contests, the first to hit a stationary target, the second to hit a target painted on a watermelon as it swung like a pendulum. He won both and caused quite a stir when he twirled the knife around his hand before giving it back to the judge.

With each show of their skill, Stuart looked more and more mutinous. Zane could feel in every fiber of his being that something was going to happen tonight. The only question was who would instigate it—Ty or Stuart?

As sunset encroached, Ty was left to handle the last event: the lasso.

"Goddammit, Zane, you should have let me throw the first knife!" Ty hissed when the event was revealed.

Zane couldn't help but laugh. Ty could handle any weapon someone put in his hands and do it with competence, if not skill. A lasso was the last thing Zane had expected, but even if they came in second place in this event, they would still win the whole thing.

Ty was shaking his head, muttering under his breath as they watched Mark take his turn. Before Zane could quell the urge, he pulled his lover close to give him a very public kiss. It caused a few gasps and murmurs, and Zane could feel all those eyes on them. He didn't care. Ty didn't flail or tense up, and Zane felt him smiling against his lips.

"Even if we don't win this," Zane said, "thank you."

Ty nodded, lingering just long enough to make Zane's heart beat faster. Then the judge called for the last contestant to take his turn, and Ty gave Zane one last glance and a smile before stepping out into the cleared arena. There were three targets, and the closer he came to the smallest target, the higher his points. The most he could get was six, and they only needed one point to beat Mark and Jamie.

Zane laughed heartily as Ty tried to get the rope settled in his left hand. He might have been able to handle the thick, heavy rope with both hands, but with his dominant hand in a cast, it was just too much for him.

The crowd began to buzz, ripples of laughter going through it.

"If I was a rodeo clown, you'd all be gored to death," Ty said as he finally got the rope in place.

There was more laughter, and Zane realized he was grinning from ear to ear as he watched his lover make a spectacle of himself.

When Ty got the rope going in circles over his head, Zane thought his partner might actually have paid attention when he'd tried to teach him. He had good form, and the rope was swinging like it needed to. But then Ty released the lasso too early, and the toss came sailing toward Zane and the other contestants instead of the targets.

Stuart didn't have time to dodge it; he just stood there as the rope dropped around his shoulders and Ty pulled it tight. He stumbled forward, arms trapped at his sides as the crowd burst into raucous laughter and applause.

"Sorry!" Ty said with a wave of his hand that pulled the lasso tighter.

"What the hell are you doing!" Stuart bawled. "You fucking moron!"

Ty pulled him forward again, and Zane could only shake his head as he watched, stunned by his partner's gall.

Ty continued to apologize profusely, making a show of being a bumbling drunken idiot, and Stuart kept up a litany of cursing and accusations as Ty inexplicably managed to wrap him up even more instead of helping him out of the ropes.

"Wow, these things are really complicated, aren't they?" Ty said over the raucous laughter of the crowd. Stuart lost his balance and tumbled to the ground. Ty stood over him. "How do you make it let go?"

Stuart's friends came over to help, strong-arming Ty out of the way. He held up both hands and took a few steps back, the picture of innocence.

"You're insane," Zane said as soon as he drew close. Ty was grinning, his eyes sparkling in the dying sunlight as they watched Stuart struggle to get loose.

"I've always wanted to do that," he said, as gleeful as a schoolboy who'd just caught a frog.

"And?"

Ty looked Zane up and down, as if sizing him up, then he gave a lecherous grin. "You think we could take one of those lassos home with us?"

"Ty, focus!"

Ty grinned. "We got him."

"You're sure?"

"Damn sure."

Mark and Jamie were declared the winners amidst a round of polite applause as Ty and Zane discussed it. When Zane was declared the individual winner of the event, he looked around in surprise as everyone cheered.

"Nicely done, Big Iron," Ty said to him.

Zane looked at him suspiciously as Ty patted him on the shoulder. If Ty had made that lasso toss, he would have won.

Harrison came up to smack each of them on the back. "Well, if it ain't Pancho and Lefty. Looks like you caught you one," he said to Ty with a big grin. He put his arm around Zane's shoulder. "That was a mighty fine show you put on. Boy, I had no idea you could throw a knife like that."

Zane felt himself blushing. Ty patted him on the shoulder and gave him a wink. "I'm going to go have a discussion with the sheriff," he said, then left Zane alone with his father.

"I guess . . . we have a lot of catching up to do," Zane said with a hopeful smile.

"You bet your ass we do."

"Have you talked to Mother?"

Harrison's jaw tightened and his eyes grew harder. He nodded curtly. "If she intends to make me choose between my wife and my son, she's got a surprise coming. I hope you and your boy decide to come down more often." Harrison threw a pointed look at Ty, who had melted into the crowd, shaking hands, laughing with strangers. He'd been accepted for the most part, whether by his own doing or Harrison's influence, Zane didn't know. Zane's mother could sign all the legal documents she wanted; it wasn't going to pierce through Zane's armor now.

Zane nodded, throat tightening. "I think we'll be able to manage that."

Harrison patted him on the cheek. "Did you catch him?"

"Ty claims he has proof enough to get the sheriff. That's what he's doing now."

"Let's hope he's right. Why do you look worried?"

Zane took a deep breath. "We think Mark's involved."

Harrison inhaled sharply. "I hope you're wrong on that one, son."

"Me too."

Zane remained there as his father walked away, the feeling of warmth and acceptance spreading deeper into him. His mother and their suspicions of Mark were a small blight on an otherwise bright day. He set off into the crowd to find Ty again, feeling somehow that if it weren't for Ty, he would never have come home, and he would have drifted through life alone until it killed him. Ty had given him a new home, and then shown him he still had his old one.

He was still musing over the twists and turns of life when a commotion broke out ahead of him. He pushed through the crowd to see what was going on, and somehow he wasn't surprised to see Ty in the thick of it. Ty stood with the sheriff and two of his deputies, facing Stuart and his three friends. Stuart was in Ty's face as the crowd cleared for them.

"You accusing me of something, boy?" Stuart was saying as Zane came up on them.

"I'm saying I know where you got that limp," Ty said.

Stuart puffed up his chest like he was trying for courage as he glared up at Ty. Both deputies put their hands on their firearms, ready for a show of force.

Everyone and his brother was armed, and the tension was gathering in the air.

Zane stepped forward, standing behind Ty and the sheriff. The others joined him, Cody, Mark, and Joe finding their way into the clearing. Zane put Mark to his side, not allowing his brother-in-law to be behind him.

"You think you know something about me? Go ahead and say it!" Stuart shouted.

"You've been poaching tigers," Ty said, as calm as the breeze. "You're running something out there, and you shot me in the chest with a dart that damn near killed me."

"You got no proof. Sheriff, this is ridiculous. You gonna let this queer come in here and tell you what to do?"

The sheriff nodded curtly. "He seems to know what he's talking about, Stuart."

"Bullshit! You got no proof!"

"You've got my knife in your boot."

Stuart took a swing. Ty leaned away from it and trapped Stuart's fist between both hands. He jabbed his elbow under the man's chin, sending him reeling back, then kicked at his thigh and caused his leg to buckle. Stuart went to his knees, and Ty kicked him in the chest, sending him sprawling into the dirt.

The sheriff and his deputies pulled their weapons, fanning out to surround Stuart and his cohorts.

Ty put one booted foot on Stuart's neck, pressing down with the heel to keep him still. It had happened so fast that none of Stuart's buddies had been able to move to help, and when the guns turned on them they each raised their hands, sinking to their knees without putting up a fight.

Harrison forced his way through the crowd. "What in the Sam Hill is going on here?"

Ty didn't lift his boot off Stuart's throat. "I put my knife into the thigh of one of the poachers who attacked me."

Sheriff Barnes looked down at Stuart. The spot where Ty had kicked him was beginning to bleed. The sheriff pursed his lips, then bent to look in Stuart's boot where Ty was pointing. He pulled a knife out of the sheath the man had tucked into his boot and held it up. It was a Strider SA model. A simple, sturdy knife about seven inches long. Zane knew the leather-wrapped handle was worn from years of use, and that the sheriff would find the words "S. SGT BT GRADY" engraved in the hilt.

The sheriff looked up at Ty and nodded. He pulled his radio from its belt and called to his dispatcher. "We caught the poachers."

Ty moved his foot off Stuart's neck as Zane joined him.

"There were more than four people involved," Zane told the sheriff.

Ty and Zane stepped back to let the deputies handcuff their prisoners. They rolled Stuart to his belly and yanked his hands behind his back.

"You think you know everything, you fucking queers?" Stuart snarled against the dirt. "You got trouble in your own damn house!"

Zane stalked forward and bent down to grab a handful of his hair. "Trouble in *my* house? Who?"

Stuart gave him a toothy grin. "You got no idea." He looked over his shoulder as he lay in the dust. "I want a lawyer."

Ty grabbed Zane's arm and pulled him up before Zane could throttle a restrained prisoner in front of witnesses.

"We need to go back to that pump house," Ty hissed in his ear as he bullied him away from the others. Zane stopped fighting him and let himself be dragged to the edge of the crowd. "We need to do it now."

Zane's eyes landed on Mark, and he was unable to tear them away as he nodded. "Let's get out there before he does."

They slipped through the crowd, lost in the excitement of the confrontation, and headed around the barn, where the family had parked their vehicles to keep them out of the way and block off certain parts of the ranch from partygoers.

The chaotic hum of the milling crowd on the other side of the barn was overwhelmed by the distinct sound of a tiger roaring.

Silence overcame the ranch. The sound ripped its way through Zane's body like nothing else he'd ever experienced, and he and Ty both froze in their tracks. The tiger roared again, the sound culminating in a low, seemingly endless rumble. It was like a purr from hell.

The crowd on the other side of the barn began to boil with panic. Screaming and shouting, people scrambled to get to safety.

Zane felt the hairs rise on his neck, a feeling of foreboding overtaking him as Ty's hand tightened on his arm. He turned his head, knowing Barnum the Bengal tiger was there before he ever caught sight of him. Ty turned with him. Barnum sat twenty yards away, watching them. He chuffed and sniffed the air.

There was a buzzing sound over Ty's harsh breaths and the sounds of the terrified partygoers, and Zane realized it was panic encroaching.

The tiger made another sound, an odd hissing that Zane soon realized hadn't come from the tiger at all. It was Ty, making the same sound he did to call Smith and Wesson.

He did it again and took a step forward.

"Oh Jesus, Ty, this is not how I want to die," Zane whispered.

"It's okay."

"No, it isn't!"

Barnum stood and lowered his head. He took a step to match Ty's. Ty took another. Barnum chuffed and drew closer, looking wary.

"He's scared, Zane."

"Well, he should join the fucking club."

"Come on, Barnum."

"Ty, you are not the tiger whisperer," Zane hissed.

Ty held out a hand to calm him, then took a few more steps toward Barnum. In the blink of an eye, Barnum lowered his body and lunged at Ty, wrapping his arms around his head and dragging his face against Ty's as he stood on his hind legs and hugged him. His massive body dwarfed Ty, and Zane could only see Ty's arms as he returned the tiger's hug. Barnum continued to rub his floppy ear against Ty's face.

Zane stood rooted to the spot, mouth hanging open, shaking his head.

After a few long moments, Barnum released Ty and sat down. Ty staggered back and leaned over, gasping for breath.

"That's the stupidest thing I've ever seen," Zane whispered, still stunned.

Ty began to laugh. "That's what he did in his enclosure." He held out his fist to the tiger, and Barnum smacked him with his paw like he was giving him a fist bump. "Loves to hug."

"You're an idiot."

"We need to get those animal control morons over here. Or call the sanctuary, let them know we found him."

"You're a fucking idiot!"

Ty straightened and Barnum sent a low grumble in Zane's direction. Ty shook his head, smirking a little. "My tiger disagrees, Zane."

"Son of a bitch."

"Go call the place, I'll stay here with him, keep him calm."

"Fuck no."

"Well, what do you want me to do with him?"

Zane stared. Both Ty and Barnum were looking at him with their heads cocked. He wasn't even sure he was awake right now. "How tame is he?"

"I don't know. Tame enough that he'd rather hug me than eat me right now, but I don't fucking speak tiger."

"Should we give him food so he won't eat anybody?"

"Zane. Why are you asking me like I know what to do? Sure, go grab a brisket off the grill and we'll see how he likes it."

"Briskets aren't cooked on a grill."

"I'm standing next to a tiger, Zane!"

"I'll go call the sanctuary."

"Thank you."

Zane took a careful step back, giving Barnum one last wary look before turning and calmly walking to the corner of the barn. He couldn't run no matter how much he wanted to. He remembered what Tish had said about playing tag with a tiger.

He was halfway to the house when his father hurried up to him. "Have you seen Sadie?" Harrison demanded.

"What?"

"We called animal control to get their worthless asses out here and got people leaving for safety, but we can't find Sadie!"

Zane went cold. He turned to look back at the barn.

If the tiger didn't have the little girl, then who did?

☙ ★ ☙ ★ ☙

Ty fought the urge to fidget. It wasn't hard, what with Barnum leaning against his leg and demanding contact. He stroked Barnum's cheek, one of the places Tish had told him was safe when handling the tigers. His heart was still racing. Tame circus tiger or not, he was still a fucking tiger and they were not in his enclosure anymore.

The seconds ticked by, and Ty imagined he could feel time expanding as he waited. What the fuck was taking Zane so long?

He looked down at Barnum, and the tiger peered up at him, tongue lolling, his golden eyes full of intelligence and trust. A chill ran down Ty's body and he fought the resulting shiver.

"What's the matter, big man?" Ty asked, maintaining a soothing tone. Barnum made a few chuffing noises, responding to his voice. Ty swallowed against the knot of nerves in his throat and began to sing. The first song that popped into his mind was one he used to sing during his Recon days: "Show Me the Way to Go Home." It was slow and soothing and easy to remember the words to when trying not to panic.

Barnum hefted his body to stand and sniffed the air again. He took a few steps away, and Ty forgot about the song. Then Barnum prowled to the side, beginning to pace.

"Oh please don't eat me," Ty whispered.

Barnum rumbled in response, sniffing the air again. He glanced back at Ty in passing, then stalked off toward the darkness, heading away from the barn.

"Barnum," Ty whispered. He clucked his tongue and made a few hissing noises, but who the hell was he kidding? If the tiger wanted to go, it was going to go. "Come on, buddy, don't leave me. I'll sing a different one," he said as he followed after the big cat. "'Eye of the Tiger'?"

But Barnum paid him no mind, slinking off into the night so quickly and quietly that Ty lost him in a matter of yards.

Ty peered into the darkness, his heart pounding hard. "Everyone's a critic," he grumbled as he backed away from the last spot he'd seen Barnum. It was just too dangerous to track the tiger in the dark, no matter how tame or friendly Barnum seemed to be. Ty needed to get to safety, and then warn the rest of the partygoers.

He continued to back away, turning once he no longer felt eyes tracking him. He made his way to the truck and climbed in, breathing a sigh of relief when he got the door closed behind him.

He found the keys under the brake pedal, where Zane often left them, and got the truck started. He drove right through the yard, not especially surprised to find that the party had dispersed. Harrison had probably taken that precaution and moved the guests inside or sent them home. The bonfire still blazed, sending ashes into the night sky. Torches were lit around the yard, marking the areas intended for the party and keeping bugs at bay. But there was no other sign of life.

Ty pushed down the creepy feeling and headed for the house, parking the truck right at the bottom of the steps. He had been chewed on by enough felines in his lifetime, thank you.

He hopped out of the truck and darted up the steps, then slung open the screen door and didn't relax until it had clicked behind him.

A gun cocked near his ear, and the distinct barrel of a .45 pressed to his temple.

Ty froze.

"Grady?"

Ty risked a sideways look past the barrel of the gun and found Cody standing there.

Cody lowered the gun and smiled. "Sorry."

Ty shook his head, growling but unable to produce a curse word appropriate for the moment. "What the hell are you doing?"

"Sadie's gone missing."

"What?" Ty asked, his heart sinking.

Cody nodded grimly. Ty noticed that he hadn't put his gun away. "They think the tiger nabbed her."

Ty looked from Cody to the gun. "So you thought I was a tiger?"

Cody shook his head. "Stuart said we got trouble in our own house. Can't be too careful."

"Where are the others?"

"I don't know. Party broke up, everyone got scattered looking for Little Bit."

Ty glanced around the quiet house, then back at Cody. "Come with me. I need you to drive me out to that pump house."

Cody nodded and headed out onto the porch. Ty followed, glancing around the yard. The night was silent. No insects sang, no horses whinnied from the barns. None of the animals made a peep.

"Why are we headed back out there?" Cody asked.

"Whatever's under that place, that's what this is about. It's not just stolen tigers. And I think whoever has Sadie might be headed there."

Ty hopped down the steps. The crack of a gunshot tore through the night, and the impact thumped into Ty, stealing his breath and knocking him flat.

Somewhere in the darkness, Barnum the Bengal tiger roared.

# Chapter 10

"**I** don't get how she can just disappear!" Harrison sounded near panicked as they rounded the dark corner of the house and headed for the front yard again.

"She didn't disappear, Dad, Mark's got her! He's running with her!"

Harrison grabbed Zane's arm and whirled him around almost viciously. "You best be damn sure before you say that out loud again."

"Yes, sir," Zane said through gritted teeth. "I have to get back to Ty and let him know what's going on before he and that damn tiger get twitchy."

Harrison nodded.

Zane turned the corner of the house in time to see Ty and Cody hurrying down the front steps. "Ty!" he called out, but his shout was drowned out by the crack of the gunshot. Ty and Cody both fell to the ground, either hit or taking cover. Zane shouted again, drawing his weapon.

Harrison grabbed him and yanked him back just as a shot thumped into the house.

"No!" Zane fought against his dad's hands.

Harrison slammed him against the siding. "You ain't no good to him dead, Z! Get inside."

Zane opened his mouth to respond, but the sudden shatter of glass and a crash from behind the house cut him off. They hit the ground, and a shadow hustled through the trees, the moonlight glinting off a shotgun. The shooters were aiming at the house and at *them*. Bullets glanced off the walls, far too close for comfort.

Harrison clamped down on the back of Zane's neck and wrenched him to his feet. "Get in the house!"

They scrambled for the French doors of Beverly's office.

Zane took the steps three at a time as bullets tore up the façade, splintering the wood and sending flowers spilling from broken pots. He ran for the den and its gun cabinets, trying not to think about the odds outside or the image of Ty falling to the ground that kept replaying in his head. He yanked a case open and grabbed a shotgun and a rifle. They were loaded and ready to go; guns in the Garrett household were meant to be used, not admired for their shiny parts.

"What in the blazing hinges of hell is going on out there!" Harrison took one of the weapons from Zane's hand.

"I have no idea!" Zane loaded up a shotgun and grabbed a handful of extra rounds. "See if you can find the family, get everyone upstairs."

Harrison grabbed him as he was turning away. "Where are you going?"

"Ty's out there," Zane said. He yanked away and ran for the front door.

When he got to the door he hit the marble, staying low as he peered out. Ty was nowhere to be seen. Only a blood smear on the front steps was left of him.

"Ty!" Zane called out. Above the commotion he heard his name called in response. He strained his ears, but instead of Ty, he heard the galloping of horses. In the flickering firelight, he caught silhouettes of horses racing into the night; the entire stock of the C and G had fled from a barn as flames licked at its roof.

Zane's mind flooded with horror at the sudden outburst of violence. Whoever had been working with Stuart didn't trust him not to give them away. They were making a break for it tonight.

Gunfire from the back of the house sounded like it was coming from outside and within. His father was firing back.

Zane picked up his rifle and crawled out the door, intent on finding Ty. "Where the fuck are you?" Zane muttered. He hurried down the steps, staying low. Blood stained the steps, but not as much as he'd feared. Ty may have been able to get up under his own power and find cover.

Zane crouched low and skirted the truck parked in front of the steps, heading for the barn. "Grady!"

"Garrett!"

Zane skidded to a halt and turned. He finally saw Ty, lying under the truck on his back. Zane dove for it, peering underneath with a relieved laugh. "Are you okay?"

"Clipped me. I'm bleeding."

"Come on, let's get inside."

"I can't."

"Ty, come on, quit screwing around," Zane said as he reached under the truck to grip Ty's arm. He pulled, but Ty didn't budge.

Ty met his eyes, the hazel looking a sickly gray in the firelight. "My cast is stuck on the undercarriage."

"That's not funny, Ty."

"You're right, Zane, it's not! Give me your knife."

"I don't have it, it's in my carry-on bag. Where's yours?"

"It's in an evidence bag!"

"Goddammit, Ty!" Zane tried tugging at him again, but Ty cried out and shoved at his hand.

"Go get me a knife!"

Zane handed him the shotgun and ran for the house. There were more gunshots, and the tiger was somewhere, roaring. He didn't have time to be confused, he was just reacting and hoping they could sort out the who and the why later. He ran for the kitchen, but almost toppled over his father as he pushed through the door.

"Dad!"

"Zane!"

Zane was shocked to see all the people in the kitchen—at least twenty, some family, some guests of the party. Annie and Beverly huddled together in the banquette, pale and drawn. Harrison held a shotgun, as did at least five other employees of the ranch. Mark was there, a rifle in his hands and blood at his hairline.

"What are you doing?" Zane asked his dad. "I told you to get upstairs!"

"If we head up, we'll be trapped," Mark said, shouting over the noise.

"Where's Sadie?" Annie screamed.

Zane shook his head, his eyes drawn back to Mark. If Mark wasn't behind it, then who the hell was? His stomach flipped. A blast sounded from the front of the house.

"Ty." Zane grabbed his dad's arm. "Do you have a knife?"

Harrison dug in his pocket and handed Zane his pocketknife. He followed Zane to the front door, where they both stopped and watched in horror as flames licked at the bed of the truck parked in the driveway. Glass broke somewhere in the house. Then another window smashed.

"Molotov cocktails," Zane said. "They're going to set fire to the house."

"I called the sheriff back. They were already halfway to Austin."

"They'll never get here in time." He shoved at his dad. "Go get the others, we have to fight back or we'll be dead. I have to get Ty."

"Where is he?"

"Stuck under the truck."

Zane took the steps two at a time and darted around the truck to dive to the gravel at Ty's side.

"Truck's on fire, Zane," Ty said, sounding urgent but calm.

"I see that, Ty," Zane said through gritted teeth. He handed Ty the knife.

"Watch your six," Ty said, then disappeared further under the truck. When Zane turned and looked up, a 4x4 was thundering toward them. He raised the shotgun in his hands, knowing the birdshot would do nothing to slow down the truck but hoping to hit the driver. The truck skidded to a stop and Joe barreled out of the cab.

Zane lowered the shotgun.

"I saw the fire," Joe stuttered when he realized Zane had almost shot him.

"Got bigger problems than that." Zane knelt back down to peer under the truck.

A bullet hit the door, striking inches from his ear. He hit the dirt. "Jesus!"

Another bullet impacted where his head had been.

"Zane, go!" Ty yelled. "He's in the corral, get inside!"

Zane and Joe scurried around the truck to the other side, putting it between them and the sniper in the corral. Zane looked under the truck to see Ty lying flat, sawing at the jagged piece of his cast that had caught on the undercarriage.

"Come on, Ty."

"It's not exactly easy under here. How close is the fire to the gas tank?"

"Too close. Come on, baby."

Ty yanked at his arm, but his elbow just hit the ground. He couldn't find any leverage to get free, and the knife was small and dull.

"It's not coming free."

"Come on, Ty!"

A shot pinged off the top of the truck.

"Where's Cody?" Ty asked through gritted teeth.

"I don't know."

"We were heading out to look for the cavern under the pump house when the gunfire started. They either shot him or he shot me."

"What?" Joe shouted as he flattened to look under the truck as well.

"Jesus Christ!"

"What cavern?" Joe demanded, his voice going higher.

"Mark's inside, it's not him," Zane told Ty.

"Then it's got to be Cody!" Ty shouted. He yanked at his hand in frustration, to no avail.

Zane reached under the truck to see if he could help, but Ty was too far away. His fingers just barely grazed Ty's shoulder, and no matter how much he stretched, Zane couldn't grasp him. It was his worst fear come to life, watching helplessly as his lover struggled to get free.

"What the hell are you talking about?" Joe demanded.

"Someone's been moving drugs on the ranch," Zane said through gritted teeth.

"And you thought it was Mark?"

"It's not. But whoever it is has Sadie."

"I told you we should have cut this fucking thing off, Zane!" Ty yelled, his voice cracking with frustration.

"I'm sorry!"

There was a scream from inside.

"Go, Zane," Ty urged as he continued sawing at the cast.

Zane was torn between staying there to cover Ty, and going inside to protect his family. He hesitated.

Ty turned his head, his eyes shadowed. "Go, Zane! Go!"

Zane stared at him for a frozen moment, then pushed off the ground and ran for the front door, Joe on his heels. Shots chased them up the steps. Pain seared through his thigh and he stumbled, pitching forward through the door. He rolled across the marble, a streak of blood following him. He grasped at the back of his leg and his hand came away bloody.

Joe kicked the door shut, then knelt with him and began yanking off his belt to staunch the flow of blood.

"Dad!" Zane called out.

"We're okay!" Harrison shouted back from somewhere in the recesses of the house. Several rooms in the middle of the house had no windows. They'd be safe unless the house caught on fire.

Harrison and Mark hurried out of Harrison's study, both carrying a shotgun and a rifle, and Harrison knelt next to Zane as Joe pulled the belt tight around Zane's thigh. Zane shouted in pain, but Joe paid him no mind as he fastened it.

Harrison put his hand on Zane's shoulder. "Where you hit?"

"Leg. I don't know if it's a bullet or a ricochet."

"Where's Grady?" Mark asked as they helped Zane off the floor.

"Stuck under the truck. There's a sniper firing from the corral."

Harrison's grip tightened on Zane's arm. "Where's Cody?"

"We think he's in the corral," Zane said, voice tight.

"What?" Harrison and Mark both cried.

"Hold on, if Ty was with the tiger, and then Cody was with Ty, who has Sadie?" Joe asked. He looked so distraught that his best friend might be behind this that even his mustache seemed to be drooping. His mind was still sharp though, and Zane could see anger and the embers of revenge starting to burn in his normally placid eyes.

Zane shook his head. He had no answer.

The fire in the barn was gaining power, roaring and crackling, and there were men outside shouting over the noise. It was impossible to make out what they were saying.

Zane pulled away from his dad and limped toward a window. He used the barrel of his rifle to push the lace curtain away and peered out. The truck was still on fire, the flames licking ever closer to the gas tank. Whether Ty was still under it or not was anyone's guess. Three men stood in the yard, shouting at the house. Why wasn't Ty firing from under the truck? He had the perfect vantage point.

As the fire grew stronger, it illuminated them. They all wore bandanas and hats to hide their faces, like old-time outlaws robbing a bank. One of them held Sadie in his arms. She had her head buried in his shoulder, grasping his neck for dear life.

Anger flooded Zane so fast and hot that his vision went white. Now he understood why Ty hadn't fired from his position under the truck.

"My baby," Mark whispered. The desperation in his voice tore at Zane's heart.

"Garrett!" Blue Bandana yelled over the sound of the fires burning.

"You recognize them?" Zane asked his father.

Harrison shook his head. "Hard to say."

Zane looked from Sadie to the truck, his heart hammering away. He tried to decide how much time they had before the fire reached the gas tank and it blew, or before it reached the undercarriage and Ty.

"We just want to talk, Harrison!" Red Bandana called out.

"That's what the telephone is for, you bastards!" Harrison shouted through the glass.

Zane grabbed him and yanked him away from the window, but the men outside didn't fire. Zane and the others pressed against the wall, waiting. There was movement outside, scuffling and talking and cursing. Every second they waited was a second Ty didn't have. And then there was Sadie.

A gunshot cracked, then another. Zane jumped with each one. When he glanced out the window, one of the men was at the truck. They'd found Ty. Zane lurched toward the door, but Joe grabbed his shoulder to keep him from going out there. Another shot came from the truck, and then Blue Bandana stood and began pulling on one end of a lasso.

He dragged Ty out from under the truck. He may as well have grabbed a crab by the wrong end, though, because as soon as Ty was free of the undercarriage and sliding across the gravel on his back, he was fighting. He was also yelling at Sadie as the other two Bandanas fought to flatten him. Sadie lifted her head.

"Run!" Ty yelled. He made a gesture with his hand, jabbing at the air with two fingers before he disappeared under the other two men.

Sadie began to squirm, and the man in the black bandana struggled to hold her. She threw herself back like all children were apt to do when they were pitching a fit, going limp and trying to slither out of his arms. When she couldn't get loose, she mimicked the motion Ty had made, poking her little fingers into the pressure point at the man's neck, just as Ty had taught her. Black Bandana let her go and she dropped to the ground.

"Run!" Ty yelled, his voice muffled.

"Come on, baby doll," Mark shouted. "Run, baby!"

Sadie crawled a few yards, then pushed to her feet and darted toward the house.

Mark dropped his gun and ran for the front door, yanking it open and leaping down the front steps in a single bound. In the driveway, Ty lurched to his feet and threw himself into the man with the shotgun, sending the shot wild and forfeiting his chance to get away in favor of covering Sadie's flight.

Mark grabbed her at the front of the burning truck and turned with her, shielding her from the gunfire and whisking her inside. Joe slammed the door behind them. A hail of bullets followed and they all took cover. Mark ducked out of the way with Sadie in his arms. There was more shouting from outside, and Zane knew without having to look that Ty was suffering for the little girl's escape.

Sadie was sobbing. Relief washed over Zane as father and daughter clung to each other. Annie ran from the study and took Sadie out of Mark's arms. They retreated to the relative safety of a windowless room to huddle with Beverly and the stragglers from the party, and Mark crawled back to the window to pick up his gun. They weren't safe yet.

"Hey, Zane!" one of the Bandanas called. "Zane, we got your little boyfriend out here! Get your daddy to come talk or we take it out on his pretty face!"

Zane's breath caught. That meant Ty was still alive.

"At least he's not under the burning truck anymore, right?" Joe whispered.

Zane closed his eyes. His heart was racing and he had to take a few breaths to calm down.

"I'll go out there," Harrison said.

"No. No, I'll go. If it's you they want, they'll need to get through me first," Zane said. He nodded at Mark and Joe. "Cover my ass."

Mark nodded and traded the shotgun in his hands for Zane's rifle. Zane took a deep breath and opened the front door.

The Three Bandanas were in the yard, using the flames from the truck as partial cover. Ty was on his knees in front of Blue Bandana, a shotgun held to the back of his head. His cast was gone, and the side of his face was bloody. In fact, he was bloody almost everywhere. A large stain was spreading at his ribcage where he'd been shot, and more was flowing from his hairline.

Zane had to fight not to rush forward. "What's this about?" he called out, trying to keep his voice even and calm.

"You know how much money you cost us?"

Zane shook his head, gritting his teeth as he stared at Ty.

"You found our stash, Zane. Ty told me. You were going to go expose us."

"I don't know what you're talking about," Zane called.

"Bullshit! We were supposed to have it all moved by now, but with all this attention we couldn't risk it. We got nothing to show for it! The money and those damn cats were all supposed to be in Mexico tomorrow."

Zane narrowed his eyes. The voice was familiar. "Cody?" he said with a sinking feeling, realizing he hadn't truly believed it until now.

Cody reached up and yanked the blue bandana down. The others followed suit. Ronnie, another of Harrison's ranch hands who'd ridden to the pump house with them, was behind the red bandana. Zane's knees went weak when his cousin Jamie pulled the black bandana off his face.

"It was you?" he asked, barely able to get the words out. "Why?"

"You said yourself, there were more than four," Cody said with a sneer.

Zane was breathless with shock and his mind was racing. It had been about drugs all along, but why? Like Ty said days ago, they were too far from the normal routes for it to make sense. Was this the first wave of some sort of cartel expansion? A chess move in a game being played hundreds of miles away? And what the hell did big cats have to do with any of it?

"Guys... you're looking at a hell of lot more time if you go through with this than you would for selling drugs or poaching exotic animals."

Cody shook his head. "You don't understand, Zane! We got us a deal down in Laredo. He wants his money, and he wants his goddamned tigers. We don't deliver, we're dead men. He'll think we swindled him."

"You'll get life for this. Attempted murder. Hell, kidnapping, assault on a federal agent."

"He'll kill us anyway!" Cody shouted, and he worked the action on the shotgun. Ty squeezed his eyes closed at the sound.

The rage and terror bubbled up and Zane snarled. "You hurt him, and *I'll* kill you."

"You can try it, Zane."

"Ty and I can help you get out of this. This isn't the way. Do you have any idea how many people are in this house?"

Cody's eyes flickered to the house and he shook his head. "We don't want no one to come to harm, that's why we want to talk."

Zane eyes were drawn back to Ty. All color had drained from his face. He was losing too much blood. The only thing holding him upright was the lasso around his neck, but he raised his head and met Zane's eyes.

"What do you want?" Zane asked Cody.

"We want the money," Jamie called out. "What Uncle Harry's got in that big safe of his. It's the only way we can get out from under the man we owe. Get Uncle Harry out here or Cody blows Ty's brains out."

Zane swallowed hard and met Ty's eyes once more. It didn't even take a moment's thought. He half-turned toward the door, but Harrison stepped out and onto the porch with him.

"Boys," Harrison called in a deep voice that carried well over the yard. "This ain't the way to go about this."

"Your meddling is going to cost us our lives," Ronnie shouted.

"They'd have gotten away with it too!" Ty said, his words almost slurred and sounding half-delirious. "If it hadn't been for you meddling kids."

Cody put his boot on Ty's back and then jerked on the lasso. Ty arched, reaching up to grasp the rope before it could cut off his air.

"Shut your damn mouth!"

"Give us the money to pay off what we owe," Jamie told Harrison. "We disappear. Stuart and his boys take the fall for the poaching and the drugs. Nobody gets hurt. If you don't, we burn it to the ground."

Zane eyed his father. Harrison glanced at him, meeting his eyes. It seemed a clear-cut decision. It was only money, after all. Money for the lives inside the house was simple.

Harrison nodded at the men in the yard. "I say yes, you know you can push me around. You'll keep coming back and taking and threatening until I'm dead and buried and got nothing but disgrace to my name. I don't need money. But I ain't giving you my pride."

"Dad," Zane whispered, both impressed with his father and terrified that they were going to shoot his lover in the head as he watched.

"It's all right, Zane," he whispered, and then, to the men outside, "You boys burn down the house, you only hurt yourselves. My money'll burn down with it, and then what will you do?"

"Uncle Harry, think about this!" Jamie shouted.

"I ain't your uncle, boy!"

"That's it," Cody snarled. He raised the barrel to the back of Ty's head.

"No!" Zane shouted, panic and rage blinding him as he lunged for the stairs. Harrison grabbed him.

Glass broke as Mark took advantage of the distraction to bust the window with the butt of his rifle.

Ty jerked his head to the side and rolled, kicking the barrel of the shotgun and knocking it aside. It went off as Ty tackled Cody to the ground. Ten feet away, Jamie was knocked to his back, screaming and bloody.

Ronnie raised his gun and Harrison pulled Zane back inside as the man fired at them. The birdshot didn't even reach the porch at that distance. Harrison slammed the front door as Ronnie switched guns.

Mark and Joe took aim and fired in return, trying to cover Ty as he wrestled with Cody in the yard and trying to deter Ronnie from peppering the house with his .45.

"Dad, go get the girls and get to your truck!" Mark shouted between shots. "Get everyone out the back!"

Harrison looked to Zane, and Zane nodded. Harrison moved away to retrieve Beverly, Annie, and Sadie and get them to safety. Zane peered around the windowsill to see how Ty was faring. He and Cody were scuffling in the dirt, but despite the covering fire, Ronnie was wading in. Ty was an injured man with one good arm and a rope already around his neck, fighting two healthy men. And he was losing. Badly.

Zane took the rifle Harrison had readied and took aim, standing above Mark and looking through the sights at Ronnie as the big man grabbed Ty and held him. Cody pulled a knife from a sheath at his thigh.

Zane let out a breath and pulled the trigger. Ty jerked in Ronnie's arms and turned both their bodies. The bullet went through Ronnie's arm and he howled, and Ty cried out too as they both hit the ground.

Cody dove to the gravel and all three men were out of sight.

"Did you just shoot your boyfriend?" Mark cried.

"Fuck!"

Joe and Mark both grabbed an extra gun and darted for the door, on Zane's heels. Harrison had returned and followed them onto the porch. They were just in time to see Cody get to his feet and grab up a revolver from the grass. He pointed it down at Ty, who was writhing in the dirt, holding his arm where Zane's shot had hit him.

Zane raised his rifle.

The others all cried out before Zane could pull the trigger. He caught a flash of orange out of the corner of his eye: Barnum the Bengal tiger speeding across the yard toward Ty and the others.

"Ty!"

Ty rolled and saw the tiger coming. He curled into a ball as Barnum rushed him. The tiger leapt over him, claws extended, graceful body long and lean as he attacked. Cody screamed and fired his gun, but the tiger hit him at full force, sending him skidding through the gravel a solid ten feet away.

Claws slashed and teeth sank into flesh. Cody screamed, a bloodcurdling sound that Zane didn't think he'd soon be forgetting.

Zane sprinted across the yard toward Ty, who was still curled in a ball with his arms covering his head. He grabbed Ty's arm and yanked him to his feet.

Ty wavered, but seemed to rally as Zane wrapped his arm around him. "Somebody shot me, Zane."

Zane nodded and pulled the rope off Ty's neck. He shoved him toward the porch, then bent to check Ronnie's pulse. The man was alive, but he wasn't moving. Zane gathered all his weapons, then left him to lie there, unconscious and defenseless, at the mercy of the enraged tiger.

He turned to follow his partner, but Ty was rooted to the spot, watching Barnum savage the ranch hand who had tried to kill him. Zane couldn't bring himself to look.

"Come on, Ty," Zane whispered. He tugged at Ty's arm.

Ty shook his head, then he gave a short whistle. "Barnum!"

The tiger jerked his head up and growled. Ty and Zane both staggered back as if it had been a warning. Ty stopped his retreat, though, and said the tiger's name again with a little more authority. Zane couldn't help but glance sideways at the animal. Barnum had Cody's hand in his mouth, and the arm was obviously broken and possibly beyond repair. There were gashes and punctures all over his body, but nothing like the damage the tiger could have done.

"Easy now. Come on," Ty said to the tiger, and after a moment Barnum released Cody's hand and began to prowl toward Ty. Zane started backing away.

Ty held his hand out, breathing out like he was trying to calm himself. His hand was trembling. Barnum approached and nosed his bloody muzzle against Ty's palm. Ty carefully scratched under his chin "That's twice you saved me. Good boy."

Barnum chuffed and then pushed onto his back feet, putting one huge paw on each of Ty's shoulders. Ty couldn't take the weight of the 600 pound tiger and they both toppled to the ground. Barnum sat down with a huff and rubbed his face against Ty's as Ty gasped for air. Then he wrapped his paw around Ty's head and began licking Ty's wounded face. Ty didn't struggle, merely closed his eyes and held his breath.

"Ty?" Zane whispered.

"Just go get someone with a tranquilizer gun please," Ty said in a soothing, almost sing-song voice. "Slowly."

Zane backed away, watching in fascination as the tiger lay down in the grass and rested his chin on Ty's stomach. Mark had already retrieved Annie, and she was readying her tranquilizer gun even as Zane reached the porch.

They tossed out the meat that had been thawing for the BBQ to lure Barnum away from Ty, and as soon as Ty was out of his reach, Annie shot the dart. They had to wait only a minute or two before the tiger was out.

Ty sat down beside him and laid a hand on his head as everyone else surveyed the damage. Harrison's men and several of the party guests who'd been caught in the house rushed to the barn to try to contain the fire. Minutes later, they could hear the police cars and fire trucks approaching, sirens blazing. Tish and several interns from the Roaring Springs Sanctuary arrived ten minutes after the police to take possession of Barnum and return him to the sanctuary.

Zane thought Ty might cry as they loaded Barnum into the truck.

"Will they have to put him down since he attacked someone?" Ty asked the sheriff as the Roaring Springs truck ambled down the drive.

The sheriff glanced at Cody's ravaged body and shook his head. "Looks like he got hit by a truck to me. Ain't that what happened, son?"

Ty stared at him, eyes wide. Then he nodded. "Yes, sir."

"That's right. A very angry truck," the sheriff drawled as he walked away.

The ambulance arrived a full twenty minutes after it had been called. By then, Cody had lost a good deal of blood and gone into shock. Annie refused to treat him, saying that the Hippocratic oath didn't extend to vets or to people who shot guns at her baby girl.

Zane couldn't blame her.

Ronnie and Cody would both live, though Cody would likely lose an arm and a few non-essential organs. Jamie had bled out from the shotgun blast to the chest, dying long before help could get to him. Zane suffered a pang of remorse over the death of his cousin, but he didn't waste much effort in mourning a man who'd been willing to kill them all just for money.

The man in Laredo, and the question of why the drug trade had veered so far off its course, were both large problems. They weren't Zane's problems, though, and even if he wanted to be involved, it wasn't his jurisdiction.

Joe was horrified and crushed by the whole affair. Cody had been his best friend. Zane felt sorry for him, even though he was more relieved to find that Joe'd had nothing to do with any of it.

Beverly sat on the porch swing with a shawl wrapped around her shoulders, staring. They had checked her for shock and deemed her in good health, then left her to sit there.

Zane eased into the seat beside her, watching the commotion in the yard in silence for a few seconds. Ty was sitting on the porch steps, his shirt gone, his arm in a sling, and his ribs patched up until they could get him to the hospital. Mark and Joe flanked him. The three of them appeared to simply be sitting there in dazed silence. Sadie perched between Ty and Mark, babbling as they nodded in response. She wasn't at all fazed, and she was recounting the events of the night as if it'd been a movie she'd watched rather than a terrifying experience she had lived through.

Zane knew one thing for damn sure: he would never make fun of Ty again for teaching a toddler how to jab a pressure point.

Annie and Harrison stood with the sheriff, relating what had happened, and many of the party guests had filtered back toward the house to tell their versions as well. The local press had not been allowed onto the property, but Zane knew they would all be loitering down at the gate. It wouldn't be long before they got the story.

Beverly turned her head and Zane met her gaze. It was excruciating to look into her eyes and see nothing there but that emotionless mask hiding what she truly thought and felt. Zane never intended to inflict that kind of pain on Ty again.

"I don't know what to say," she whispered.

"How about 'good job'? Or 'thank you'? How about telling me Ty's a good man and you're happy for me?"

Beverly stared for long minutes. Zane tried to find some hint of emotion in her icy blue eyes, but there was nothing there. She nodded curtly and looked away, holding her chin high, stubborn and proper as ever.

Zane sighed as the cold settled in his chest. Beverly had never known anything but ranches. Like frontierswomen before her, protecting the homestead was first and foremost, even if it meant sacrificing the things they loved. She was still doing that, protecting her ranch and her family's legacy. She had simply lost sight of what her family meant.

He looked down at the bandage wrapped around his thigh. The bullet had gone straight through, narrowly missing an artery. He'd been lucky and would only be limping for a while. Ty had fared much worse, all for the sake of Zane's family.

He nodded, looking over at Beverly one last time. "Good-bye, Mother," he murmured before standing and limping away.

Ty and Zane spent most of Sunday night, Monday, and the majority of Tuesday in the hospital. Each of them had several bags of IV fluids pumped into them, and when Zane heard a commotion down the hall, he knew that someone had just ordered a new cast put on Ty's hand. Since Ty had lost a lot of blood and had nowhere to run, Zane was fairly certain he'd wind up in another cast.

Wednesday was almost worse than the hospital—from which Ty had checked himself out early, against medical advice—spent filling out official statements. Ty cursed and muttered the entire time they sat in the barely air-conditioned trailer that served as the sheriff's outpost for the ranch community. The sheriff had offered to come to them, but Zane knew Ty wouldn't make a very credible witness while still confined to a hospital bed.

After some intense questioning, one of the Cactus Creek hands had revealed where the stolen tigers were being kept. Tish and her people had already transported the other three tigers back to their homes. Barnum had been deemed a hero by several local news stations, and Ty and Zane were both in a hurry to get out of town before the national press caught wind of the story.

The sheriff's deputies had gone with Harrison to the pump house, and after a little searching they'd found an entrance to the underground system of caverns carved in the limestone. The river that had been the source of the spring was still trickling; it had merely dug deeper as it beat through the soft stone.

Within the caverns, they found hundreds of thousands of dollars' worth of cocaine.

Zane knew Laredo was controlled by the Gulf cartel, the same cartel that had dealings with Colombia, Venezuela, and Brazil. The tenuous connection to his work in Miami was frightening, as was the mystery of why that much product had been shipped so far into the Hill Country. He left the sheriff and the San Antonio field office with enough information to watch over the connection in case it wasn't a coincidence.

When they were finally able to leave the sheriff's office, all that was left for them to do was tell Zane's family good-bye and go home.

# Chapter 11

Harrison dismounted and wrapped his horse's lead around the deck railing, then pulled a large manila envelope out of the saddlebag before he walked across the stone pavers toward the guesthouse. Zane chewed on the inside of his lip as he watched from the kitchen window.

Beverly hadn't changed her mind after the attack on the ranch, too stubborn and too proud to admit that she might have been wrong. Or the alternative: she didn't think she was wrong at all. If Harrison supported Beverly's decision to write him out of the will and essentially out of the family . . . Zane shook himself, not even able to think about it.

"Hey," Harrison said, voice gruff.

"Hey." Zane's wounded thigh pulled as he held himself straight and tall.

Harrison shook his head and reached out to pat Zane's shoulder. "Relax, son," he said.

Zane thought he might drop in relief right there. He swallowed hard and nodded, stepping back to let Harrison into the house.

Harrison walked to the kitchen table and dropped the envelope onto it. "You two doing okay?"

Zane glanced up the stairs to the loft. "Yeah. Ty hit the bed and fell asleep before I could make him take his boots off. He lost a lot of blood."

Harrison pursed his lips, which made his mustache twitch. Zane smiled fondly. "Got a little time?" Harrison asked.

"We've got another hour or so until we need to go to catch the plane."

"I'm glad I came right over, then. Sit down, Z. We need to talk."

The apprehension hit Zane again like a hammer. He edged into one of the chairs, babying his leg.

Harrison sat opposite him, drumming his fingers on the tabletop. "I'm proud of you, son. What you did was damned brave."

The words warmed Zane to his toes. "I could say the same of you. I never realized how lucky I was to have you as a role model."

Harrison raised an eyebrow, and his mustache twitched again.

Zane grinned. "Thank you for teaching me how to stand my ground, Dad."

"Garretts got iron in their spines. You remember that."

Zane nodded.

"What your mother's done is a terrible thing, Z, and I won't excuse her for it." He sighed and shook his head. "Not that it matters much to her what I think."

"Dad, what happened to her?"

"She's always been a person who saw things in black and white, Z. Either it's good for business, or it ain't. You must remember what that felt like."

Pain shot through Zane's chest. He did remember. It had been a cold world. The only people who'd ever been able to see through his own icy exterior had been Becky and Ty. Was his father able to do the same with his mother?

"Are you happy, Dad?"

"I always have been."

"But—"

"The love of my life is my ranch, Zane. It's all I need to be happy. Beverly runs the money side of it and she's good at it. I run the people side. Horses run themselves."

Zane nodded, finally seeing a glimpse of the real marriage between the two of them. He didn't understand it, but he believed his dad when he said he was happy. He stared out the glass wall over the rolling hills, seeing nothing but blurry grass and trying to ignore the awful, hollow feeling in his chest.

"I don't put my nose into her side of the business, and she leaves her opinions out of mine. But this is one decision she won't be making alone. I won't allow it to tear my family to pieces."

Zane blinked at him in shock.

"If she wants to take the Carter name and all that goes with it from you, she can." He reached out and clasped Zane's shoulder. "But you'll *always* be a Garrett. Nothing she does or says can ever change that."

Zane nodded, blinking against the stinging in his eyes.

"Now, when you were born, your granddaddy set up the Garrett Ranch in a revocable living trust," Harrison said, his grip on Zane's shoulder loosening. "I'm the successor trustee, so I've run the Garrett Ranch right along with the Carter Ranch ever since your granddaddy passed. But they're still two completely separate entities."

Zane frowned. "So you own the Garrett Ranch separate from the Carter Ranch?"

A smile played around the corners of Harrison's mouth. "No, Zane. *You* own the Garrett Ranch."

Zane stared at Harrison, his mind gone blank. "What?"

"You own it. You're the beneficiary of the trust."

Zane shook himself. "That's not possible. There would have been paperwork."

"Oh there is, and there has been since you were a baby. Trust takes care of itself," Harrison said as he pushed the envelope under Zane's hand.

"I own... *own* half the ranch?"

"The Garrett half. The Carter half was originally Garrett land, deeded to the Carters when we married as a dowry. Your mother inherited it and it folded back into the Garrett Ranch. Now, if something like, say, divorce papers got filed, the Carter half would revert back into the Garrett name, and that half is in my name alone. Beverly would walk away with nothing."

Zane gaped, unable to say anything.

Harrison smirked. "We Garretts, we may be a lot of things, but we ain't stupid."

"Jesus, Dad."

"Now, Beverly knows all that, and she knows if she raises a hand against you, or speaks against Ty as long as you're with him, I got no need for her."

"So... I own the Garrett half, and you own the Carter half?"

"That's right. Meaning, one day, you'll own the whole thing."

Zane opened his mouth to speak, but failed. He'd never had any inkling the Garrett half of the ranch was the ranch in power. His mother always ruled the roost as if her family's money fed it. It made sense now, all those years of her heavy-handed ways; she was compensating for having no monetary importance in the alliance of the families.

Harrison's mellow temperament made it easy for her to control things, and her savvy business sense had made it a good arrangement.

Now, though, Harrison was flexing his muscle. And it was a lot of muscle.

"Dad," Zane whispered. He shook his head.

"Your granddaddy wanted you to have it, wanted you to know you had a place, no matter what."

"What about Annie?"

"He left a significant cash inheritance for her. And I'll do the same when I pass. She and Mark used it to set up her vet business. But the ranch follows the Garrett name."

"Why didn't you tell me?"

Harrison sighed and leaned back in the chair. "I wanted you to live the life *you* wanted, Z. Texas held more bad memories for you than good. Becky was gone, Beverly wouldn't leave you alone, and I knew *here* was the last place you wanted to be. But if you'd found out, you would have dropped it all and come back here, no matter how miserable it made you in the end, simply because it was your granddaddy's doing."

Zane inhaled sharply, trying to swallow down the swell of emotion. "Yeah. You're probably right."

"Well. Now you know. The Garrett Ranch, and the Garrett name, are yours to do with what you will. The envelope's got copies of all the legal paperwork, banking information and so on, but there's really nothing you have to do. Beverly and I got it all set up to sustain itself and then some. I just need a few new hands, is all. Just like Cody."

Zane laughed in surprise at his father's rueful words.

Harrison winced. "Too soon?"

"Probably."

"Ah, well. Three-quarters of profits are folded back into operations, the other quarter splits into three accounts: one for Annie, one for Sadie, and one for you to do whatever you want with."

They sat in silence for long minutes while Zane tried to let it sink in.

"What about you, Dad?" he finally asked.

"What about me?"

"If the Garrett Ranch is mine, and Mother is . . . what do you have?" Zane was sure there were more questions to ask, but that one loomed large.

Harrison waved a hand. "What do I need when I'm running the place anyway? I got a son and daughter who love me. I got a grandbaby whose eyelashes are going to take over the world someday. And I have my horses." He leaned forward and covered Zane's hand with his own. "Don't worry about me, Z."

Zane laughed despite himself. "And I thought I was a stubborn ass."

"You come by it honest." Harrison sighed and patted Zane's hand a couple times, and then glanced up at the loft. Zane could hear the topic change coming a mile away. Harrison met his eyes and smiled. "You hang onto him with everything you've got. Not every man gets a second chance."

Zane eyes strayed to the loft, where Ty probably still lay sprawled on the bed. Zane smiled as the warmth of contentment spread through him. "I know."

They lucked into plane tickets that took a short hop from Austin to Houston, and then carried on in a single leg to Charleston, West Virginia. Zane even upgraded himself and Ty into first class.

They both looked like they'd been dragged behind a tractor, and trudging through the airport in Houston didn't help either of them. As they sat waiting for the connection, they watched the local news about the heroic tiger outside of Austin and sank lower in their seats. After the news story was over, the man beside Ty joked about his bandages, asking him if he'd been mauled by a tiger too.

Ty managed a smile as the stranger chuckled, then gave Zane a look that said if they didn't move he was going to end up with blood on his hands.

The rest of the flight home was uneventful. It was dark and quiet as Zane drove up the last mountain road before they got to the Grady's winding driveway.

Ty kept glancing over at him, as if he wanted to ask if he was okay but already knew the answer. He gave Zane directions instead. Zane pulled the rental beside the old truck in the gravel driveway and turned off the car. They sat in the darkness, the engine clicking as the silence settled over them.

Ty cleared his throat. "Should we tell them about the shooting and violence and tigers, or just stick to the basics?"

Zane rubbed his thigh. He could feel bruises and strained muscles all over his body, little bangs and cuts that you never noticed when you were scrambling for dear life. Ty looked and probably felt even worse. Zane sighed and pointed at Ty's brand new cast and the sling he now wore because of the gunshot to his shoulder. "They'll figure it out anyway."

"Alrighty," Ty said. He unbuckled, but stopped and glanced at Zane again before getting out of the car. "Tell me something, Zane."

Zane stared at him in the darkness, wallowing in the relief of simply being with Ty. "Anything."

"Was it you or Mark who shot me?"

Zane bit his lip, trying not to smile. "Totally Mark."

Ty narrowed his eyes. Then he smiled and leaned over for a quick kiss. Zane couldn't help but laugh. He had a feeling Ty knew he was lying. It was one lie he didn't mind paying for later.

Ty lingered over the kiss for another moment, then pressed their foreheads together. Calm settled over Zane, and then Ty pulled away and slid out of the car. As soon as the car door shut, the porch light came on and the front door of the house opened.

Zane waited for the anxiety to strike, but it never came. He was happy to be here, and the relief was overwhelming. Even the uneasiness between himself and Earl didn't register as important anymore.

He opened the door to climb out of the car, stifling a groan as the stitches in his thigh pulled.

Earl stood on the top step. "You boys look like something the cat dragged in."

"The cat jokes lost their luster a while ago, Dad."

"Not 'round here they didn't."

"Wait 'til he hears about the tiger," Zane muttered.

Ty laughed, not even trying to stop himself. Zane grinned, falling victim to Ty's infectious laughter and beginning to chuckle. Suddenly, it all seemed funny.

Ty was still snickering as he trudged up the steps. Earl offered his hand to Ty in greeting, but Ty bypassed it and hugged his father instead. Earl looked shocked for a moment, but he hastily returned it, gingerly patting Ty on the back at first, and then truly embracing his son.

Zane merely smiled as he watched. Mara came out just as Ty let Earl go, and she shouldered past Earl and pulled Ty into another hug. Ty gave a pitiful cry as she grabbed his arm.

"Oh my good gracious, what happened?" She took Ty's face in her hands, then turned her sharp eyes to Zane. "You too! What did you do to yourselves?"

"Just a little scuffle," Zane said as he dropped his bag on the front step and turned back to the car for Ty's.

"Zane Garrett, you get back here and give me a hug!" Mara called after him. "Earl, get their bags."

Zane spun in place and returned to the porch, a little bemused by how he reacted to her orders without thinking. "We're fine," he said as she pulled him down into a tight hug. It was still awkward for him, but he was beginning to realize just how special it was.

"Both of you are liars," Mara grumbled, though her voice was affectionate. "Come on in and tell us what happened. We wasn't expecting you back." She turned and led them into the house, where they could smell something with cinnamon cooking. Mara hooked her arms through both of theirs and dragged them into the house.

The smell of cinnamon was stronger in the kitchen. Mara pointed them toward the table and then sat across from them. "What happened in Texas?"

Zane met Ty's eyes, wondering what Ty wanted to tell them. Zane wanted to tell them every word of it. He wanted to speak it to someone who would understand and give him a hug to make it better.

"Well," Ty started out, glancing at Zane and then looking at his mother carefully. Zane could see his gears turning. "There were guns. And tigers. And horses, Ma, the horses were *horrible*. And basically, people wanted to kill us. Well, not us specifically, but—"

"All right!" Mara interrupted, waving her hand at Ty. She turned to Zane and pointed her finger at him. "He's too full of bologna. You tell me."

Zane released a sigh and smiled. Chester ambled in and took a seat, looking them both over but not commenting on their injuries. Earl joined them, and they gathered around the table as Zane related the entire story from beginning to end.

When he was done, it was nearing dusk. Mara stared at Zane for a long moment, then shifted her eyes to Ty suspiciously.

"And you thought I was lying," Ty said, clearly satisfied. He pointed at the breadbox and stood. "Is that cinnamon bread? Is it warm?"

He turned toward the counter and Mara started fussing at him not to touch anything in her kitchen, leaving Zane at the table without further questioning. Surprised and grateful, Zane let out a long, slow breath and relaxed back in his chair as he watched mother and son verbally spar.

Earl's hand came to rest on Zane's shoulder, drawing his attention. Zane tensed as he turned to look at him, expecting the worst.

"You okay, boy?" Earl asked softly.

Zane blinked rapidly to cover the surprise and gave a curt nod. Then he shook his head. "No, sir."

Earl nodded and gave his shoulder a brief squeeze. "You will be."

He left it at that, and Zane found the words and his simple delivery oddly comforting.

He sat back and observed the Gradys, finding it soothing. Eventually Chester shambled off to bed, and Earl and Ty left the kitchen under the auspices of checking the roof they'd rebuilt.

Zane found himself alone with Mara. She sat across from him and narrowed her eyes before talking. "Now I know Ty ain't exactly diligent about it, so I'm telling you. You need to know I expect certain things from my boys."

Zane raised an eyebrow. He wasn't certain he could stand another lecture from a disapproving mother. "Okay."

"We do Christmas, Thanksgiving, and sunrise service at Easter. If you have to go to Texas for some of those, that's just fine, but I expect a phone call. Chester's birthday is in April, and do not bring him anything that fires projectiles or is sharp. Or, God forbid, sharp projectiles. Understand? Because Ty does it every year."

Zane blinked. He wasn't quite sure where this was going, or why she was telling him instead of scolding Ty about it. "Yes, ma'am."

"Okay then." She nodded and sat back. "Now, there's supposed to be a cold snap coming, so be a doll and go out back and get some firewood for me, would you?"

"Yes, ma'am," Zane said, bemused.

He pushed open the creaky screen door and stepped outside into the cool night, lit by a half moon and a ton of stars above him. He limped to the woodpile and looked up at the sky to let it sink in that Mara meant it when she'd said "my boys." Including him.

It was more than he had any right to hope for, but he realized that deep down, he'd wanted to come here for exactly that reason.

A soft whistle from above cut into his thoughts, and when he looked up from the woodpile to investigate, he saw Ty and Earl both sitting on the new roof of the outbuilding, legs dangling over the edge. They were sharing one of Ty's cigars. And they were laughing at him.

"She sent you out for firewood?" Ty called, incredulous.

"She said there was a cold snap coming."

Ty's infectious laughter rang out in the night, accompanied by Earl's deeper chuckling. "Zane! It's July!"

"But it's the mountains!"

"It's still July!"

Zane shrugged and waved them off, resisting the urge to gesture rudely. He realized what Mara was doing: distracting him while making him feel like part of the family instead of a guest. It had worked.

Earl still chuckled as he got to his feet. He began to slide along the new roof, heading toward the hill and the precarious way down. His voice carried in the night. "She thinks I'm building a fire in the middle of July, she's off her rocker."

Ty remained on the edge of the roof. Zane balanced the small stack of wood on his hip and walked up to him, able to return his lover's smile without any added weight to his heart. Zane's home was with Ty, even if he was sitting on a rickety tin roof framed by the smoky light of a summer moon.

"How'd you get up there?" Zane asked.

"Either stupidity or codeine, I'm not sure," Ty answered amidst a blue ring of smoke.

"Should I call you Juliet or Rapunzel?"

"That which we call a rose." The genteel words were so unexpected, uttered in Ty's low, gravelly voice, Zane couldn't help the shiver that ran through him. Ty leaned forward and smirked. "Are you ready to go home, my love?"

Zane bit his lip and nodded. "I'm ready for anything."

Ty's grin was slow and mischievous. "I certainly hope so."

When Ty pushed through the door of their row house, the first thing he did was make the hissing noise to call for Smith and Wesson.

Zane shook his head. He would just have to come to terms with the fact that he would always play second fiddle to killer felines.

"Oh God, it's good to be home," Ty said with a groan as he eased himself onto the couch and sprawled. Zane sat next to him with a sigh. They were both so banged up it was nearly impossible to do anything but lean against each other. Ty pressed his lips to Zane's temple. "You want to talk about it?"

Zane stared at the room around them. They'd already made so many memories here, some of them stored in photos and trinkets, others only residing in Zane's mind. It was a life he'd never expected to have, colorful and easy and bright. He shook his head. "I just keep wondering . . . would I have been like her? If Becky hadn't died, if you hadn't . . ."

"Zane."

"Would I have turned into her, Ty? Would that have been me?"

Ty wrapped his arm around Zane's shoulders and ran his fingers through his hair. "I don't know, Zane. There are . . . there are so many paths in life. Some we choose, and some are chosen for us. We walk our paths without looking down and that's the life we lead. The only things you'll get from guessing where another path would have gone are questions you can't answer and heartache you can't ever soothe."

Zane met Ty's eyes, gazing at him as a sense of calm seeped into his bones. He smiled. "You're like a damn walking fortune cookie, you know that?"

Ty smiled, and Zane kissed him. He was right; it was good to be home.

Ty broke the kiss with a gasp when it got too heated for his injuries. He hummed and cocked his head. "Do you hear the cats?"

"No, actually."

Ty sat up and called for Smith and Wesson again, then got up and headed for the stairs, looking up and frowning. Usually when the door opened, the cats came running. If it was Ty, they would swarm his legs, rubbing against him, purring so loudly they seemed to vibrate the floor. If it was Zane, they would both sit down to stare at him disapprovingly. They would watch him as he moved around the house, growling or hissing if he came too close to one of Ty's things, and they wouldn't leave him unattended until Ty got home.

It was odd that they hadn't come when Ty'd called the first time. Even more so that they'd allowed Zane to cuddle with Ty on the couch for that long without trying to bleed him dry.

Ty headed for the basement door, but he stopped short when he passed the kitchen counter. He picked up a manila envelope and his breath caught.

"What is it?" Zane asked. He stood and followed. A sense of dread settled in the pit of his stomach as he watched Ty's expression fall.

Ty shook his head and cleared his throat. "It's from Cross. He says thanks for watching his boys. He came and got them." Ty pressed his lips together hard as he read the rest of the note.

"Oh, Ty," Zane said as he moved closer. He put his arm around Ty's shoulder and hugged him. He had dreaded this day, knowing it would break Ty's heart when those stupid, scheming, evil cats were gone.

Ty nodded, still looking at the note on the envelope. Zane thought he might be fighting back tears. First, he'd had to leave Barnum behind, and now Smith and Wesson were gone too.

"What's inside?" Zane whispered.

Ty shook his head and handed the package to Zane. Zane squeezed his shoulder before taking it and reading the rest. Cross's note was longer than the original he'd scribbled when he'd left Smith and Wesson and a bowl of cat food in Ty's kitchen. The prose was odd and stilted, but it didn't strike Zane as unusual for Julian Cross. That was the way the man spoke. He'd thanked them for treating the cats well, wished them both the best in life, and apologized for taking so long. He ended by saying, "Nice car."

Zane looked out the window of the back door, frowning. "Nice car," he said, beginning to smile. His father had made good on his promise to have the Mustang delivered to Baltimore. That would ease some of Ty's distress.

He opened the package from Cross and slid the contents onto the counter. A picture frame slid out. It matched the frames on Ty's walls perfectly, down to the color and style of the matting. In it was a photograph of the two massive orange cats, green eyes staring at the camera like they could burn a hole through the lens.

Ty reached for the picture. He *was* close to tears, but he was smiling too.

There was more in the package, and Zane dumped the rest out. Several heavy metal emblems slid onto the counter. Ty picked one up, turning it over. They were classic Mustang emblems, the patina and weight marking them as originals and not recasts.

Ty began to laugh, shaking his head. "Bastard," he said, almost fondly. "Somewhere there's a Shelby owner who is very pissed off right now."

Zane reached under Ty's chin to lift his head and meet his eyes. "I'm sorry about Smith and Wesson."

Ty gave him a sad smile and nodded. "I knew he'd come get them eventually. I'm sorry your mom's a raging bitch."

Zane shrugged. "We all have our little problems."

Ty snorted and stepped closer, resting his chin on Zane's shoulder with a sniff.

Zane hugged him tight. "I have something that might make you feel better."

Ty turned his face into Zane's neck and inhaled deeply. "Does it involve you in a Stetson?"

"That too." Zane moved away, heading for the bags they'd dropped at the door. He rummaged through his laptop case and came out with a thick plastic protective sleeve. He couldn't help but grin when he handed it to Ty.

Ty took it warily. He'd no doubt been expecting something fun like glow-in-the-dark spurs or a stolen lasso. He popped the sleeve open and pulled the contents out without asking any questions. As soon as he saw the picture, he began to laugh.

Zane grinned wider. Before they'd left Texas, Tish had sent it to the house as a thank-you and Harrison had brought it to Zane along with the legal papers. It was a picture taken by one of the Roaring Springs interns when Ty had visited the second time. In the photo, he stood inside Barnum and Bailey's enclosure, and all that could be seen was the side of his face and his broad shoulders, his stance wide to hold the weight of the tiger. Barnum was standing on both feet, hugging him. The tiger's massive paws held onto Ty's back and his head rested on Ty's shoulder. His floppy ear lay against Ty's hair.

Zane had laughed and laughed when he'd seen the photo, and he hadn't been able to resist making a call to the sanctuary.

Ty looked at the picture for a long time, a melancholy smile on his face, before he lifted it to look at the papers underneath. He frowned before looking back up at Zane, mouth open.

"You adopted Barnum?"

"And Bailey."

"Zane!" Ty lunged at him and gave him a ferocious one-armed hug, forcing him to stumble back.

"Thank you," Ty whispered against his ear.

"Anything you love that much . . . it's worth any price."

Ty stepped back, his eyes shining. "I love you."

Zane smiled, and then rolled his eyes as Ty practically vibrated in front of him. "Okay, go hang up your kitty pictures and pet your car."

"Thank you!" Ty said in an excited rush as he bounced away.

Zane watched his lover go, the smile still playing at his lips. He shook his head and laughed. Life with Ty. He was in for one hell of a wild ride.

# Acknowledgments

I would like to acknowledge the staff and volunteers at the International Exotic Animal Sanctuary in Boyd, Texas. They do amazing work to provide a permanent sanctuary for big cats that have been abused, abandoned, neglected, or saved from dangerous situations, and they have been working tirelessly to improve the plight of these magnificent creatures since 1988.

I went to visit IEAS while writing this book, and I was surprised to find a real-life Barnum the Bengal tiger there! Over sixty animals are being cared for in this amazing facility, and the price is high to give them the lives they deserve. If you're interested in helping, or just finding more information, you can go to www.bigcat.org/how-to-help to see the many ways you can help give a big cat a better life. I also encourage anyone who is near a big cat sanctuary to visit, donate, and take a stroll. There are many across the United States, and all of them need every bit of help they can get.

I will be donating 10% of my earnings from all 2012 sales of Stars & Stripes to IEAS in honor of Ty and Zane, my loyal readers, and Barnum the Bengal tiger and all his brothers and sisters who deserved better than to be born in a cage.

# ALSO BY ABIGAIL ROUX

### The Cut & Run Series

Cut & Run (with Madeleine Urban)
Sticks & Stones (with Madeleine Urban)
Fish & Chips (with Madeleine Urban)
Divide & Conquer (with Madeleine Urban)
Armed & Dangerous

### Novels

According to Hoyle
Caught Running (with Madeleine Urban)
Love Ahead (with Madeleine Urban)
The Archer
Warrior's Cross (with Madeleine Urban)
Gravedigger's Brawl (coming October 2012)

### Novellas

A Tale from de Rode
My Brother's Keeper
Seeing Is Believing
Unrequited

# ABOUT THE AUTHOR

Abigail Roux was born and raised in North Carolina. A past volleyball star who specializes in sarcasm and painful historical accuracy, she currently spends her time coaching high school volleyball and investigating the mysteries of single motherhood. Any spare time is spent living and dying with every Atlanta Braves and Carolina Panthers game of the year. Abigail has a daughter, Little Roux, who is the light of her life, a boxer, four rescued cats who play an ongoing live-action variation of Call of Duty throughout the house, a certifiable extended family down the road, and a cast of thousands in her head.

To learn more about Abigail, please visit www.abigailroux.com.

Enjoyed this book?
Find more love and laughs at
RiptidePublishing.com!

*Country mouse meets city cat.*
ISBN: 978-1-937551-34-6

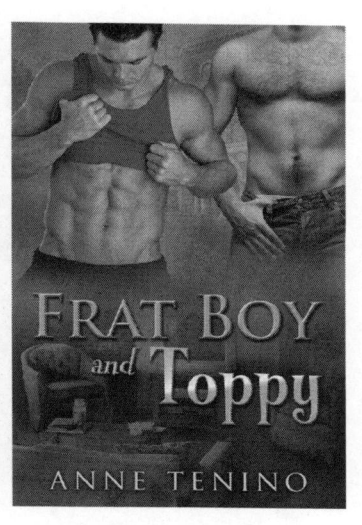

*Let the gay life commence.*
ISBN: 978-1-937551-27-8

RIPTIDE PUBLISHING

Printed in Great Britain
by Amazon.co.uk, Ltd.,
Marston Gate.